Spine loose 27/07

CSA

FIELD OF PREY

JOHN SANDFORD
FIELD OF PREY

**SIMON &
SCHUSTER**

London · New York · Sydney · Toronto · New Delhi

A CBS COMPANY

First published in the US by G. P. Putnam's Sons, 2014
A division of the Penguin Group (USA) Inc.
First published in Great Britain by Simon & Schuster UK Ltd, 2014
A CBS COMPANY

1 3 5 7 9 10 8 6 4 2

Simon & Schuster UK Ltd
1st Floor
222 Gray's Inn Road
London WC1X 8HB

www.simonandschuster.co.uk

Simon & Schuster Australia, Sydney
Simon & Schuster India, New Delhi

A CIP catalogue record for this book
is available from the British Library

Trade Paperback ISBN 978-1-47113-485-2
Hardback ISBN 978-1-47113-484-5
eBook ISBN 978-1-47113-487-6

Book design by Meighan Cavanaugh

Printed and bound by CPI Group (UK) Ltd, Croydon, CR0 4YY

For Gabriel

YEARS AGO . . .

The fifth woman was a blond waitress who enhanced her income by staying late to do kitchen cleanup at Auntie's, a diner in Faribault, a small city on Interstate 35 south of the Twin Cities. The diner had excellent qualities for a kidnapping. The blacktop parking lot was wide and deep in front, shallow and pitted in back, which meant that nobody parked there. When the fifth woman finished her cleanup, at midnight, she'd haul garbage bags to a dumpster out back.

In the dark.

She was out there alone, sweating in the summer heat, sickened by the odor from the dumpster, with no light except what came through the diner's open rear door and two pole lights in the front lot.

R-A waited for her there, hidden behind the dumpster. He was carrying an old canvas postal bag, of the kind once used to carry heavy loads of mail in cross-country trucks. The bags, forty-eight inches long and more than two feet in diameter, had eyelets around the mouth, with a rope running through the eyelets. The rope could be cinched tight with a heavy metal clasp.

R-A also carried a leather-wrapped, shot-filled sap, in case something went wrong with the bag.

Horn sat in his truck, in an adjacent parking lot, no more than a hundred feet away, where he could see the action at the dumpster, and warn against any oncoming cop cars. When the waitress came out with her second load of garbage bags, R-A waited until she was standing on tiptoe, off-balance while throwing one of the bags into the dumpster. He stepped out behind her, unseen, and dropped the canvas bag over her head, like a butterfly in a net.

The woman struggled and fought, and screamed, but the screams were muffled by the heavy bag, and two seconds after he took her to the ground, R-A slipped the locking clasp tight around her legs.

Horn was coming, in the truck. He stopped beside them, blocking the view from the street. Together, Horn and R-A lifted her and threw her in the back of Horn's extended cab truck. Horn climbed in on top of her with a roll of duct tape, and threw a half dozen fast wraps around the woman's ankles. Sort of like calf-roping, he thought.

As he did that, R-A jogged a half-block down the street to where he'd parked his own truck. When Horn had finished taping the woman's ankles, he jumped out and slammed the narrow door, ran around the back of the truck and climbed into the driver's seat, and they were gone, Horn a half-block ahead of R-A.

The system had worked again.

In three minutes, they'd gotten to the edge of town and were starting cross-country toward a hunter's shack in the backwaters of a Mississippi River impoundment. There, they'd rape the waitress and kill her.

R-A trailed a half-mile behind Horn. That was part of the system, too. If a cop car came along, and showed any interest at all in Horn's truck, R-A could provide warning, and support. If worse came to worst, R-A would drive recklessly and way too fast past the cop, provoking a chase, while Horn would re-route.

THE SYSTEM HAD WORKED BEFORE, and would have worked again, except that Heather Jorgenson had always worried about being alone in that parking lot in the night. She carried a Leatherman multi-tool, which included a three-inch-long serrated blade, in the pocket of her waitress uniform, and while her feet were restricted by the locked bag and the duct tape, her hands were free.

For the first minute or so of the truck ride, she fought with a panic-stricken violence against the heavy bag, without making any progress at all. In the thrashing, her hand slapped against the Leatherman.

The knife!

She fumbled it out and broke a nail trying to get it open, but hardly noticed; three minutes into the ride, she had the knife out and open. Jorgenson knew she'd only have one chance at it, so she continued to shout and scream, and thrash with one hand, as the truck drove through town. At the same time, she slit the bag with the razor-sharp blade, and at the bottom end, cut the binding rope around her legs. Finally, she carefully sliced through the duct tape at her ankles.

She took a moment to get her courage up, then pushed herself up in the back of the truck, and screaming, "You sonofabitch," she stabbed Horn in the neck, and then stabbed him again, in the back, in the spine, and then in the arms, and in the neck again, and Horn was shouting, screaming, trying to swat her away, while struggling to control the truck. He failed, and the truck swerved to the left edge of the road, two wheels dropping off the tarmac. They ran along like that for a hundred feet, then the truck began to tip, and finally rolled over into the ditch.

Jorgenson, in the back, felt the truck going. A former cheerleader, still with a cheerleader's suppleness, despite the extra pounds she'd picked up in the diner, she braced her feet against the roof of the truck and locked herself in place as it went over. When it settled, driver's side down, she found the handle on the back door, unlocked it, shoved it open, and crawled out.

She ran across the roadside ditch, tumbled over a barbed-wire fence, ripping her clothes and hands, into a cornfield—she was afraid to run down the road, because the kidnapper could see her, might come after her.

They'd just left town, and there were house lights no more than four or five hundred yards away. She ran as hard as she could, choking with fear, through the knee-high corn, then fell again and found herself in a mid-field swale, a seasonal creek, dry now.

Breathing hard, she crouched for a moment, listening, fearing that the kidnapper was right behind her. When she heard nothing, she got to her feet, stooped over so far that her hands touched the ground, and groped forward in the dark, toward the house lights.

She had no idea how long she'd been in the field when she made it into a tree line, the branches of the saplings slapping her in the face and chest. She crossed another fence and a ditch, out onto a road, then ran across the road toward the house lights. She was now so frightened and exhausted that she took no care about waking the house. She leaned on the lighted doorbell and pounded on the door while screaming, "Help! Help me!"

THE COPS were there in five minutes.

They found an upside-down truck with lots of blood in the front seat, and the cut-open mail sack in the back. They traced the truck in another five minutes, and were on their way to Horn's house in ten.

WHEN R-A GOT TO Horn's truck, the woman was gone.

Horn groaned, "I'm hurt, man, I'm hurt bad."

"Where is she?" R-A asked.

"She ran off, she's gone, man, we gotta get out of here." Horn was crumpled onto the driver's side window of the truck. R-A was kneeling on the narrow back door on the passenger side, looking down into the truck, the front door propped half open. "Help me out, help me."

Horn was covered with blood, down to his waist. R-A pulled him out of the truck, but Horn couldn't walk: "Did something to my legs, they don't work . . ."

R-A carried him to his own truck, put him in the back, and told him to stay down. "The hospital . . ."

"Fuck that. Fuck the hospital," Horn said. "They're gonna find my truck. The bitch knows my face, from the scouting trips. She'll pick me out."

"Then where?"

"Your place," Horn groaned. "They'll be at my place, sure as shit."

R-A GOT HIM BACK to his place, managed to half-drag, half-carry him down to the basement bomb shelter. Put him on a cot, plastered his wounds the best he could.

Thought about killing him. Horn's legs didn't work, he could never be anything but a liability. But R-A couldn't do it: Horn was the closest thing he'd ever had to a friend.

HORN MADE THE TV the next morning: Heather Jorgenson, according to police reports, said she'd been attacked by *a man* in the parking lot behind Auntie's, and had stabbed *him*. The police were looking for Jack Horn, of Holbein. Jack Horn, singular. No mention of two men. R-A cruised by his house, and the cops were all over it.

Horn himself, down in the bomb shelter, was drifting in and out of consciousness. In one of his lucid moments, he saw R-A staring at him.

"What're you staring at?" he mumbled. And, "Water. I need a drink. Need some . . . medicine."

R-A ran a country hardware store, with veterinary medicine in a locked cabinet at the back. Horn was out of it, so never felt the horse-sized needle that R-A used to give him the penicillin.

.   .   .

HORN WAS still in and out. During one of his lucid moments, R-A told Horn that the cops had taken his truck away, and that there was a warrant out for him, for kidnapping. "They're looking for you everywhere between Chicago and Billings. You can't look at the TV without seeing your ugly face."

"Water," said Horn. R-A went away and came back with a glass of water, but Horn found he couldn't even lift his hand. R-A poured it awkwardly into Horn's open, trembling mouth.

"How long?" he said, when he found his voice again.

"You've been up and down for two days," R-A said. A pause. "Mostly down."

"No hospital . . ." Horn said.

"If I don't, I figure you'll die," R-A said. "Then what'll I do?"

"No hospital . . ." Horn repeated. And then he was gone again.

It went like that for two more days; by the end of the second day, the bomb shelter smelled like an unclean hospital room, with the stink of human waste and corruption.

Then, on a Friday, R-A got back from the store and found Horn deathly still, his face as pale and gray as newsprint. At first, R-A thought him dead. That would have . . . made things easier. He could get rid of the body, and still feel he'd filled the requirements of male comradeship.

Then Horn opened his eyes and said in a calm voice, "You been thinking about choking me out, haven't you?"

"The thought crossed my mind," R-A admitted.

"No need, now. Things are different now."

"Yeah, I . . ."

"I been thinking about it. This is the perfect place. You're going to have to start bringing the girls here."

"I . . . thought I might stop."

Horn grunted: "Roger—you can't stop. But there's no more banging them out in the woods. That's all done. . . . Now you'll have to bring them down here. Look around. It's perfect. Down here, we can keep them for a while. Half the trouble, twice the fun."

And it'd worked. For a very long time.

1

There comes a crystalline moment in the lives of most young male virgins when they realize that they are about to get laid, and they will clutch that moment to their hearts for the rest of their days.

For some, maybe most, the realization comes nearly simultaneously with the moment. With others, not so much.

For Layton Burns Jr., of Red Wing, Minnesota, a recent graduate of Red Wing High School (Go Wingers!), the moment arrived on the night of the Fourth of July. He and Ginger Childs were wrapped in a blanket and propped against a tree of some sort—neither was a botanist—in a park in Stillwater, Minnesota, looking down at the river, where the fireworks were going off.

Fireworks were not going off in Red Wing, because the city council was too cheap to pay for them.

In any case, Stillwater *did* have fireworks. Layton, a jock, had his muscular right arm wrapped around Ginger's back, then under her arm and in past the unbuttoned second button on her blouse, where he was getting, in the approved parlance of the senior class at Red Wing High School, a bare tit. One of those hot, nipple-rolling bare tits. Not only a bare tit, but a semi-public one, which added to the *frisson* of the moment.

While intensely pleasant, this was not entirely a new development. They'd taken petting to a fever pitch, but Layton was the tiniest bit shy about asking for the Big One.

Ginger had her hand on Layton's thigh, where, despite his shyness, his interest was evident, and then as the final airbursts exploded in red-white-and-blue over the hundred boats in the harbor below, Ginger turned and bit him lightly on the earlobe and muttered, "Oh, God, if only you had some . . . protection."

UNTIL THAT VERY MOMENT, one of the few people in Red Wing who wasn't sure that Layton was going to get laid that summer was Layton himself. His parents knew, her parents knew, Ginger knew, all of Layton's friends knew, all of Ginger's friends knew, and Ginger's youngest sister, who was nine, strongly suspected.

But Layton, there in the park, wasn't organized for the moment. He groaned and said, in words made memorable by thousands of impromptu daddies, "Nothin'll happen."

"Can't take a chance," said Ginger, who was no dummy, and for whom, not to put it too bluntly, Layton was more or less a passing bump in the night. "Do you think by tomorrow night?"

Wul, yeah.

· · ·

BY THE NEXT NIGHT, Layton was organized.

He'd gotten the green light to borrow his mom's three-year-old Dodge Grand Caravan, which had Super Stow 'n Go seating in the back, converting instantly into a mobile bedroom. He'd stashed a Target air mattress and a six-pack of Coors with a friend. And he'd stolen three, no make it four, lubricated condoms from a twelve-pack that his father had conveniently left unhidden in the second drawer of his bedroom bureau, for the very purpose of being stolen by his son, his wife being on the pill.

Layton also had the perfect spot, discovered a year earlier when he was detasseling corn. The perfect spot had once been a farmyard with a small woodlot on the north side. The farm had failed decades earlier. Most of the land had been sold off, and the house had fallen into ruin and had eventually been burned by the local volunteer fire department in a training exercise. The outbuildings had either been torn down or had simply rotted in place. Still, the home site had not yet been plowed under, though the cornfields were pressing close to the sides of the old yard.

A narrow track, once a driveway, led across a culvert into the site; and there were good level places to park. An hour before he was to pick up Ginger, Layton signed onto his computer and went out to his favorite porn site to review his knowledge of female anatomy; which also reminded him to put a flashlight in the car in case he wanted to . . . you know . . . *watch.*

LAYTON HAD BUILT a sex machine, and it worked flawlessly.

He got the beer and air mattress from his friend, picked up Ginger, and they headed west on Highway 58, out of the Mississippi

River Valley, up on top, then down through the Hay Creek Valley, up on top again, and out into farm country. The ride was short and sweet in the warm summer night, with fireflies in the ditches and Lil Wayne on the satellite radio, which was a good thing, because Ginger was hotter than a stovepipe, and had her hand in Layton's jeans before they even got off the main highway and onto the back roads.

They found the turnoff into the farm lot on the first try, pushed aside some senile, overgrown lilacs as they wedged into a parking space, pumped up the air mattress with an air pump powered through the cigarette lighter, and got right to it.

There was some confusion at the beginning, when Layton un-rolled the first rubber, rather than rolling it down the erect append-age, and was reduced to trying to pull it on like a sock. A bit later, if Layton had been more attentive, he might have noticed that Ginger knew a good deal about technique and positioning, but he was not in a condition to notice; nor would he have given a rat's ass.

And it all went fine.

They did it twice, stopped for a beer, and then did it again, and stopped for another beer, and Layton was beginning to regret that he hadn't stolen *five* rubbers, when Ginger said, demurely, "I kinda got to go outside."

"What?"

"You know . . ."

She had to pee. Layton finally got the message and Ginger dis-appeared into the dark, with the flashlight. She was back two min-utes later.

"Boy, something smells really bad out there."

"Yeah?" He didn't care. She didn't care much either, especially as she'd reminded him about the flashlight.

So they messed around with the flashlight for a while, and Ginger said, "You're really large," which made him feel pretty good, although he'd measured himself several dozen times and it always came out at six and one-quarter inches, which numerous Internet sources said was almost exactly average.

Anyway, the fourth condom got used and stuffed in the sack the beer had come in, and Layton began to see the limits of endurance even for an eighteen-year-old—he probably wouldn't have needed the fifth one. They lay naked in each other's arms and drank the fifth and sixth beers and Ginger burped and said, "We probably ought to get back and establish our alibis," and Layton said, "Yeah, but . . . I kinda got to go outside."

Ginger laughed and said, "I wondered about that. You must have a bladder like an oil drum."

"I'm going," he said. He took the flashlight and moved off into the trees, wearing nothing but his Nike Airs, found a spot, and as he was taking the leak, smelled the smell: and Ginger was *right*. Something *really* stank.

It was impossible to grow up in the countryside and not know the odor of summertime roadkill, and that's what it was. Something big was dead and rotting, and close by.

He finished and went back to the car and found Ginger in her underpants, and getting into her jean shorts. "I want to go out and look around for a minute," he said. In the back of his mind he noticed his own sexual coolness. Even though her breasts were right there, and as attractive and pink and perky as they'd been fifteen minutes ago, he could have played chess, if he'd known how to play chess. "There's something dead out there."

"That's the stink I told you about."

"Not an ordinary stink," Layton said. "Whatever it is, is big."

She stopped dressing: "You mean . . . like a body?"

"Like something. Man, it really stinks."

When they were dressed, and with Ginger holding onto the back of Layton's belt, they walked into the woods—as if neither one of them had ever seen a *Halloween* movie—following the light of the flash. As they got deeper in, the smell seemed to fade. "Wrong way," Layton said.

They turned back and Ginger said, "Hope the light holds out."

"It's fine," Layton said. Fresh batteries: Layton had been *ready*.

They walked back toward the area where the house had been, and the smell grew stronger, until Ginger bent and gagged. "God . . . what is it?"

Whatever it was, they couldn't find it. Layton marched back and forth over the old farmstead, shining the light into the underbrush and even up into the trees. They found nothing.

"Don't ghosts smell?" Ginger said. "I saw it on one of those British ghost-hunter shows, that sometimes ghosts make a bad smell."

Every hair on Layton's neck stood up: "Let's get out of here," he said.

They started walking back to the car, but by the time they got back, they were running. They jumped in, slammed the doors, clicked the locks, backed out of the parking place, and blasted off down the gravel road, not slowing until they got to the highway. The bag with the used condoms and the empty beer cans went into an overgrown ditch, and fifteen minutes later, they were headed down the hill into the welcoming lights of Red Wing.

LAYTON LAY IN BED that night and thought about it all—mostly the sex, but also about Ginger's best friend, Lauren, and what a wicked threesome that would be, and about that awful odor. Ginger called him the next morning to say it had been the most wonderful night of her life; and he told her that it had been the most wonderful night of his.

The night had been wonderful, but not quite perfect. There'd been that smell.

LAYTON'S BEST FRIEND'S older brother was a Goodhue County deputy named Randy Lipsky, who was only six or eight years older than Layton. If not quite a friend, he was something more than an acquaintance.

Layton got up late, shaved, ate some Cheerios, and still not sure if he was doing the right thing, called the sheriff's office and asked if Lipsky was around. He was.

"I need to talk to you for a minute, if I could run over there," Layton said.

So he went over to the law enforcement center, found Lipsky, and they walked around the block.

Layton said, "Just between you and me."

"Depending on what it is," Lipsky said. "I'm a cop."

"Well, *I* didn't do anything," Layton said.

"What is it?" Lipsky asked.

"Last night, my girlfriend and I went up to this old farm place, out in the country, and parked for a while."

"Ginger?"

"Uh-huh."

"She's pretty hot. You nail her?"

"Hey . . . But, yeah, as a matter of fact." He was so cool about it that ice cubes could have rolled out of his ears.

"Anyway . . ."

"Anyway, there's something dead up there. Something big. I never smelled anything like it. I thought it was a cow or a pig. The weird thing is, we couldn't find anything, and there aren't any dairies or pig farms around there. We could smell it, like it was right *there*: like we were standing on it. It made Ginger throw up it was so strong. I was thinking last night, what if we couldn't find it because . . . somebody buried something?"

"You mean . . ." Lipsky stopped and looked at Layton. Layton was a jock, but not an idiot.

"Yeah. I thought I should ask," Layton said. "Now you can tell me I'm a whiny little girl, and we can forget about it."

Lipsky said: "I'll tell you something, Layton: ninety-five percent it's nothing. Probably somebody shot a buck out of season, and you were smelling the gut dump. Those can be pretty hard to see in the dark, once they go gray. But, five percent, we gotta go look."

Lipsky went to get a patrol car and Layton called Ginger and told her what he'd done. "Well, God, don't mention me," she said.

"If it's something, I'll probably have to," he said.

"Well, if it's something . . . sure. I worried about it, too, last night," she said. "Like you were saying, it smelled big. What if it's a dead body?"

"I'll call you when we get back," Layton said.

THE DRIVE IN THE DAYTIME was even faster than the drive the night before, out into the countryside and the hot July sun. Layton pointed Lipsky into the abandoned farm lot and Lipsky said, "What a great place to park."

"Yeah, it'd be okay, if it didn't stink so bad," Layton said. "Over here."

He led the way back where the old house had been, and the smell was like a wall. They hit it and Lipsky's face crinkled and he said, "Jesus Christ on a crutch."

"I told you," Layton said.

"Where's it coming from?" Lipsky asked.

They quartered the area, kicking through the underbrush, and eventually always came back to the yard where the house had been, and finally Lipsky pointed to the edge of the clearing and said, "Go over and pull out that old fence post, and bring it back here."

THE FENCE POST WAS a rusting length of steel still attached to a single strand of barbed wire. Layton wrenched it loose, pulled the barbed wire off, and carried it back to Lipsky. Lipsky was walking around a patch of fescue grass twenty feet across, a distracted look on his face.

"What do you think?" Layton asked.

"Might be an old cistern here, or an old well," Lipsky said. "You see that line in the grass?"

"Maybe . . ."

Lipsky took the fence post from Layton and began probing the patch of grass. He'd done it four times when, on the fifth, there was a hollow *thunk*.

"There it is," Lipsky said. "Should have been filled in, doesn't sound like it was."

He scraped around with the fence post and found the edge of the cistern cover, which was a circular piece of concrete. A whole pad of fescue lifted off it, in one piece, and Lipsky said, "Just between you and me, I don't think we're the first ones to do this."

"Maybe we ought to call the cops," Layton said. Lipsky gave him a look, and Layton said, "You know what I mean. *More* cops."

"Let's just take a look," Lipsky said.

They pulled the grass off, and Lipsky said, "Check this out."

One edge of the concrete cover showed what seemed to be recent scrapes, perhaps made with a pick, or a crowbar; and all around the edges, older scrapes. Lots of them. Lipsky found a place where he could get the good end of the fence post under the rim of the cistern cover, and pried. There was a *pop* when it came loose, and the gas hit them and they both reeled away, gagging, vomiting into the grass away from the cistern.

When they'd vomited everything in their stomachs—Lipsky had gone to his hands and knees—they went back and looked into the cistern, but all they saw was darkness.

"Let me get a flash," Lipsky said. "Don't fall in." He spit into the weeds as he went, and then spit again, and Layton spit a couple times himself, his mouth sour from the vomit.

Lipsky got the flashlight and walked back to where Layton was standing, his forearm bent over his nose.

They looked into the hole and Lipsky turned on the six-cell Maglite, and they first saw the two white ovals.

"Is that . . . ?" Layton asked.

"What?" Lipsky looked like he didn't want to hear it.

"Feet? It looks like the bottoms of somebody's feet," Layton said.

Lipsky turned back toward the squad car.

"Where're you going?" Layton asked.

"To call the cops," Lipsky said. "*More* cops. *Lotsa* cops."

2

The Bureau of Criminal Apprehension is housed in a modern red-brick-and-glass building in St. Paul, Minnesota. Lucas Davenport had once explained the somewhat odd name to an agent of the Federal Bureau of Investigation this way: "In Minnesota, see, we actually *apprehend* the assholes, instead of just investigating them."

The fed said, "Really? Doesn't that get you in trouble? I'd think the paperwork would be a nightmare."

Lucas parked his Porsche 911 in the lot below his office window, where he could keep an eye on it. The last time he'd parked it out of eyesight, somebody had stuck a vegan bumper sticker on it that said: "Beef: It's What's Rotting In Your Colon."

He hadn't found it until he pulled off the interstate, wondering why other drivers were honking at him: A tire problem? Something about to fall off? When he saw the sticker, he crawled home in shame, through the back streets, and then spent a half hour peeling it off, cursing the rotten bastard who'd stuck it there.

Today, he would park within pistol range.

.   .   .

His office was on the second floor, in a corner, and when he got there . . . there was nobody home. He walked back out to a conference room, where the door was open. One of his agents, Del Capslock, was sitting at the conference table, looking solemn, part of a crowd of solemn agents. Lucas was sure he hadn't missed a scheduled meeting, so . . .

Del looked out through the door, saw Lucas, and crooked a finger at him.

Lucas had been out of the office since the previous afternoon. Before leaving, he'd heard that the BCA crime-scene crew was leaving for a murder site west of Red Wing, a small Mississippi River town something less than an hour south of St. Paul, famous for boots and country crocks and the state reform school: "If you don't eat your Cap'n Crunch, the cops will send you to Red Wing."

Something about a cistern, with a body in it.

Lucas slipped into the conference room. All the chairs were full, so he propped himself in a corner. Henry Sands, a bald man of limited emotional dimension, sat at the head of the table, the flats of his hands pressed to his temples, as though he were trying to hold his head together. Not a good sign, since Sands was the director of the BCA.

Rose Marie Roux, the commissioner of public safety, and Sands's boss, whose office was in a different building entirely, was sitting at one corner of the table, rubbing her forehead with the tips of her fingers. Another bad sign.

Almost everyone else—a dozen people, ten male, two female—were staring at them, waiting, or looking at a variety of yellow legal pads, laptops, and iPads. When nobody else spoke, Lucas did. "How bad is it?"

Roux looked up and said, "Lucas. Good morning. They've got fifteen skulls. They don't have them all, yet. They're not even sure that they've got most of them. We just had Beatrice Sawyer on the phone, and she said it's like excavating ten feet of cold bean soup. She says there might be four feet of bones at the bottom."

"Holy shit."

"That's the prevailing sentiment," Roux said. She was a heavyset woman with a notorious smoking habit and hair of an everchanging color. A politician and former prosecutor, Minneapolis police chief, and, briefly, a street cop, she was one of Lucas's oldest friends and a longtime ally.

"Have they identified anyone?" Lucas asked.

Sands said, "Mary Lynn Carpenter. She disappeared from Durand, Wisconsin, two weeks ago. They found her car at the Diamond Bluff cemetery, across the river from Red Wing. She'd go there every once in a while to clean up her grandparents' graves. The cemetery's on the Mississippi, above a slough. They'd been looking for her body in the river."

"Who else?" Lucas asked.

Sands shook his head. "Don't know, but Beatrice said that judging from the skulls, they're all women. Carpenter had been strangled with a piece of nylon rope. It's still around her neck. What's left of her neck. She's probably been in the well for two weeks."

"Cistern," somebody said.

"Can't they pump it out?" Lucas asked.

"They're trying, but the bottom of the cistern is cracked and the crack's below the water table," Sands said. "Water seeps back in almost as fast as they can pump it out. They can't pump too fast, because they don't want to lose any of the . . . material."

"WHAT TOWNS ARE down there? Besides Red Wing?" Roux asked.

One of the agents was looking at a laptop and said, "Not much—closest town, besides Red Wing, is Diamond Bluff, across the river in Wisconsin, less than five hundred people. That's where Carpenter was when she disappeared. Ellsworth is fourteen miles away, also in Wisconsin, three thousand people. In Minnesota, there's Lake City, seventeen miles south of Red Wing, Holbein, fourteen miles southwest, Zumbrota, eight miles past Holbein, Hastings, more or less twenty-five miles north, and Cannon Falls, twenty miles west. The cistern is eight miles from Red Wing, nine miles from Holbein, eleven from Lake City, quite a bit further from Cannon Falls and Hastings."

"Are we talking to the Wisconsin DCI?" Lucas asked.

"We are," Sands said. "They already had an agent involved, on the Carpenter disappearance. He's down at the scene now."

Another agent, a woman, jumped in: "On a sheer numbers basis, the killer's probably from Red Wing. Next most likely is that he's from here in the Cities—we're fifty miles from the cistern. But if you were originally from that area, and knew about the cistern, and you were living up here and needed a body dump . . ."

A third agent: "We don't have the facts. We've got to identify more of the bodies before we can start talking about where the killer's from. Right now, with one identifiable body, picked up in that area, I'm betting he's from down there. If we find a couple more from down there . . ."

That set off a round of squabbling, until Roux held up a hand and said, "Okay, okay, okay. You guys can do the numbers later. Henry, we need a structure here. We need the most intense investigation we've ever run, because, my friends, this is pretty much it. You are all standing in front of the fan that the shit just hit. They'll be screaming about this from every TV station in the nation tonight and they will continue screaming until we get the killer. Is that perfectly clear to everyone?"

Everyone nodded.

SANDS SAID, "Bob Shaffer will run the investigation. There'll be a lot of ins and outs to the case, so he'll need a lot of guys. Anybody who isn't closing out a case, Bob'll be talking to you. The only exemptions are Lucas's crew . . ."

He looked over at Lucas: "Can you switch off the Bryan case?"

Lucas shook his head. "Not really. We still haven't figured out whether he's dead."

"He's dead," somebody said.

Somebody else disagreed: "No, he's not. Ten-to-one he's in Honduras, or someplace like it."

Lucas said, "I just don't know."

"What's Flowers doing?" Roux asked.

Lucas said, "Vacation, down in New Mexico. He left two days ago, pulling his boat. He won't be back for three weeks."

"New Mexico's a fuckin' desert," somebody offered.

"He says there's a musky lake," Lucas said. "He said he's gonna clean it out."

"He ought to bring the boat back. We could use it in the cistern,"

Roux said. And: "All right. Bob, get your crew together and get going."

Shaffer, who had been sitting silently taking notes, nodded and stood up and said, "I want to talk to Jon and Sandy right now, my office. Everybody else, we'll meet back here in a half hour."

Roux stood up and said, "Lucas, I want you to take a look at whatever Bob comes up with. Henry, I want updates every couple of hours today, and then every morning and evening until we close this out. Let's get this done, guys. Let's get it done in one big hurry."

While they were all there together, so they'd all hear it at once, Lucas pushed away from the wall and said, "I don't think that's going to happen, Rose Marie. If there are really that many dead women, and we didn't know about it, didn't connect the disappearances, then the killer is smart and careful. I mean, really careful. This could take time."

"I don't want to hear that," Roux snapped.

"You need to," Lucas snapped back. He looked around. "We don't want anyone hinting to the media that this is gonna be a walk in the park, that we'll get the guy next week. If we do, that's fine. But if we don't, the media's gonna be a hair shirt, and we're all gonna be wearing it."

All the cops looked at him for a moment, then Roux said, "Okay. He's right. So: we have one guy talking to the media. Anybody else talks, you'll be manning the new bureau down in Bumfuck, Minn. Everybody understand?"

LUCAS SPOKE TO SHAFFER for a few moments after the meeting broke up, with Del orbiting around them. Shaffer and Lucas didn't particularly like each other, but had worked several ugly cases together, with good results. They agreed that Lucas would be on the distribution list for everything coming out of the investigation, but would stay away from the main case.

"I might talk to a few people, if I come across any that are interesting," Lucas said.

"That's fine," Shaffer said. "If you get anything, be sure to update the files."

"I will do that," Lucas said.

Shaffer started to step away, then said, "Lucas: I appreciate what you said to Rose Marie. This could take a while. You were the right guy to tell her that."

Lucas nodded: "Had to be said."

LUCAS AND SHAFFER had been successful, when they worked together, precisely because they were so radically different in style.

Shaffer was a data collector and a grinder: with enough data, he believed, you could solve anything. His files were wonders, his spreadsheets were remarkable, his decision matrices were monuments to game theory. And they worked. Anytime his agents could collect enough relevant data, his clearance rate was exceptional.

Shaffer looked like a grinder: neatly dressed at all times, in short-sleeved shirts in the summer, blue or white oxford cloth in winter, with bland neckties, wrinkle-free khaki trousers from Macy's, and blue blazers. He exercised extensively and efficiently, ate right, didn't drink or smoke. Married to his high school sweetheart, he was slender, of average height, with pale brown hair.

He'd come up the hard way: a patrol officer in Duluth, then a detective, then up through the ranks at the BCA, until he'd become one of the go-to investigators. He knew statistics: he'd taken college courses in statistics and geography at the University of Minnesota's extension school. He'd kept his nose clean.

LUCAS WAS A connection collector, an investigator who liked to knit people together, to put one source with another and let them fight it out. He thrived on mysteries.

A tall, brooding man with dark hair, friendly blue eyes, and a sometimes frightening smile, Lucas was hawk-faced and heavy in the shoulders, and scarred from encounters with the misbegotten. Like Shaffer, he'd gone to the University of Minnesota, where instead of statistics, he'd studied hockey and women.

He'd never had to work his way up. He'd spent a short time on patrol, and then jumped over three dozen senior men to become a Minneapolis detective. Nor had he tried very hard to keep his nose clean. He'd been pushed out of the Minneapolis police department after beating up a pimp who'd church-keyed one of his sources.

He'd gotten back into the department when Roux, the new chief, made him a deputy chief, a political appointment. That job ended when Roux quit to become the state's commissioner of public safety. But as soon as she reasonably could, Roux had dropped Lucas into the BCA, right into a top slot.

His clearance rate, like Shaffer's, was excellent. Lucas exercised, but inefficiently: running frequently, but not every day, playing basketball and senior hockey. Lucas had once had a reputation for chasing skirts; and catching them. He had a daughter out of wedlock, two children from his only marriage, and an adopted daughter. He'd drink a beer in the evening, and knew his barbecue.

WITH ALL THEIR natural differences, in career path and personality, Shaffer and Lucas were never going to be close: but with all the important differences, their real distaste for each other came on relatively minor issues. Shaffer was a natural socialist, who'd grown up in an Iron Range union family. He didn't like rich people, not even self-made rich people.

Lucas was self-made rich.

Even worse than the money was Lucas's whole lifestyle: the Porsche, his history with women, the wardrobe. Lucas bought his working clothes in men's boutiques, and every couple of years, went to New York.

To shop.

Lucas thought of Shaffer, when he thought of Shaffer at all, as a clerk.

Shaffer knew it.

WHEN HE'D FINISHED talking to Shaffer, Lucas and Del went down to his office, where Shrake and Jenkins were waiting. They were both big men, in suits that were too sharp, as though they'd fallen off a truck in Brooklyn. Both had even, extra-white teeth, and for the same reason: their real, natural, yellower teeth had been knocked out at one time or another. Lucas told them about the find at Red Wing.

"We're throwing Bryan out the window?" Shrake blurted.

"No, Shaffer's doing the work," Lucas said. "We'll be mostly talking."

"I hate to see that officious prick get all the glory," Jenkins said. "He's the kind of guy who wouldn't give you a six-inch putt."

"He does good records," Del said.

"He's also exactly the right guy to run this case," Lucas said. "It's gonna be all sorting bones and extracting DNA and running the spreadsheets."

"Still wouldn't give you a putt," Jenkins said.

"Probably because he's not fuckin' stupid enough to play golf," Lucas said. "Anyway, if Shaffer doesn't find this killer in a hurry, they'll be sniffing around our asses, looking for help. Let's close out Bryan."

BRYAN.

Bryan had run a St. Paul investment company that turned out to be a Ponzi scheme, a scheme that had eventually come up a couple of Ponzis short. He'd been arrested and the state attorney general's office was trying to get back the thirty-one million dollars that had been entrusted to him by 1,691 small investors, most of them elderly. Bryan said the money was gone—spent on fast Italian cars, slow Kentucky horses, and hot Russian women, along with a $250,000 RV, which lost half its value when he turned the key on it, and an unprofitable ostrich ranch in Wyoming. Rumor said that a good deal more of the cash had gone up his nose.

There were doubters.

Bryan had divorced three years earlier, and his ex-wife, Bloomie, now lived in a house very near, but not quite on, the Atlantic Ocean in Palm Beach. According to the local conspiracy theorists, Bryan had seen the trouble coming, had given an overly generous divorce settlement to his wife, who would support him when the problems became public and the company went broke. There was also talk that he owned a Cabo San Lucas estate under a Mexican corporate shadow.

That may have been true, but apparently had become irrelevant when Bryan's court-ordered ankle monitor went dead, and his BMW M6 convertible had been found parked near the St. Croix gorge at Taylors Falls with the front seat soaked in his blood. No body had been found. There were, at latest count, 1,691 suspects in Bryan's disappearance.

"Well, we've already interviewed twelve of them, so that only leaves one thousand six hundred and seventy-nine to go. We should have that done by 2020," Jenkins said.

"Start with the ones young enough to move a body," Lucas suggested. "That'll cut the workload by ninety-eight percent."

"Are you gonna help?" Shrake asked.

"First, I'm gonna go down and take a look at this cistern, this well, where they found all the bodies," Lucas said. "Then this evening, I'll be talking to the beautiful Carrie Lee Pitt, about Bryan's missing clothes. I'm hoping she'll let me peek in her closet."

"How come *we're* not talking to Carrie Lee Pitt?" Jenkins asked.

"Because that will take some *savoir faire*, which you don't got any of," Lucas said.

Jenkins looked offended, lifted an arm and sniffed his armpit, and said, "Yes, I do."

. . .

JENKINS AND SHRAKE LEFT, and Lucas turned to Del, who had taken Lucas's visitor's chair and put his feet up on a file cabinet.

Del was a thin man, with a sun-darkened face of knobs and wrinkled plains, a little more than average height: a dusty guy in his mid-fifties, who looked like he lived on the street. He was wearing a long-sleeved turquoise cowboy shirt and faded jeans over hiking boots. "We're going down to the well?"

"Cistern," Lucas said. "Yeah, I guess we better. But Jesus, that shirt makes me want to pluck my eyeballs out. You been hanging out at Goodwill again?"

"From what I hear, if we're going down to the well—the cistern—we're gonna want to burn the clothes afterwards," Del said. "I'd rather burn a polyester shirt than a two-thousand-dollar Italian suit. Or three-thousand-dollar Romanian shoes."

"British shoes. And when you're right, you're right." Lucas pushed himself out of his chair. "We'll stop at my place on the way out. You ready?"

"As ever."

"Fifteen skulls so far," Lucas said, as he turned off the office lights. "And there are more down the well."

"Somebody's been a bad, bad boy," Del said.

ON THE WAY OUT of the building, they ran into Sands, the BCA director. He was looking harried, and said, as they walked down the stairs to the first floor, "This can come to no good end. Remember I said that."

"It already did, for at least fifteen women," Del said. "But we'll get him."

"Not soon enough," Sands said. He breathed in Lucas's direction, and Lucas had to fight an impulse to step back: Sands's breath was notorious. "It's already not soon enough. Charlie's already getting calls from the *Today* show."

Charlie handled the BCA's media relations.

AT HOME, Lucas changed into worn Levi's 505s and a blue chambray work shirt from Façonnable; he let the shirt hang loose to cover the .45 in his beltline.

He and Del loaded an Igloo cooler into the back of his black Mercedes SUV, and Lucas threw a nylon daypack on top of the cooler. On the way out of town, they stopped at a BP station for gas, and picked up ice, bottled water, Coke and Diet Coke, and headed south across the Mississippi.

"I have a psychological observation," Del said, as they crossed the water.

"Nobody's more qualified to make one," Lucas said.

"It's just this. You say, 'fifteen skulls,' and I say, 'Somebody's been a bad, bad boy.' If an outsider had heard that, they'd think we had no feelings at all. I'd have sounded like an asshole."

A Prius passed Lucas, doing ninety, and then cut in front of him and slowed. Lucas tapped the brakes and said, "Blow me." And to Del, "Not you, the Prius. And what you say is true. Not a new experience, for you, though."

"Or you. We sit around and bullshit about this stuff, like we're reading a bus ticket, but when we start finding out about the victims, we're gonna get pissed," Del said. "We're not pissed now, but we will be. We'll find out about their lives, about what they wanted to do, and all the misery this killer caused, we'll start brooding about it, and we'll get pissed."

"Get to the point. I want to put on my Pink album."

"The point is this—Henry and Rose Marie are already pissed. They're pissed because the politics might hurt them. They're not pissed about fifteen women down the well, they're pissed about how they're going to look on TV. You know, the big-shot cops who let this happen right here in River City."

"In the interest of your continuing employment," Lucas said, "let's keep this psychological observation between you and me."

"You know what I'm saying," Del said.

"I do," Lucas said. "It's the way of the world, man. There are the worker bees, and the manager bees. The worker bees take care of the work, the manager bees take care of themselves."

THEY WERE HEADED OUT on a good summer day, but hot, down Highway 52, through Cannon Falls, and on south. The cistern site was in rolling farm country west of the Mississippi River Valley, on a gravel road off Goodhue County 1. They spent a few minutes wandering around, after an off-map shortcut didn't work out, and so took an hour to find the site.

The road was blocked by two cop cars five hundred yards out, and a half dozen TV vans were parked on the shoulder of the road, reporters and photographers clustered on the shady sides of the vans.

"Lot of TV," Del said. "It's been a while since I've seen this much."

"Gonna be rough," Lucas said. "Shaffer's gonna be hip-deep in bullshit before he's through."

"Better him than us," Del said.

THE COPS AT THE ROADBLOCK, both sweating furiously in their long-sleeved uniforms, looked at Lucas's ID. Lucas said, "I got ice-cold Coke, Diet Coke, and water in the back."

"Cokes," the cops said simultaneously, and Del dug them out of the cooler and passed them to Lucas, who handed them through the window to the cops and asked, "Who doesn't get speeding tickets in Goodhue County?"

"You're good up to ag assault, far as I'm concerned," the cop said, and they went on through.

"TOO MANY PEOPLE," Del said, as Lucas pulled onto the shoulder of the dusty road, fifty yards short of the site. The shoulder was filled with cop cars, civilian cars and trucks and vans, and an empty heavy-equipment trailer.

"Everybody's gonna want to be here, just to say they were," Lucas said.

They got out of the truck, into the hot midday air smelling of roadside weeds. Lucas stuffed Cokes and bottles of water into the daypack, and they ambled along the gravel road toward the farm turnoff. Halfway to the cistern site, they ran into a BCA agent named Don Buford, who saw them coming and said, "I don't suppose you got a beer in there?"

"Got a Coke or a Diet Coke," Lucas said. "Or a bottle of water."

"I'll give you ten dollars for a Diet Coke."

Lucas gave him the Coke and Buford looked around and said, "Ain't this a great day? Hot, sunny, no wind. Tell you what, when you get up there, you'll be praying for cold, wind, and rain. The smell . . . half the guys up there have been pukin' their guts out."

"What's there to see?" Lucas asked.

Buford shrugged: "Just the site. They're calling it the Black Hole of Goodhue. You know, like . . ."

". . . the Black Hole of Calcutta. We get it," Del said.

"The whole crime-scene crew is up there," Buford said, rolling the cold Coke bottle across his forehead. "It's a nightmare. Got boxes of skulls. Nothing for me, though. I'd eat a sandwich, if I could keep it down."

"We're wasting our time?" Lucas asked.

"Oh . . . no. You gotta go look, and look around," Buford said. "Maybe tell you something about the guy who did this. Got to be some kind of crazy farmer. Somebody who butchers his own meat, or something. Some kinda . . ." Buford shuddered. ". . . monster."

THEY LEFT BUFORD in the road and walked up a slight rise to the turnoff, showed their IDs to another cop, and walked up the grassy track into the heart of the old farmstead. There they found four people in hazmat suits peering into a hole in a concrete slab, and a dozen cops scattered through the trees and brush, watching.

A yellow front-end loader's lift bucket dangled over the hole, with a steel cable dropping into the hole itself. Off to one side was a stack of semi-transparent plastic tubs, the kind you can buy at Target, with paper stickers on the top-covers: human remains. A skull grinned out of one of them. A hundred feet from the hole, an air compressor was working, and in the other direction, a Honda generator. Power and air lines led to the hole. As they got closer, the stink hit them, and Lucas turned away.

"Buford was right," Del said. He dug into his pack and came up with a jar of Vicks VapoRub, opened it, and offered it to Lucas, who took out a bit on the end of a finger and rubbed under his nose. Del did the same, and they walked up to the hole, and a woman standing next to it in a dark blue hazmat suit with the hood down. Beatrice Sawyer, head of the crime-scene crew.

Lucas said, "Hey, Bea."

She turned and said, "Lucas, Del. Nice day, huh?"

Breathing through his mouth, Lucas peered into the cistern, which was illuminated with LED work lights. He could see another person in a hazmat suit, ten feet down, suspended on a wooden platform over a murky gray liquid that could hardly be called water. The suit was sealed, with air lines leading into the helmet.

"You've been down there?" he asked.

"Yeah. That's Hopping Crow down there now. We're trying to find a way to get the water out, without disturbing the remains too much," Sawyer said. "Larry's placing pump lines with filters that we got from a septic-supply place in Red Wing. We're improvising. Don't know if it'll work."

"Why wouldn't it?"

"Oh, we could get the water out with any pump that's large enough," she said. "Everything else would come, too. We need to *gently* remove it, with a flow fast enough to replace the inflow of groundwater. This cistern is essentially sitting on a spring."

"Hmm." Lucas didn't know about farm stuff.

"How's the skull count?" Del asked.

"Seventeen, now," Sawyer said. "There are more. We can feel them, but we can't see them, and we don't want to damage them. We need to see the dental work."

Del said, "Bobbing for Satan's apples."

"Pretty fuckin' poetic, Del," Sawyer said.

"Any more IDs?" Lucas asked.

"Yes. One. A probable, anyway. When we were using another pump, it got jammed up, and when we pulled it, we found it had sucked up a plastic Visa card, still readable, issued to a Janice Williams. A Janice Williams from Cannon Falls disappeared eight years ago. She was a student at Dakota technical college. Her friends thought she might have gone to Miami—she knew some guy down there, and she'd talked about going down. Her parents thought she'd been kidnapped, and she's never been back in touch. That's all I know at this point, but I think it's likely her, down there."

"Will we screw anything up . . ." Lucas paused when a man a few feet away suddenly bent over, then rapidly walked away, still bent, and began retching against a tree. They looked away and Lucas started again: "Will we screw anything up if we walk around here? To look the place over?"

"Possibly, but I wouldn't worry about it," she said. "There have been five hundred people here today, and if there's anything that hasn't been stepped on, I don't know what it would be."

Del asked, "Can you get DNA out of vomit?"

Sawyer nodded. "Sure."

"If the killer popped the top off this thing two weeks ago, when this last woman disappeared, is it possible that he puked into the dirt, right where we're standing?"

They all looked at their feet and Sawyer said, "I wish you'd asked that question yesterday afternoon."

SAWYER HAD BEEN SWEATING heavily in the hazmat suit, and she greedily sucked down one of Lucas's Diet Cokes. A man stepped up behind them and said, "Hey, Lucas, Del. You guys got another Coke?"

Lucas turned: "Hey, Jimmy. We were told there was a Wisconsin guy here. Didn't know it was you."

"Yeah, I'd been poking around the Carpenter disappearance, over at Diamond Bluff." James Bole was an agent with Wisconsin's Division of Criminal Investigation, an earnest, square-shouldered, stocky man with strawberry blond hair and a neat strawberry blond mustache. He was familiar enough around the Minnesota BCA, working cross-river cases. He took one of Lucas's Cokes and said, "Don't have much. We didn't know whether she'd been kidnapped or had gone down to the river and fallen in. Now she . . ." He gestured at the hole.

"We heard," Lucas said. "You take her car apart?"

"Yeah, but there was no sign that anything happened to her inside the car. Didn't find anybody's prints but hers and her mother's—nothing was wiped—so she probably drove it down there herself. One thing: when she was reported missing, her car was spotted by a Pierce County deputy. It'd rained not long before she disappeared, and when he found her car, he noticed that her tires had made tracks in the mud, and they were still pretty clear. He figured if she had been kidnapped, the kidnapper must've had a vehicle down there in the cemetery . . . otherwise, he would have had to carry her up a bluff, or down to a boat. There weren't that many other tracks around, so he had casts made of all the different tire tracks."

"Good move," Del said.

"It's thin, but it's what we got," Bole said. "All the tire tracks were probably made by trucks, all-weather tires, four different patterns, four different brands. I gave a list to Buford, he was here."

"Saw him down on the road . . ."

SHAFFER SHOWED UP, spotted them, lifted a hand, talked to Sawyer for a moment, then walked over. "Isn't this something?"

"It is," Del said.

"Get anything at all?" Lucas asked.

Shaffer's crew had interviewed the owner of the farm that surrounded the site, a woman named James, and from her had gotten a number of ideas that might help locate the people who'd known about the hidden cistern. Shaffer himself had interviewed the two kids who'd first smelled the decomposing body down the cistern, and the deputy who'd pried the lid off the hole.

"You can't see it now, but the whole site was covered with grass, with sod. The cistern was invisible: had to know it was here before you could put somebody into it, and not many people knew about it."

"That could help," Lucas said.

"Yeah. I hope. Have you seen . . . There they are. Gotta go talk to these guys."

He walked away, toward two guys who had a laptop propped against a tree trunk, entering . . . data.

THEY'D DRIFTED AWAY from the hole as they talked, mostly to get away from the stink. A squabble started at the hole, and they turned around to see Sawyer, in the hazmat suit, still holding the Diet Coke, faced off with a woman in a Goodhue County deputy's uniform. The deputy was tall and pretty enough, but rangy like a basketball or volleyball player, with wide shoulders and a small butt. She looked like she'd been in a few fights; her nose wasn't quite on straight. She had one hand resting on her pistol, like she might have to shoot her way out of the farm site.

Sawyer was saying, ". . . everything goes through our office, and if you want reports, you'll have to get them there. We can't get them out to every Tom, Dick, and Harry—"

"I'm not every Tom, Dick, and Harry—this is my jurisdiction and my job," the deputy snarled. She'd come primed for a fight, Lucas thought, or perhaps spent her life angry. She was red-faced and angry now. "I want copies of everything, and I want them as soon as they come out."

Lucas stepped toward her and said, mildly enough, "Everything has to go through one system, or we'll all get confused. If you're authorized to get the reports, it's not a problem: we just make an extra set of copies."

"Who're you?" she asked, looking him up and down.

"I'm a BCA agent," Lucas said. "I've been assigned—"

"And we're second-class citizens?"

"Hey—you'll get the crime-scene stuff as fast as I do," Lucas said. "You need to talk to Bob Shaffer to get on the distribution list. He'll be the agent in charge. He's around, I just talked to him."

"Bob Shaffer?" She took out a notebook. "How do you spell that?"

Lucas said, slowly, "B-o-b . . ."

Her eyes snapped at him and he'd had the sense that she'd almost smiled. Instead, she rasped, "Are you giving me a hard time?"

"S-h-a-f-f-e-r," Lucas said. "He'll be happy to hear from you."

He backed away, to where Del and Bole were standing. She watched him go, then folded the notebook and stalked off across the farmyard, toward the cars.

"Wouldn't want to meet her in a dark alley," Del said.

"Ah . . . Catrin Mattsson. She's okay. Well, some of the time," Bole said.

"You know her?" Lucas asked.

"Yeah, I run into her occasionally," Bole said. "She's the lead investigator for Goodhue. Pretty much known for her attitude. Not dumb, though. Good investigator. She just doesn't have a smooth, Del-like personality."

"It's a tragedy," Del said, as they watched her go.

"Yeah, well . . . her looks somewhat make up for it," Bole said. "The thing is, you BCA guys have a teensy-weensy tendency to throw your weight around on a deal like this. Busy, busy, busy. Don't have a lot of time for the local-yokels."

Lucas: "Really?"

"Well, like I said, it's teensy-weensy."

ALL CASES LIKE the Black Hole murders start slow. The investigators needed to know what they had, before they could start working patterns, asking questions, figuring out who might be a person of interest.

Figuring out what they had was up to the crime-scene people and the medical examiners. That would not happen on the first day. Lucas and Del hung around the hole for a while, watching, passing out Cokes, then walked across the old farm site, getting a feel for cover and dimensions and views.

The place was a perfect square, with the road at the south end. The other three sides were guarded by the remnants of a barbed-wire fence and a few old steel fence posts. The north side was covered with the remnants of a wood lot, and dozens of trees were scattered around the rest of the plot, apparently having grown up since the farm was abandoned. Everything else, except a thin clearing in the middle, was covered with a variety of brush and weeds.

A single track, probably along the old driveway, crossed the ditch over a rusting culvert. The spear-like tops of a few old irises grew along the edge of the ditch, and a line of ancient lilac bushes lay along the line of what had been the driveway.

There were probably a thousand identical plots in Minnesota, Wisconsin, and Iowa.

When they were done walking it, Del said, "You couldn't have invented a better place to get rid of bodies. Back country road, invisible cistern, nearest farmhouse a half-mile away. Roll in here at night, knowing where you're going, pop the lid, drop the body, put the lid back down, and roll on out. Knowing it ahead of time, you could be in and out in five minutes, with never a trace of what you'd been doing."

"But you'd have random kids coming up here to park, like the kids who found it," Lucas said. "It looks a *little* used, anyway. It's possible the killer ran into somebody up here, one time or another."

"If he did, he'd just back out . . . drive around, wait until they were gone."

"Yeah. Probably not much there," Lucas said. "If there's anything, Shaffer'll find it."

Del asked, "What do you want to do?"

"Go home," Lucas said. "But first, let's go talk to the farm lady."

Del took a last look around: "The asshole really did fuck up a great place to park. Did I ever tell you about the time Cheryl and me—"

"Jesus . . . noooo. . . ."

THE LAND AROUND the Black Hole plot belonged to a farmer named Sally James, who'd inherited it from her father twelve years earlier. James was in her mid-fifties, a stout red-faced woman whose blue eyes carried the glazed look of someone who'd been whacked in the forehead with a board.

Lucas and Del found her at her own farmstead, a half-mile away, visiting with a couple of reddish-brown horses in a corral next to her barn. "I think they're called sorrels, but I'm not sure I'm pronouncing it right," Del muttered, as they walked up to her.

When Lucas introduced himself and Del, James said, "I've already been interviewed three times by the police. As soon as they take the roadblocks down, there'll be fifteen TV stations in here, knocking on the door. I don't know what more I can say."

Lucas explained that there were two teams of BCA agents working the case, as well as the sheriff's office and the Wisconsin DCI. Since the crimes had gone interstate, he expected that the FBI might take a look. "We like to talk to people in person, because something they say may ring a bell with something else that we find, later on," Lucas said.

"You don't think *I* had anything to do with it?"

"We don't think anything in particular," Lucas said. "We're just getting started."

"How many do they have now? It was sixteen this morning," she said.

"Seventeen, now," Del said. "There are more to come."

"My lord, my lord. Ah, come on in. We can sit in the kitchen."

THE HOUSE WAS COOL, a relief from the day's heat. The kitchen smelled like bread and cooked carrots, with an undertone of cabbage and pork chop. James fired up a coffeepot, and passed around thick china cups, and they drank coffee and talked about it.

James started by sketching out a history of the place: the previous owner had sold his land to James's father, but nobody wanted the house or outbuildings. Eventually, title to the land was taken by the county for back taxes. "The county tries to sell it every once in a while, but nobody wants it. Four acres in the middle of nowhere, old septic tanks in the ground, that cistern, old foundations . . . it'd probably take twenty grand to clean it up. So, it sits."

"Kids park there, to make out," Lucas said.

"From time to time, in the summer," James said. "We've had Cub Scouts and Girl Scouts do overnighters there. And corn detasselers, like the kid who found the bodies."

"Does everybody around here know about the cistern?" Lucas asked.

"No way," she said. "I didn't know about it. That cistern probably hasn't been used for sixty, seventy years."

"Then how would the killer find out about it?" Del asked.

"That's a puzzle, and I've been thinking about it," she said. "There are these guys, treasure hunters, they go around to these abandoned farm sites with metal detectors and such, looking for old junkyards and buried treasure. Somebody like that could have found it. When this all came up, a deputy took me down there to look at it. I'd been in there a hundred times, and it never occurred to me that the cistern was still there. You couldn't see it, all covered up with sod. Nobody found it by accident."

"This is good stuff," Lucas told her. "From what you've told us, the killer has to be somebody who's familiar with the place, and there aren't many."

"Well . . ." There was doubt in her voice. "You know, this boy who found it, knew about the place because he was a detasseler."

Lucas smiled at her and said, "I was a city kid. I don't totally understand detasseling. I've heard of it."

James explained that corn plants have both male and female parts, and are self-fertilizing. "When you're hybridizing corn—

crossbreeding it—two varieties of corn will be planted in alternating strips. Because the corn is to be crossbred, you don't want one strip of the corn self-fertilizing. Instead, you want it to be fertilized only by the second variety. To do that, the tassels from the target variety are removed from the cornstalks, by hand, by pulling them out of the top of the stalk."

"Like castrating the corn," Del said.

"Exactly," she said.

The work was short-term, hot, tedious, and low-paid, usually done by high school kids sitting on detasseling machines that are driven up and down the rows of corn.

"Me and my dad have always contracted out part of the farm to grow hybrid seed, so there are detasseling crews taking breaks in that old Clemens place, eating lunch, every summer. That could be twenty or thirty people at a time, mostly boys. Over the years, there have been hundreds of them—hardly anybody does detasseling for more than a year or two."

"Would the hybrid company have a list of employees?" Del asked.

"Mmm, probably not," she said. "The way it works is, you need a lot of kids for a real short time, and the work is nasty. So, the seed companies recruit people who can recruit kids—and that usually means teachers. A teacher might contract to detassel, say, a hundred and twenty acres. Then he'll recruit a bunch of kids from his school, the company supplies the machine, and when the tassels start to pop, they go in and start pulling."

"Would the teachers have a list?" Lucas asked.

"Maybe . . . and it's the same teacher every year, usually. I'm sure the hybrid company would have that list, of the teachers. It's Marks's Best Seed Corn, over in Red Wing."

"Okay. That's a place to start," Lucas said.

"What good would it do you? You're going to investigate hundreds of people?"

"With this many dead, we might," Lucas said. "What you hope is, you punch the names into a computer, push a button, and your database kicks out names of sex offenders who match the names you put in."

"Ah," she said. "Of course. Computers."

THAT WAS ALL SHE HAD: scouts, lovers, treasure hunters, and detasselers. "Or teachers, I suppose. I'd go with the treasure hunters, myself. You get these bottle hunters, they love to find old outhouse pits. They'll get in there with a shovel and dig them right out. They can get a hundred bottles out of a good one, and they're worth some money."

"That happen over there?"

She shook her head: "Not that I've ever seen. But you know, those people can be sneaky. They find a good spot, get a friend to drop them off early in the morning, and they can dig out a whole pit in a day. Fill it back in, I might never know. I doubt that I'm in there twice a year, mostly during detasseling season. If somebody dug in there during the fall, I probably wouldn't go back in there until the next summer. It could be completely grown over."

"So . . . treasure hunters," Lucas said.

"Yup. Or a detasseler."

·   ·   ·

THEY PUSHED HER A bit more, but she couldn't think of anyone else who'd be familiar with the place. She'd had a boyfriend for fifteen years, she said, but he lived in Holbein and rarely came out to the farm. "He's a city boy, like you. When we do an overnight, I've got to go to *him*. He doesn't like the quiet out here. I'll tell you, though, he wouldn't hurt a flea."

"I'd like to get his name," Lucas said. "For the record, you know?"

OUT IN THE CAR, Del said, "He's a city boy like you. Likes to hear them cars."

"Hey. She's right."

"Holbein, if I'm not mistaken, is about the size of my dick," Del said. "There's probably only one car."

"Let's go look," Lucas said. "It's not exactly on the way home, but it sort of is, and we're not wasting our time backtracking."

HOLBEIN WAS LARGER than Del's dick, unless Del had been hiding his light. It was an older place, once a milling town on the East Fork of the Zumbro River, population now 5,706, according to a sign just outside of town. Driving through to the business district, the place seemed . . . usual.

Radically usual.

White- and blue-pastel clapboard houses on small lawns, most of the houses built sometime not long after the turn of the twentieth century. As they drove through the older neighborhoods around the business district, they saw only a handful of houses, obviously in-fills, that might have been built after World War II.

The East Fork of the Zumbro twisted along one edge of town, piling up in a small lake, behind what had probably been a miller's dam a century and a half earlier. The dam was not original, and was now a heavy, inelegant chunk of mossy concrete. The lake was sur-rounded by the city park, with an unoccupied kids' play area and a band shell, and a thumb-like protrusion of dirt and grass that stuck out into the lake, with a sign that said, "Ol' Fishin' Hole."

"I could live here," Del said.

"No, you couldn't. You'd turn into a coot and hang out at the general store, with your fly down," Lucas said. "You'd be known for goosing middle-aged women. You'd be the town embarrassment."

Del nodded. "Yeah. You're probably right."

They did a loop through the business district, which covered maybe a dozen square blocks. As Lucas had noticed before in small-town Minnesota, there seemed to be one of everything. Not many choices, but one of everything: one car dealer, one farm implement dealer, one hardware store, one lumberyard, an off-brand cell phone store, a computer repair shop, a fern restaurant, one diner, a VFW for the Lutherans, a Knights of Columbus for the Catholics, and for those who preferred getting hammered in secular surroundings, a bar. Sometimes more than one bar, even in towns no bigger than Del's dick.

"Remember when Flowers did that survey in a small town, to see who they all thought might be the bomber?" Del said, as they cruised. "Maybe we could do something like that."

"It's a thought. Virgil will be back in three weeks, and if Shaffer doesn't have anything by then, we could ask him to set it up. The problem is, the killer probably isn't from here." Lucas looked out the window at the small, innocent houses. "He's probably from Red Wing. Red Wing has a lot bigger population, is closer to the cistern. A lot more of the detasseler kids would come from there, than from here."

"We gotta call the people at this Marks's Seed Corn, see who's who," Del said.

Lucas shook his head: "No. That's not us. That's Shaffer, and I'd bet he's already all over it. He's got the clerks to handle it."

"What are we going to do?"

"Think about it, mostly. See what Shaffer gets, read the reports. What we really need to know is who the victims are. Where they came from, what's the earliest killing. The earliest killing is going to be close to the killer's home ground. It'll also give us some idea of how old he is now. He probably started as a young man, late teens, early twenties. If there are twenty dead, and he's doing four a year, then he's probably in his mid- to late-twenties. If he's doing one a year, he'd probably be in his forties, or close to it."

"He's not dumb, he's been getting away with this for a long time, with nobody suspecting," Del said. "I think that means he probably wasn't a teenager when he started. He's not reckless, he's thought about it. And if he was doing four a year, and they're all local, we would have noticed."

"So move the ages a little, make him a little older . . . We'll know, when we start putting names on the victims."

"A lot of names, man."

"Yeah." They'd made a circle through some of the back neighborhoods, with newer houses, then turned back onto Main Street and rolled down the hill toward the business district. "You seen enough?"

"Mostly. And one of the things I've seen is that supermarket. I bet they got donuts. All these small-town markets got bakeries."

"Aw, for Christ's sakes," Lucas said. He went on for a block, down a gentle hill, and turned into the supermarket parking lot. "Two cherry-filled, if they've got them. Or raspberry."

"Right."

"Don't let them know you're a cop," Lucas said. "It's embarrassing."

Del disappeared into the store, came back out with a white paper bag, and they sat in the parking lot for five minutes, eating the donuts, looking up the hill at the hardware store, and the lumberyard, and Sally's Paws and Claws, "For All Your Kitty and Doggy Needs."

Del said thoughtfully, "I'd like a little pussy."

Lucas chewed and swallowed and said, "Yeah? Have you talked to Cheryl about it?"

3

Lucas and Del were back in St. Paul by mid-afternoon. Other than reading some of the incoming reports from the crime-scene team and Shaffer's group, and talking to Shaffer's crew, they did nothing more about the Black Hole for three weeks.

Three weeks of an odd, edgy summer.

The cops all wanted to get the killer, of course, but it seemed at first that they'd never get any work done. Everybody wanted updates. The FBI sent around a profiler, and the profile was leaked, and the populations of all the small towns south of the Twin Cities began speculating about how well their neighbors fit the profile. That led to a couple of bar fights, screaming front-lawn confrontations, and unnecessary investigations prodded by round-the-clock media coverage.

Media reporting led to further problems. Both Fox and CNBC put investigation teams on the story, and both came up with lists of sexual offenders who fit "serial killer profiles" invented by the news teams with the help of *experts* from the West and East Coasts.

Disclosure of the lists led to disclosure of specific names, and the kind of conspiratorial "he could have done it" stories that had the cops jumping through their butts just knocking down the stories.

Three weeks in, Shaffer's crew had turned up almost nothing that they hadn't known about after the second day. The media, running out of easy stories, began sniffing around for those responsible for what was obviously an incompetent investigation. Rose Marie Roux took the brunt of the attacks. Henry Sands, without saying much about it, took off for a week-long Alaskan fishing trip right in the middle of it. Smart, some people said. Chicken-shit, said others.

All the attention, and the lack of progress, began to have an impact on morale: agents working off the clock, arguing, scratching their fingernails on blackboards of futility.

LUCAS'S GROUP wasn't working the Hole, and so were out of the line of fire. Instead, they focused on finding Bryan, the Ponzi guy.

They'd had a minor breakthrough earlier in the investigation when Lucas read through a long list of Bryan's American Express card purchases from the year before, and on that list he found . . . suits from Gieves & Hawkes, a dozen neckties from Ermenegildo Zegna, a dozen more from Hermès, and boots from John Lobb.

He'd been through Bryan's house, including his walk-in closet, after Bryan disappeared. Lucas knew his clothes—and he hadn't seen anything that'd really rung his bell, as those labels would.

To make sure, he and Shrake went back, and Lucas sifted through the clothes hangers, jacket by jacket. Nice threads—Ralph Lauren Purple Label, etc., but nothing from Gieves & Hawkes, no boots from John Lobb.

Lucas had interviewed Carrie Lee Pitt, Bryan's last-known lover, the night he got back from the Black Hole.

Carrie Lee was an unnatural blonde with a Missouri accent. She was almost, but apparently not quite, hot enough to be a rich guy's trophy wife. She was taking on-camera lessons in hopes of becoming a sideline interviewer for NFL broadcasts, trying to pick up the all-important hooker vibe.

"Y'all come right in," she'd said at the door of her condo in downtown Minneapolis. Her red lipstick was slightly smeared, as by a cocktail glass, and she smelled of Chanel 5. "I want to cooperate in every way possible."

She left the pink tip of her tongue parked outside of her upper lip, which made Lucas think of oral sex, as it was supposed to.

"What I really need to do is look at Mr. Bryan's clothes," Lucas said.

"You're welcome to it. I don't think he'll be needing them."

"We'll see," Lucas said.

They went back to the shuttered double closet, and he went through the labels. Carrie Lee helped him look, one breast pressing comfortably against the back of his arm. The missing clothing was still missing; Lucas went home and jumped the old lady.

"THAT SONOFABITCH IS ALIVE," Lucas said the next day. "He's not hiding out in a jungle. More like Paris."

Shrake and Jenkins developed a theory: Bryan had among his

conquests, somewhere, a nurse. The nurse had taken a pint of blood out of Bryan's body, just like she would a blood donor, and he'd smeared it around the inside of his car and then snuck away.

When pressed, Jenkins admitted that they had not one scintilla of evidence that would directly suggest that. They couldn't find a nurse, and Bryan, healthy as a horse, who went to a clinic on the rare occasions when he needed a tetanus or flu shot, had never established a regular doctor.

They continued to push, interviewing Bryan's bankers, friends, business associates, and his ex-wife. They looked at his known phones, credit cards, the places he'd taken vacations. They had a watch on with Homeland Security and customs.

Bryan had a son going to Yale, and when they checked on him, found that his tuition had been paid in advance—way in advance—and during the school year, he lived in a small house in New Haven, Connecticut, that his father had bought for him. That seemed to suggest that Bryan didn't think he'd be around to pay the bills on a monthly basis. Asked about it, the kid shrugged: "I guess Father knew he was in trouble, and made arrangements in advance, expecting to go to prison. I don't think he expected to be killed."

He didn't seem to be all that broken up by his old man's possible demise, Shrake said.

Del suggested that the names of all the money-losing investors be typed into a computer program and run against an FBI database of known associates. That had taken a secretary the best part of a week, and she'd moaned and complained the whole week. When they pushed the button on the computer program, nothing happened.

Like . . . nothing.

． ． ．

Lucas had two other, non-related cases hanging out there.

Del was watching two elderly couples named Case and Waters, from Sartell, Minnesota, who traveled together in an oversized RV, towing a Jeep Wrangler. According to sources on Lucas's Asshole Database (ADB), they financed their travels—indeed, their entire retirement lifestyle—by buying high-end black rifles on the northern plains, between the Rockies and the Great Lakes, where the cops were few and far between and the weapons were abundant. Once they had a hundred rifles or so, they'd transport them in the RV to the Texas border, where they sold them to a selection of underground dealers, both American and Mexican.

Lucas's sources said they'd unload batches of twenty or thirty rifles at a time, making anywhere from $400 to $800 each, depending on brand and condition, in profit. If you wanted to pay cash, that was great. If you wanted to pay in cocaine, that was even greater, since the two couples had a tight connection to the Washington Avenue Set of the Black River Lords of Chicago. On cocaine deals, the profit went to $1,500 per rifle. They'd make five or six trips a year.

"That's getting up to a half-million dollars a year, not counting their Social Security checks," Del said. Del was coordinating with both the ATF and the DEA on tracking the senior citizens. "Don't tell anybody I said this, but I think they might be doing some wife-swapping, too. The right spouses don't always go home together. And sometimes they have sleepovers, where nobody goes home. . . ."

"Yeah, Jesus, I don't want to hear about it," Lucas said.

. . .

IN ADDITION TO the gun peddlers, Lucas was dealing with a . . . peculiarity. A week after the Black Hole discovery, Lucas got an arrest warrant for Emmanuel (Manny) Kent, the brother of a serial bank robber named Doyle Kent.

Doyle Kent had been tentatively identified by Jenkins, after consultation with the ADB, and loosely tracked by the BCA and a variety of metro-area police departments for four months.

When he'd begun to focus on a bank in suburban Woodbury, the tracking got tighter. On a misty day in July, he'd gone into a Wells Fargo branch, wearing a fedora, one leg of a pair of sheer nylon panty hose over his face, carrying a bag for the money and a Colt .45. He'd been killed by the Woodbury cops when he came out of the bank shooting.

In the subsequent round of self-congratulation, Jenkins and Lucas had been credited with the identification of Doyle Kent, while the Woodbury cops got credit for taking him down.

The week after the shoot-out, the Minneapolis cops began picking up talk that Emmanuel Kent was telling his street friends that he was going to kill Lucas and Jenkins as soon as he could get a gun. If he couldn't get a gun, he was going to stab them to death, with a knife that he already had.

Lucas and Jenkins did some research on him and found that Emmanuel Kent was a thirty-two-year-old schizophrenic with four convictions for assault, and twenty-two arrests over sixteen years for possession of small amounts of marijuana.

Nobody had been badly injured in the assaults, which actually appeared to be street fights, rather than straightforward attacks.

Several doctors had also testified on Kent's behalf in the drug cases, telling the courts that his use of marijuana was an attempt at self-medication, because the use of antipsychotics made his thinking so fuzzy that he couldn't care for himself.

As one doc put it, "He'd rather be crazy than helpless, and the weed makes him less crazy."

In any case, Lucas and Jenkins found enough people to testify about Emmanuel Kent's threats that they were able to get a warrant and have him picked up for another psychiatric evaluation, to determine how serious the threats might be.

The Minneapolis cops were familiar with Kent and his habits, and where he usually slept, and so picked him up immediately. He was held at the Hennepin County Jail, and evaluated by a contract psychiatrist named Betty Calvin, who returned a report that said Kent was basically a gentle individual who spent his days collecting recyclable cans, and donations of dog and cat food, which he distributed to stray dogs and cats during the evenings.

When pressed, Kent told Calvin that he really didn't intend to stab anybody.

But, she said, he was also prone to acting out, and in a specific set of circumstances, might be a threat. She did not think he was capable of planning an attack, but if he should encounter Lucas or Jenkins at random, might be capable of some level of violence.

His animus toward Lucas and Jenkins was based on a news story in the Minneapolis *Star-Tribune* that noted that Lucas had been involved in another fatal bank-robbery shoot-out, which had been controversial at the time, at least among progressive legal theorists.

Two female bank robbers had been gunned down after robbing a bank and shooting one of the customers. Lucas and his team had trailed them for quite a while, being morally certain that the women had been involved in other robberies and shootings, but without evidence to arrest them.

Lucas had then *allowed* the women to go into the bank, and their killings outside the bank had been only thinly disguised summary executions, even though the two women had opened fire first. The surveillance without supporting evidence had been a violation of the women's *civil rights* . . . according to the theorists.

Not much was said about the customers and bank employees who'd been shot during the two-state robbery spree.

Emmanuel Kent, who might be crazy, but who was not illiterate, read the article and picked up on the concepts of "summary execution" and "civil rights."

Lucas, he said, had done it again, this time, to his brother.

Doyle had been Manny's only source of financial support during his life on the street. He used the money to feed himself and the cats and dogs, and to buy the weed he used to self-medicate.

Lucas and Jenkins, he said, had gotten his hero brother killed in cold blood.

"NOT TOO WORRIED," Jenkins had said, after reading the shrink's report.

"Not about being stabbed," Lucas said. "But Jesus, we sort of fucked him, didn't we? What's he gonna eat?"

"There are five hundred people out there tonight who are worried about that, Lucas, and none of them are threatening to stab us to death," Jenkins said. "If we want to worry about somebody, let's worry about them first."

But, Lucas thought, he didn't personally fuck the other five hundred. While he didn't worry obsessively about Kent, the guy remained like a small dark cloud that occasionally passed over Lucas's consciousness, bringing rain.

On the night of August 1, with Lucas still occasionally brooding about Emmanuel Kent, they finally got a definitive indication that Bryan, the Ponzi guy, was still alive, even if not kicking.

He stopped kicking when Inga (Bloomie) Bryan, the ex-wife, shot Bryan in the groin in the living room of her not-quite-oceanfront house in Palm Beach, tearfully explaining to cops that he'd entered the place in the night, without telling her that he was coming, and she'd mistaken him for an intruder.

Well, not really mistaken him—he *was* an intruder.

"Two shots," Jenkins told Lucas the next morning. "I'm told the surgeons were unable to make the necessary repairs, and went to amputation."

Lucas winced, and Shrake added, "Our current theory is, Bryan and his ex were not cooperating."

An hour after that, Rose Marie Roux called and said, "I hear Bryan is . . . mmm . . . available for questioning."

"Yeah, as long as he isn't talking with his dick," Lucas said.

"I heard that," she said.

"Yup. Shot with a very efficient double-tap, a .410 shot-shell followed by a .45 Colt, from a gun called the Governor, on the less expensive of two Persian carpets in his wife's living room, according to the Palm Beach police," Lucas said. "They know all about Persian carpets down there."

"Probably the one that held the room together," Roux said.

"*Dude.*"

"Okay. You're done with that, you can let somebody else do the follow-up, getting Bryan back here, and all of that," Roux said. "I want you on the Black Hole. Starting tomorrow. Or this afternoon. Shaffer's moving too slowly and people are getting pissed."

"Man, that case is dead in the water," Lucas said.

"If that was a deliberate pun, you're fired," Roux said.

"Sorry," Lucas said. "It wasn't deliberate. But it's Friday, I can think about it over the weekend—"

"No. I want you on the case right now. You know: *before* noon."

"How bad is it?" Lucas asked. "All the bullshit? I haven't been paying that much attention."

"Bad," she said. "We've got people from Fox and CNN renting apartments in Minneapolis. Old friends are getting nervous about talking to me. I think Henry . . . that asshole, that fishing trip was a disaster . . . I think Henry's put out some résumés."

"How about the governor?"

"We talk every day. The thing is, Minnesota's supposed to be squeaky clean, and the closer we get to the next presidential primaries, the less he wants people talking about all those boxes full of skulls. He doesn't want it to be a *thing*, if you know what I mean."

The Minnesota governor wanted the vice presidential nomination, and was in fairly good shape to get it. He had a lot of money, which could be used in a primary campaign, pulling in the national recognition; and he was far enough left to balance out a more centrist Democrat.

"I know what you mean," Lucas said.

"Yeah. When he leaves the job, I'm gone. When I leave, you're gone. Probably. But if he makes it as vice president, we get taken care of, one way or another. Life could be very interesting, if we can pull that off."

LUCAS PASSED OFF the Bryan follow-up.

Jenkins and Shrake talked with the Palm Beach cops, who said they'd found several hundred files in the trunk of a rental car that Bryan had been driving, along with a couple thousand dollars in cash, two ounces of cocaine, and three fake IDs, including a Honduran passport under the name of Rolando Smoke.

Jenkins suggested that both he and Shrake would be needed to question Bryan about the whereabouts of any remaining money, and to review all that paper.

Lucas got them authorization, and that afternoon, as he and Del began a methodical rereading of all the crime-scene and investigative reports on the Black Hole, they watched, from Lucas's office window, as the two agents loaded their golf clubs into Shrake's truck for the ride out to the airport.

"Gonna be a high-quality investigation down in Palm Beach, you betcha," Del said.

LUCAS DIDN'T CARE; Bryan was disappearing in the rearview mirror. He turned back to the pile of paper in front of him.

"Twenty-one skulls now," he said. "Twenty-one girls, before the well went dry."

"You know, if we take this on, the media will find out, and we're gonna have media shit raining down on us, too," Del said.

"We don't have a choice," Lucas said. "But let's try to sneak into it quietly."

SHAFFER'S GROUP had identified seven of the victims, which left fourteen unknown. Of the seven, two had been identified through dental work, two through credit cards found in the Hole among a layer of rotting cotton and polyester, one through a driver's license, and two through DNA samples matched to worried parents or siblings of missing women, who'd volunteered to supply cell samples.

The bodies that had been identified through dental work, credit cards, and the driver's license had been confirmed through additional DNA comparisons.

All of the identified women came from Minnesota, except the most recent one, and from a roughly trapezoidal area ranging as far north as the southern suburbs of St. Paul, and as far south as Rochester, as far east as the Mississippi River, and as far west as I-35—an area roughly sixty miles long and forty wide. The one exception, Mary Lynn Carpenter, from Wisconsin, had apparently been taken from the banks of the Mississippi across from the Minnesota town of Red Wing. All victims' homes had been spotted on a map included with Shaffer's paper.

The earliest known victim had disappeared ten years earlier, but with fourteen yet to be identified, and with the other seven spaced a minimum of a year apart, Shaffer's team thought it likely that they hadn't yet found the earliest victim.

"ALL SEVEN OF THE WOMEN disappeared in mid-summer, ranging from June twenty-second to August eighteenth," Shaffer had told Lucas, two weeks into the investigation. They were in Lucas's office: Shaffer had come by to chat, to see if Lucas had been thinking outside the box. He had not been. Shaffer was looking beat-up, though in a tidy way. His clothes were ironed and his shoes were polished, but the dark loops under his eyes were the size of bicycle tires.

"None of them disappeared in the same year," he said. "Our statistician says that's probably not a coincidence although it could be—we have a weak theory that he kills every summer, and only once. If that's true, and he's killed this year, then the first murder was twenty years ago. That's not a sure thing—he might have killed more frequently in the early years. If the theory's right, he's probably in his late thirties or early forties, and lives somewhere in that trapezoid between Minneapolis and Rochester. I suspect it's close to the center of it. If he's smart enough to get away with all these killings, then he's smart enough not to make long-distance trips with a body in his car."

"What about the detasseling thing? Or the treasure hunting?"

Shaffer shook his head. "Nothing. We located and talked to a half dozen treasure hunters, pretty much ruled them out. They call themselves 'detectorists.' The detasseling information is so fragmented that we can't say much one way or another, but the ones we've been able to check, haven't panned out. But that's well under half of the potential detasseling suspects."

"What about technique? Does the killer scout the girls?" Lucas asked.

"Can't tell yet. Three of them, at least, seem to be opportunity-based. Women out partying, maybe drunk, alone, at night. He might have scouted them, but he didn't have to—they were ripe for the picking. When their disappearances were investigated, nobody remembered seeing anyone with the women."

"Observant and careful," Lucas said.

"And bold," Shaffer added. "Maybe with a backup excuse, if somebody should question him."

"Like what?"

"We've been picking around the idea that it could be a cop," Shaffer said. "We haven't found anything that would make us think we're right."

"Hope not," Lucas said.

"We all do," Shaffer said. "But we're having trouble picking up patterns, which makes it seem more likely that he was killing spontaneously—no pattern except opportunity, which is the next thing to random."

"All blondes," Lucas said.

"Yeah, and not dishwater—mostly all pale blond. That's a pattern, but it doesn't mean much in Minnesota, in terms of prediction."

"Anything on the ropes?" Lucas asked. They'd found more than a dozen ropes in the cistern, dumped with the bodies.

"Not much. A variety of brands, a variety of materials. Could be . . . this is weak . . . from marinas. Half of them are nylon, which you don't see that much of, outside marinas. The rest are polypro, which is everywhere."

"Plenty of marinas around Red Wing," Lucas said.

"Yeah, and we've been in all of them," Shaffer said.

They talked about some miscellaneous possibilities, all thin, and then Lucas asked, "How much trouble are you having with the TV people?"

Shaffer grimaced. "Ah, you know: they're waiting outside every morning. I've actually had them follow me around town."

"Be cool," Lucas said.

"Oh, yeah—but you know, if you could just count on the newsies being as competent as we are, things would be a lot easier."

THAT HAD BEEN the last extended conversation they had about the case, although the rumor mill said Shaffer was choking. Lucas doubted that: it had seemed from the beginning that, barring a fantastic piece of good luck, the investigation would be a long one. Shaffer was patient.

The news media, on the other hand, wasn't. They were looking for a hero, not an accountant.

AFTER THE DEPARTURE of the golfing twosome, Lucas and Del continued plowing through the Black Hole paper, looking for something they could get their fingernails beneath, something that might suggest a trail.

"Gotta be something in common with the girls," Del said. "They're all under twenty-five. Most of them were known to party. . . ."

"They weren't known to go to the same clubs, or even the same parts of town . . . any town," Lucas said. "They weren't known to hang out with the kinds of guys who'd intersect. None of them went to the same school. Ever. They don't have any relatives in common. Their jobs weren't similar, so it wasn't like a UPS man was picking them out. One of them had a night job, and was probably picked up in the early morning . . . so it's not a cable guy, snatching them out of their apartments."

THEY WERE STILL AT IT when Hopping Crow stuck his head in the door. He was vibrating. "We have a developing anomaly in the DNA tests."

"Is an anomaly the same thing as a break?" Del asked.

"Could be."

"Since you're standing in my door, it must be interesting," Lucas said, leaning back in his chair.

"Not so much interesting, as batshit crazy," Hopping Crow said. "Getting clean DNA has been a problem. With those water-soaked bones and all the meat that came off them, it was like a DNA stew down that cistern. We're mostly getting the clean stuff out of teeth, and even then, we haven't had much to match it to. Three hours ago, we got a cold hit from the criminal database."

"Really," Del said.

"Yeah, really—the skull came from a woman named Doris Mead, the mother of Roger Douglas Mead, who was convicted of first-degree sexual assault four years back."

Lucas's chair came upright with a bang: "I'd call that some kind of break."

"Eh, it's more complicated than that. For one thing, he obviously couldn't have killed Carpenter or Fisher, because he was locked up when they disappeared. And he has no history of violence. He was a high school social studies teacher, and the girl was sixteen, and cooperative. Anyway, he's in Stillwater, and Buford talked to him. He says his mom is definitely dead. She died thirteen years ago, of a stroke. She was buried in a cemetery at Demont, which is over by Owatonna. When she went in the ground, her head was still attached."

Lucas and Del both stared at him for a second, then Del said, "Her skull was . . . grave-robbed?"

"Looks like it," Hopping Crow said. "The good thing about it is, apparently not all the skulls belong to people who were murdered. The bad thing is, we don't know yet which is which. That's going to take some more lab work."

"Who's going down to the cemetery?" Lucas asked.

"Shaffer. Got in his car and took off like a big-assed bird. Shaffer told me to tell you about it, in case you wanted to go down yourself—everybody's heard you're done with Bryan."

"How's he doing?" Del asked Hopping Crow. "Shaffer?"

Hopping Crow said, "He seems to be calm. Unnaturally calm. Especially for a guy who has about fifteen people screaming at him, from the governor on down."

Del said to Lucas, "Probably why we got the invite. All those screaming people."

Lucas said to Del, "I'm going. You want to come along? What's happening with the old folks and the rifles?"

"They're buying. Betty Case bought two mint Bushmasters from a guy up in Anoka yesterday. They're pretty close to a full load. Her old man took the RV in for servicing yesterday, probably won't get it back before tomorrow. So, today . . . I could go."

"Then let's."

SHAFFER WAS FIFTEEN MINUTES ahead of them. Lucas called him and Shaffer said, "It's the Valley View cemetery, just west of I-35 at Demont. You don't go into town, you take a left on the first street you come to, after the exit. That's Twelfth Street. The cemetery borders the street, about a half-mile down."

"Are you pulling the coffin?"

"That's the plan," Shaffer said. "Buford got authorization from her son—Doris Mead's husband took off for the Florida Keys after she died, and Roger doesn't know how to get in touch with him. So, we're good on that. I talked to the guy at the funeral home down there, they should be digging now."

"We're right behind you," Lucas said.

THE DRIVE TO THE DEMONT EXIT took forty-five minutes, and another five down to the cemetery, which was between the town and the freeway, on a flat square of ground with cornfields on three sides, and the approach road on the fourth.

Shaffer's blue Chevy Equinox sat with a couple of sedans on the left side of the square, where an orange Kubota tractor/backhoe sat motionless next to a pile of yellow dirt. Lucas pulled up and he and Del got out, and found Shaffer and two middle-aged men in sober blue suits watching a third man, in coveralls, who was down in the grave, using a spade to scrape dirt off a coffin.

When Lucas came up, Shaffer turned and said, "We're not going to pull it yet—we're just going to open it and see what's inside." He gestured at the two men in suits: "This is Joe and Leon Murphy, they run Murphy's Funeral Home in Owatonna. They arranged Mrs. Mead's funeral."

"Any idea of what happened?" Lucas asked.

Shaffer said, "Two theories: one, the killer is weird . . ."

"Good call," Del said.

". . . and two, he was literally grave-robbing. Roger Mead told Buford that at the funeral, his father put their wedding rings and Mrs. Mead's engagement ring into her hand, to be buried with her. They were gold. He thinks the engagement ring might have been worth a couple of thousand dollars, and whatever gold is worth in the wedding rings."

"Not more than a couple of hundred," Del said.

Shaffer said, "Yes, but: treasure hunters. We've been looking at treasure hunters, and the guy who dug this up, in the middle of the night, looking for diamonds and gold . . . what's that, if it's not a treasure hunter?"

THE FUNERAL HOME OPERATORS were brothers, and looked alike, with nearly identical comb-overs, except that one was thin and the other was fat. The fat one, Leon, said, "You don't often see that— putting valuables in the coffin. A lot of times, with a cremation, for example, the relatives will ask for the gold that comes out of the loved-one's teeth. Most people are pretty practical: they don't bury money."

"If the grave was robbed, the robbers must've known about the jewelry," Lucas said.

"Had to," Joe Murphy said. "It might be possible to rob one grave out here with nobody noticing, but you couldn't go around digging up a whole bunch of them. They had a specific grave in mind." They all looked around the flat, windswept cemetery. There were only two other graves showing raw dirt; extensive digging would have stuck out like a sore thumb.

The guy in the hole, who hadn't been introduced, said, "Hand me the key," and Joe Murphy passed him a slender crank, a long metal handle with a right-angle stem. Murphy said, "Four latches . . ."

"Got 'em," the guy said. In digging up the grave, he'd cut out a small platform to one side, where he could stand while he opened the coffin lid. He undid the latches with the coffin key, and Lucas looked away when he pulled open the lid: the whole procedure, messing with buried bodies, disturbed him.

He looked back when Shaffer said, "Well, there you go."

The body remained in the coffin, still preserved, though shrunken. The head was missing, and the hands, which had apparently been crossed over the woman's midriff, had been turned over. Her hands were empty.

"Took the jewelry and the head," said Shaffer. "Both a robber and weird."

"Possible that she had gold fillings," Leon said.

Lucas looked at the brothers and asked, "Do you know about any other grave robberies around here?"

Joe said, "Years ago . . . not long after Mrs. Mead was buried, so it could be the same bunch. There were some sepulchers over in Holy Angels that were broken into, some body parts were taken."

"One or two over in Holbein about the same time," Leon said.

Shaffer asked, "Where's Holy Angels? How many years? Skulls?"

"It's in Owatonna. Yes, skulls, I think. Maybe fingers. This must've been"—he looked at his brother—"around the turn of the century?"

His brother shook his head. "After that. Remember, we saw that one break-in when we had that boy back from Iraq. First one back, must have been near the beginning of the war."

Joe snapped his fingers and said, "Ah, right. You're right."

"Any suspects?" Del asked.

"Not as far as I ever heard," Leon said. "And I would have heard. Nobody was ever caught. There were several break-ins, all about the same time, and then they stopped, and there weren't any more. It's possible that the robbers found out that the risk wasn't worth the rewards they were getting."

"What about the other ones?" Shaffer asked. "The Holbein ones."

Leon shrugged. "Don't know about those. Just heard about them. Probably ought to ask at Doncaster's, up in Holbein."

"That's the Holbein funeral home?"

"Yes." Leon nodded.

"Okay." Shaffer looked into the grave and said, "We'll have to pull the coffin. We'll want to close it and lock it to protect it, and then get it out so the crime-scene people can work it over. There may still be fingerprints inside, so you gotta be careful. Can you guys handle that?"

Leon Murphy nodded. "We can."

"All really odd," Joe said.

Shaffer said, "I need somebody to take me to those other . . . what do you call them? Sepulchers? Those are the things that look like little stone cabins, right?"

"Right," Leon said.

"I'll want to look inside . . . want to get a feel for them."

"We can take you there. You want to go right now?"

"I do," Shaffer said. "I'll want to look at everything you've still got on the Mead funeral . . . names, people who paid for stuff, flowers, whatever. I want to know who was there."

"We can look up that at the office, we'll still have some of it," Joe said. "They were Catholics, and it was a Catholic funeral, if I recall . . ."

"It was," Leon said.

". . . so you could probably find the officiating priest, he might be some help."

"I need it all," Shaffer said.

SHAFFER WAS ALMOST TREMBLING with excitement. On the way back to the cars, he said to Lucas, "This is our first solid lead. The killer knew the Meads. Had to. Probably was at the funeral. We'll go back to Roger Mead, try to contact Mrs. Mead's husband. I'll start working the funeral angle right now. You got any ideas?"

"Those sound like the best ones," Lucas said. "Some cop had to work those earlier grave robberies. Maybe they had some ideas about suspects, even if they never arrested anyone. Del and I could talk to whoever it was."

"Do that. Be sure to update us," Shaffer said. "Bless me, this is something."

BACK ON THE ROAD, Del said, "I don't think I've ever seen Shaffer that wound up."

"He's got a sniff of the guy, after a hard month," Lucas said. "That's always good."

"Gettin' the sniff," Del said. "Yeah, it is."

LUCAS CALLED FROM the car, and was passed from the Steele County sheriff's office to the Owatonna police department, where they talked to a detective sergeant named Ralph Bellman.

"I remember that, those break-ins. Pretty darn creepy," Bellman said. "Let me see . . ." They could hear him tapping on computer keys, and then he said, "Okay, I got it. Never made any arrests. Talked to some kids, we thought maybe it was some kind of, you know, Harry Potter thing. I don't think the kids we talked to knew anything about it, so . . . we came up empty. We've got a bunch of reports, you're welcome to them, but they don't say much."

"Like to take a look anyway," Lucas said. "We'll be there in ten minutes or so."

BELLMAN WAS RIGHT: there wasn't much. Three sepulchers had been broken into, and the heads were stolen from the female bodies interred inside—four heads, total. Two of the female bodies were missing ring fingers. Three of the four male bodies had not been touched; the fourth was missing a ring finger.

"Two of these places were really old—went back a hundred years," Bellman said. He was a husky, cheerful man, balding with a long pale face. "The other one was from the forties. We think probably the missing fingers meant the bodies were buried with some jewelry, which was stolen. That made us think it wasn't kids, but the missing heads made us think it might be. You know, midnight rituals and all of that."

"There were only three?" Lucas asked. "Only three of these things, and they broke into all of them?"

"Right. I guess they're not used much anymore," Bellman said. "More of an old-timey thing."

"Could we get printouts of the reports?" Del asked.

"Coming right up," Bellman said. Then, hushed, "You think whoever did this is the Black Hole killer?"

"We're hoping it's something," Lucas said. They'd told Bellman about the grave and missing skull in Demont. "We were kinda hoping we could hook the three sepulchers down here to the grave up there."

Bellman kicked back in his chair, his forehead wrinkling. "Mead," he said. "There are a few of them around, but I don't know if they're related to your Mrs. Mead. The people in these sepulchers died a long time before Mrs. Mead, though. I think probably the link was the valuables. Maybe they scored when they dug up Mrs. Mead, but didn't want to do all the work, and the sepulchers looked like easy targets. If that's it . . . the link wouldn't go anywhere."

"Except that the robbers would have to know who was well-off enough to bury valuables," Del said. "You'd have to be local to know that."

"Or well-off enough to have sepulchers," Lucas said. "Those things can't be cheap. At least not compared to just sticking somebody in the ground. And you could figure that out by driving by the cemetery."

Del said, "Okay. But they had to know about Mrs. Mead, and the rings in her hand. Wonder what Shaffer's getting?"

4

Shaffer was on the cusp of solving the Black Hole killings, he thought. The idea came to him as he stood in front of one of the sepulchers at Holy Angels cemetery in Owatonna. He confirmed it by backtracking to the other two. He didn't want to talk about it, because it sounded . . . too easy. Possibly even stupid. Should that turn out to be the case, he didn't need Davenport or Capslock gossiping about it.

He said good-bye to the Murphys and headed north and east to Holbein. He'd just gotten into town, when he saw a young woman loading her kids into a van. He slowed, rolled his window down, and said, "I'm a police officer with the Bureau of Criminal Apprehension. Could you point me to the cemetery?"

"Sure," she said. She pointed down the street and said, "Take this street down about four blocks, one block past the stoplight, and you'll see the turnoff for 19. Take that about, oh, a little ways. You'll go over a bridge on the Zumbro, and the cemetery will be right there on your left."

"Thank you," Shaffer said.

The cemetery was on a piece of high ground above the East Fork of the Zumbro, which, at this point, downstream from the dam and fishing hole, wasn't much more than a creek. The cemetery was smaller than Holy Angels, but bigger than the one at Demont. There were two sepulchers, both of a gray limestone stained with age, both with iron gates, both surrounded by ankle-high grass and weeds. He paused at the first one, and moved on to the second, which was just as old as the first.

They confirmed what he'd seen in Owatonna.

He said, "Huh," but with a clutch in his stomach. He'd worked a lot of hard cases, and the tightness wasn't unfamiliar: he was on to something.

On the way out of the cemetery, he took a call from his wife: "Will you be home in time for the game?" she asked.

"Probably not for the first few innings. I've got something going here. You better take him, and I'll try to get up there as soon as I can."

"You've got something going?"

"Maybe. It's thin, but maybe," Shaffer said.

HE DROVE BACK into Holbein, found the funeral home, and talked to the owner, who'd taken over two years before, after half a lifetime in Texas. He was not around at the time of the sepulcher break-ins, and had no idea of who might know about them.

Back in the car, he drove over to the police department, but there was nobody home. Earlier in the investigation, he'd learned that there were usually only two officers working at a time, and they spent most of their time patrolling. When somebody needed to call them, they went through City Hall, but City Hall was already closed. In an emergency, they could be reached through the Goodhue County sheriff's dispatcher, but this wasn't exactly an emergency.

Shaffer was hungry. He hadn't eaten since breakfast, so he drove back to Sperry's, the supermarket, parked, went inside, and after a one-minute look-around, guiltily bought a couple of jelly-filled bismarcks. He took them out of the bag and threw the bag into a trash can outside the door. Back in the truck, he sat eating a bismarck with his left hand, while he made a couple notes in his notebook. He managed to drip a pinhead-sized drop of cherry filling on the page, said a rare bad word—*fuck me*—licked his little finger, and wiped it off.

When he put the notebook away, he sat in the truck and ate the second bismarck, and at some point, realized he was looking up the hill at a Hardware Hank store.

Another idea. He started the truck, drove up the hill to the store, parked, went to the entrance, and found it locked. He looked at his watch: ten after six. A sign in the window said summer store hours were seven to six. An unusually early closing, for a farm town, he thought. But he was an urban kid, like Lucas, and wasn't sure about that.

Below the "Closed" sign was another, handwritten one that said, "In case of emergency, contact Roger Axel." Below that was a phone number and an address. The address included a house number on First Avenue, and Shaffer turned away from the door and walked

back to the street. Main Street was down the hill; First Avenue was
fifty feet uphill.

He walked up and looked at the closest house number: Axel
lived in the next block. Shaffer went that way, shadows now length-
ening across the sidewalks. He was feeling the energy of a possible
solution: thin, but maybe something.

ROGER AXEL was having his regular after-work drink with Horn
when there was a knock at the door, a metallic *rap-rap-rap* of the
horseshoe knocker. R-A, as the locals called him, paused halfway
between the kitchen and the living room, bourbon in hand, and
said, "Who in the hell would that be?"

"One good way to find out," Horn said.

It was well after six o'clock. R-A put the glass down and went
to the door, pulled the curtain aside, and peered out at an unfamiliar sandy-haired man. The man said, "Hello?" and seemed pleasant
enough, so R-A opened the door and said, "Yeah? Who're you?"

The man showed him an ID case and said, "My name is Shaffer,
I'm an agent with the Minnesota Bureau of Criminal Apprehension.
Could I have a word with you?"

"What's this about?" R-A asked, stepping through the door and
onto the front porch. R-A was a small man, with a soft belly but
a bench-lifter's hard shoulders and arms. He had the red nose of a
hard drinker, and slack, grainy skin around protruding eyes. He was
balding, a scrim of thin blond hair brushed over a freckled scalp; his
fingers were stained with nicotine.

"I'm looking for the answer to a peculiar question, and I thought
you might be able to help me," Shaffer said.

He asked the question, and R-A frowned and said, "Hmm. I'd have to think about that for a moment. C'mon in."

He left the door open behind him and Shaffer stepped inside. R-A said, "Push that door shut, will you? We got flies. I was just getting a bourbon and ice for myself and Horn. You want one?"

"Oh, no, thank you . . ." Shaffer stepped into the living room and looked up at the walls: the ceiling was high, eleven or twelve feet, and ringed all around with stuffed heads: deer, antelope, a couple of bears, a mountain sheep, moose antlers minus the moose head.

Shaffer stepped farther into the room and in the back of his head, barely at the conscious level, he thought, *Headhunter.* Then he noticed the figure in the wheelchair. Horn was looking right at him, and Shaffer blurted, "What the hell?"

R-A had taken a .45 off a bookshelf, where he kept it cocked and locked. He flipped the safety off and shot Shaffer in the back, through the heart. In the small room, the blast was deafening; but with all the walls and shelves between them and the nearest neighbors, R-A was almost sure he'd get away with it.

Shaffer essentially died on his feet, the hollow-point .45 slug clipping his spinal cord and blowing out his heart. He never had another conscious thought, but took a half-step forward and did a slow pirouette and sank to the floor, then went flat.

R-A put the .45 back on the bookshelf, between *The L.L. Bean Game & Fish Cookbook* and Bill Gardner's *Time on the Water,* and looked down at the body, which was still trembling and shaking, as Shaffer's brain died. R-A was familiar with the phenomenon.

There was blood to be considered. "Goddamn blood'll get in the floor cracks and smell to high heaven if we don't clean it quick," R-A told Horn.

"Plastic garbage bag," Horn suggested.

R-A hurried into the kitchen, got a bag, laid it flat on the floor, and heaved Shaffer's body onto it. The body was as loose as a sack of Jell-O; there was a pool of blood under it, which had left a huge blot on Shaffer's shirt. More blood was seeping into the oak-plank floor, and he hurried back to the kitchen to get paper towels and a spray bottle of Scrubbing Bubbles, and cleaned it up.

"Now what?" he asked, when that was done. Shaffer was staring up at him.

"I wouldn't put those paper towels in your trash can, that's for sure," Horn said. He was a shriveled, dark-complected old man. "Best to burn them."

"I have to get rid of the body. I could use his car, if I can find it," Horn said.

"Look at his keys," Horn said. "If it's got one of those remote opening things, it'll beep and blink its lights at you."

"Good idea," R-A said. He stooped, as if to look for the keys right then, but Horn snapped: "Stop. You fuckin' moron. Didn't you spend about a hundred hours reading about DNA? Use some gloves. And don't go flashing those car lights with the remote, and then going right over to it. Wait until dark, anyway."

R-A said, "Right." He looked out in the street. There were no unfamiliar cars parked in front of the house. But it had to be close by, he thought. Maybe at the store. "What else?"

"The slug probably went through him and hit somewhere over by the fireplace. You might want to find the hole and patch it."

"Yeah. Keep talking."

"Town's too small to leave the body here. I'd move it somewhere. Zumbrota, maybe."

"Yes, but . . . how would I get back here? Without somebody noticing?"

"Run? Walk?"

"That's eight miles," R-A said.

"You just shot a police officer. You'll get life for that, without parole, even if they never did connect you to the girls, which they would," Horn said. "Walking eight miles is out of the question? What would it take you, three hours, maybe?"

"Hmm . . . I'll think about it," R-A said, looking at the body. He was in fair shape, he thought, for a man who smoked and drank too much. Three hours was not impossible—he walked that far, over rougher ground, during deer season. "In the meantime . . . where'd I leave that drink?"

JUNE SHAFFER called Lucas at eleven o'clock and asked, "Have you heard from Bob?"

"No. I haven't seen him since we left Demont," Lucas said. He was sitting in his study, reading a book called *How Much Is Enough?* He'd already determined that he had enough. "Last time I saw him, he was headed over to a cemetery in Owatonna."

"I'm getting really worried," she said. "He hasn't called me. He told me he'd miss supper, but he'd be here for at least part of Todd's ball game. He didn't make it and his cell phone is turned off, and sends me to the answering service. I've left messages, but he hasn't called."

"I don't know what to tell you," Lucas said. "The last time I saw him, he was with a couple of guys from a funeral home. I could give them a call."

"Could you? This is really not like him, and with him investigating a crazy man. And the last thing he told me was that he might be getting somewhere."

"Yeah? Okay, let me check."

LUCAS CALLED JOE MURPHY, who said he'd last seen Shaffer as he was leaving Holy Angels cemetery. "I don't know what was up, but he looked at the sepulchers out there, and all of a sudden, he was in a hurry. He looked . . . intense . . . about something. I don't know what."

"Did he take any phone calls while you were with him?"

"Hmm. He was talking on his cell when we first got to the cemetery, and he got out of his truck. I didn't hear what he said."

Murphy didn't have anything else—Shaffer had looked at all three sepulchers, and had walked back and forth between them, then had enough and went hurrying back to his car.

"Never called or came back," Murphy said.

"And you don't know where he was going?"

"No, but he asked about the sepulchers up in Holbein. The break-ins up there. He could have been headed that way."

WHEN LUCAS FINISHED with Murphy, he woke up Bellman, the detective sergeant from Owatonna, and asked if Shaffer had stopped by. He had not. "If he had, I would have seen him—the boss was gone all day up to the Cities, and any investigative inquiries would have come to me. You lose him, or something?"

"I don't know," Lucas said. "He's not a guy to get lost. He's the last guy in the world who'd ever get lost."

"What kind of car is he driving? We've got a dozen hotels here, I could send a couple cars around to look at parking lots."

"That'd be good. I think Holbein's in Goodhue County, maybe you could call them, too?"

"Not a problem."

"Let me call his wife about the car." He remembered that Shaffer had been driving a blue SUV, but hadn't noticed exactly what kind.

He called June Shaffer and she picked up instantly. Shaffer hadn't called. His car was a Chevy Equinox, a year old, and she found the car registration in a file and gave him the tag number. "Do you know what phone service he was with? AT&T? Verizon?"

"Verizon," she said. "And he had some kind of lost-phone service."

"I'll get back to you," Lucas said. He called Bellman back and passed along the information about Shaffer's SUV.

"He having trouble with the old lady?" Bellman asked. "He's not out on the town?"

"Nope. No, I don't think so," Lucas said. "That's one reason I'm getting worried."

LUCAS'S ADOPTED DAUGHTER, Letty, wandered into the study, carrying a bottle of red vitamin water and a book. She was a slender girl, and athletic, and, Lucas had noticed, much admired by the jocks at her high school, whom she admired back. More things to worry about . . .

She asked, "Did you know that the Davenport family has a crest?"

"Great," he said.

"What happened?" she asked, picking up a *tone*.

"Ah . . . can't find a guy. He should have been home hours ago,"
Lucas said.

"Del?"

"No, no . . . Shaffer."

Letty knew most of the people Lucas worked with, including
Shaffer. "He's the lead on the Black Hole case."

"We maybe got a break on it this afternoon," Lucas said. "We
were down around Owatonna. He never came back."

"Have you called the cops?"

"Yeah, they're checking the motels," he said. "I gotta make a call."

He called the BCA duty officer, explained about Shaffer, and
then said, "He's carrying an iPhone, and his wife said they've got
some kind of lost phone function on it. Get in touch with the Apple
people, see if they can activate it. While you're doing it, call Verizon. He's with them, and maybe they can spot it."

He gave the duty officer Shaffer's cell phone number: "Give me a
call back the instant you figure out where he is."

BELLMAN CALLED BACK an hour later and said that the Owatonna
cops had checked all the motels and bars, and the main streets, and
had found a few Chevy Equinoxes, but not Shaffer's. "I called over
to the sheriff's department and asked them to talk to the patrol
guys, tell them to keep an eye out. Goodhue's doing the same."

Lucas passed the word to June Shaffer, who was becoming
panic-stricken. "Something terrible has happened," she said.

Lucas said, "It's too early to think that. I'll head on down there myself and wake some people up. If he calls, you can get me on my cell phone."

LUCAS'S WIFE, Weather, was already in bed. She was a surgeon, and would be cutting in the morning. He woke her, said, "I have to go out." He gave her a quick explanation, and she sat up and said, "God, I hope nothing happened."

Lucas went back downstairs and called Del. "What are you doing? You in bed?"

"No, I'm up in North Oaks. They got the RV back early and they're loading up the guns. I'm here with Stuckney from the ATF. What's up?"

Lucas told him, briefly, and Del said, "I'm sorry, man, but we're pretty busy around here."

"That's okay, stay with it—I was looking for company, more than anything," Lucas said. He hung up and pulled on a jacket.

Letty had been lingering near his study, and now asked, "Can I go?"

"I might be all night," Lucas said.

"That's okay. I'm not doing anything tomorrow. If you get sleepy, I could help drive."

"Bring a jacket," he said.

THEY WERE ON I-35 south of the Cities, coming up to the town of Faribault, when he took a call from a Steele County dispatcher: "Agent Davenport?"

"Yeah. What's up?" He had the call on the car's speaker.

"Uh, well, we've got some pretty bad news. Your duty officer gave us a general location on Shaffer's phone. It's down in Zumbrota, in Goodhue County. We passed the word to a Goodhue deputy. They found the car, and there's a body inside. The deputy opened the door to make sure the victim was dead, and then stepped back, because he doesn't want to mess up the scene. The victim was shot to death."

"Ah, Jesus, ah, goddamnit," Lucas said. "How do I get there?"

ON THE WAY to Zumbrota, which was east of the interstate, a half hour from their I-35 turnoff, Lucas shook Rose Marie Roux out of bed. "You're sure it's Shaffer?" she asked.

"No, but it probably is. We've got to get somebody going, to notify June Shaffer." Lucas looked at his nav system, which predicted he'd be in Zumbrota in thirty-six minutes. The nav system didn't know that he had a siren and lights. "I'll be there in half an hour. I'll confirm then."

"My God, Lucas, did he find the Black Hole killer?"

"Must have. Must have," Lucas said.

"How?"

"I have no idea," Lucas said. He told her about the break earlier that day, and also how thin it was.

"Call me when you know for sure it's him," Roux said. "I'll start kicking people out of bed."

THEY WERE RUNNING fast through the night, on a rural highway, past balls of gnats swarming over the warm road, past fireflies in the meadows, the highway stripes flicking by, and Lucas glanced once at Letty and saw her tight, eager face willing the road to *pass*, to get there.

And he thought, *Shit, she likes it too much. She's gonna be a cop, one way or another.*

He would have preferred that she do something else. She'd even talked about applying to West Point, and he'd grudgingly agreed that for a person of her . . . inclinations . . . it wouldn't be a terrible idea. Now, glancing again at her face, he thought it would be a terrible idea. She needed the same kind of daily rush that he did. She needed a gun on her hip and somebody to hunt.

THEY FOLLOWED Highway 52 to Zumbrota, then threaded their way through town, taking directions from a cop by cell phone, turned north on Main, crossed the North Fork of the Zumbro, left on Pearl, then down a long lane guarded on both sides by twenty-five-foot-tall arborvitaes. As soon as they made the turn onto the lane, they saw the gathered flashing lights of a half dozen cop cars, and assorted civilian sedans and SUVs. When they pulled in, the faces of twenty men and a few women turned toward them.

"You know what to do," Lucas said to Letty.

"Be nice and keep my big fat mouth shut," she said.

"Couldn't have put it better," Lucas said. They got out and a cop stepped over and Lucas held up his ID. "BCA. You got my guy?"

The cop said, "I hope not. C'mon this way." He glanced at Letty, but said nothing.

They walked between cop cars, killing the conversation that had been going on. The Equinox was on a cemetery road, just to the right of the last tall arborvitae. The cemetery extended on both sides of the street, and in the reflected light from the cluster of cars, they could see the heavy canopies of large trees, and pale tombstones scattered across the neatly trimmed lawn.

A tall blond woman in civilian clothes—Catrin Mattsson, the Goodhue County investigator whom Lucas had met at the Black Hole—was talking to a couple of uniformed cops at the back quarter-panel of the Equinox. Mattsson, in blue jeans and a letter jacket, broke off when Lucas and Letty came up. "Davenport."

"Yes. He's in the car?"

Instead of answering, Mattsson swiveled to Letty: "Who're you?"

"My daughter," Lucas said. "She's okay, she's been before."

Mattsson nodded: "If you say so, but it's an unhappy thing to look at." To Lucas, she said, "It's him. It's Bob."

LUCAS AND LETTY stepped over to the Equinox and looked through a back window, which had been lowered. Shaffer was lying faceup on the backseat. His sport coat was pulled open, revealing a huge bloodstain on his shirt. In the pale illumination of cops' LED flashlights, his eyes were wide open and dirty gray. He didn't look surprised: he just looked dead.

Letty said, "Shot once."

Lucas was still reacting to the sight of the body: not a friend, but a colleague he'd known for years. A prickling sensation ran through his skin, like goose bumps, but a tighter, tenser feeling. After a few seconds, he caught up with Letty's comment and asked, "You're sure?"

"Not without a doc saying so, but you can see only one pucker in his shirt, and it's right in the middle of the bloodstain. Looks like he was shot in the back with a hollow point. I've seen a lot of wounds like that," she said. "Hit him square in the heart. Whoever shot him probably doesn't know that much about shooting, or he would have hit him at least twice."

Lucas turned away from the car and rubbed his face. Didn't want to look back, and didn't; instead, he spoke sideways to Letty, who was still looking at the body. "Maybe he was trying to keep the noise down," Lucas said. "You can almost always get away with one shot. With two, somebody might come looking."

She turned her face to him: "You never told me that."

"You never needed to know," Lucas said.

Mattsson was next to Letty: "You said you'd seen a lot of wounds like that. How would you . . . ?"

"Used to run a trapline up north," Letty said. "Bang the coons with a head shot, .22 hollow points. Go in small, come out bigger, when they came out at all. Like this. Except this was a bigger slug." She turned to Lucas and said, "It looks a lot like the holes your .45 makes, when we're shooting paper."

Lucas was rubbing his forehead, and he said, "Yeah, yeah." He wasn't ready for analysis. He said to Mattsson: "We got a break today. Maybe. I think Shaffer followed it right in to the killer, and this is what he got."

"He didn't call me," Mattsson said.

"He didn't call anyone," Lucas said. "I suspect he had a really questionable lead, and it just took him . . . to this. He was a smart guy: it could have happened."

"I know. I talked to him six or seven times in the last month. I'm sorry," Mattsson said.

"So am I," Lucas said. "He was a good cop. He had a nice family, and most of the time, when I was dealing with him, I was an asshole."

Mattsson said, "Well." And then, again, "I'm sorry."

R-A HAD BEEN HOME for two hours before Shaffer's body was found. The initial high from the killing had worn off, and the walk home had cooled him off even more.

Horn was waiting: "How'd it go?"

"Perfect," R-A said. "I had a lot of time to think. Know what? I don't want to get caught."

"We'll have to work on that," Horn said.

"I mean, I *really* don't want to get caught," R-A said. "Unless I can think of something smart, I probably will be."

"Got a couple of ideas . . ."

"Not tonight. I'm too tired. I need a drink or five," R-A said.

"I got a question for you. Did killing that cop—that *male*—did that give you a boner, too?"

"Fuck you," R-A said.

"Gave me one," Horn said. "I gotta tell you, I liked watching him die. Not as good as the girls, because it was so quick. But you know, old Horn got boners like nobody got boners."

"Ah . . . shut up." R-A poured a drink.

That night, in bed, a peculiar thought crossed R-A's mind. Horn was a nasty, cynical remnant of the man he'd once been—but he was a great help, from time to time. Now, he might have become a liability. There was a warrant out for Horn, and there had been for years. Horn, in fact, hadn't been outside for years, except twice when R-A had gotten extraordinarily drunk and had taken him out for a quick roll in the night.

That was crazy-dangerous. If anyone had ever seen them . . .

Horn had been a cop, of a kind. He worked out of the police department, and even carried a gun, a .22, that right now was in R-A's gun safe. He also carried a spray can and a lasso on a pole and drove a truck. He could issue tickets—but only if your dog was running loose, or didn't have a license.

Horn was the dogcatcher.

And not *just* a dogcatcher. He was the skunk remover, the cooncatcher, the possum-shoveler, the gopher trapper, the dead-animal remover. You got a squirrel killed on the sidewalk, as the cops said, get on the Horn.

Horn and R-A had met at a rifle range. Horn was interested in death, and R-A was interested in big-game hunting. They were both interested in sex, and both of them had to pay for it. Both were interested in the altered states brought on by alcohol; both were alcoholics. Neither had other friends.

Their friendship was careful, but over some time, mutual interests emerged. R-A was a treasure hunter: he was the one who'd found the cistern at the abandoned farm. He was the one who knew about the diamonds and gold in the Mead coffin—he'd heard about it from a customer at the hardware store.

The raids on the sepulchers started as a joke and a dare. They'd continued until they realized that the risk was too high for the small rewards they were getting.

That's how it started with the women, too. As a joke and a dare. Not quite believing that they'd ever do it.

Then doing it.

There weren't twenty-one skulls, as the cops thought. There were twenty-three—but the first two were rotting bone somewhere in the deep woods in Wisconsin, lying under a few inches of dirt and oak leaves.

After the first two, they'd worked out a system for taking the women. They were proud of the system, and it worked perfectly. They sat around at night, watching baseball on TV and working out their strategies.

Everything went well, until the accident.

Until woman number five, Heather Jorgenson, rose up out of the backseat of Horn's truck with a blade in her hand.

R-A could still see the scars in Horn's thin, bony neck; could put his fingers in them, if he'd wanted to.

Didn't do that.

He touched Horn's shoulder and said, "I'm going to bed. We'll talk in the morning."

"Got ideas," Horn said.

5

With a murdered cop, a lot of stuff had to happen, but after identifying the body, not much of it was Lucas's job.

He was shaken by Shaffer's murder, more than he would have thought. He wandered away from the group at the truck, sat down for a minute on a tombstone. He couldn't shake from his mind the first sight of Shaffer: a yellowed-out vision like the photo of a dead man on an old postcard. Would somebody be looking at him like that, sometime in the future?

He sat like that for a moment, the heels of his hands braced on his thighs, then sighed and pulled his cell phone from his pocket and called Roux. Shaffer lived north of the Twin Cities, and it would take a while to get the notification done.

"Lucas, you need to take this over," Roux said, after he gave her the news about Shaffer.

"No, I don't. I need to catch this guy, but I'm not good at

organizing a big crew like Shaffer's," Lucas said. "Get somebody else to run the crew, but I'll find the guy. I promise you."

After a few seconds of silence, she said, "Okay. That's the deal, then. Somebody else takes the crew, but you find him. In the meantime, we got the preacher on his way up to Shaffer's house."

The preacher was a BCA agent who was also an ordained minister; a hard-nosed cop and a soft-nosed minister, for a Baptist, anyway.

AFTER TALKING TO ROUX, Lucas heaved himself off the tombstone and walked back to Mattsson and Letty and the other cops. He said, "Shaffer's wife will be notified pretty quick."

Mattsson nodded and said, "We thought we better leave this to your crime-scene people. Our guy is here, but with the possible link to the Black Hole killer . . ."

"I'll get them down here. Bob should have a notebook in his jacket pocket," Lucas said. He'd seen Shaffer take it out any number of times. "You think your guy could go in there and slip it out, without messing anything up?"

Mattsson turned to one of the deputies, who nodded and said, "Let me get my stuff."

As the cop went to get his crime-scene kit, Lucas called the duty officer and ordered up the crime-scene team.

"What a fuckin' disaster," the duty officer said.

"Yeah."

THE COPS ALL STOOD AROUND and watched as the crime-scene deputy slipped on surgical gloves and, after looking at the handle on the back door with a flashlight, popped the door. They all looked inside, but there was nothing on the floor or the seat near Shaffer's body.

Lucas said, "Left side."

Moving as carefully as he could, the deputy slipped his fingers under the lapel of Shaffer's jacket, lifted it, and with his other hand, slipped the orange-covered notebook out of Shaffer's inside pocket. "I'll bag it. We can look at it through the bag," he said.

As he carried the notebook back to his car, Lucas's cell phone buzzed. He took it out of his pocket and looked at the screen: Shaffer's wife was calling. She hadn't yet been notified.

Lucas flashed the screen at Letty, who blurted, "Don't answer it."

"I think I gotta," Lucas said.

"No, no, let it go, let it go . . ."

He let it go; he could call back. When the phone stopped ringing, he asked, "Why?"

"Because we know there's nobody there with her, except her kids. She shouldn't hear he's dead on the telephone, from somebody who's a hundred miles away."

"When I don't answer . . ."

"There could be a lot of reasons you don't answer," Letty said. "You might have left the phone in the car . . . Dad, somebody should be there with her. Believe me."

He thought about it for a minute, then said, "Okay," and put the phone away.

THE CRIME-SCENE DEPUTY had the notebook sealed inside a transparent plastic bag, and Lucas and Mattsson put it on a car hood and bent over it, and the other cops shone a half dozen flashlights on it.

Lucas turned the pages, awkwardly because of the bag, but got it done. There were brief notes on the grave opening at Demont, and the interview with the funeral directors in Owatonna. Then Shaffer had gone to a new page and had written *Holbein* at the top of it, and underlined the name. Beneath that were brief, unhelpful notes from an interview with a man named Robert Gibbons. Lucas didn't immediately recognize the name, but Gibbons had told Shaffer that he hadn't been in Holbein long enough to know about the break-ins at the local cemetery's sepulchers.

Lucas remembered something one of the other funeral directors had said about the funeral home in Holbein, and said to Mattsson, "I'm not sure, but I think this guy works as the funeral director over there."

Mattsson called over her shoulder to one of the deputies and told him to check the name.

"Is that blood?" Letty asked.

They looked at a pinkish smear at the bottom of the Holbein page. There hadn't been blood anywhere else on the notebook.

"Could be. Have to check," Lucas said. He closed the book gently, to preserve the stain, and handed it back to the crime-scene guy. "Careful with it," he said. "We need to get it into our lab as quick as we can. If that's not Shaffer's blood . . ."

A deputy came over to Mattsson and said, "That guy, Gibbons— he's the Holbein funeral director, like you thought."

"Let's figure out what we're doing here, and then we oughta run up and talk to this guy," Lucas said. Mattsson nodded.

A Goodhue County deputy named Mackey lived in Zumbrota, just around the block. He and Mattsson and a couple other senior deputies, and the Zumbrota chief of police, with Lucas and Letty, went over to Mackey's house. They were the last car in the caravan over, and Letty couldn't stop talking about the murder until Lucas said, "You want to shut up for a while? I'm having a hard time over here."

She said, "Okay," and shut up.

Mackey's wife made them coffee and took some hot cross buns out of a refrigerated tube and put them in the oven, and the whole bunch of cops, and Letty, sat around the kitchen table and talked about the murder.

They agreed that unless something very strange had happened, Shaffer had found the killer.

"Had to be dark by the time he got to that cemetery," Mattsson said.

"Maybe," Letty said. "He wasn't killed there, though. Somebody drove him there."

You could almost hear the eyebrows go up. Letty continued: "He was shot once in the heart, from the back, and was lying there faceup. He wasn't shot in the truck—didn't look like there was enough blood anywhere. Somebody had to put him there. I suppose he could have been shot outside the truck, in the cemetery, but then, why bother to carry a heavy dead guy to the truck, and get blood all over your-self, and leave your own DNA behind? It would have been easier and safer to put him in some weeds, or drag him behind a tree, or walk away. He was shot somewhere else, and driven to the cemetery."

The convocation of cops looked at her, without saying any-thing, and then the deputy's wife chirped, "Makes perfectly good sense to me."

Letty said, "Thank you."

Lucas: "You might be right. But you might be wrong, too. A lot

of things that happen at crime scenes don't have good reasons: killers get scared, freaked out, like anyone else. They do things in a
panic. I'll tell you one thing: the guy's not a traveler. He's not somebody from the Cities or Red Wing, come down to get rid of the
bodies. Whether he drove Shaffer down here, or came separately
and killed him here, he's from somewhere close by. Shaffer found
him in Owatonna, or in Holbein, or here in Zumbrota, or somewhere in between. Shaffer was in at least four cemeteries, and left at
least two of them alive. How Shaffer got here, I don't know. But the
killer is close by."

The cops all looked at each other, nervously: biggest serial killer
at large in America, right now, and right here.

"Something else," Lucas said. "If Letty's right, and somebody
drove him here, that means he knew what Shaffer was doing today—
that he was looking at cemeteries. They had to talk, and the killer
had to know what Shaffer was thinking, and that it was worth killing him about. Somehow. Some way. They had to talk."

THERE WAS A KNOCK on the screen door, and a young cop stepped
into the kitchen. He looked at Mattsson: "I ran around to those
houses, like you said, and nobody heard any shots tonight. It's cool
enough so that people aren't running their air-conditioning, but two
of them had windows open. No shots."

Mattsson nodded and said, "Thanks, Terry. Go all the way up the
road, hit the rest of them." The cop backed out the door and Mattsson said to Letty, "You're looking better."

One of the deputies asked Lucas, "What're we doing tonight?
Other than covering the scene?"

"That's about it," Lucas said. "Stay away from the car, keep people away from the area until the crime-scene crew gets here. We need to talk to people who might have seen a car coming and going, and ask who they think it might have been."

Another of the deputies said, "Something just occurred to me—I need to talk to Jeff. Excuse me."

He went out on the back porch, and they could hear him on his cell phone as they worked through other possibilities. A couple minutes later he stepped back in and said, "The guy's from here. Zumbrota."

"Why?" Lucas asked. The cop sounded so sure that it felt like a break.

"I was thinking about what Letty just said, about the guy driving him here. Assuming there's only one guy involved, and if he drove the body here, how'd he get away? Where'd he go? The answer is, he'd have to walk. On the other hand, if they met here—if the killer had his own car—and Shaffer was killed here, he could have been pretty much from anywhere."

Lucas: "And?"

"I called Jeff, our crime-scene guy, and told him to look at the steering wheel on Shaffer's car. It's plastic—and it's been wiped. The front seats are leather, and they've been wiped, too. Everything in the front of the car has been wiped. He can tell just by looking at them with a flashlight. If he'd never been in the car, why wipe it? Didn't wipe the backseat."

They all considered that for a moment, and Letty said, "He drove Shaffer's car with the body in it, and then had to walk away . . . unless he has an accomplice."

"That's happened with a couple of serial killers," Lucas said.

"The Hillside Strangler in L.A. was actually two guys, related some-how, I'm not sure how. But it's rare."

Mattsson said, "He was driving Shaffer's SUV, so he could have had a bicycle in the back, or even a small motor scooter."

"Didn't wipe the back," the other deputy said.

"Could have, but it doesn't feel quite right to me," Lucas answered. "Can't sneak on a bike or a motor scooter, you have to go on roads. People would remember seeing a stranger on a bike, after dark. He was probably on foot."

"He's not only from around here, like Lucas said," the deputy said, knocking on the kitchen table. "He's from right here—from Zumbrota."

Mattsson asked, "Who in Zumbrota could be a serial killer? Couldn't be too many possibilities . . . single male, probably in his late thirties or early forties, if his killing goes back as far as the grave robberies."

"*Probably* single," Lucas said. "There have been a few married killers, even happily married. But probably single."

The Zumbrota chief said, "Boy, I'd have to think about that. I know everybody in town, just about, all the long-timers, anyway. There are a few single guys . . . not anybody I'd suspect of this."

"Get a list going," Mattsson said. "Think about it more. If we get some DNA out of the car, it could be important."

MATTSSON ASKED LUCAS, "How are we going to coordinate this? It's our jurisdiction, too."

"Our crime-scene crew will do the science," Lucas said. He

paused as the deputy's wife started a tray full of hot cross buns around the table. He took one and passed the tray on. "But I guess what we really need tonight is exactly what you're doing: talking to as many people as you can, asking about unusual sightings. Guys walking or running on their own. We need every speck of information we can find. We'll take rumors, even. Anything we can hook onto. I won't be running the operation, they'll appoint a new team leader first thing tomorrow."

"It is tomorrow, Dad," Letty said.

THEY TALKED ABOUT other immediate needs—Lucas would tell the new crew leader to pull all of Shaffer's cell phone records, and take his phone apart. He had an iPhone, so it probably had a file of his phone-call locations. "That might tell us where he was, and when, and who he was talking to. I'll tell them to get that information to you as fast as we can pull it out. We need everybody pulling together to limit the confusion."

"We can do that," Mattsson said. "I gotta tell you, I'm a little pissed about not being included in that exhumation at Demont. You BCA guys aren't paying a hell of a lot of attention to what us folks are doing. I've been running my ass off all over the county, talking to people, and Shaffer acted like I was some loony on the sidewalk."

"He was . . . focused," Lucas said. "He did what he did."

"I'm sorry he's dead, but I didn't like the way he handled things," Mattsson said.

"Well, I'm sorry," Lucas said. "When the new guy takes over, I'll tell him to work with you. To pay some attention to what you're thinking."

"If you're not important enough to run it, why would they pay any attention when you tell them to work with me?" Mattsson asked.

Lucas shrugged: "That's the way it is."

Mattsson looked at him, without saying anything, then Letty reached out and touched her hand and said, "Dad's good friends with the governor and with Rose Marie Roux. The BCA people pay attention to him."

Mattsson looked at him for another moment, weighing him, then glanced at Letty and said, "All right."

Lucas said, "Listen, for your guys out here, the ones who'll be doing the walking. Make sure they go in pairs. Nobody out there alone. This guy . . . well, you know."

"Yeah. But you—what're you going to do?"

"I'm going up to Holbein and talk to the funeral home guy. You might want to come along."

She nodded again.

"If we get anything, we'll follow it up. You might want to keep some guys handy, in case that happens. If there's nothing there, I'll head on home, get some sleep," Lucas said. "Then tomorrow, I'm going to look at everything everybody got, then I'm going back to Demont and Owatonna and Holbein, walk the same ground Shaffer did, talk to the same people in the same places, and see if I can figure out what Shaffer found that got him to the killer."

"Careful," one of the deputies said. "Like you said, you don't want to come up on him, without knowing it."

.   .   .

THEY WENT TO HOLBEIN in three cars, Lucas in his SUV, another deputy chosen by Mattsson in a second car, and then Letty and Mattsson in Mattsson's car. When Letty asked if she could ride with her, Mattsson shrugged and said, "Sure, if you want to."

"Tired of me?" Lucas asked.

"I talk to you all the time," Letty said. "I'd like to get another viewpoint."

They didn't call ahead: in an excess of caution, they decided they wanted to talk to the funeral home director without his knowing they were coming.

"Though I can't see that he did it," Letty said, as they walked out to the cars. "Looked like Shaffer's notes on him were finished."

Mattsson nodded: "Yup. But then, there was that smear of blood, right after he finished writing. Maybe the funeral guy was right there."

THE DRIVE TO HOLBEIN took ten minutes, and another couple of minutes to find the funeral director's home. They knocked and rang the bell, and Gibbons's wife showed up first, and then Gibbons, wearing blue flannel pajamas with little rocket ships on them. "He was murdered?" Lucas had seen the phrase "his jaw dropped," usually in not-very-good novels, but he saw it now in both Gibbons and his wife. Their jaws dropped, and Letty looked at Lucas, and Lucas nodded: the funeral director was out of it.

"We didn't talk for very long, and he was perfectly okay when he left—I don't think he was much interested in talking to me when he found out that I moved up from Texas only a couple years ago," Gibbons said. "He seemed to be kinda in a hurry about something. He wanted to know if Neil Parsons—he was the former owner here—had told me anything about the sepulchers out at the cemetery, but Neil never did."

"Where's Parsons now?" Mattsson asked.

Gibbons tipped his head to the south. "In the cemetery."

He recapitulated the whole interview with Shaffer, and after twenty minutes, Lucas, Letty, Mattsson, and the other deputy were back out on the sidewalk. "I got nothing out of that," Mattsson admitted. "Didn't even scratch up an idea."

"Me neither," Letty said.

Lucas said, "All right. We're heading home. I'll be back tomorrow morning. We're close to the guy, whoever he is. That's new. Here's something to sleep on: Shaffer saw something, and it took him straight to the guy. What did he see?"

Mattsson: "Did he know what he was seeing?"

ON THE WAY HOME, Lucas took a text from June Shaffer that said, "Find him and kill him."

He passed the phone to Letty: "June Shaffer's been notified."

"Ah, jeez," she said. "If I ever get to be a cop, I'll never be a notifier."

LUCAS USUALLY SLEPT LATE. He and Letty hadn't gotten back home until four in the morning, but he was up at nine, not rested but alert. Weather had taken the two small children, Sam and Gabrielle, to the park, but had left a note: *call me when you get up.* He called her and told her about Shaffer.

"Oh my God. That poor June. How many kids did they have? Two, I think? Both in school?"

"I think so," Lucas said. "From what we could see, there were no defensive wounds, no struggle, and Shaffer was in shape, and did that aikido stuff—whoever did it shot him down in cold blood. I suspect he never saw it coming. Had to have been indoors, I think. He had to have gone somewhere, pretty much on impulse. He's such a compulsive record-keeper that if he'd developed a serious clue, he would have made a note of it, or called someone. Anyway, I'm going back down there. I might be late getting back."

"Do not—DO NOT—take Letty."

"I'm not planning to, though I suspect she's already sitting in the truck," Lucas said.

"Don't take her," she said. "Just find this guy."

Lucas finished cleaning up, and before he left the bathroom, saw on his shaving-TV a photo of Shaffer, with the report of his murder. The news report was light: they didn't know much yet. He turned off the TV, got dressed, including a .45 that he carried in a belt rig, and went downstairs.

Letty was sitting in an easy chair, legs casually crossed, pretending to read a magazine, and he said, "No."

She dropped the magazine. "Why not?"

"Because you're a kid. Besides, your mom made me swear I wouldn't take you. Otherwise, I might."

"Listen, Dad—"

"I don't have time for an argument," Lucas said. "I'll be back tonight. Ask me again, when I get back. Though I'm not the one you have to convince. You need to work on your mom."

WITH LETTY WATCHING from the garage door, Lucas backed out of the driveway and headed across town to BCA headquarters.

The place was crawling with agents; he had to thread his way through a crowd listening at the conference room door. Henry Sands, the director, just back from Alaska, had already appointed an agent named Jon Duncan to run Shaffer's crew, and Duncan was briefing the crew on Shaffer's murder. When he saw Lucas, he waved him in and asked, "What do you know?"

Lucas told them about the scene the night before, what he thought had happened. "I'm going down there now, and I'll go over the same ground that we know that Shaffer covered. Do we have anything from the crime-scene crew yet?"

Duncan shook his head: "Nothing definitive, nothing good. They're working the front seat for DNA. We're going to flood Zumbrota this afternoon, start talking to as many people as seems reasonable. Start checking off the single guys. But, a woman named"—he flipped a page in a notebook—"Cathy Irwin called here an hour ago and said she saw Shaffer's picture on TV this morning, and she spoke to him for a couple of seconds in Holbein. He asked her for directions to the cemetery, and she told him where it was, and he drove away. That was about ten minutes to five. You already talked to Gibbons, the funeral director. We talked to him again from here, and he told us the same thing he told you: he had the impression that Shaffer was on to something. He even asked, but Shaffer brushed him off. But, he got that impression. We do know he was alive and operating then, a little before six o'clock."

Lucas took out his notebook and made a note of Cathy Irwin's name. "I'll talk to her," he said. "Nothing from the Goodhue sheriff's people?"

"Nothing," Duncan said. "By the way, we can't find Bob's main notebook. That little one was mostly names and numbers, but he had a big one, too. One of those leather folders with a yellow legal pad in it. You didn't see anything like that?"

"No. Sounds like something we need," Lucas said. "I'll call Catrin Mattsson at Goodhue and have her run some people around to the places we know he stopped."

Lucas told them about Mattsson: that she was thorny, but seemed bright, and suggested that Duncan treat her with care.

"I will do that," Duncan said. "I met her last month, and we talked some."

"Then I'm outa here," Lucas said. He turned at the door and said, "There was some blood on Bob's notebook. We weren't sure if it was his."

Duncan waved him off. "We checked it first thing, wanted to get some DNA going. Wasn't blood at all. It was jelly."

"Jelly."

"Yeah. No DNA. No break," Duncan said.

Lucas took another step and turned back again: "I don't know if you guys got it, but one of the funeral guys from Owatonna told me that Shaffer made a call just as he was arriving at the cemetery there."

Duncan said, "He was calling here, checking on the crew."

· · ·

BACK IN HIS OFFICE, Lucas called Del: "I'm going down to the Hole. What's happening with the old folks? Are you free?"

"Ah, man, Shaffer," Del said. "I mean, Jesus Christ. He had kids, I mean . . . I really need to go with you, but I can't. I was up all night, I'm dying, but they're getting ready to roll. Me and Artie are watching them load up. The guns are all on board, now it's food and water and talking with the lady who feeds the cats, and all the stuff you can do in the daylight."

Artie Martinez was another agent with the ATF.

"All right. Talk to you when you get back," Lucas said. "Take care."

"And you. Cocked and locked," Del said.

THE DAY WAS a good one, with puffy dry clouds, the countryside beginning to show color as they got into August. Lucas had been tempted to take his Porsche for the run south, but wound up in the Mercedes again, with the feeling that he could be banging around on some back country roads: the 911 didn't like gravel, or, for that matter, any bump or divot more than two inches high or deep.

He'd planned to go through the cemeteries in the same order as Shaffer had, but found himself curious about the woman Shaffer had talked to. Instead of stopping at Demont and Owatonna, he went straight through to Holbein, calling ahead to the woman, Cathy Irwin. She was waiting when he arrived at her big white two-story home a block off Main Street.

She was a pretty woman, and smart, and Lucas learned nothing from her. She was eager to help, but she'd spoken to Shaffer for only a few seconds, and had never seen him again.

"Did he seem like he was in a hurry? Like he was excited?" Lucas asked.

"No. He was just sort of . . . friendly. He seemed like an ordinary guy. He was polite, seemed perfectly relaxed, and thanked me, and went off toward the cemetery."

"Where's that?" Lucas asked.

"Down by the East Fork."

LUCAS DIDN'T CARE for cemeteries, but Holbein's was a pleasant-enough place, as cemeteries went, and if somebody had told him that he'd be buried there, after a life of, say, a hundred forty years and much more sex and barbecue, he would have been content with the prospect.

The land lay above the narrow river, fenced off from the surrounding fields by ordinary barbed wire. The grass looked like it was probably cut every couple of weeks, and was now a little shaggy. Clumps of wild black-eyed barbecue and purple coneflowers grew here and there along the fence line. Bobbing their heads in the light breeze.

Most of the graves were modest, with low tombstones, and the two sepulchers stood out as grim monuments to death: they were gray and age-stained—limestone, he thought, something Poe might have written about—with rusty iron gates. He walked around them, scratching for any kind of insight they may have inspired in Shaffer. He was still doing that when his phone rang.

He took it out of his pocket and looked at the screen: Mattsson, the Goodhue County investigator.

"Yes," he said. "This is Davenport."

"You better get down here, to Zumbrota," Mattsson said. "We might have a witness. We might even have a suspect."

"I'm in Holbein," he said. "I'll be down as quick as I can."

"That'd be seven or eight minutes," she said. "Unless you hurry."

Lucas hurried. Mattsson gave him directions, but as he accelerated out of Holbein, he had the uneasy feeling that he'd just made a mistake, or had missed something important. He didn't know what it was, and the feeling was fleeting, gone before he got to Zumbrota.

THE WITNESS LIVED in what Mattsson called the Sugarloaf neighborhood north of town, in a stone-and-clapboard ranch-style house with a front-yard flower garden lining the walk between the garage and the front door. Mattsson was there with another deputy named Tom Greenhouse, and the witness, and the witness's parents: the witness was eight years old.

"It's something," Mattsson said. She met Lucas in the driveway. "It's a kid, but there's no reason to think she's not reliable. She brought it up on her own, and her parents confirmed that she saw the guy last night."

"Let's talk to her," Lucas said.

The witness, Kaylee Scott, was waiting in the living room with her parents, Reggie and Carol Scott, all three of them honey-blonds, all a little portly, more than a little anxious. The first thing Reggie asked Lucas was, "Do you think we should get out of town? Can you put us up?"

"Let's see what we've got," Lucas said. "I'm not really up to speed on this."

The story was short and sweet: the night before, the Scotts had been returning from Red Wing, late, after visiting Carol Scott's sister's family. They'd driven down Highway 58 from Red Wing, then cut cross-country north of Zumbrota to County 6, and down County 6 to Sugarloaf Parkway. Just before they got to the parkway, they all agreed, Kaylee, who'd been sitting in the backseat, had blurted, "There's Mr. Sprick!"

Reggie, who was driving, said he hadn't seen anything, and Carol was dozing.

"I was looking right, where I was turning," Reggie Scott explained. "He was in the left ditch—the east ditch."

When Kaylee said, "There's Mr. Sprick!" Reggie had turned and asked, "What?"

Kaylee said, "Mr. Sprick was down in the ditch."

"What?"

"Mr. Sprick was walking in the ditch." She said she'd seen him just as her father started to turn.

Reggie and Carol had blown off the claim, thinking that Kaylee was sleepy and must have been imagining things. They went home and they all went to bed.

Then, the next morning, they'd seen stories about Shaffer's murder, and about police officers going through town, looking for someone who might have been seen late, in the area of the Zumbrota cemetery. The cemetery was only a few hundred yards north of the Sugarloaf area, and Highway 6 went directly past the turnoff to the cemetery.

"Who's Mr. Sprick?" Lucas asked.

Kaylee said, "Mr. Sprick, the mailman."

"Mark Sprick, the letter carrier for the neighborhood," Mattsson said. "I've got a guy keeping an eye on him, on his truck. He's down south right now. We've been putting together a file, but there's not much. Never been arrested as far as I can tell. He's been married, he's divorced now. Apparently threatened violence to his ex-wife but wasn't arrested."

"How old?" Lucas asked.

"Forty-one: right in the age slot."

Reggie Scott said, "We're gonna need protection."

Lucas looked at the kid, who was sitting on a red velveteen couch, and asked, "Honey, how sure are you that you saw Mr. Sprick?"

"I saw him," she said positively. "I said so right away. I saw his face looking at me."

"We need to talk," Mattsson said to Lucas.

MATTSSON, LUCAS, AND GREENHOUSE talked on the front lawn. Mattsson said, "I think we pick him up, and squeeze."

"Is there any way to figure out who his friends are, if he has any?" Lucas asked. "Maybe touch them first, or at the same time? See what they have to say?"

Greenhouse said, "After I found the girl, I talked to Catrin and then I called the chief of police. He knows Sprick, says as far as he knows, he's an okay guy. He came here in high school, his parents still live here. He rents a house on the south side of town, apparently got in a loud argument with his ex once, when they were in the process of getting divorced. He was warned to stay away from her, but nothing official was ever done."

"Pure negligence," Mattsson said. Greenhouse looked a bit uneasy, and she snapped, "What?"

"The chief said his ex was a hell of a lot meaner than Sprick, and Sprick denied doing anything violent or that he threatened anyone," Greenhouse said. "The chief said he thought Miz Sprick might have made some of it up."

Lucas said to Mattsson, "Better talk to the ex-wife, if she's around."

"The chief says she's in Faribault, works at a florist over there," Greenhouse said.

"I hate to leave Sprick running around loose," Mattsson said. "If he gets a whiff of a witness . . ."

"But it'd be best if we had something to hit him with, before he knows we're coming," Lucas said.

"We could keep an eye on him, if you want to run over to Faribault," Mattsson said.

Lucas said, "Well . . . I could do that."

"You think it's something?" Greenhouse asked.

"It's something. The girl saw somebody," Lucas said.

"And she sees Sprick all the time," Mattsson said.

"If it was Sprick, and he lives south of here, why was he north of the cemetery?" Lucas asked. "What's out there that would have had him walking in the ditch?"

They all looked north: they couldn't see it, but beyond the heavily treed neighborhood, there wasn't much but the cemetery, a couple of farm equipment dealers, a fairground, and then a lot of farm fields, stretching out for miles.

"I don't know," Mattsson said. "Maybe he ditched a car up there? I do believe Kaylee."

MATTSSON CALLED the Faribault cops and had one cruise by Busch's Florist Shoppe. Andi Sprick was working. Lucas talked to Kaylee for a couple more minutes, and then to her parents, and left fairly sure that somebody had been in the ditch the night before. He suggested that Mattsson call her crime-scene deputy and have the Scotts show him where Kaylee had seen the man in the ditch.

While they did that, he would go to Faribault, a fast run straight west. He got an address for the flower shop from the Faribault cops and punched it into the car's nav system.

ON THE WAY, Lucas found himself losing faith in the sighting. He couldn't have explained exactly why, except that the suspect, Sprick, was simply in the wrong place. Why would he have been in a ditch more than a quarter-mile north of the road to the cemetery, when, if anything, he should have been walking south? Lucas could make up any number of reasons why that might have happened, but they would be just that: made up. Didn't feel right. Then there was the question of how Sprick could have run into Shaffer. Shaffer had been nowhere near Zumbrota, as far as they knew from his notes in the little notebook. Again, he could make up a reason that they collided . . .

It was all very foggy.

Busch's Florist Shoppe was in a yellow-brick building on the edge of Faribault's business district. The nav system put him at the front curb thirty-eight minutes after he left Zumbrota. He climbed out of the truck and went inside.

Andi Sprick was a tall, thin, dark-haired woman who was not happy to see him. "I don't have anything to do with Mark anymore," she said, her voice shrill with resentment. "I'm having my name changed back to Shroeder."

"We're not implying that this has anything to do with you," Lucas said. They were in the back room of the flower shop, which smelled like a funeral. "We're trying to get an idea of what your ex-husband was like."

"He's a lazy, self-centered jerk without a single ounce of ambition," she said. "He'd rather sit home and play video games than go outside and . . . and . . . have the wind blow on him. He doesn't do *anything*."

"You didn't see a violent streak in him?" Lucas asked.

"Well, when we were getting divorced, he *screamed* at me . . ."

"Miz Sprick . . ."

"Shroeder . . ."

"Miz Shroeder, we're looking for somebody who might have strangled twenty young women."

She snorted. "You're wasting your time with Mark. He wouldn't make the effort. He . . ." She paused, then backed away from it. "I'm not being fair. Mark is everything I've said. He is snarky, lazy, unambitious. He once played an online space game for thirty-six straight hours, right through our second wedding anniversary."

"Ouch," Lucas said.

"But I've been in the car when he stopped to get out and carry a turtle across the road," she said. "He'd never hurt anybody, or anything, not on purpose."

"You think you've seen deep enough into his . . . psychology . . . to say that for sure?"

"His psychology is about ankle-deep," Shroeder said. "And no, he didn't do it. Even thinking he might . . . it's just ridiculous."

They talked for a few more minutes, then Lucas said good-bye: and she'd convinced him.

BACK IN THE CAR, he called Mattsson: "I talked to Sprick's ex-wife, and she said that there's no way that Sprick's involved. I believe her."

"Well, I'm talking to Sprick himself about that," she said. "We decided we couldn't wait. I'm at his house now."

"Oh, boy . . ." Lucas said.

"That make you nervous?"

"Makes me want to stay away from Zumbrota for a while," Lucas said. "With a small town like that, everybody knows everything. Believe me, there are already five people on their phones to the TV stations. You'll be up to your knees in media in an hour."

"I can handle that," she said.

"I hope so. If Sprick's innocent, they could give you a hard time."

"I really do believe Kaylee," Mattsson said. "I'm sure she saw something, and she says it's Sprick."

Lucas was less sure. Eyewitnesses were often useless—or even worse than useless, because they could point you in the wrong direction. Kaylee had seen something, but it was impossible to know what. The man in the ditch might have been wearing the kind of hat Sprick wore, or might have walked the way Sprick walked, or carried a shoulder bag, if Sprick carried one of those . . . almost anything might have triggered off a pre-programmed *Sprick* response in the little girl's brain.

"Go easy," he said. "You want me there? Or do you want to take it?"

"We can take it. Not a problem. If you want to sit in, that's okay, too."

"I'll stop by," Lucas said. "Just to hear his voice."

ON THE WAY back to Zumbrota, Lucas took a call from the *Star-Tribune*'s lead crime reporter, Ruffe Ignace. "So . . . you down in Owatonna?" Ignace asked.

"No," Lucas said.

"Let me rephrase that," Ignace said. "Are you somewhere down south of the Twin Cities, investigating the Black Hole case and the murder of Robert Shaffer?"

"Maybe."

"That sounds like a big 'yes.' Anything new?"

"Yeah, but don't feel like telling you what it is," Lucas said.

"Thanks. Another thing. I'm sure you've heard of Emmanuel Kent, who's threatening to kill you and Jenkins. Or maybe Shrake. I get those guys confused."

Lucas smothered a groan. "Yes, what about him? He's probably harmless."

"Yeah, well, he might not be physically dangerous, but he might be, media-wise. He's sitting outside City Hall, on a rug. He's gone on a hunger strike, and says he won't eat anything until you and

Jenkins are fired. He's got a big sign around his neck. He will drink water and a variety of donated fruit juices, to drag it out. His death."

"Aw, for Christ's sakes," Lucas said. "And you're gonna blow this up into a crisis?"

"No, not me, but we've got a feature writer working it—Janet Frost. She did that story on the guy who got stuck in the chimney last winter. She could jerk a tear out of a brass monkey. And a photographer, of course. I'm told Emmanuel's quite articulate, not to say picturesque."

"What's she gonna say?" Lucas asked. "We should have given a free pass to a bank robber, so the crazy guy can get a cheese sandwich once a week?"

"I don't know what she's doing, but I thought I'd warn you, so that you'd owe me one. She'll be calling you. I would counsel you not to use the phrase 'the crazy guy.' It reeks of the incorrect. Possibly even the Republican."

"All right, I owe you one."

"So what's new?" Ignace asked.

Lucas thought for a moment, about the fact that all the TV stations probably knew about it: "Off the record. Didn't come from me."

"Sure."

"The Goodhue County sheriff's investigator is questioning a Zumbrota man about his possible involvement in Shaffer's murder."

"Stop the fuckin' presses," Ignace said. He said it in a way that wouldn't stop any presses. "I'm thinking you sound skeptical."

"Maybe. That's all I'm saying."

"But you think it's bullshit."

"I'm sure the Goodhue County sheriff's department has good reason to question the gentleman in question."

"Okay, I won't put quotes on you thinking it's bullshit," Ignace said. "When Janet calls, remember: you're a liberal, she's a liberal. These are complicated issues, and though Kent's story is a tragic one, and mental health care is certainly an issue deserving of additional serious funding by both the federal and state governments, his brother, in robbing those banks, was putting in danger the lives of many innocent people, including rug rats and chicks, maybe even hot chicks with serious boobies."

"I'll keep it in mind," Lucas said, and clicked off.

Fuckin' media.

SPRICK'S HOUSE WAS a small white clapboard place on the south side of town. A Zumbrota cop car was parked outside, with two Goodhue County cars. Lucas left his truck at the curb and went up the walk and knocked on the door. A Goodhue deputy came to the door, said, "We're almost done," and pushed the door open.

Sprick and the cops were in Sprick's living room.

Sprick was six feet tall, blond and slender, wearing a T-shirt, jeans, and a frightened expression. He was sitting on a broken-down love seat. The only other furniture in the living room was a giant stereo system, with two five-foot-tall speakers and three smaller ones, a fifty-inch television, and an array of boxes with blinking lights. The cops were sitting on folding chairs, and Lucas, looking into the kitchen, saw a folding card table, apparently used as a dining table, that matched the chairs; and there were no other chairs in the kitchen.

Post-divorce clean-out, Lucas thought.

Mattsson said, "Mr. Sprick says he was home asleep last night."

"I was," Sprick said. "I gotta get up at six o'clock. I got mail to sort, you can ask anyone."

Lucas said to Mattsson, "Let's talk out front for a minute."

They went back through the front door, and Lucas asked: "What do you think?"

"Well, he's got an unbreakable alibi—he was home asleep—and he's sticking to it. Won't move at all."

"But what do you *think?*" He emphasized the *think.*

"I don't know," she said. She looked back through the screen at the clutch of deputies. "We just can't move him off the spot. Didn't get up to pee, didn't get up for a drink. He drank some beer last night, watched the last part of the Twins game—he got the score right, and what happened in the last couple of innings—then he went to bed, and didn't move until the alarm went off at six. Period. End of story. His story. But Kaylee . . ."

"You ask him to give up some DNA?" Lucas asked.

"Yes. He says he'll do it. Or fingerprints. Whatever we want," Mattsson said.

"Not a good sign," Lucas said.

"But Kaylee . . ."

". . . Saw something," Lucas said. "You're right there. I gotta tell you, though, you don't have an arrest. Not that I see. Not unless he blurts something out."

She bit her lip, glanced sideways at the screen door, and the sound of Sprick's voice, then nodded. "You're right."

"And you've got trouble," Lucas said, looking past her.

She turned, and saw the mobile broadcast truck rolling down the street toward them. "Ah, boy."

"Tell them the truth—that you're talking to a lot of people around town, and Sprick was one of them. Don't commit to anything, don't say Sprick's a suspect. You're doing the routine."

"I can do that," she said, hitching up her gun belt as she looked down the street at the approaching van. "What are you going to do?"

"I'm gonna run for it," Lucas said.

SPRICK LACKED the intensity of the Black Hole killer. He was a mistake, now trailing away in Lucas's rearview mirror. In the same rearview mirror, he saw the TV van stop next to Sprick's house, and Mattsson walking out to meet it.

What next?

He decided to start over, to do what he'd planned to do when he left St. Paul. Visit each of the four cemeteries, and talk to the Owatonna funeral home brothers, to see if Shaffer had left any clues behind, if they'd said anything to point Shaffer in a particular direction.

He turned a corner and headed out to the main drag; another TV van turned the corner and rolled past him.

Mattsson said she could handle it. Maybe she could. Maybe not.

Not his problem.

6

R-A was having his early-evening drink, one of five or six he would have after work, and watching television with Horn, when he saw Catrin Mattsson on the evening news. She was talking to a TV reporter about the murder of Bob Shaffer.

"Hoochy-coo," R-A said. "Take a look at this one."

Mattsson was saying, "We are talking to everybody in the community who . . . who *monitors* the life of the community, looking for factors that might point us at the killer. Mr. Sprick, as the mail carrier, is one of those people."

The reporters didn't believe her. They'd had it from the locals that Sprick might be the Black Hole guy. Mattsson tap-danced: she did not consider Mr. Sprick a suspect, she said, although, "to be plain, we don't rule anyone out. It's my feeling, and this is just a personal feeling, that we are very close to the killer—close physically, I mean. He's close by, right now."

The cameraman zoomed in on a window in Sprick's small house and caught the crinkle in the venetian blind, where Sprick was peering out. You couldn't see anything but a black spot that might have been an eye—and of course it *felt* like a killer's eye.

"What about the witness? How much credibility are you giving her?" the reporter asked.

"We haven't identified the witness as a woman—" Mattsson began.

The reporter interrupted: "Every person here knows who the witness is. We haven't identified her because of her . . . demographics, so to speak. Given those demographics, how reliable do you think she is?"

"I really can't address that question . . ."

"DEMOGRAPHICS? What the fuck is she talking about?" R-A said to the TV. "Nobody from Zumbrota saw me. Demographics? Does that mean she's from somewhere else? Or maybe she's a hooker or something?"

"Don't know," Horn said. "They're being weird about it."

"Maybe just jerking my chain," R-A said. "They probably figure I'm watching."

On the TV, somebody asked a semi-witty question, and Mattsson grinned at the reporter, a girlie grin. When she turned half-away from the camera, you could see her figure.

R-A rattled the ice through his bourbon and took a nip and said to Horn, "Look at this woman, Horn. Look at those tits. Look at that *uniform*. That's primo boner material right there. Isn't she something?"

After a long silence, Horn said, "Roger, you can't do that. You can't go killing this woman. You'd be a hell of a lot better off figuring out who this witness is, and what you might do about her. Figure out how she identified this Sprick guy. And who the fuck is Sprick, and why do they think he's you?"

R-A said, "I just, uh, I just . . ." He slumped back in his chair, and Horn recognized the attitude. R-A couldn't think about the witness, not right now: he was purely fantasizing about what he'd do to Catrin Mattsson, down in the basement.

"They're going to get you, Roger, if you don't pay attention," Horn said. "You don't have much more time, now. I thought that a month ago, when they lifted the lid off the cistern. They'll get some of that DNA stuff and they'll start checking everybody. God knows you put enough of it in those girls. They'll ask every man in town for his DNA, and if anybody says 'no' . . . They'll get your name, and they'll come through those doors with guns, and they'll kill you, because you killed one of theirs. Won't be a trial."

"Oh, bullshit . . ." R-A tried to think seriously about that, but he couldn't, as long as Mattsson was on the screen. R-A had a certain model woman that he went for: a kind of tight-looking blonde. Not all of them had been natural blondes, because he was careful, and sometimes he had to take what he could safely get . . . but he'd take a blonde anytime. And Mattsson certainly was blond.

"Wonder if she shaves?" he said to Horn. "Remember when we pulled the underpants off what's-her-name? Barbara? You remember?"

"Oh, yeah," Horn said. "I do remember that."

THE TV INTERVIEW ENDED, and R-A picked up the remote and clicked around the other major channels and she popped up again and he groaned: "Look at this *woman*, Horn. Just think what she'd be like, bent over that ottoman, screaming her lungs out. It's just, just . . ."

Just that blondes, without their clothes on, looked so *naked*. R-A excused himself, went back to the bedroom, and left Horn staring at the TV. He was back ten minutes later, and sat back down, and Horn asked, "Feel better now?"

"I know, it's disgusting, for a grown man," R-A said. He finished the now-watery bourbon in one gulp, and sucked on the slim remnants of the ice cubes.

"Everybody jacks off once in a while," Horn said. "Well, except me. But three or four times a day? You're going to break it off, you're not careful."

"You know what's going on," R-A said. "I need . . ."

The weatherman came on, smiling out at them as he talked about continuing hot and dry, and the meteor showers that were coming up and how, if the weather held, they'd have a good view of them.

They waited in silence until he finished—weather was a big deal in Minnesota, even for insane serial killers in the middle of the summer—and then picked up again: "I know what you need, but that's even crazier than it usually is," Horn said. "What I don't like, is you're putting both of us at risk."

"Yeah, what do you have to lose? You haven't done anything in years, you haven't done anything since we broke that head off old Gunter's neck."

R-A laughed at the thought. Gunter had been one of the early sepulcher residents. Twisting off old Gunter's head had been messy; he sometimes still dreamed about the neck tendons popping like a bunch of cornstalks, and then that dusty, nasty smell. "I'm going down the basement," he said. "Gonna look around."

THE BASEMENT DOOR came off the kitchen, and the basement itself was down a narrow twisting set of steps. R-A's house had been built in 1882, in a style called Carpenter Gothic. The original foundation had been made of local stone, but in the 1960s, R-A's grandfather had the house jacked up, rolled onto the back half of the lot, and he'd dug a new, deeper basement, with a foundation of concrete block.

As a Carpenter Gothic, the exterior form of the house had been determined by whim as much as anything, and the foundation necessarily followed it. That meant that it had been possible to build a long, narrow room not obvious to the eye, entered through a steel door around a sharp corner, and behind a rack of Ball jars filled with canned fruit and vegetables.

R-A's grandfather had designed it as a bomb shelter, for the day when the Russkies dropped the Big One. The neighbors didn't know about it, because after the bombs fell, they'd be out there with guns, looking for food.

R-A was as meticulous about home care as his grandfather and father had been, and the basement remained dry, clean, and orderly, divided into separate spaces for a home shop, a mechanical room for plumbing and heating fixtures, and a large and orderly storage area.

The bomb shelter had become a cell, where he beat, raped, and murdered his victims.

. · .

Now, DROPPING DOWN into the basement, R-A pushed the rack of jars aside—the rack didn't look like it, but it was quite sturdy, with casters on the legs. He pushed open the steel door and looked around.

He quite liked it down in the bomb shelter, because it was so quiet. He kept a stack of pornographic bondage magazines on a cot, and now he sat down and picked one of them up. The bound victims in the magazines were usually blond, his personal preference, and he spent some time paging through them, revisiting old favorites. He'd actually duplicated some of the scenes portrayed in the magazines, but his memories weren't as sharp as the magazine pictures.

Now he found a tough-looking blonde, nude, bent over a bench in the photo, her hands tied behind her, her face turned toward the men disciplining her . . . R-A closed his eyes and visualized Catrin Mattsson in the same position.

Closed his eyes and saw it all, and groaned, slipped one hand into his jeans. Deep in his heart he thought Horn might be right, that it was all coming to an end. The cops would never quit. But if he could have Mattsson first . . .

He knew nothing about her, where she lived, what she did when she wasn't working. He'd have to figure out a way to ambush her, or perhaps to draw her in. If she came to the door as Shaffer had, unaware, tracking a lead, he could take her right there in the hallway.

But how to bring her in, without bringing in a troop of cops behind her?

How would he do that?

. . .

A STEEL BAR ran from one side of the concrete wall to the other, a little more than seven feet off the floor. It had nothing to do with the bomb shelter—R-A had put it there, because he'd fantasized about hanging the girls up there, the better to whip them. He'd done it a few times, too, but it never worked out as well as he'd hoped it would—they usually fainted, and they'd bleed all over the place.

He wasn't a big fan of actual *blood*. He wanted submission, and sex, and . . . admiration? Well, fear, anyway. Respect.

He went over and stood under the bar, and did five pull-ups. Stood under the bar, waiting for the burn to subside, and then did three more. Not bad: most American men his age couldn't even do two.

If he could get Mattsson down here . . . He looked around.

You know what? What he'd do, he thought, was *fight* her. Get everything out of here, so she couldn't build a weapon somehow, strip her buck naked, then get naked himself, and lock the door, and tell her what he was going to do to her.

Tell her to fight for the key.

Fight her.

That's what he'd do, he thought. He was handling himself now, the urge growing again. Before his mind went completely blank, he made two resolutions. He would figure out a way to beat the cops; and he'd have Catrin Mattsson.

7

ucas spent four futile hours driving between and walking the cemeteries, checking out the sepulchers in Owatonna and Holbein, ending outside the cemetery in Zumbrota, where Shaffer had been found. He was alone for most of it—he'd had the Murphy brothers in Owatonna come out to Holy Angels, got them to recall everything that Shaffer had said, which led him nowhere—and finally he wandered through the Zumbrota burial ground, his hands in his pockets, feeling a little foolish.

Cemeteries couldn't talk, he thought. Yet . . .

At four-thirty, he called Duncan, who was still at the office.

"You going home?" Lucas asked.

"Sooner or later. I talked to Mattsson about this Sprick. She thinks it's something, but says you disagree."

Lucas told him the story, then asked, "How long are the murder books now? How many pages?"

"Lord, I don't know. Twenty-five hundred pages, for everything. Most of it's junk."

"Do you have any staff around?"

"Why?"

"I'd like to get somebody to xerox it all, for me, tonight. You can charge it to my group."

"Let me check, I'll call you back," Duncan said. He was back in a minute. "Maizy says she'll do it, but it'll take some time."

"It'll take me a while to get back. Tell her to bind it up in those blue report covers, leave it on my desk if she's finished before I get there."

"What're you doing?"

"I can't see what Shaffer was up to," Lucas said. "It has to be a combination of what he already knew, from the files, and what he saw, or maybe . . . *somebody* he saw. I'm lost down here, this isn't working. I need to study it, I need to soak it up."

"Okay. By the way, I'm supposed to tell you that Del crossed the Iowa line about an hour ago, heading south with the ATF. And there's a note on your office door that says you should call Virgil."

LUCAS CALLED VIRGIL FLOWERS, one of his agents. Flowers worked on his own, out of Mankato, Minnesota. He'd been on vacation in New Mexico, where, he said, he'd caught all the muskys in the state's only musky lake.

"What's up?" Lucas asked, when Virgil answered.

"Man, I hate to ask this, with Shaffer dead and you working the Black Hole. But you know my friend Rick Johnson?"

"Yeah, I know him," Lucas said. *"There's* a goddamn accident waiting to happen."

"Actually, it's happened several times already . . . anyway, Johnson needs some help on, mmm . . . a non-priority mission," Flowers said. "I'm not doing anything heavy, and nobody's called me for the Black Hole group, so I'd like to run over there. It's down south of La Crescent."

"You're not telling me what it's about," Lucas said.

"No, but if Johnson is telling the truth, and I make a couple of busts, it'll bring great credit upon the BCA."

"We don't need credit," Lucas said. "The legislature's already adjourned. But, go ahead, on your best judgment. From the way you're talking, I don't want to know what it is. If it blows up in your face, it's your problem."

"Deal. I just wanted you to know where I was," Flowers said.

"You taking your boat?" Lucas asked.

Long pause. Then Virgil said, "Maybe."

"Let me know if you get in trouble," Lucas said. "But before then . . ."

"You don't want to know."

"That's right."

LUCAS WAS BACK in St. Paul in an hour. Weather called as he crossed the Mississippi and said that the housekeeper had picked up a rotisserie chicken and some potato salad, and when would he be home?

"Half an hour, hold on for me," he said. "I've got to stop at the office, and then I'll be home."

"Learn anything?"

"No. I'm missing something, though. I can feel it. Give it a week, and it'll be driving me nuts."

THE BLACK HOLE books were sitting in a pile on his desk, two red, two black, and one blue. He picked them up and headed home, talked to the kids, ate chicken and potato salad, and then went and sat in the den with the five books.

An hour into it, Letty came by and asked if she could read behind him: "Feel free," he said. He explained that he was reading from beginning to end. She picked up the last book, and said she'd read from end to beginning.

"Did you see Catrin on TV?" Letty asked, as she settled into the other reading chair.

Lucas looked up from the book: "No. She do good?"

"She's good, for a cop without any training," Letty said. Letty had interned at Channel Three for four years, from the time she was in ninth grade. "And she really, really liked it. Even when Jim Burns got on her case, about pulling the trigger on the mailman guy. You can tell when they like it: their eyes shine."

"Mmm. Hope she doesn't like it too much—that can get you in trouble."

"Or a good job in PR," Letty said.

They sat comfortably together in the den, reading. Weather looked in at ten o'clock to say she was going to bed. Lucas read until midnight, then went to bed, leaving Letty reading in the big leather chair.

. . .

HE WAS BACK DOWNSTAIRS at nine o'clock the next morning when she rolled through the kitchen door in her nightgown, yawning, and Lucas asked, "Find anything good?"

"Lots of interesting stuff—the autopsies were pretty awesome—but nothing that goes anywhere. Not, at least, until you've got a serious suspect. They think they might have his DNA."

"Yeah, I saw that. Not a sure thing, though."

"But it's male. No male bodies, yet," she said.

Lucas scratched his neck and then said, "When those sepulchers were broken into . . . they only took female heads. I wonder why? Could there be something in that?"

They both thought about it for a minute, then Letty laughed and said, "If there is, I'm not smart enough to see it, and we both know I'm smarter than you."

Lucas said, "You know, I could still get you into St. Thomas." St. Thomas University was only a couple miles from their house.

"Fuck a bunch of Tommies," she said.

"Uh . . ."

"Sorry," she said, without being sorry. "To get back on topic, I don't see anything in the missing heads."

"Wonder if the killer's some kind of spooky creep? Is that redundant? Spooky creep? Anyway, if he is, people would know," Lucas said. "Maybe we could leak that to Ruffe, or to Channel Three. People tend to know about personalities like that."

"Are you going down there again today?"

Lucas yawned and said, "No. I'm gonna hang out with you guys, and do some reading, go shopping, maybe watch a ball game, and try to think. I'd like to go up north and do some fishing. No time for that, though."

"It's crazy," Letty said. "It's like a huge crisis, and there's not much to do."

"There's a lot to do: we've got several thousand pages to read, though most of it seems like junk."

For the rest of the Sunday, Lucas basically screwed off; went shopping for new running shoes, watched a ball game, ditched the kids to eat with Weather and friends at the Town and Country Club.

That night, he started reading again.

Duncan & Co. had tracked down every registered sex offender in Goodhue County and every bordering county (Dakota, Rice, Steele, Dodge, Olmstead, and Wabasha), and had done modus operandi checks on every registered sex offender in Minnesota and Wisconsin. They'd posted notices in every Minnesota prison with rewards for any inmate who could point them at a credible suspect. They'd found, now, a dozen serious treasure hunters and were working through the treasure-hunter chain to find any they'd missed.

They had DNA studies of all the victims. Sprick's life history had been taken back to his teenage years; they'd reviewed every police report of missing women for twenty-five years. They'd gotten lists of all the people known to have detasseled corn at the James farm, and run them against sex offender lists. They'd found two, but both were currently living out of state, one in the Nevada State Prison.

One of the detasseling contractors refused to speak to cops, and had demanded a public defender to represent him. That had stirred some interest, until it turned out that he was a member of the Socialist Workers Party who'd been in New York the week that Carpenter was killed. He'd demanded a lawyer because, he said, he was sure the Black Hole case was a government setup to crush the workers and forerunners of the coming anticapitalist revolution.

Whatever.

Shaffer had traced the phone records of all the Black Hole women who'd been identified. The result had caused some argument: the most recent victims had last been registered at cell towers between Rochester and the Twin Cities, but there was a cluster around the University of Minnesota. Some of the agents argued that they might be looking for an ex-student; others argued that the bars around the university were simply the best hunting grounds for somebody looking for young blond women. That brought up a subsidiary argument: if he came from the south to the university area, but mostly took women who also came from the south . . . did he scout them as high school students, or children? Could he be a teacher, or somebody who dealt with young women? A coach, perhaps, who'd see young women from a variety of different schools?

And a bewildering variety of other information, facts and theories and speculation and rumor, everything that ten or twelve hardworking cops could dig up in almost a month of relentless work, and every bit of it reported upon.

Lucas went to bed with his mind churning.

THE NEXT MORNING, with Weather already gone to work, he was debating whether to go back south, or to spend the time reading, when his cell phone rang: Hopping Crow, from the crime-scene crew. "Yeah? What's up, Larry?"

"You know that Black Hole site?" Hopping Crow asked.

"You mean the one west of Red Wing? Where they found all those skulls?"

"Yeah, that's the one. Bea and I just got here, with Rick Johnson from the U. Shaffer wanted us to do some GPR surveys, see if any other bodies popped up." GPR—Ground Penetrating Radar.

"Yeah? Did some?"

"No, but there's a dead woman lying on top of the place where the cistern was. She's been strangled."

"Larry . . ."

"I'm not joking, Lucas. I've already called Duncan and the team's on the way. And I mean . . . Jesus Christ, Lucas . . ." Hopping Crow was freaking out.

LUCAS WAS OUT of the house in five minutes, and on the phone to Catrin Mattsson, who was at home, eating breakfast, as Lucas had been. "The crime-scene crew just pulled into the Black Hole site, and say they've found the body of a young woman there, apparently strangled."

"What!" Mattsson was screaming. "Why didn't anybody tell me?"

"We are telling you, right now," Lucas said. "They just got there, I just found out, and you're the first person I called. I'm on my way, I'll see you there."

"Wait, wait . . . Any ID on the body?"

"Catrin, we called you so fast, we don't know shit about anything," Lucas said. "You can find out everything we know by going over there."

"I'm going," she said.

"Those are crime-scene people there—you probably ought to get some more deputies out there, to control the site. Don't let them trample over everything."

"Right, right, right, I'm on the way."

LUCAS LET HIS NAVIGATION SYSTEM take him to the Black Hole, running fast down the welter of highways south of the Twin Cities. On the way south, he talked to Duncan, who was running a few minutes behind Lucas, because he was coming down from a northern suburb.

"I've been talking to Bea," Duncan said. "She says they've taped off the scene, but they may have run over some stuff going in, before they found the new body. Anyway, what do you think?"

"I've got to look at it," Lucas said. "The guy has been so quiet for so long, it's hard to believe that he's come out of the woodwork to taunt us."

"Maybe he figures that since everybody's looking for him anyway, and since he nailed Shaffer, he might as well. And he *is* nuts."

"Yes, he is. I've dealt with a couple of crazies who were talking directly to us, so all that's possible," Lucas said. "I've been reading the paper again. One of the newer bones that they took out of the hole, left radius nine, had a break that preceded the killing, and was healing badly, which means the victim hadn't been to a hospital. The docs said that healing had just begun, had been under way for no more than a couple of days at most. Shaffer thought that meant the killer was holding the women for a while before strangling them, and that he was probably raping and torturing them. Most of them were apparently nude, since the clothing remnants turned up don't contain bones. This new victim is clothed. So that's out of kilter. If this woman hasn't been raped . . ."

"That's good and bad. Good for her, I guess, but if she's been raped, there'll be some DNA. Bea told me the body didn't look like it had been washed, what they can see of it. They can see a bra strap. Can't tell about rape, because they haven't moved the body yet. From what I'm hearing from Bea, the body seems to have been treated with some respect. Placed neatly on the ground. I gotta say, that doesn't sound like somebody who'd throw a body down the hole."

"Okay. I'm thirty miles out. I'll be there in twenty minutes."

THE DAY WAS another good one, with a few fair-weather clouds floating overhead, and warm and humid. Here and there, in the ditches, the sumac was showing orange leaves, and the dust from gravel roads hung in the air for a while, as it does on the windless, humid days; a good day not to be dead.

When Lucas arrived at the Black Hole, the crime-scene van was parked across the entrance, and three Goodhue County patrol cars were arrayed across the road, along with Mattsson's SUV. Lucas parked and walked around the tape, and then along a taped pathway that swung wide of probable entry lanes, to the former hole, which was now just a large square of raw earth.

The woman's body had been placed exactly in the middle of the square, on her back, arms along her sides, with the palms turned up, as in a yoga corpse pose. She had been in her mid- to late-twenties, mid-height, maybe five-six or five-seven, with narrow shoulders and short-cut black hair. She was wearing a pink cotton blouse, inexpensive fashion jeans, running shoes with white socks.

The crew was working inside a circle of tape. Mattsson was standing outside the tape, looking in, and when she saw Lucas approaching she suppressed what might have become a scowl, and said, "Davenport."

"What's the story?"

"She was murdered, strangled," Mattsson said. "Not by the Black Hole guy. Whoever killed her, dumped her here, so we might think that. A really, really dumb guy. She's got an old black eye, and an old cut lip, like she might have been in a fight, maybe a week ago. Just eyeballing it, I'd swear it was a domestic."

Bea, the crime-scene chief, came over, heard the last part of what Mattsson said, and nodded to Lucas. "Manually strangled. You can see the finger bruising. Every one of the Black Hole killings was done with a rope, as far as we can tell—we actually have several of the ropes, and we have a lack of hyoid damage that is consistent with rope. Also, just from what we can see, the bruises, she may have been in an abusive relationship. Almost all the women we've identified from the Hole were women who were blond and busty— she's thin and dark-haired. She'd also be toward the older end of the victims . . . So I agree with Officer Mattsson. Probably not the Black Hole guy."

"Anything in her pants pocket?" Lucas asked. "ID . . . anything?"

Bea was shaking her head. "Pockets are empty."

To Mattsson: "Anybody call with a missing person?"

"First thing I checked," Mattsson said. "Not here, none of the counties around here, including across the river. But . . . I think she's from Red Wing. I don't know her, but I think I've *seen* her, and more than once. Not with any crime thing. I think she might work someplace I go shopping. Maybe Target or Walmart or Walgreens or Econofoods."

"Like a cashier?"

"Something like that," Mattsson said. "I spend some time in the hospitals, too—could be a nurse."

"Maybe we should try to get a photo."

"Already done," Mattsson said. "We transmitted a mug down to the office, printed them out, and we've got a couple of guys running around trying to nail down who she is . . . if she actually works in town."

"Well, shit, Catrin, what do you need us for?"

She looked at him for a moment, then shook her head and said, "I don't think we do—not on this one."

BEA TOLD THE STORY of how they found the body—nothing to it, they drove into the site, and there she was. "There *will* be DNA, when you find the guy who did this."

"What about the GPR—you gonna go ahead with that?" Lucas asked.

"We're doing it now, but we haven't seen anything," Bea said. "I mean . . ." She gestured at the body.

She went back to work, doing an inch-by-inch search down the path from the road to the dirt patch. Lucas turned to Mattsson and asked, "Anything more from Sprick? Or about him?"

"Got a flat tire there," she said. "I still think there's something going on with him, but I don't know what. The thing is, I've been back to Kaylee twice, now, and she's rock solid that she saw Mr. Sprick in the ditch."

"Sometimes—" Lucas began.

Mattsson rode over him: "Which reminds me, I got some kinda bad news about all that."

Lucas grinned at her: "Bad news in a case with this many dead . . . that's gotta be really bad."

"More of an annoyance, than bad," she said. "First of all, Kaylee's parents told everybody they met yesterday that Kaylee had seen Sprick, and half the people in Zumbrota believe he's the killer."

"Ah, jeez. Is there a second-of-all?"

"Yeah. They've been grooming Kaylee for beauty contests and they're sort of . . . exploiting . . . this whole thing. She's being interviewed by Channel Three this afternoon. I tried to talk them out of it, but her father said that this was her 'big chance.' Could put some pressure on us."

"We've already got pressure, couldn't be much more. If you're careful about it, when you're interviewed—they'll come to you, because you're the one Kaylee's parents know—you might be able to embarrass the interviewer enough to tone down the whole thing."

She thought about it for a second, then said, "Maybe I'll do that."

"And I need to ask you something, kind of half-seriously," Lucas said.

She cocked her head.

Lucas asked, "Is there any possibility that somebody'll get drunk and decide to eliminate the killer? I mean, Sprick?"

"What an interesting question," she said. "I don't know the answer to that, but I'll talk to the Zumbrota chief."

· · ·

THEY WATCHED BEA for another minute, then Lucas said, "I'm gonna go talk to the GPR guys."

The GPR guys were dragging the bright orange ground-penetrating radar antenna through small openings in the brush of the farmyard, well away from the body. They were sweating from the work, and stopped when Lucas came up. "Anything?"

"Nothing. Not so far . . ."

He watched for a moment, then saw Duncan walking across the site, to the body. Mattsson was still standing there, watching the processing of the body. Lucas turned back to the GPR guys and asked if he could get a printout of the radar map, and one of them said, "Sure."

"You ever find any buried treasure?"

"I keep thinking I might, but I never do," the other one said. "I found a misplaced gas pipe, once." They came up to an end-marker and turned to drag the antenna back down the field. Lucas glanced over at the body, and saw Mattsson and Duncan, Mattsson with her hands on her hips, Duncan barking at her.

He thought, *Uh-oh*, and considered going over, but then Mattsson walked away from Duncan and pulled her cell phone out of her pocket and put it to her ear. She listened for a minute, then looked wildly around the yard, saw him, shouted, "Davenport! Davenport! We got her . . ."

Lucas said, "Excuse me," to the GPR guys, and trotted after Mattsson. As he passed Duncan, he said, "I got this, Jon."

·   ·   ·

HE CAUGHT MATTSSON at the road. Their cars were parked at opposite ends of the abandoned farmstead, and as she turned toward hers, she shouted, "Follow me: I'll call you."

Lucas jogged down to the Benz, climbed in, did a U-turn, and followed her down the dusty road toward the blacktop. A half-mile down, his phone rang and Mattsson was there.

"Her name is Harriet Card and she lives a mile south of town, south of Red Wing. She's a cashier at Target. She got a restraining order against her partner a year ago, but withdrew it a couple of months later. A friend of hers at Target says they got back together, but they've been having trouble again. They lived at Card's place."

"You got his name?"

"Her name. Her girlfriend's name is Glenda Hannah Shales and she has two convictions for assault and battery and on the last one, did a year and a day in Shakopee. You know that old dykes-on-bikes business? She's like that. She's a drinker and a mean bitch. I've dealt with her before."

"We're going to her place?"

"Yes. We've got the ERU on the way now, they'll wait for me before we go in," Mattsson said.

"Not the Black Hole killer," Lucas said.

"No, I guess not."

LUCAS THOUGHT ABOUT turning around, but figured he'd only further annoy Mattsson if he dropped out of what must be a fairly rare murder arrest for Goodhue County. Before he rang off, he asked, "Is she a shooter? Does she carry a gun?"

"Never has. She's more of the brass-knuckles type."

When Mattsson rang off, Lucas called Duncan and told him what he'd been told. "Sounds about right. Nobody here thinks it's the Hole guy—but keep me up on it," Duncan said.

Mattsson knew where she was going, but Lucas didn't, so he stuck close behind her as she rocketed along the back roads west of Red Wing, avoiding the town with its clogged-up traffic, to come at the city from its south side.

Card's house was off Highway 61 a couple of miles south of town, on a frontage road facing the highway, a simple one-story clapboard box with a detached garage in back. A concrete-block stoop led to the front door, which was right in the center of the house. A squat yellow truck was waiting for them at the south end of the frontage road, along with a couple of patrol cars. Mattsson pulled off in front of the truck, and Lucas was pleased to see several guys climb out, carrying rifles; the Emergency Response Unit.

"I didn't ask for them," Mattsson said. "I don't think we need them."

The team leader said, "Catrin, she *murdered* a woman last night and dumped the body on the nation's hottest crime scene. She's batshit *crazy*. Nuckin' futs. She could be in there suckin' on a gun right now, or she might decide to let us do it for her. Or take a few of us with her."

"Yeah, yeah, yeah . . ." Mattsson wasn't convinced.

THE TEAM LEADER was a short black-haired guy with muscles in his face. He nodded when Lucas introduced himself, said to the two of them, "We've contacted the neighbors. She's in there. We've got two guys watching the back, they went up through the woods." He pointed back behind the line of houses that faced the highway. "There's a hardwired phone inside the house, and we've got both their cell phone numbers. Plan is, we'll set up out front and call her, tell her to come out, and go from there."

"Far as I know, she's not a shooter," Mattsson said, repeating what she'd told Lucas. "Never had a weapons charge. She gets drunk and beats on people."

"Yeah, maybe, but I'll give you ten to one that she's got a gun in there. Everybody on this road will have one," the team leader said.

Mattsson nodded: "Probably. So take it easy."

The team leader looked at Lucas then back to Mattsson: "We'll ask you and Agent Davenport to wait until we're set up. Then, we see what happens."

Lucas said, "You guys be careful."

"Always."

THE TEAM HAD already worked out the approach. Two cars carried several team members north on the highway, and once past the target house, they came back across to the frontage road and then south to the house. The team leader and three more of his men drove the six hundred yards up the road, parked in a neighbor's empty driveway.

The leader called Mattsson and said, "We're making the call."

"Let's go on up," Mattsson said. Lucas followed her truck up the road, and they both pulled into the driveway in the visual shadow of the SWAT van, and got out.

The team leader had moved to the corner of the neighbor's garage with the talker, who was on the phone. The talker was saying, ". . . in which case, you have nothing to fear. But we're a little nervous out here, you know, given the circumstances. If you'll just come on out, we'll check you out, and have a talk. No point in getting everybody upset . . . Uh-huh, uh-huh, well, if you look out the side window to the Pauls' place, you'll see our truck, you know, that's no practical joke . . . Uh-huh, uh-huh, listen, Glenda, you know how this works, you're a smart gal. We really, really don't want anybody to get hurt here, that's our one and only mission, to make sure nobody gets hurt."

Mattsson snorted, and the team leader turned to her and raised his eyebrows in a gesture that meant, "Please don't do that."

The talker said, ". . . okay? Okay? No point in dragging it out, once we know you're okay, that nobody's going to get hurt, we can let you have lunch . . . uh-huh . . ."

It went like that for a couple more minutes, then the talker said, "That's great. That's a great decision, Glenda. You come on out, and when you come out, you don't have to put your hands up, we don't want to embarrass anyone, just a chat . . . Uh-huh. Okay, I'll look for you."

He looked up at the team leader and said, "She's coming out."

The leader spoke into a shoulder microphone, and a few seconds later, the screen door on the front of the house pushed open, and a tall, heavyset woman stepped out, chunky arms up over her head. She was wearing a T-shirt, worn loose, and Lucas said, "Watch the T-shirt," and the team leader repeated that to his men, who were moving in on the red-faced woman, rifles not quite pointing at her, but ready.

They ordered her to kneel, and she did, putting her hands up over her head, but when one of the ERU team members stepped toward her, she snapped, "Hey, hey, hey, hands off the merchandise. You want to feel me up, get Blondie to do it."

She was looking at Mattsson. Mattsson walked over to her and patted her down. More ERU guys came from behind the house, and then Mattsson told Shales she could get back on her feet.

Lucas moved in closer. Shales's T-shirt said, in gold letters, "Playing for the Other Team," and under that, in smaller letters, "Since '69."

She looked exhausted and was drunk, on wine, and stood with her head down while one of the helmeted deputies read her rights and asked if she understood them. "Yeah, yeah, I heard it all before," she said. She asked, "Why're you pickin' on me? I haven't seen Harriet since she got pissed off and walked out of here."

"When was that?" Mattsson asked.

"Couple days ago . . ." She peered at Mattsson, seemingly confused; maybe not seeing so well through the fog of alcohol. "Who in the fuck are you, anyway?"

"I'm the investigator for the Goodhue County sheriff's department, Miz Shales," Mattsson said. "I've talked to you before, when you beat up that guy at the VFW parking lot."

"I remember you, you're that fuckin' Nazi who went to court and lied."

"You nearly beat the guy to death," Mattsson said.

"I didn't beat up nobody," Shales said, rocking on her feet. "That was a straight-out fight, the guy jumped *me*."

"Yeah, right," Mattsson said. It was the next thing to a sneer, and Lucas thought, *Uh-oh*, and edged forward.

"You're trying to pin this one on me, too. I didn't have nothing to do—"

"With what, Glenda? With strangling your girlfriend and dumping her body like she was garbage? You know, there's going to be DNA all over her. That's better than fingerprints, and there's no way to strangle a woman without . . ."

Shales's face was getting redder and redder. She gestured at Mattsson, who was four feet away, at the same time turning to face Lucas, as though she was about to say something about Mattsson, and Lucas thought again, *Uh-oh*, and he took another step forward, sensing the sucker punch that Shales was winding up, but he was too late.

With more speed than any of them had suspected, Shales lashed out at Mattsson, hit her on the side of the head below her right eye, and Mattsson went down on her ass. Shales's belly flopped on her, and she got in three or four good head shots before the other cops ripped her off the cop, rolled her, piled on, bent her arms behind her back, and cuffed her.

"Ah, shit." Mattsson rolled onto her stomach, then pushed up, dripping some blood from her nose as the team leader knelt next to her. Most of the blows had been to the side of her face, which was already going blue. The team leader helped her to her feet and she looked down at Shales and said, "Tell you what, you piece of trash, even if we don't get you for Harriet, you'll do a few years for this."

"Awww . . ." Shales said, and then she began to cry, big harsh drunken sobs going *huh-huh-huh*. She was still facedown, and Lucas prodded her with the toe of his shoe and when she looked up at him, craning her neck, he asked, "You kill Harriet on purpose? Or was it some kind of an accident?"

"I didn't mean it," she said, into the dirt. "I never meant to hurt her."

"So it was an accident?"

"Yeah, it was, it really was."

All they wanted was confirmation. Shales could explain later how she strangled somebody by accident.

"Get her out of here, and start processing the house," Mattsson said to one of the cops.

The team leader said, "You need to get somebody to look at your nose."

"Yeah, yeah."

Lucas, still standing over Shales, prodded her with his toe again and asked, "How old are you, Glenda?"

After another moment of weeping, she mumbled, "Twenty-seven."

Lucas stepped away and Mattsson asked, "What?"

"Too young to be the Black Hole killer," he said, his voice quiet. "Besides, the Black Hole guy is a guy."

"She's too goddamned dumb, anyway," Mattsson said.

"You've got to get to the hospital and have them take a look at you," Lucas said. "If nothing else, get some ice on your face, and pretty quick. If you don't, you're going to look like a pumpkin."

"You think I fucked up, there?"

"No. I think you pushed her button, which was a good thing to do," Lucas said. "We got her for killing the woman, ten seconds after we all witnessed her rights being read to her. You got popped, but you didn't fuck up."

"Rough way to get it done, though," one of the ERU cops said.

"Shut up," Mattsson said.

Lucas showed a thin smile—couldn't help himself—and Matts-son snapped, "What? You think it's funny?"

Lucas made the mistake of trying to go all comradely with her: "You know . . . you might have moved just a teeny bit faster. Or stood just a teeny bit further away."

She looked at him for a moment, then said, "Fuck you. I got her."

Lucas's smile went away. "Yeah, you did," and he walked away. Fuck him?

The team leader touched Mattsson on her shoulder and said, "Come on. I'll have one of the guys drive you in. Get some ice."

8

ucas was pissed when he got back to his truck, but it quickly wore off. Cops tended to have confrontational personalities, and Catrin Mattsson was an exaggerated version of that. It wasn't all one way, either.

The BCA teams were probably the best in the state, though both Minneapolis and St. Paul might have an argument with that—but too often, when dealing with sheriff's departments, the BCA specialists tended to give off more than a whiff of superiority. Lucas himself had once gotten in a fistfight with a sheriff's deputy, one that he probably could have avoided if it hadn't been for a certain big-city attitude.

To say nothing of his expensive suits and the big-titted mouthy cop-girlfriend he'd had with him. He smiled a bit as he remembered it.

.   .   .

FROM THE TIME he spent walking the cemeteries, without finding anything specific, he'd almost concluded that whatever Shaffer had discovered, hadn't come only from the cemeteries: it'd come from some combination of information from the murder books, plus the cemeteries, or even something that had popped up in a random conversation somewhere. Because Shaffer had gone to the last two cemeteries alone, it was even possible that he'd actually encountered the killer face-to-face, purely by coincidence.

He came to the highway, stopped, got on the phone and called Bea Sawyer, the crime-scene crew chief, and asked if Shaffer's clothing had been processed for clues as to where he'd been killed.

"Not completely processed, but they've been eyeballed," she said. "We think it was probably indoors—there's no obvious dirt, twigs, grass, anything that would suggest that he fell on the ground. He was wearing Ecco shoes with a distinct heavy tread on them, and there's no significant dirt. They're clean. Of course, it's been dry, so even walking on streets and across lawns, he wouldn't pick up much, but they were so clean that I suspect he was last walking on a hard surface. I think, indoors—I didn't see any concrete dust, no pieces of blacktop, nothing like that. Nothing from a road or driveway. That could change, after we start looking at the fabric with a microscope."

Something to think about, Lucas thought, after he ended the call. Probably shot indoors. Shaffer had no indoor appointments that Lucas knew of, other than at the funeral homes. The last funeral home he was in was run by a man who'd just arrived two years earlier from Texas, and was distinctly not a suspect. Shaffer had to have gone inside a building again, after that. Where had he gone? And why?

He thought about going back to the Hole, but he had no reason to.

Another thing occurred to him. They'd been looking for similarities between the victims, that might point to the killer, but they hadn't really thought about *dis-similarities*, if there was such a word.

The last victim, Mary Lynn Carpenter, somewhat stood out: physically, she fit with the other victims, but she hadn't been a party girl. She'd lived on the far edge of the circle—or even beyond the far edge—that Shaffer's investigators had defined as the killer's territory, and she'd apparently been taken in daylight hours, rather than at night, as the others apparently had been.

She'd come from Durand, Wisconsin, he knew, a good distance east of the Mississippi. The question was, did the killer meet the woman in Durand? If so, what was he doing there? Durand was a small town, and isolated. If you were going someplace other than Durand, and crossing the river at Red Wing, there would be a better way to go to that other place than through Durand.

But Carpenter hadn't been killed in Durand. She'd been picked up at the tiny town of Diamond Bluff, right on the Mississippi, while cleaning up her grandparents' graves.

Then he thought, *Well, of course. Another cemetery.*

Still sitting at the highway stop sign, he called Duncan and asked, "Listen: you know we arrested a woman from down south of Red Wing?"

"Nobody's said anything to me."

Lucas filled him in, and Duncan asked, "No possibility that she did the rest of them, then?"

"Almost none. She would have had to start killing when she was about twelve," Lucas said.

"Shoot. Too bad—it was a possibility, even if it was a thin one. Sorry to hear that Mattsson got hit about nine times. I'd have been happier if it'd been fifteen."

"Yeah, right. Listen, another thing popped into my head. The last victim, Carpenter, was not like the others."

"Yeah, we know that, but it hasn't worked into anything."

"She was probably picked up in a cemetery, and Shaffer was killed after looking at either three or four cemeteries."

After a moment of silence, Duncan said, "Jesus. We've been so stretched, we didn't even think of that. That might be something. The guy could be a cemetery worker, or maybe just a weirdo who hangs around them. Either way, we might be able to isolate him."

"Maybe. I'm going to run over to Durand and talk to Carpenter's folks and maybe the cops and the mayor. I've read all the interviews, but I'm going to come at it from a different angle, not so much the personal stuff about her, as about the town, and what she did there."

"All right. If Mattsson already picked up the killer on this one, I'm going back to town to jack up the team on the cemetery angle. Stay in touch."

LUCAS TURNED NORTH on Highway 61. He had the murder books in the back of the truck, and in town, he found a cafe, carried the relevant book inside, and ordered a hot beef sandwich with mashed potatoes, brown gravy, and green beans. He read through the interviews with Carpenter's parents as he ate, and when he was done with that, called her mother, Sandra Carpenter, and was told that her husband was at work, but could come home for an interview.

The drive to Durand took forty minutes. Lucas had been through the place a couple of times in the past, and it always reminded him of a TV version of an old Western town. The main street ran along the bank of the Chippewa River, with the shoulder-to-shoulder business buildings backing up to the water.

The odd thing about it, to Lucas's mind, was that there was almost nothing on the other side of the river. Most river towns form a circle around both ends of a bridge; Durand stretched for almost a mile and a half along Highway 25, from southwest to northeast, right along the water for much of it, but on the other side of the bridge, there was almost nothing.

He crossed the bridge shortly after one o'clock, in bright sunlight, followed the navigation system through the town, right on Main Street, left past a park, to a small blue cottage a few streets back from the river. A man was standing in a picture window, watching, when Lucas parked in front, and came to the door as Lucas walked up the sidewalk.

Clark Carpenter was a tall man, too heavy, with thinning blond hair and an untidy blond mustache. He held the door as Lucas walked up, said, "I'm Clark. Come on in."

Sandra Carpenter was waiting in the living room, sitting on a couch, in front of a silver-plated tray of cookies. She stood up when Lucas came in, with Clark trailing, and said, "Mr. Davenport? Sit down, please."

Lucas took the easy chair that faced the couch, and Sandra pushed the cookie tray toward him. He took a cookie.

"We heard about Agent Shaffer. We met him here, once. He seemed like a very nice guy," Clark said. "Smart guy."

"He was nice, and he was smart," Lucas said. "We think he tripped over the killer. He had a lot more, mmm, knowledge of this case than I do, and I suspect something that he knew, with something that he saw that last day, led him to the killer. But he might not have known that, somehow, he was a threat to the killer. He turned his back on whoever it was, and was shot."

"That's awful," Sandra said, as Clark sank into the couch next to her.

"Not as awful as what happened to our daughter," Clark said. "We haven't been very happy with the investigation over there. Nothing seems to be happening . . . until Agent Shaffer got killed."

"Not much was," Lucas admitted. "But Shaffer got right next to this guy. We'll get there, too. This time, we won't turn our backs."

"I hope you kill him," Clark said.

OVER THE NEXT fifteen minutes, they told him almost nothing that was directly useful, but he noted all of it down, because he didn't know that for sure. They hadn't seen their daughter in the three days before she died. She had no boyfriend—she'd broken off a relationship with an Ellsworth man several months before she died, and hadn't yet started over. The Ellsworth man had been investigated from his scalp down to the soles of his feet, and he was clean.

Mary Lynn Carpenter had run a candy store on Main Street, and told her parents that while she wanted to meet a good man and have children, right now, she wanted to build her business. She'd taken business classes at the University of Wisconsin–Stout, in Menomonie, Wisconsin, a half hour north of Durand, and had bought the store with a loan from her parents.

"She did great with it," Clark said. "I mean, it was never going to be a *huge* money-maker, but she was already doing pretty darn well, and she had this idea for a whole chain of these small places, in small towns. See, they're really efficient: you don't need much capital to start one, and basically, one person can run it most of the year, with a half-time high school kid in the summer and at Christmas, when you do most of your business."

"I don't think Agent Davenport wants to know about the candy business, dear," Sandra said, touching her husband's thigh.

"Well, I'm just telling him," Clark said. "She figured she could put together ten of these places, all within a hundred miles or so, and be pulling down a half-million a year. That's real good money."

"Yes, it is," Lucas said. "What happened to the business?"

"She had this girl working for her, Cindy Tucker, she lives here in town," Clark said. "Cindy was going to a junior college, and she was gonna run the store when Mary Lynn branched out. Anyway, Cindy bought it from us—got a loan from her folks, and we took back part of the price, she'll pay it off over five years. We were Mary Lynn's only heirs, and we gave Cindy a good deal on it. She's a good kid, and that's what Mary Lynn would have wanted."

"Is the store open now?" Lucas asked.

"Sure."

"And Cindy saw Mary Lynn the day she disappeared?"

"The day before," Sandra said. "She didn't work the day Mary Lynn disappeared. Something broke at the store . . ."

"Pipe . . ."

"They weren't going to be able to do some of the cooking," Sandra said. "Cindy wanted to go shopping up in the Cities, so Mary Lynn told her to take off."

"Who else saw her before she disappeared?"

"Oh, Lord, lots of people," Sandra said. "Your investigators made a whole list. Half the people in town were in there."

WHEN LUCAS WAS LEAVING, Clark asked, "You really think you'll get this guy?"

"Yes. We will."

Clark showed a grim smile, more than a little skeptical: "You're pretty sure about that."

Lucas stopped just below the porch. "Mr. Carpenter . . . if we don't have this guy sewed up in two weeks, I will come to your house and give you a thousand dollars."

"I don't need a thousand dollars, but I like the concept," Clark said. "If you get him, I'll tell you what: I'll give a thousand dollars to whatever charity you want."

Lucas nodded: "It's a deal. Or a bet. Whatever. But I'm gonna get him, so get your money ready."

Carpenter started laughing, an odd whinnying laugh, and tears started running down his face.

THE CANDY STORE was in the middle of the downtown business strip, a narrow shop, just wide enough for a candy case to one side, an aisle for the customers, and a counter with a cash register at the end of the aisle. It smelled like sweet chocolate and caramel, and featured a row of caramel apples in the glass case.

Two women were working the shop: one maybe twenty, and one who might have been eighteen. Lucas asked the older one, "Are you Cindy Tucker?"

The woman nodded: she was short, fair-haired, with a quick smile. "Yes, I am. Who are you?"

Lucas dug his ID out and said, "I'm with the Minnesota Bureau of Criminal Apprehension. I need to talk to you for a few minutes about Mary Lynn."

She grimaced: didn't want to do it. "I've got to tell you, I've already talked to three different agents."

"I know, I need to hear some of it myself," Lucas said.

"Is this because that other agent was killed?" the younger girl asked.

"Not exactly," Lucas said. "I would have gotten here sooner or later, if we didn't catch this guy first." To Cindy, "It'll just take a few minutes."

SHE SUGGESTED that they walk across the street to a cafe. The place was nearly empty, and they took a corner table, ordered a Diet Coke and a root beer.

Lucas said, "The killer we're looking for chose a particular kind of person to prey upon . . ."

"I know. Blondes."

"Not just blondes. Young blond women who liked nightlife. Liked bars. The thing about Mary Lynn, and the reason she interests me, is that she doesn't fit that model. The other women who were killed were probably out drinking when they were picked up. He got to Mary Lynn some other way. Why would he go there, at that moment, when she was there? It is possible that it was an outlandish coincidence, and he acted on it. But if you're going to kidnap someone, which is a lot more complicated than simply killing them, you've got to be ready. You've got to have some way to intimidate them, to keep them quiet, you've got to handcuff them or tie them up, you have to transport them."

"So . . . what? You think he saw her in the shop?" She looked around, with a shadow of fear in her eyes: she was pretty and blond.

"I thought it was a good possibility, when I started over here today," Lucas said. "I think it's even a better possibility now that I see what her job was—she was in your little store, and all the time, I understand. It's an attractive place, for anybody who wants a quick cheap sugar hit—fudge, chocolate peanut bars, candy apples."

"We do have a lot of regulars."

"The guy could have been in and out any number of times, checking her out," Lucas said. "Even making friends. I don't think he's from here, in Durand. I think he's from Minnesota, from Zumbrota, or Holbein, or Red Wing . . . in that area. So—did you or Mary Lynn know anybody like that? A Minnesotan, probably in his thirties to mid-forties, who came over here from time to time? Maybe some kind of job thing, who'd stop and talk to you? Buy a candy apple and talk to Mary Lynn?"

She bit her lower lip, turned and looked out the front window, her eyes unfocused, and after a minute she said, "Oh, God, there must be people like that! I can't think of any right off the top of my head, but there must be."

He let her think another minute, then said, "I'm going to give you a card. If you could ask anyone who knew Mary Lynn . . . I know she'd broken up with her boyfriend, so maybe she mentioned somebody who'd come on to her a bit? Just ask around."

Then she said, "I just thought of one guy from Minnesota who's here every week, and he comes to our store almost every time. Doesn't seem like the killer type, but then, what do I know?"

"Who is it?"

She tapped Lucas's Diet Coke. "The Coke guy."

THE COKE GUY.

Lucas thought, *Of course.*

And the Pepsi guy, and the bread guy, and the meat guy and the beer guy. Durand was a small town, and anything that came into the stores would be delivered by truck. With perishable stuff, probably on a weekly or even daily basis.

"You think the Coke guy in particular?" Lucas asked.

"No, it's just that he usually comes in, when he's in town. He didn't really come on to us, he's always paid more attention to the candy case than he does to us. He's heavyset: he likes his candy. He buys it and leaves, but sometimes, he takes a while to make a choice."

"Know his name?"

"It's Andy, something. He works for a distributor in South St. Paul, and he has a route through the towns around here."

"All right. See, this is something," Lucas said. "We can check the regular distributors through here. That's good. Anybody else you can think of? Anybody?"

"Not right now. Let me talk to people, I can probably find a few."

"Good. Here's my card: call me as soon as you think of somebody. If you can point me at the police station, I'll go have a talk with the people over there. But I'm really kind of leaning on you. You know how serious this is."

She shivered, and clutched her arms, her eyes welling up. "Yes. My God, when you think about what happened to Mary Lynn. She was just always . . . so . . . lively."

HE LEFT HER at the store after getting directions to the police department. She said it'd be quicker to drive over, than to walk.

When he walked back to the car, he found a tall unbent elderly man looking at it. Lucas said, "How ya doin'?" and the old man nodded at him.

"What kind of truck is that?" he asked.

"Mercedes-Benz."

The man said, "Huh."

"Let me ask you something," Lucas said. "When you come into town from the west, across the bridge, almost the whole town is built south of the bridge, and only on this side of the river. Why is that? Most towns, they're on both sides of the river."

The old man looked up toward the bridge, which wasn't visible from where they were, and then back at Lucas. "'Cause they moved the bridge. Used to be right in the middle of town, but when they built the new one, they put it up there."

"Why didn't I think of that?" Lucas asked.

"I dunno," the old man said. And, "Pretty fancy, that Mercedes."

. . .

THE RIVER RAN down a V-shaped valley and the police department was in a long tan county government building on top of the east valley wall, across from the golf course. The chief, whose name was Carr, was walking out the door when Lucas was walking in—Lucas spotted him because his badge said "Chief"—and when Lucas identified himself, and said what he wanted, Carr suggested that they go back inside.

They walked past a sheriff's department window with nobody behind it, down the hall to the city police department office. A cop named Lucy was fiddling around with some paperwork. The chief called her over, and they all found chairs around the chief's desk. Lucas told the same story that he'd told Cindy Tucker. "To sum it up," Carr said when he finished, "you think the Black Hole guy might visit here from Minnesota, and go to the candy store often enough to get friendly with Mary Lynn. He's probably in his late thirties or forties."

"That's about it," Lucas said.

The Durand cops looked at each other, then Lucy said, "I don't see that many Minnesota plates here. Every time we see one, we could just call it in and get a list going. We could ask the people in town here to chip in names. There might be quite a few, though."

"We can handle that," Lucas said. "It's not the length of the list that kills us, it's not having the information."

"So let's do that," Carr said. "We can bring it up to the city council, and the Optimists and so on, and get everybody to spread the word around town, and call in to us. We could probably hand you a pretty good list in a couple of days."

"That would be excellent," Lucas said.

. . .

LUCAS HAD TURNED his phone off while talking to Cindy Tucker and hadn't turned it back on before he left the police department. When he did, in the truck, he found a couple of calls from Catrin Mattsson.

He called her back and she said, "I might have been a little grumpy this morning."

"You're apologizing?"

"You were sort of smirking about me getting hit, so I'll apologize if you will," she said.

"I'll have to think it over," Lucas said. "You started it."

"Ah, Jesus."

"All right, I apologize for that, and everything else I might have done, or will do, in the future."

"Okay," she said. "I apologize for being grumpy."

"How's the face?"

"I look like somebody hit me six times," she said.

"That can't be a first," Lucas said.

"It wasn't. Anyway—where'd you go? Back to the Hole?"

"No, I'm over in Wisconsin, in Durand, looking into Mary Lynn Carpenter." He told her the story, and she said, "That could be something. We've got too many somethings, though, that keep coming up nothings."

"We'll get him."

"Listen. One thing. I know you don't believe Kaylee about seeing Sprick in the ditch—"

"I do think she saw *something*," Lucas said.

"Well, I've got a digital photo of Sprick right here—I'm at my desk. If I sent it to your cell phone, could you run it by this Cindy woman? I know you don't believe—"

"I'm going right past the store on my way out of town," Lucas said. "Send it to me."

"You'll have it in ten seconds," she said.

WHEN LUCAS GOT BACK to the store, Cindy Tucker was waiting on an elderly woman stuck like Buridan's ass between two piles of chocolates, one with pecans, and the other with almonds. The woman kept glancing at Lucas, feeling his impatience, then made a forced choice of the almond ones. As they were being loaded onto a candy scale, she seemed to be reevaluating the choice, her eyes drifting back to the pecans.

"Tell you what," Cindy whispered to her. "I'll throw in a free pecan, so you can think what they might have been like to have a whole bunch of them."

The elderly woman brightened at the deal, got her white paper sack, and waddled out the door.

Lucas looked after her, and when she was gone, said, "One more thing. The sheriff's investigator out of Red Wing was looking at a particular guy. She sent along a picture. I wonder if you could take a look?"

He brought the photo up on his cell phone. Cindy took the phone, looked at the photo, a wrinkle creasing her forehead, and she looked up at Lucas with her mouth in an "O" shape. After a few seconds, she sputtered, "Oh my God! I've seen this guy. He comes in here two or three times a year. I mean, not regular, but I recognize him. I don't know what he does . . ."

She looked back at the photo again. "I think."

"You think? On a scale of one to ten, how sure are you?" Lucas asked.

She studied the photo and then said, "Seven. Or eight. Not nine."

"How big is he? How does he dress? Has he ever said what he does?" Lucas asked.

"He's . . . a little short. He wears just regular button shirts and jeans. Pretty sure about the jeans. He's never said what he does . . . mmm . . . I got the feeling that he's well off, but he also works with his hands. He's got that building-contractor look. The time before last, when he came in, he was wearing this watch, and Mary Lynn told me it was either a real Rolex or a fake Rolex, but the watch said Rolex on it."

"He was friendly with Mary Lynn?"

"Well, he was trying, but she didn't like him. I remember her saying that he seemed a little *queer* to her. She didn't mean gay. She meant queer the other way." She was still studying the photo, and after another moment said, "Six."

"Six?"

"Yeah. I think it's him, but the longer I look at it . . . the more I think it might not be. But at first . . . jeez . . ."

"All right. Listen, keep this under your hat," Lucas said. "Don't even tell your folks. For a couple of days, it's important that you keep quiet."

"Oh . . . Oh my God," she said, her hand at her mouth. "This might be the guy."

9

R-A was in the parlor, where, in the olden days, visitors would be taken to chat. R-A had stripped out the furniture and put in beige accordion blinds for privacy, and moved in a weight bench and a few hundred pounds of bars and plates, plus speed and heavy bags.

In the morning, before he went to work, he'd go to the weights for half an hour, in a custom routine he'd created after several hours of Internet research. He'd end with a hard ten minutes of punching.

And a cigarette.

Get his lungs open, punching, and the nicotine hit like a pack of razor blades.

"You need to work out harder," Horn said. He was in his wheelchair at the entrance to the parlor, watching. "Need to do something about that gut. When the cops come for you, they're gonna put you in prison forever. The big black boys in there are gonna look at your fat white ass, and if you ain't ready to defend yourself, they're gonna wear you out."

"Fuck you," R-A said. "How am I gonna get out of this?"

"You gotta go proactive," Horn said.

R-A mocked him: "Proactive? What's a shitkicker like you doing with five-dollar words?" He sat down on the end of a weight bench, dangling a forty-pound dumbbell from each hand. He stood—finishing a squat—curled the dumbbells, thrust them overhead, un-curled them, and sat down slowly. When he was solid on the bench, he did it again.

"Shut up," Horn said, showing some teeth, glittering and crooked like fresh-water pearls behind his dry lips. "I've been think-ing about this. You want to take this Mattsson? How about this? You know that old typewriter up in your mom's closet?"

"Yeah?"

"You go up there and write you a note. The note says, 'It's hardly worth killing women anymore, when all that's on the other side is a bunch of dumb flatfeet. No fun in fooling you. You couldn't find your own pussy with two hands and a flashlight.'"

"That's gonna impress her," R-A said.

"Get her attention, for sure," Horn said. "Then you say, 'You can't even figure out who's down that Black Hole, and I didn't even try to hide who it was. You want some names? There's Shawna Riv-ers from New Prague, I took her off four years ago, her skull's down there. Then there's Melissa Scott, she was eight years ago, and she was a fun little thing. I turned that girl every way but loose, and I still get a big ol' boner just thinking about it. She was begging for more by the time I got tired of her and choked her out. Here you were on the TV whining about twenty skulls—you haven't even fig-ured out the pits in Alexandria and Eau Claire. I've been doing this for a long time, honey. I'd be embarrassed if it were only twenty, after all the work I've put into it.'"

R-A dropped back onto the weight bench. "Okay. That will get her attention. Why do I want to do that?"

"Let me finish. Tomorrow, you tell the boys at the store that you've got to run up to the Cities. You run right through the Cities to Sauk Centre and mail that letter. Don't go licking any stamps or any envelope glue, or they'll get you on that DNA. When she gets that letter, she'll *be* someone. You could tell when you saw her on the TV that she wants to *be* someone. So she'll be waiting to talk to you. You tease her, and tease her . . . We get her turned around, get her on TV, get her running around like a rat, sooner or later, we'll figure out a way to pull her in, and take her."

"Take her in Sauk Centre?"

"No, dumbass. You mail the letter from Sauk Centre to pull the attention up that way. They'll still be down here, some, but they've been down here for a month and they ain't got shit. They'll be worried because you mentioned Alexandria, and another pit, and Sauk Centre is the next place down the highway. They're already panicked. If there's more pits out there, and they don't get you quick, they'll all lose their jobs. You let them worry about that for a couple of days, *then* . . ."

"This is gonna be nasty, isn't it?" He grinned at Horn.

"Then you go up to Alexandria and take a nice little blond girl, and you choke her out, and you leave a note with her. From the same typewriter," Horn said. "The note is in one hand, which is pointing out somewhere, and the note says, 'The Alex pit is over that way . . . but pretty far. When I take the next one, I'll point to her, too. Maybe the lines will cross over close enough that you'll find it. It's not like the Black Hole, it's something completely different. Good luck!' See, the thing is, they do all that analysis shit, and they'll see it's the same typewriter. They'll believe you, and the next thing you know, they'll be marching through the streets of Alexandria."

"So." R-A sat on the bench, dropped the dumbbells. He'd just lifted a total of two thousand pounds with each arm; both his arms and legs burned with acid buildup. "Everybody is up there looking . . . and Miss Big-Tit Goodhue County Sheriff's Deputy is out of the action. Then we feed her something that'll get her out in the open . . . and she comes in. What do we feed her?"

"Don't have that yet," Horn said. "I'll think of something."

R-A THOUGHT ABOUT IT all morning, working around the store, and sitting in his office, figuring out inventory and bills. One of the bills, for nine hundred dollars, covered the wholesale cost of six aluminum Wave-Busters, used by boaters when back-trolling. He bought twelve a year, and reliably sold them. Still had four left. When he sold three of them, he'd run over to Greg's Machine, five miles north of Durand, and get six more. Probably wouldn't have to do that until February, he thought.

Wouldn't have to stop at the candy store . . . although . . . Mary Lynn's assistant had been cute, if he remembered her right. A little flat-chested, but a possibility.

He punched the "pay" button on his computer-books program, and the printer spit out a check for nine hundred bucks.

Mary Lynn had been a disappointment. She'd given up too quick.

But this deputy, this Mattsson . . . she looked like a fighter.

. . .

HE WALKED HOME at noon, and wrote the note, using his dead mom's old Royal typewriter. The ribbon was crappy and dry, but the words were clear enough. He called Roy, at the store, said he was feeling a little rocky, and was taking the afternoon off.

"You going to Sauk Centre?" Horn asked, when R-A got back home.

"Worth a try," he said.

"Rolling the bones," Horn said. "It's getting interesting, now."

R-A got in the car just about the time Lucas crossed the Mississippi on his way to Durand. Sauk Centre was two and a half hours away. If he dropped the letter as soon as he got there, Mattsson could get it as early as the next day.

10

Lucas didn't want to tell Mattsson about Cindy Tucker's identification of Sprick on the telephone: face-to-face would be better, he thought. He called her, said something interesting had turned up, and where was she, anyway?

Sitting at home, she said, with a Blue Ice pack freezing her face.

MATTSSON HAD AN APARTMENT in downtown Red Wing, the only apartment on the second floor of a brown-brick building, above Bunny's Nail Parlor. If you stood in just the right place at a back bathroom window, and pushed a curtain aside, and looked at just the right angle, you could see a tree on the far side of the Mississippi.

Lucas came out of the bathroom after washing his hands and said, "You can almost see the river from the bathroom."

"Yeah. When I rented it, it was called a 'view apartment,'" Mattsson said. "I told the landlady if she planned to charge me extra for the view, I'd bust her for fraud."

Mattsson was sitting on a plaster banco in the kitchen, which smelled pleasantly of a peppery tomato soup. The Blue Ice bags were back in the freezer, getting cold again; the bruise on Mattsson's face was the size of Lucas's hand. He pulled out a chair at the kitchen table, sat down across from her, and said, "You always want to have a good start with a new landlady."

"Ah, she wanted me in here," Mattsson said. "Reliable job, so she gets paid, and it's always good to have a cop around, keeping an eye on the place. I wanted it because it's got space. So . . . you figured something out?"

"What happened with Shales?"

"She spilled her guts. She's a sad case. She said Harriet Card was the only person who ever loved her. Last night, Card told her that it wasn't working out. They started fighting, and Shales choked her. Won't be a trial—she'll eventually plead out, probably take ten."

"Good when that happens, cuts all the crap out," Lucas said. "So listen . . . I showed your photo of Sprick to the candy store girl. She says it's six-out-of-ten Sprick was over there three or four times a year."

Mattsson sat bolt upright: *"What?"*

"Yeah. She sorta half-ass identified him."

"Jesus! Davenport!"

"Calm down. I don't think he's the guy," Lucas said. "The question is, why did Kaylee identify him from the ditch, and why did Cindy Tucker identify him as a guy who was in her store several times a year?"

"I could think of one really good reason," Mattsson said. "It's him."

"But it's *not* him. For one thing, Cindy said he's on the short side. Distinctly on the short side. Sprick must be six feet tall. I mean, we should go over there and talk to him, but I'll bet he's as confused as we are. So we want to ask, does he have male relatives of the same age? A brother? Somebody who could be mistaken for him? Somebody shorter?"

"Let's do that," she said. "Let me get my Blue Ice and some gloves: I can hold it on my face driving over."

THEY DID THAT.

Lucas followed her over, a half hour from downtown Red Wing. Ten minutes out, he took a call from Rose Marie Roux. "Where are you?"

"Down by Red Wing," Lucas said.

"How's the hunt?"

"We're getting some movement—I'm keeping Duncan up to date," Lucas said. "You probably already know this, but the body found at the Hole this morning doesn't have anything to do with the guy we're looking for."

"I heard. The thing is, the media were saying at noon that we probably had caught the killer," Roux said. "Now they're having to say that we haven't caught the killer, and you know how annoyed they get when they're wrong. They start looking for somebody to blame that's not them."

"Yeah, well, fuck 'em."

"Yeah. Sometimes I wish I could run into Channel Three with a dynamite belt and blow the whole place to kingdom come," Roux said.

Lucas: "Did something happen?"

"Three has out an editorial. They're saying the investigation has been incompetent, that this killer is going to kill more people," Rose Marie said. "They say I should fire Sands. If I don't, the governor should step in and fire both of us. They say we're an embarrassment to law enforcement."

"Oh, boy. Why don't they blame the FBI? They had that profiler guy talking to Shaffer every day."

"Because they're not going to get the FBI fired," Roux said. "Me, they could bag."

"Is it serious?"

"It's getting that way," Roux said. "If we don't get this guy soon . . ."

"But you and the governor are asshole buddies," Lucas said.

"He won't fire me—but I'll have to go."

"I'll tell you what," Lucas said. "I bet Mary Lynn Carpenter's father a thousand dollars that I'll have the guy in two weeks. Can you hold on that long?"

"Maybe. Can I tell the governor you said that? He trusts you."

"Go ahead. Tell him two weeks, not more," Lucas said.

"Could he say it on television? Two weeks?" Roux asked.

Lucas had to laugh: "Jesus, it's *that* bad?"

JUST BEFORE THEY GOT to Zumbrota, where Sprick lived, he took another call, this time from Ignace, the *Star-Tribune* reporter: "Janet Frost is trying to get you, for that story on the crazy hunger-strike guy, but she hasn't been able to get your phone number. I told her I didn't have it, but I'd call around the BCA and try to get it. Can I give it to her?"

"Ah, jeez, I don't want to talk to her."

"Well, her next move is to come over to your house tonight and pound on the door. So . . . She's going to get you one way or another."

"Give me her number, and I'll call *her*."

LUCAS TOOK THE NUMBER as they crossed the Zumbro bridge into Zumbrota. Five minutes later, they were parked outside Sprick's house behind a Channel Three van. The lights were on in the house, but all the shades were pulled.

When Lucas and Mattsson got out of their trucks, a reporter hopped out of the van and said, "Officer Mattsson . . . Agent Davenport. What's up?"

"Mr. Sprick invited us over to play canasta," Lucas said, and he continued up the sidewalk.

Mattsson, trailing behind, asked the reporter, "Are you still doing that story on Kaylee?"

The reporter looked at his watch: "Should be running in ten minutes."

The cameraman had come around from the driver's seat with a camera on his shoulder. The reporter, stopping short of Sprick's property, called, "Is it true that you were hospitalized after the fight with Glenda Shales this morning?"

Lucas turned to Mattsson as she came up behind him. "If you talk to these guys, they'll bite you in the ass. I promise you."

"I kinda like it," she said.

"Yeah. Until they bite you. They're like crocodiles. They will bite, sooner or later," he said.

Sprick came to the door, peered out, then opened it. "What?"

Lucas said, "We need to talk to you, but that camera's running out there, and the microphone could probably pick up an ant walking across the sidewalk."

Sprick stared at them for a moment. He was haggard, and maybe a little drunk. Lucas could smell the beer from the porch. Sprick looked past Lucas to the TV truck, then said, "Come on in."

He shut the door behind them, and pointed to the living room, where the chairs were. "I still didn't do it."

"I've only got one question for you," Lucas said. "How often do you go to Durand, Wisconsin?"

"Durand? Wisconsin? I've heard of it, I've seen it on addresses on envelopes, but I don't know exactly where it is," Sprick said. "I've never been there."

"Never?"

"Never. You find another body?"

"No, but a woman there said she recognized you as having been in her store, a few times every year."

Sprick rolled his head back in exasperation. "I've *never* been there . . . never in my life."

Mattsson said, "We've got two people identifying you as being associated with crime scenes. If we believe you . . . have you ever seen anybody around here that could be mistaken for you? Do you have a brother, or a cousin, or somebody like that?"

Sprick was shaking his head. "I've got two sisters, and they don't look like me. I've got a couple of cousins, but they live over by

Milwaukee, and they don't look any more like me than anybody else does."

"You don't know anybody that looks like you? From right around here?" Lucas asked.

"No. I know about every single person in town, and I don't think anyone looks enough like me that Kaylee would make that mistake."

"The Kaylee interview is going on the air tonight," Lucas said.

"I know, they've been promoting it all afternoon," Sprick said. "That fuckin' *Little Kaylee*, that's what they're calling her, is gonna hang me up by my nuts. I can't even go outside."

LUCAS WENT HOME after the interview with Sprick. He was tired. He'd gone running out that morning to look at a dead body, and hadn't stopped since. On the way north, he looked at the number that Ignace had texted him, the woman who was doing the story on Emmanuel Kent. He punched it into his phone, listened to it ring three times, and was about to hang up, when she answered: "Janet Frost."

"This is Lucas Davenport, with the BCA. I understand you've been trying to get in touch."

"Thank you, thank you, thank you for calling back," she said. She had a nice sexy voice, with a suppressed giggle in it. "You know about Emmanuel Kent? He's on a hunger strike, outside City Hall. He says he's on it because you set up an ambush to kill his brother."

"I wasn't even there," Lucas said.

"No, but you were obviously behind it—the smart guy behind

it," Frost said. "The Woodbury police told us that you or this other agent, Agent Jenkins, were passing on surveillance to them that led up to the shoot-out."

"That's partly true," Lucas said. "But we weren't doing the surveillance—that was all done by the local police forces, and as Kent moved around the Twin Cities, they kept an eye on him, and let us know what he was up to. All we did was keep everyone informed. Then, he started cruising the bank out in Woodbury, and we notified the Woodbury force that he appeared to be coming their way."

"Instead of killing him, why didn't you just stop him? Warn him?" Frost asked.

"Because he would have laughed us off. We had word that he was the guy doing this, but we had no proof at all," Lucas said. "Remember, he'd robbed five banks—he was a very efficient robber, very skilled at it. But sooner or later, he was going to run into a problem, and he was going to kill some innocent person trying to get out of it. He went into the banks with a gun, and sooner or later, he'd pull the trigger. That was our belief. He certainly seemed prepared to do so. When he was confronted by Woodbury officers, he pulled the trigger first."

"He was shot seven times by Woodbury officers. The officers admit that they fired at least twenty bullets."

"Yes. I thought they showed great restraint," Lucas said.

"Restraint? Shot seven times?"

"Sure. Have you ever fired a semiautomatic pistol?"

"No, I—"

"The feds say a novice shooter can fire three times in a second—

and a trained man can fire twice that many," Lucas said. "With four trained officers there, all shooting, twenty rounds total, they probably were firing for a second or so. Not as much as two seconds."

Frost was silent for a moment—taking notes, Lucas hoped— then said, "Somehow, though, it doesn't seem fair, four policemen, behind their cars . . ."

Lucas hesitated, then said, "Well, Janet, it wasn't supposed to be fair. This wasn't *High Noon*. The Woodbury officers were attempting to stop an armed bank robber who opened fire on them. This is not a video game where you get a do-over. When Kent opened fire, somebody was going to get shot, and the police officers involved were desperately anxious that it not be them. Go look at a gunshot wound sometime, and you'll see why."

"You know what Doyle was using the money for? He was supporting his brother on the street—"

"That's not exactly the whole story," Lucas said. "When he hit the bank in Golden Valley, he took out twelve thousand dollars, and he apparently spent it all during the month before he hit the Woodbury bank. As close as I can tell, from the psychiatrist's report on Emmanuel Kent, Doyle Kent might have given his brother two hundred dollars during that month. So he wasn't exactly supporting him in style. That's two percent of his take."

"And yet we have this result: a street person starving in front of City Hall," Frost said.

"I can't solve that problem," Lucas said. "That's somebody else's job. My job is to try to keep the assholes from robbing banks and killing innocent people."

"You don't feel sorry at all for Manny?"

"Of course I do," Lucas said. "I've known a lot of those folks, ever since the beginning of my career. If somebody could figure out a way to help them, that they'd go along with, I'd say, 'Go ahead, bump up my taxes, take care of them.' But it's a complex problem, and so far, nobody's come up with a solution."

They talked for a few more minutes, and then Frost, apparently satisfied, thanked him for his help and rang off. He'd done all right, Lucas thought, although he probably shouldn't have used the word "assholes."

He drove on for a while, thinking about the interview, and eventually decided that the most worrisome aspect of it was that Frost kept referring to the Kent brothers by their first names, Doyle and Manny.

He GOT HOME too late for dinner, had a turkey sandwich and a glass of orange juice and told Weather and Letty about the day, and the dead body, and the interview in Wisconsin, and talking to Sprick. Weather said she had an interesting operation the next day, a revision of a breast enhancement botched by a cosmetic surgeon. As a board-certified plastic surgeon, Weather looked down on doctors who called themselves cosmetic surgeons; but happily reworked their mistakes.

"This guy," she said, talking about the other surgeon, "has a signature tit. I'd recognize it anywhere. All rounded and sculpted, nipples pointed up . . . doesn't make any difference what your body looks like, that's the tit you get. This woman now looks like she's got bowling balls in her shirt. She's a lawyer, used to be an A cup, she wanted to go to something like a C . . ."

Lucas ate his sandwich and said the right things, and thought

about the killer and what he might be doing, how he might be reacting to the pressure.

When the meal was over, Letty went to go online with some
friends, and Lucas and Weather went for a walk on the nice warm
summer night, kids out on the sidewalks, convertibles cruising the
boulevard. Weather said she thought they should get a dog from
the humane society because she'd grown up with dogs, and she
wanted the small kids to do that, too. Lucas said, "Uh-huh," and
wondered if the killer might be out taking a walk, thinking about
blond girls . . .

Back at the house, he told Weather he was going for a run, and
he went upstairs to change clothes. About the time he put his right
foot through the leg of his running shorts, he thought, *Wait . . .
a dog?*

11

Lucas needed to talk to Duncan about the trip to Wisconsin, and the Sprick identification by Cindy Tucker, and talk to the Minneapolis cops about Emmanuel Kent, the hunger-striker.

He was shot off his horse before he even got started.

He'd slept late, as he usually did, rolling out of bed after nine o'clock. He got cleaned up and dressed, read the papers as he ate breakfast, talked to the kids for a while, and then called Duncan.

Lucas told him the whole story about the Sprick identification. When he finished, Duncan said, "So . . . you're saying it's a dead end."

At that moment, an incoming call beeped through. Lucas said to Duncan, "I've got a call from Mattsson coming in. Let me get back to you."

"Hope it's something . . ."

He clicked over to Mattsson, who said, "Davenport? I got something really weird, man. I don't know if it's real or not, but my hair is standing straight up."

"What?"

"I got a letter, here at the office, from somebody who says he's the killer," she said.

"That'll happen on these kinds of cases," Lucas said. "We've already had a couple of confessions—"

"I know, I know, but this is different. He names two victims that we don't know about."

Lucas said, "Huh."

"Huh? What does that mean?" Mattsson asked.

"Any indication that these . . . ?"

"Yes. I've checked. Both women have been reported missing, one five years ago, one six. Both blondes, both young. Both drinkers."

"All right, that's serious," Lucas said. "I'll call the lab. Put the letter and the envelope in separate evidence envelopes—"

"Already did that," she said.

"Drive it up to the BCA. You know where that is?"

"Give me the address."

He gave her the address, and she said, "Give me forty-five minutes."

"Catrin? Lights and siren."

He called Duncan and told him Mattsson was on the way.

Duncan said, "I don't need any false hopes. If this is a fake, my ass is gonna fall off."

LUCAS SAID GOOD-BYE to the family and headed for the BCA. He and Duncan were waiting when Mattsson arrived with the letter.

Lucas met her at the front door, and they carried it up to Duncan's office. Mattsson was tense: "I don't pray. All the way up here, I was trying to remember some prayer I could say that this is a break."

Duncan read through it, peering through the side of the evidence bag. When he was done, he read it again, then said, "He's got pits in Eau Claire and Alexandria? If this gets out before we get him . . ."

"We've got to start processing it, like right now," Lucas said. "Almost all of the jawbones are intact. We need to find out if these women had dentists."

"What about DNA?" Mattsson asked.

"Takes a few days," Lucas said. "If we can find their dentists and get some X-rays, we could know by noon."

"I've got the guys who could find out," Duncan said.

Mattsson: "The note's written on a typewriter."

Lucas said, "There's something wrong about that. Who's even got a typewriter anymore? The guy doesn't seem like an idiot, but even an idiot knows that you can identify individual typewriters from the key strikes."

Duncan said, "Maybe he doesn't watch those CSI shows."

They all stared at the note and talked about the possibility of fingerprints and DNA, until Hopping Crow came down to get it, and then Duncan went to assign investigators to talk to the relatives of the two missing women.

"What do you think?" Mattsson asked Lucas.

"It had a feeling of reality about it," Lucas said. "But I don't see a motive for sending it. He's been lying low all these years."

"Maybe he's getting stoked by the publicity."

"Maybe . . ."

.   .   .

THEY GOT COFFEE and donuts from the team room, and sat and talked about the killer, and how his psychology might work, that would cause him to create the letter: killing time.

Talked about Letty for a while: "You got a smart kid there," Mattsson said. "She told me she's thinking about a law enforcement job, or intelligence. She says she's going to Stanford."

"And much too soon," Lucas said.

"If she graduates from Stanford and goes for a law enforcement job, it's gonna be something big-time: FBI, CIA." Mattsson said that she'd graduated from River Falls: "Didn't have the money for a really top-end school, so . . . here I am."

"Tone your act down about fifteen percent, kiss Duncan's ass a little—he's on his way up—and you could come work here," Lucas said. "You're smart enough, but you rub some of the guys the wrong way."

"'Cause this is a macho—"

"No, no. There are women all over the place. It's because you're a little . . . snappish. On occasion."

"You're saying I'm an asshole."

"A little snappish," Lucas said. "That's what I said, and I'm sticking to it."

THEY'D BEEN TALKING for fifteen minutes, including a brief dispute about the definition of "snappish," and Lucas said, "See?" and Mattsson said, "Fuck you," when Duncan came back and said,

"We've had some luck. We got to the parents of Melissa Scott and they said their daughter only went to one dentist all of her life, down in New Prague. We got his number, and he's still got her X-rays. He says they're the old kind, the film kind, but he thinks he can put them on a view box and shoot a close-up with a digital camera, and then e-mail them up here."

"How long?" Lucas asked.

"Fifteen minutes," Duncan said. He looked at his watch. "Nine minutes now."

They walked up to Duncan's office, and he checked his e-mail, nothing there, and they talked about nothing, and he checked again, nothing there, and then his computer made a chirping sound and the e-mail came in.

The dentist's shot was in color, but the X-ray was in black and white, and sharp and clear, the girl's fillings standing out like white icebergs in a dark sea. Duncan printed it, and they hurried upstairs to the lab, where one of the techs had a digital file of all the jaw-bones taken from the Hole.

Five or six investigators gathered around the tech's chair, peering over his shoulder. They found a match in two minutes.

"Okay, okay. He's real, he's live," Duncan said, and everybody started talking at once, what to do, where to go, what it all meant. Duncan looked at Lucas and Mattsson: "Where does this get us?"

"If there's anything on the paper or the envelope . . ." Mattsson began.

Duncan shook his head. "The lab people aren't optimistic. The envelope has fingerprints, but it's probably just mailmen . . . and yours. One set looks like a woman's."

"How do they know the prints aren't his?" Mattsson asked.

"He used a self-stick envelope and there are no prints, even smeared, where you'd normally find prints. It looks like he sealed it under another piece of paper or maybe used gloves. If he was that careful when he sealed it, he was probably careful whenever he handled it."

"Shoot. No DNA from spit. How about the stamp?" Mattsson asked.

"Stamps are all self-stick now—and this one is."

"Which makes me worry even more about the typewriter business," Lucas said. "There's something going on there."

"What?" asked Mattsson. "What could he be doing?"

Nobody could suggest an answer to that.

MATTSSON WANTED to hang out with the team for a while, to speculate on the motives of the killer. Lucas said good-bye and headed south again. Something, he thought, was getting away from him. He'd spoken to everybody that Shaffer was known to have interviewed. When he'd left Shaffer, the day he was killed, Lucas had gone off to a police station where he'd learned nothing. Shaffer had gone to an Owatonna cemetery. The funeral home guys said he left there in a hurry, like he might have figured something out.

From there he'd gone to the cemetery in Holbein, and maybe Zumbrota. . . . Why was that? What was he searching for in cemeteries? He'd professed himself excited by the discovery of the grave robbery, as a possible break, but that hadn't worked out . . . had it?

Lucas had started to walk the cemeteries, but had gotten

diverted and hadn't walked those at Demont and Owatonna. But Shaffer had figured something out by doing the cemeteries in a certain order. . . .

So Lucas would.

AN HOUR LATER, he stood by himself next to the raw earth of Mead's violated grave at Demont. The cemetery was small and barren, and Lucas looked down at the now filled-in grave, and then around at the other graves, and nothing occurred to him. What had they done that day, the day of the exhumation? He closed his eyes, swayed a bit in the wind, and rewound the tape of his memory. They'd watched the coffin being opened, and Lucas had turned away, and then they'd all looked at the headless body. . . .

Still nothing. He tried to find something in that experience, but failed, and walked back to his truck. As he fired it up, something began pecking at the back of his mind, and he remembered a similar experience a few days before, when he was leaving the cemetery at Holbein.

He had seen something, down in that grave. What was it?

HE MOVED ON TO Holy Angels in Owatonna, and again, spent some time looking around. He hadn't been there with Shaffer, so there was no memory there to lean on. He walked around the sepulchers, looking for anything that might bring up Shaffer's vision.

Felt the pecking again. What was he seeing, but not recognizing?

On to Holbein.

Alone in the cemetery, he stood back and looked at the sepulchers and said, aloud, "What the fuck is it? What happened here?
We have an asshole breaking into the sepulchers and . . ."

The tumblers snapped into place.

Keys.

"Kiss my ass," Lucas said aloud.

THE GRAVEDIGGER at Demont had to do some gymnastics to get
the grave open; and he'd had to use a special key to open the casket.
The casket had been undamaged, which meant the robbers had a
key. Where would some random asshole get that key? How would
he even know about it?

And out here, they'd kept saying that the grave robbers had *broken into* the sepulchers, but when he'd looked at them . . .

Not quite sure of himself, he hustled over to one sepulcher, and
then the other. They both had old-style wrought iron doors with
old locks. One lock was integral to the door, the other was locked
shut with a chain, the links the thickness of his middle finger, the
padlock the size of his hand. They looked like they'd been there
since the nineteenth century, but nothing was broken.

Keys.

That's what Shaffer had seen. The locks on all the sepulchers
were different, and different still from the casket keys—somebody
had to have access to a whole wide variety of keys, including
casket keys.

They'd thought the killer was a cemetery worker, but a cemetery worker wouldn't have access to all those keys. So—a locksmith?

Lucas got on the phone to Duncan, but Duncan was out of touch: "He'll be right back," the group secretary said, when Lucas checked with her. "I could hear his phone ringing on his desk. He has a Waylon Jennings ringtone."

"I might have something on the Hole. Tell him to call me as soon as he can."

LUCAS HAD BEEN FOCUSING on his phone, and felt something like a chill wind blowing down his shirt. His hand went to his gun, and he looked around. Still all alone, standing next to the grave of Baby Boy Wilson.

That chilled him even more, and he hurried off to his truck; and called Mattsson.

"I got something," he said. "I need to talk to somebody who knows everybody in Goodhue County."

"Tell me."

He told her, and when he'd finished, she said, "Coffin keys. Who'd have coffin keys? We're back at cemetery workers? Where are you?"

"In my truck, just backing out of the cemetery at Holbein," Lucas said. "I was thinking locksmiths."

"I'm on my way back to the office, but I can cut over there. I'll meet you."

"I'll meet you in Red Wing," Lucas said. "The Bobcat Cafe. I need to get lunch, anyway. And I want to go over Diamond Bluff. See if anybody has anything to say about cemetery workers."

"I'll be there in twenty minutes," she said.

. . .

SHE TOOK A LITTLE LONGER than that, but not much. She had a thin stack of printer paper in her hands as she slid into the booth across from him and said, "Something occurred to me."

"What?" He was swirling ice cubes around in a half-empty glass of Diet Coke.

"If the killer took Carpenter at the cemetery, just because he could, and because he was due . . . how does this fit with the candy shop girl identifying Sprick or a Sprick look-alike, that Little Kaylee also saw in the ditch after Shaffer was killed?"

Lucas: "Because he's a cemetery worker who looks like Sprick? But I don't know how that fits with him going over to Durand."

"I'll tell you—it doesn't," she said. "I suppose he could have seen her in the cemetery sometime earlier, and found out she was from Durand, and then checked back from time to time to find out when she was going to the cemetery. He'd know that it was isolated down there . . . I mean, if he was a scouter kind of guy."

Lucas said, "That's . . . pretty complicated."

Mattsson eyed him for a minute, said, "You mean, unlikely."

"Not impossible."

"Okay." She looked at the menu and asked, "You got any recommendations? For lunch?"

"Yeah. I'd recommend that you stay away from the open-face roast beef sandwich with mashed potatoes, brown gravy, and string beans. I was here yesterday, and my wife almost made me sleep outside last night."

"Too much information," Mattsson said. And, "I stopped at the office and pulled this off the computer. List of locksmiths within seventy-five miles."

She handed him the paper she'd brought in, and Lucas took it and scanned it: "Not many down here."

"But a whole load of them on the south side of the Cities," Mattsson said.

"I don't think he's up in the Cities—I think he's here."

"But he's a locksmith?"

"Or a cemetery worker. Or both. Somebody who could get a key to a coffin, and a bunch of sepulchers."

They ate lunch in a hurry, then crossed the river in Lucas's truck and turned north to Diamond Bluff. As Lucas came off the bridge, he took a call from Duncan, and told him what they were doing. "That's interesting. We're already looking at every cemetery worker in the world. This certainly seems to confirm that idea. You got any interviews set up in Diamond Bluff?"

"Not yet, but we'll be there in one minute."

"Let me see what I can find out from up here," he said. "I'll call you."

Diamond Bluff was an unincorporated settlement, in which the major public establishment seemed to be the bar. They asked in the bar, but nobody could identify a town official of any kind, or even a better place to ask. Nobody in the bar knew who might run the cemetery.

Out in the parking lot, Mattsson looked across the highway at the short clutch of streets between the highway and the river— there were only two, or maybe three—that made up the town. She put her fists on her hips and said, "I can't believe *nobody's* in charge. How could they get anything done?"

"Maybe everyone just takes care of himself," Lucas suggested.

They went down to the cemetery. It was both pleasant and pre-dictably melancholy, with big trees and grass that had been cut, but not recently.

"Now what?" Mattsson asked.

"We're not doing any good, standing around like this," Lucas said.

"Tell you what," Mattsson said. "You can drop me at the office and I'll start calling people. I'll have a list of names by the end of the day. I'll call all the funeral homes. They gotta know who's running these places."

"Look for locksmiths," Lucas said. "I'll give your list to Duncan, and have him run them all."

"YOU EVER THINK it might be like this?" Lucas asked, as they walked back to his truck.

"What?"

"Investigating. You get what feels like a hot lead, but you can't find anyone to talk to?"

"It's worse than that, in my job, anyway. You get a hot lead, but the crime was so low-rent that the lead bores you," she said. "So—what're you going to do?"

"I'm going to read the murder books again. Shaffer knew more than I do—I'm pretty sure the key thing is what he figured out. The question is, how'd he take the next step? It's gotta be in what he knew."

"Okay. That's boring."

.   .   .

THEY NEVER DID any of that, because as they were leaving, Duncan called and asked Lucas where he was.

"Over in Diamond Bluff."

"Look—I never could find who takes care of the cemetery at Diamond Bluff, but we've had something else come up. There was a funeral down in Zumbrota this morning—just wound up a few minutes ago. We're being told that the funeral party found Shaffer's wallet and the other notebook. The big one. They say it looks like somebody threw them in a patch of long grass. One of the funeral party picked up the wallet—they thought somebody had lost it— but they haven't touched the notebook. We're hoping for prints or DNA. Could you get that Goodhue crime-scene guy and go get it?"

"Yeah, but don't we have a few guys still up at the Hole? They'd be closer."

"No. They wound that up this morning, they're already back," Duncan said. "Besides, I want to know what's in that notebook just as soon as I can."

"On my way," Lucas said.

Mattsson had been listening, and she said, "Take me back to my truck, and I'll follow you over. Actually, if you follow me over, we'll get there faster. I know the shortcuts. I'll call Johnston now." Johnston was the Goodhue County crime-scene investigator.

THE RUN WAS a fast one: down across the river through Red Wing with Lucas's flashers going, and then a two-truck caravan rocketing cross-country to Zumbrota. When they arrived at the cemetery, they saw a hearse, a line of civilian cars, a Zumbrota cop car, a Goodhue sheriff's car, and a cluster of people in suits and somber dresses. Off to one side, an open grave and a rank of folding chairs.

Mattsson pulled up and hopped out, with Lucas a few steps behind. She turned and said, "Johnston's already here. He was cleaning up at the Hole from yesterday, taking some site photos."

Johnston was, in fact, taking photos of the wallet and the notebook, which lay by a tree ten yards from the still-open grave; the mourners were spread around him in a semicircle, watching him work. The notebook was actually a yellow legal pad, inside a leather cover.

When Mattsson and Lucas walked through the semicircle of mourners, Johnston looked up and said, "Almost done. I need another two or three shots."

"You got any of those plastic see-through evidence bags?" Lucas asked.

"Yeah, sure."

"When you're finished with the photos, let's get the notebook in a bag. I want to take a look."

MATTSSON WALKED OVER to the mourners, Lucas a few steps behind, and asked, "Who found the notebook?"

A white-haired older man, in a dark blue suit, white dress shirt, and shiny blue necktie, raised his hand and said, "That'd be me."

"Tell us about it," Lucas said.

The mourners had come to the cemetery in a short convoy, he said. When they got to the new gravesite, they'd all gotten out, sat in the folding chairs, and listened to a few words from the Lutheran minister who was presiding. When he mentioned the minister, the minister raised his hand, and Mattsson nodded at him.

". . . was talking about Gillian and her good works, and I happened to look over there by that tree, and I saw it. The wallet. I wasn't sure it was a wallet, but it looked like one. When we finished here, I walked over there to check, and it was, and I picked it up."

He automatically checked the cash compartment, which was empty, then opened it to the driver's license window. When he saw the name, he replaced it where he found it and told the crowd.

They'd called the local cops, who'd come over in five minutes or so, and shooed everybody away from the tree. One of the cops had spotted the notebook, which was lying fifteen feet away, in a patch of long grass behind a tombstone. Nobody had touched it.

Johnston finished the photography, chimped the photos to make sure they were correctly exposed, and present on both the main and backup memory cards, then put the camera in his car. He took plastic gloves out of his kit, pulled them on, and carried two evidence bags over to the wallet and notebook.

They did the notebook first, and when it was safely isolated in the oversized evidence bag, Lucas asked Johnston to open to the last pages. There wasn't much from Shaffer's last day—names, mostly, written in blue ink.

On the last page was the enigmatic notation "Horn," surrounded by a double-lined box.

Lucas asked Mattsson, "What does that mean? Horn?"

The Zumbrota chief of police, standing behind him, looking over his shoulder, said, "You gotta be shittin' me."

Lucas turned: "What does it mean?"

The chief said, "That's the killer: he was saying that Jack Horn is the goddamned Black Hole killer?"

Lucas and Mattsson, simultaneously: "Who's Jack Horn?"

THE CHIEF TOLD THEM.

"Years ago, jeez, must've been ten or eleven years, a woman was attacked over in Faribault, by a guy named Jack Horn. From Holbein. He was the dogcatcher over there, I believe."

"He was," said one of the mourners.

The chief went on: "Anyway, he attacked this waitress. Can't remember her name, off the top of my head. It was at night, he threw a bag over her head, I think a postal bag, it was, and tied up the bag and threw her into his truck. She had a knife with her, and she cut her way out, and then she stabbed him while he was driving. Maybe several times. He crashed the truck, and she managed to get out and ran away. Got to a house and called for help. When the Faribault police got there, they found the truck upside down in the ditch, and lots of blood, nobody there. They went to his house, but Horn was never seen again. Never tried to get to any of his stuff. A lot of people thought he'd crawled away from the truck and gone off somewhere and died in a hole. Never found a body, though. Everybody for a hundred miles around was looking for him, including us. Hell, not a hundred miles—all over the state, and down in Iowa."

"This woman, the waitress?" Mattsson asked. "Do you remember anything about her?"

"A couple things," the chief said. "You're gonna have to check me on this, but she was attacked in the summer, I believe, and she was young and blond."

Lucas took his phone out and stepped away.

Mattsson: "You calling in the team?"

"Yes."

Before Lucas could call, the chief said, "I'll tell you something else. The seat cover was taken out of the truck, and the Faribault cops put it somewhere, as evidence. I don't think they did DNA at the time, but I remember hearing from somebody that they compared the blood from the truck with some, mmm, stains they found on his bedsheets, and it was the right guy. The blood came from Horn. Then, a few years ago I heard that you guys, you BCA guys, came down and took samples of his blood to do the DNA thing, and put it in your database."

A tall, elderly man cleared his throat and said, "Jorgenson. Heather Jorgenson."

Mattsson: "Excuse me?"

"The woman who got away from the killer was named Heather Jorgenson. She was a relation of Luther Jorgenson, who used to live here in town, but he moved up to the Twin Cities years ago. Luther came over to my house to service the water softener, and we talked all about it. Biggest thing that ever happened to their family."

The chief said, "I think John's right. Now that I think about it, I talked to Luther about it myself. Jorgenson."

Lucas said to Mattsson, "Why don't you call the Faribault police, see what they've got. We can go on over there when we're done here."

The chief said, "If Horn's still out there, hiding out after all these years, that kinda scares the shit out of me. There's a lot of us around that he don't like."

R-A HAD BEEN PARKED near the fairgrounds when the white-haired guy picked up the wallet, and a moment later, showed it to the rest of the people in the funeral party. R-A should have left then, but he couldn't: he had to see how it came out.

Now the cops would have two hard pieces of evidence: a name associated with an earlier sex crime that fit the precise pattern of the Black Hole killer, and a letter mailed from Sauk Centre, which was a hundred miles away, to the northwest. Horn hadn't cared about being identified, because if he was ever seen, the jig was up anyway. The important thing was to move the cops away from Holbein. With any luck at all, the BCA would shift the center of its investigation up there, looking for a man they wouldn't find.

They'd go because they'd know for sure that Horn couldn't be in Goodhue County, where he'd be known and chased on sight. . . .

Horn had suggested another step: killing a woman from the Alexandria area, still farther to the northwest. That would really pull the investigators away from Holbein . . . but any killing was a risk. Risk was interesting, but now he had another goal in life.

Mattsson.

Sheer foolishness, Horn had said. He was right, but Mattsson had entered R-A's thoughts and dreams, and she wouldn't get out. When the BCA investigators left for Sauk Centre, she'd be almost alone, working the case.

He watched the funeral party as they all moved over to the tree where the white-haired man had found the wallet, and as one of the men got on his cell phone. A few minutes later a Zumbrota cop car rolled into the cemetery.

Still, he waited, watching through a pair of image-stabilized hunting binoculars as the rest of the troops arrived.

Including Mattsson. She got out of her SUV, waited for a tall, well-dressed guy to catch up with her, from another truck. After that, he couldn't see much, as Mattsson and the cops were surrounded and obscured by the funeral party.

Mattsson. Yum.

12

D uncan's team met at nine o'clock the next morning. Lucas arrived at eight-thirty, and made some calls: Jenkins and Shrake, still in Florida, said that the papers they'd found in the truck of Bryan's car would hang him for fraud, no question about it. They'd also found an account from the Cayman Islands, and had talked to a fed about it.

"He's stashed better than fifteen million in the bank, and the feds have got a hold on it," Jenkins said.

"I thought those offshore guys wouldn't talk to us," Lucas said.

"They won't tell you anything new, but the feds say if they have the proof, the bank'll give it up—they're scared to death that the islands will go on an embargo list. So, if you've got the facts and figures, and put a gun to their head, they'll cooperate. We put a gun to their head. All it took was a call to the IRS."

"Good move," Lucas said. "How's the golf weather?"

.   .   .

FLOWERS WAS WORKING down on the Iowa line: "I'll have something for you in the next couple of days. Alert the media."

DEL WAS IN TEXAS: "They've off-loaded a few guns, we got them in
Technicolor. The big meeting is probably two or three days away
yet, down near El Paso. The ATF is recording everything going in
and out of their cell phones. As soon as the deal goes down, we're
gonna throw a net over them."

"You buy a cowboy hat yet?"

Long silence, then, "It's really hot and sunny down here."

"Ah, Jesus," Lucas said. "How about the boots? You buy the
boots?"

Another long silence.

ROSE MARIE ROUX leaned in his office doorway: "You haven't got
him yet."

"I was there when we opened Shaffer's notebook," Lucas said.

"That wasn't really you," she said. "That could have been
anybody."

Lucas said, "Yeah, but it wasn't."

Roux said, "Lucas, I don't give a wide shit about who got where
first. I *want* the guy. *Now.* And I'll tell you something else—you
might have your own media problem. I talked to this Janet Frost
from the *Strib*, and she seems to have a problem with you, involving
this shooting in Woodbury and the hunger-strike guy."

"Aw, for Christ's sakes," Lucas said. "I tried to help her out."

"Don't feel sorry for yourself, feel sorry for me. I mean, what could I do that I haven't, to get the Black Hole guy? It's not like I didn't drive the squad car fast enough."

"Yeah, but you politician assholes swim in the media sea—you love it, when it's on your side," Lucas said. "I might get whacked for doing the right thing."

"You could still solve both problems if you caught this guy in the next day or two. You'd be the big hero, and I'd still be your boss."

THE MEETING WENT OFF precisely at nine o'clock. Mattsson showed up and took a chair next to Lucas, leaned toward him and said, "I talked to every cop shop in the county. Nobody's ever had a hint of Horn. A lot of cops knew him personally, and so did everybody in Holbein, but nobody's had even a sniff of him, after that night in the truck."

"According to the original reports from Faribault, the victim said she stabbed him several times," Lucas said. "I am really curious about what happened to him . . . how he walked out of there, after being in a bad car wreck and getting himself stabbed."

"I'm curious about why he'd go to Sauk Centre," Mattsson said.

"We don't know that he did," Lucas said quietly. "I don't think a guy smart enough to pull off this many killings, and tough enough to walk out of the wreck of his truck, and get away . . . I don't think he'd mail that letter from his hometown. Or type it."

"Huh," she said.

Lucas grinned at her: "What? You don't think a killer would be rotten enough to lie to us?"

"You think he's still down in Goodhue?"

"I didn't say that. You couldn't hide Horn anywhere around Holbein, but you get up north, in tourist country," Lucas said. "Up north, you could hide him. And it's possible . . ." He scratched his head.

She prompted him, "What?"

"You've got to look around Goodhue to see if he had any friends."

"I've already asked about that," Mattsson said.

"Good. Because I'd think he might have needed help, from someone willing to keep a really ugly secret."

Henry Sands, the BCA director, and victim of one of the most serious rounds of backbiting in BCA history, post Alaska, said, "All right, folks, let's get this going. . . ."

DUNCAN TOOK OVER as soon as Sands finished outlining what everybody knew at that point.

"As everybody knows," Duncan said, "we've finally got a suspect, Jack L. Horn, formerly of Holbein."

Duncan outlined Horn's history. When the police raided his house after the kidnapping attempt, they didn't find much in the way of personal possessions, but they did get a link to his past through his Social Security number. The number had been issued in 1984, but his age at the time of issuance was uncertain. It had been issued so he could take a job at a taco restaurant in Des Moines. Subsequent jobs put him in Council Bluffs, Iowa, and Cheyenne, Wyoming. The Cheyenne job was with an over-the-road trucking company, as a driver.

"Nobody knew him very well at any of his jobs," Duncan said. "We haven't been able to track down his parents or any relatives, but we're still working on that. We'll be interviewing everyone who knew him around Holbein, so that may come to something."

Duncan had decided to shift half of his crew to the Sauk Centre area, where the letter had been mailed from. "We have Horn's photo—Dick, pass those copies around—although they are pretty dated, and not very good. Various licenses and so on. We'll be plastering the media with them."

They all looked at the photos, then Sands asked, "Since we know for sure that he was around Sauk Centre, and since we know for pretty sure that he's not living in the Holbein area . . . why are you keeping so many people down south?"

"Because we've developed a number of other possibilities," Duncan said. "We know that he broke into one casket and several sepulchers down there, but Lucas says each one of those things needs a different key. He believes that's what Shaffer figured out. He thinks Shaffer then used that insight to . . . to . . ."

". . . figure out who might have all those keys," Lucas interjected.

"Right," Duncan said. "He figured something out, or talked to somebody about it, and then, based on what that hypothetical person said, Shaffer found Horn, or vice versa, and was murdered."

Sands said to Duncan, "You said 'possibilities.' The key thing is one. Are there more?"

"Yes. The last woman murdered was kidnapped from a cemetery. Shaffer was killed after visiting four cemeteries. You put that with the cemetery key thing, and we conclude that there's a tight connection between somebody who works at these cemeteries, or is some kind of cemetery freak, if there is such a thing. That gets noticed by small-town folks, so we're going down for a whole run of interviews on that point: short, single guy in late thirties or forties, who works in cemeteries or has something to do with them, or has a special interest in them. Maybe collects or makes keys."

They talked about those possibilities for a while, and then Roux asked, "Lucas—what are you going to do?"

Lucas said, "I don't know. We're at the point where anything I could do, Jon and his crew can do better. We need lots of interviews, we need lots of legwork. I've got some things I've got to catch up on here. Virgil's working a case down in the southeast corner of the state that I'd like to take a peek at, and Del is in Texas—"

"Screw that," Roux said. "I need you thinking about this case."

"As I was going to say, I'll be thinking about this case," Lucas said. "One thing befuddles me: Where did Shaffer take his insight about the keys? I'm going to mark every note that he took. . . . He made some kind of mental leap."

"Make the fuckin' leap," Roux said.

A SECRETARY STUCK her head into the room and said, "Excuse me?"

Everybody looked at her. "We have a Sergeant McGraff on the phone from Goodhue County, for Catrin Mattsson. He says they have another letter, to her, that could be from the killer. A typewriter, from Alexandria."

Duncan said, "Okay. Put him in here on the speakerphone."

The secretary went away and a moment later, McGraff came up on the speaker and said, "Yeah, Catrin, it looks just like the first one you got. Kathleen was sorting through the mail and spotted it. We haven't opened it, so everything inside should be clean."

Duncan identified himself and then said, "Get it up here, in an evidence bag. Like right now. Don't let anybody else touch it."

McGraff said he would.

When McGraff had gone, Sands said to Duncan, "You might review your staffing plans. This guy seems to be up in that Alexandria–Sauk Centre area."

Duncan nodded: "I'll pull a couple more guys off and get them up there. Today. I'm going to run over to Eau Claire and interview this Heather Jorgenson, see what she has to say about Horn."

THE MEETING ADJOURNED, but most of the agents milled around the open bay area, waiting for McGraff to show up. Lucas went back to his office, with Roux. "You're not just going to sit in your office, are you? You going to Goodhue, or up north?"

"Probably down to Goodhue, not up north. The guys going north might find him, but it'll be walking door-to-door. I'm not good at that. I've got a feeling that these notes are all wrong. He might be trying to divert us away from the real opportunity."

"Good luck," she said, and sighed. "If Elmer gets picked for vice president, I was thinking I might run for governor as a law-and-order Democrat. That's a lot harder, if you're blamed for not being able to keep law and order."

"I'd vote for you, anyway," Lucas said. "Probably. Depending on who the Republicans put up."

MCGRAFF SHOWED UP with the letter in the bag, gave it to a CSI guy called down from the lab, and a few minutes and a couple of changes of bags later, they got the letter and a clump of blond hair tied with a red ribbon.

It said:

Hi, there, Catrin. Got another name for you. Alice Wolfe, from Cannon Falls. Look for her in 2001, went dancing in Minneapolis and never came home. Never got to Minneapolis, either, ha-ha. You won't find her at the Black Hole. I put her in the other pit. Oh, that's right, you haven't found that one yet. No problem, I'm sending some of her hair that I kept as a keepsake. Shake it out of the envelope, have your scientists do the DNA thing. It will keep them busy, anyway.

That was all of it.

"I'll tell you all something," Duncan said. "We'll get DNA out of this hair, and we'll match it to Wolfe's relatives, and if it doesn't match any of the DNA from the cistern and if Alice Wolfe is blond and did disappear, in 2001, that means, there *is* another pit."

"Another pit," Roux said. "It's a fuckin' nightmare."

LUCAS HUNG AROUND the office for a while, flipping through the murder books. He tried to call Flowers, but Flowers didn't answer his cell phone. He left a message for a callback. He called Del, who answered but said he had nothing new to report, except that women in Texas had big hair.

"I knew that," Lucas said.

He finally told his secretary that he was heading south, to listen to people who'd known Horn. He got a list from one of Duncan's crew, and took off.

He spent the rest of the afternoon either driving or talking—four cops, and a half dozen other people in town who had a variety of relationships with Horn: two landlords, the owner of the liquor store, and the owner of Croakers, a bar and grill where Horn would go to drink.

Horn, he knew, was a tall man and thin, and everyone remembered him that way. He had odd-colored hair; that was mentioned by a couple of people. It was gray, but not old-gray—rather, slate-colored, tending almost to blue.

He was a solitary character, like a gunfighter in a movie, a former landlady said, and had suspicious black eyes. Never saw him with a woman. She had been in his rented house a few times, when he wasn't there, and had taken a look around. He had about a million comic books, but she'd never seen anything like porn, or anything else that might suggest he was obsessed with sex. He wore jeans and work shirts and boots, but always with a black sport coat, as though he were covering up a gun.

"Was he?" Lucas asked.

"Don't know—never saw him with his coat off," she said. "He had a metal safe in his bedroom. A gun safe, I'm pretty sure."

ONE OF THE COPS SAID, "I don't believe he had any close friends. I don't think he had any friends, period. For one thing, he smelled like a skunk half the time. The other thing was, he was an asshole. Just fuckin' mean. To animals. Dogs. I'll tell you what, you didn't want your dog to get loose in Holbein, because Horn would flat break its neck, or soak it down in that dog-spray stuff. He even shot a couple."

The owner of the liquor store said that Horn had been a regular customer: "We don't like to see anyone going alcoholic, but Horn would put away two or three fifths of vodka a week; plus, he'd be drinking over at Croakers. Weren't many nights he'd go home sober—but with his job, can't say I'd blame him. Picking up dead animals all day."

The owner/bartender at Croakers said that he always sat by himself at the bar, by choice, and drank slowly, but thoroughly. "I felt kinda sorry for him, at the time, but every time I tried to chat with him, he'd kinda cut me off. After a while, I figured that was just the way he was, and let it go."

If told that Horn was a killer, they all agreed that they wouldn't be particularly surprised.

When Lucas talked to Letty that night, he said, "It was a curious thing—of all the assholes I've known in my life, I've never met anyone that *someone* didn't have a good word for. Out of simple charity. Because they were nice people, and wouldn't say a bad word about anybody. Not with Horn. Nobody liked him. Not one single person."

"Can you trust that? Maybe they liked him before he attacked that woman."

"That's a point," Lucas said.

"It seems like he does have some kind of interest in sex," she said. "There's a tone in his notes. Like, I hate to say it, *playful*. Or kind of weird-flirty."

Lucas shook his head. "If you have somebody interested enough in sex that they're kidnapping women, and they have the Internet, they're gonna have some porn around."

"But we *know* he was kidnapping women," Letty said. "That is absolutely nailed down. The truck, the blood, the fact that he disappeared. Maybe he was a kind of super-secret guy, or knew that the landlady was a snoop, so he kept the porn hidden."

"You make a good case, and it's completely wrong," Lucas said.

"How?"

"I don't know."

LUCAS WENT TO BED at two o'clock. Weather got up early, as usual, to go in to the hospital. He was sleeping soundly when she sat on the corner of the bed and rubbed the back of his neck.

That woke him, and he rolled halfway over.

"Good morning," she said.

Too early: he was confused. "Morning?"

She dropped a newspaper on his chest. "Guess what? You made the *Star-Tribune*."

13

Lucas didn't operate well on four hours of sleep, but as Weather left for work, he propped himself up in bed and turned on the reading light behind his head. The story in the center of the front page, by the feature writer Janet Frost, was what the crime reporter Ruffe Ignace called "a weeper." It began with scene setting— Emmanuel Kent's cardboard-box shelter that he set up every night beneath an overhang on the steps of a local Lutheran Church.

The church no longer let him come inside for the night, because he tended to wreck the place. Before locking up at nine o'clock, they let him fill his empty two-liter plastic Pepsi bottles with water, and in the morning, they let him in to wash and use the toilet in a basement restroom.

Sitting in the stygian darkness beneath the concrete overhang, partly concealed by the ivy, he carefully removes his boots before he goes to bed, and washes his feet with a rag he left to dry on the railing. "During the Great War, you could be shot on the spot if you got trench foot," Manny said in his high-pitched, yet gravelly voice. "That's a big danger for those of us forced to live outside. If you don't take good care of your feet, you could get gangrene. I don't know how many times I've seen that, it's endemic among the street population."

Guy sounded like he graduated from Harvard, Lucas thought, except that he had no idea about trench foot and World War I. And he thought, Janet Frost wouldn't know a stygian darkness if one jumped up and bit her on the ass.

The story recounted the beginning of the hunger strike, and the shooting that preceded it.

Doyle could be impetuous, but he was not a dangerous man. Everybody liked him, Manny said. "The Woodbury police executed him. I'll ask you this: What is the penalty for bank robbery in this state? Is it execution without a trial? No, it's not—but that's what was done to my brother. He was executed, shot down in cold blood."

The Woodbury police claimed that Doyle Kent fired a shot when he emerged from the bank, but no bullet was found.

Lucas thought, *Uh-oh.*

Down further in the story, Manny rolled a marijuana cigarette, which he uses to self-medicate. He lit it with a pink Bic lighter, and then, dry and warm, he said, "I'm definitely feeling weaker. I haven't had anything but fruit juice since Saturday, but I'll never quit until I get justice, or die," he said. He added, "I went so far as to buy a gallon of gasoline, and I hid it. If I ever get the feeling that the police are about to remove me, or put me in jail, I will get my gas can, and I will immolate myself on the steps of City Hall. Won't that make the mayor proud?"

Then,

Lucas Davenport, the senior BCA agent involved in the tracking of Doyle Kent, admitted that he had "no proof at all" that Kent had done the earlier bank robberies, and though the Woodbury police admitted firing twenty shots at Kent, striking him seven times, including three shots in the chest, three more in the shoulders and neck, and one in the stomach, Davenport joked that "I thought they showed great restraint."

Davenport was involved in a similar incident in which two women were shot down outside a bank. . . .

Lucas said it aloud: "Ah, shit."

The story ended with a protracted scene in which Emmanuel Kent hunkered down under his blankets and looked up at the stars, and visualized a better life for himself, after he'd gotten his justice. Frost concluded with a statement that "a number of prominent attorneys" were considering filing a suit against Woodbury and the BCA, on Kent's behalf, for excessive violence.

LUCAS TRIED TO GO back to sleep, but failed. He had decent relationships with most of the media, and earlier in his career, had had a child with a prominent female reporter for Channel Three, although they hadn't married. He'd always been suspicious of television, because of the ways news got compressed to comic-strip chunks, but he'd been less suspicious of newspapers, because they seemed more professional; he hadn't often felt deliberately victimized.

Janet Frost had deliberately screwed him. She attributed a few partial quotes to him, and he couldn't really disavow them, because they were correct, as far as he remembered—they just weren't in context. And she'd left out critical bits of information, such as the fact that the women shot down outside the bank, in the earlier case, had shot a man inside the bank and had killed another victim in Wisconsin.

AT EIGHT O'CLOCK, groggy and annoyed, he got up, spent some time in the bathroom, looked at a suit and tie, then said, "Fuck it," and put on jeans, a golf shirt, and a black sport coat.

Downstairs, Letty said, "I read the story. I mean, *Wow*. Not even Channel Six would do that to somebody. You think it has anything to do with the Black Hole thing?"

Lucas considered: "Maybe. It does feel like open season on the cops."

"You talk to Ruffe about it?"

"He's the guy who asked me to talk to her," Lucas said.

"*That fucker.*"

"Hey! Language!"

"Live with it," she said.

RUFFE IGNACE CALLED precisely at nine o'clock: "I would have called earlier, but I know you don't get up early."

"Fuck you."

"Man, I'm really sorry," Ignace said.

"That makes me feel a lot better," Lucas said. "I'll tell you some-thing, Ruffe: she's a loose cannon. Sooner or later, she's gonna screw the paper. She said I was joking when I said Woodbury showed great restraint, but she didn't put in the explanation. She didn't tell people that we had good reason to track Kent, and she didn't say that Candy and Georgie LaChaise murdered that poor sonofabitch in Rice Lake and shot another one here in the Cities—"

"I know, I know, I know. Listen, you're pissed, and I don't blame you," Ruffe said. "I'm going to file a complaint with the ombuds-man, so expect a call from him. In the meantime, I'm going to write a piece about how your guys are going to recover money from Bry-an's account down in the islands and how you're hunting down the Black Hole guy now. Honest to God, Lucas."

Lucas was quiet for a minute, then said, "Ruffe, I appreciate it."

"It was a fuckin' hatchet job," Ruffe said. "I can't stand it when people do that shit. I took this fuckin' job because . . . fuck it, never mind. They'll put my piece on the front page tomorrow, or I'm gonna fuckin' quit. And believe me, they don't want me to fuckin' quit."

Ruffe slammed the phone down.

Letty was looking at Lucas and said, "He was screaming. I could hear it from here."

Lucas grinned his coyote grin, the one that showed just a rim of white teeth: "Yeah. He's almost a friend."

Letty asked, "You've been running around in circles. What're you going to do?"

Lucas said, "I don't know. I've got an idea, but I don't want to do it. It's to look at the ADB, see who knows what."

"What would any of the assholes know? The guy has to be a deep dark secret—because if he wasn't, the word would have gotten around, and even the assholes would have ratted him out."

"I'm afraid you're right, but what else have I got?"

THE ADB—The Assholes Database.

Lucas had taken two years to put it together, and was still working on it. It contained more than eleven hundred names, with addresses and phone numbers, of Minnesota assholes, along with several dozen more from Wisconsin and Iowa, and a couple from the Dakotas and Canada. Most came from the Twin Cities, but there were at least a few from every county in Minnesota.

A number of people knew about it, outside his own circle, but he was careful about sharing anything. The problem was, it wasn't just a list of assholes, it was a list of people who'd deal with Lucas, but expected, with limitations, to get some payback, if they needed it.

Quite a few of them needed it. Payback came in the form of testimony to judges: even though this particular dickweed did, in fact, loot the local Walmart, he has been a reliable source for Minnesota law enforcement, so instead of three years, how about one year plus time served?

Lucas made a call before he left home, setting up a face-to-face talk. At noon, he was in Owatonna, talking to a guy named Toby in the back of Antoine's bar and grill.

Toby dealt in illegal python skins and black-bear gallbladders and paws. He paid a dozen farmers across the state to run snake barns. The skins went to Europe. A dozen bow hunters in northern Minnesota and Wisconsin kept the gallbladders flowing; shooting bears is not a problem in parts of the North Woods. Toby once told Lucas that he could get $1,500 for a really good dried gallbladder—they'd sell for up to $3,000 in China—and handled four to five hundred a year, shipped by UPS to a Chinese connection in San Francisco.

He was staring into a glass of beer when Lucas came in. Lucas got a Coke at the bar and carried it back.

Toby wore an old Army ball cap and a short-sleeved camo shirt over jeans. He would have a pistol strapped to his ankle, Lucas knew. He was a short, thick-set man with a three-day beard and a watery blue walleye. When Lucas sat down, Toby leaned forward and asked, in a low voice, "What do you hear about Maxine?"

"She called me three weeks ago," Lucas said. "I told her you were dealing out of Madison."

Toby bobbed his head. "Madison. That's good. Maybe she'll kill a couple of fuckin' hippies and the Madison cops will put her in prison."

"Not gonna happen, Toby," Lucas said. "There's only one guy on her list right now, and she knows what you look like."

Maxine Knowles was a radical animal-rights activist pledged to kill Toby. She'd been warned off, but she continued to look for him. She owned a Remington Mountain Rifle in .243, and was reportedly an excellent shot.

"Fuckin' crackpot," Toby said. Then, "What's up?"

"It's this Black Hole killer. We're looking for a guy named Jack Horn."

Toby nodded: "Seen it on TV." He pointed his beer bottle at a TV in the corner. "They have been talking about it all morning. First thing up, every time."

"People who knew him said he was a serious hunter," Lucas said. "I wondered if he ever hunted with you."

Toby shook his head: "Never worked with him. Heard about him, talking to guys this morning. Supposedly a pretty good shot, a reloader, used to go out to Wyoming two or three times a year, to shoot prairie dogs."

"Right: So who would have shot with him, around Holbein? Or Zumbrota?" Lucas asked.

"Oh, boy: none of this gets back to me, right?"

"Right."

Toby scratched his head. "Blair Tucker would be number one. He's a well driller, got a place just outside of Holbein. He's big on reloading and prairie dogs. Roger Axel would be another possibility, runs the hardware store in Holbein, though he's mostly into head-hunting: you know, a one-of-everything guy. But he's mostly into big game, so he might not have had much to do with Horn. Dan Weil is another one. Dan has a private two-thousand-yard range out of Holbein towards Red Wing. Horn used to shoot there."

"This range is up toward the Black Hole?"

"Well, yeah. More or less. Not real close, but that direction," Toby said.

Lucas wrote the names down, and asked if there was anything he could do for Toby, who said, "I don't know. Maybe."

"What happened?" Lucas asked.

"You heard of the Raleigh Duane Cornwall case, up in Canada?"

Lucas looked around the bar, then leaned closer to Toby and said, "Am I wearing a Mountie hat? Look around, Toby. We're not in Canada. My jurisdiction stops at the border."

"Yeah, but if somebody could put in a word . . . Raleigh's one of my best boys, and what happened to him isn't fair."

The story was about as stupid as any Lucas had ever heard. According to Toby, Cornwall had known the location of an extremely large, extremely old black bear—the best kind for gallbladders. The bear lived on an island in the Rainy River, which was the border between the U.S. and Canada. Cornwall paddled out to the island in a car-topped canoe, set up a lightweight tree stand, spread around a can of bear bait, which consisted of stale donuts and a quart of bacon grease, and climbed up in the tree stand with his bow, to wait.

The bear showed up ten minutes later, moving fast. Cornwall drew on it, but as he was about to let the arrow fly, the bear sensed him, and stopped quick. Cornwall reacted by yanking the bow off his lead, and let the arrow go. He'd reacted too much—the arrow hit the bear in the ass. The bear let out a yelp, spotted Cornwall in his tree, trotted over, and started climbing.

Cornwall had just the instrument for such an occasion: a .357 Magnum. The bear got halfway up the tree to the stand, Cornwall shot him twice, and the bear dropped like a rock.

"The thing is," Toby said, "the island turned out to be in Canada. I mean, just across the line. Who was to know? There aren't any markers. And there was a goddamn provincial game warden who heard the shots, and come up on Raleigh from behind."

He caught Raleigh standing there with a gallbladder in his hand, a pistol in his holster, and a twist of cocaine in his shirt pocket.

"They got him for illegal entry, importation and possession of an illegal firearm, importation and possession of illegal drugs, and shooting a bear out of season. He could be looking at fifteen years."

Lucas said, "Toby, man, I'd like to help. But I gotta say, with a guy like that . . . the rest of us are probably better off without him walking around loose."

Lucas left Toby looking morosely at his beer, and headed toward Holbein.

The first guy on the list, Blair Tucker, was sitting in his office, which was surrounded by flatbed trucks loaded with pieces of well-drilling equipment. He was counting twenty-dollar bills, when Lucas stuck his head in.

"Yeah, I'm Blair," Tucker said, sliding the stack of bills into his desk drawer. "What can I do for you?" He had an environmental likeness to Toby, the spare dry face of a man who spent his time working outdoors.

Lucas showed him his ID. "I'm looking for a guy named Horn."

"I figured somebody'd be coming around," Tucker said. He'd known Horn, but said he hadn't hung with him. "I knew he was some kinda fruitcake. The thing is, he didn't get off on the shooting, he got off on the killing. The guy would kill a hummingbird if he had a chance. With a hammer. Knew another fellow who went squirrel hunting with him, said old Horn shot a heron, walking along a pond. Just to see the feathers fly. Then didn't even pick them up. The feathers."

Tucker didn't know anything good, but confirmed Lucas's picture of Horn as a killer. When Lucas left Tucker's place, driving into town, he thought about Horn's disappearing act: not many people could simply walk away from their house, and never again use an ID or a credit card or a cell phone, and set up again in a new town, and start a new life all over.

Though it had been done . . . the mob guy from Boston had done it.

He was on the outskirts of Holbein when Mattsson called: "Where are you?"

"Holbein."

"Good. I just got a call from Reggie Scott, Kaylee's father. Kaylee was out riding her bike with a girlfriend, and says she saw Mr. Sprick staring at her from his car. Said he drove by really slow, staring at her. She said he looked at her in a really mean way, and scared her."

"Have you talked to Sprick?"

"On the way. I'll be there in a half hour," Mattsson said.

"I'll be there in eight minutes," Lucas said. "Exactly when did she see him?"

"Five minutes ago."

Lucas looked at his watch, noted the time, and said, "I'm on the way."

Kaylee or Sprick? Sprick first, Lucas decided. He had Sprick's cell phone number and as he drove into Zumbrota, called him. "Where are you?"

"At the office. They pulled me off my route, they got me subbing, sorting mail. What happened?"

"Where's the post office?"

LUCAS PARKED at the Shell station across the street and walked over to the post office and found Sprick sitting in the back, not doing much of anything. "Now what?" Sprick asked.

"Where were you fifteen minutes ago?" Lucas asked.

"Right here."

"A half hour ago?"

"Right here," Sprick said. "I've been here since six o'clock this morning. I had a break at ten and walked up to the Shell station and got some coffee. That took five minutes. Then I came back and I've been here ever since. Three guys here with me."

One of the three other guys, who'd been listening while trying to look like he wasn't, glanced at Lucas and Lucas asked, "Was he?"

"Right here," the guy said. "And he's a guy who wouldn't hurt a fly."

"What happened fifteen minutes ago?" Sprick asked.

"Kaylee said she saw you, in your car. Said you were stalking her."

"Aw, for Christ's sakes. What'd I do to deserve this? What the heck did I do?" He threw his hands up.

FROM HIS CAR, Lucas called Mattsson: "Sprick was at the post office, sorting mail, since six o'clock this morning. He has three witnesses, and they don't look like a criminal conspiracy."

"Meet me at the Scotts' house," Mattsson said. "I'm getting tired of this."

"I'm way past tired of it," Lucas said.

"I saw that story in the paper this morning," Mattsson said. "You sound like quite the fashionable gunslinger."

"Hey, Catrin? Stick a sock in it."

"In what?"

"See you at the Scotts'."

. . .

KAYLEE SCOTT insisted that she'd seen Mr. Sprick. She had a witness. "We were riding our bikes over to the swimming pool," Kaylee said. "He went by in his truck real slow. He looked out the window at me, a really mean look. It was him."

Another little girl, with a bobbed blond hairdo, her bangs right down to her eyebrows, nodded solemnly as she said, "He did. Look mean at us."

Her name was Jane Windrew, and she was sitting between her parents, Marge and Lanny. Mattsson asked Jane, "Do you know Mr. Sprick?"

"Mr. Sprick. Yes. We'd see him in his truck, every day, until he scared Kaylee."

Reggie Scott said, "I'm telling you, the guy's a maniac."

Lucas said, "I'd appreciate it if you'd keep that talk to yourself. Sprick has three witnesses who say he never left the post office today, except for five minutes at ten o'clock, to walk across the street to the Shell station."

"We prefer to believe our daughter," Carol Scott said.

Mattsson asked, "Who else was around there, on the street? Just you two, or were there more girls?"

"It was just us," Jane said.

"Were there any other adults around? If you'd yelled or screamed, would anybody have heard you?" Lucas asked.

The girls looked at each other, and then Kaylee turned back to Lucas and said, "I dunno. I didn't see anybody. We were just riding down the street."

"Sprick drives a Subaru," Mattsson said to Kaylee. "You said he was driving a truck. What kind of truck? Like a truck like your dad's, an SUV? Or a pickup, or . . ."

"A pickup," Jane said. "It was dark brown."

"Black," said Kaylee.

"I think it was dark brown," Jane said.

Reggie Scott said, "Whatever. What color's Sprick's Subaru?"

Mattsson said, "Silver. Silver and gray. Nothing like black or brown."

"It was him," Kaylee said. Her mother gave her a hug and asked Lucas, "Why don't you believe us? It's not like Sprick would be stalking her in his own truck."

Mattsson said, "We do believe her—the girls—that they saw someone. We just know it wasn't Sprick that they saw."

"You know, you'd think you guys never heard the phrase 'Going postal,'" Carol Scott said. "Who knows what they're cooking up down there."

"Down where?" Lucas asked. "The post office?"

"We *know* what our daughter saw," Carol Scott said again.

Lucas turned to Jane and asked, "When he went by, did you look at him right in the face?"

Her eyes shifted. Lucas glanced at Mattsson, and she'd picked it up. Jane said, "Not exactly. I saw him go by, and Kaylee said, 'It's Mr. Sprick,' and I saw it was him."

"Did you actually see his face?"

Again, the eye shift. "Well, Kaylee said—"

"Pretend that you were riding the bicycle on your own," Mattsson said. "Close your eyes and pretend. Did you see his face?"

She didn't close her eyes, but she said instead, "Kaylee . . . I believe Kaylee."

Jane's mother said, "Okay. That's enough. I think we better hit the road."

Carol Scott said, "Hey, you know what they saw."

Marge Windrew said, "I'm not exactly sure what Jane saw, but we'll take some steps to make sure she's safe." She nodded to her husband. "Let's go. I really don't want Jane to be more traumatized than she is already."

Mattsson said to the Scotts, "I talked to the sheriff when I was on the way over here. He's going to put some unmarked cars in the neighbors' driveways for the next few days, just in case the prowler should come back."

"When are they going to start?" Carol Scott asked. "How'll we recognize him? I even hate to answer my door."

"They'll come by and introduce themselves, tell you where they'll be," Mattsson said. "You and the Windrews will both get a phone number, in case you should be . . . disturbed. You call, we'll have somebody at your door in a half minute. Literally half a minute, maybe less."

LUCAS, MATTSSON, and the Windrews left at the same time, walking out to the curb where Lucas and Mattsson had parked. The Windrews lived a block away. Lucas caught up with them and asked, "You seemed a little skeptical about this. I don't want to cause you any trouble with your neighbors, or with your daughter's friend, but . . . I was wondering why you sounded that way."

The Windrews looked at each other, and then Lanny Windrew said to his wife, "You better tell them."

Marge said, "Before the kids left for the pool, I heard them talking, and Kaylee said that if Mr. Sprick came around again, and looked at her, they could both go on television. We don't care if Jane ever goes on television. The Scotts . . . think differently about that."

Mattsson brushed her hair back and said, "Damnit." To Jane: "You never actually saw Mr. Sprick at all?"

Jane said, "I saw the truck."

"But not Mr. Sprick."

"Not exactly. But it *could* have been him."

WHEN THE WINDREWS walked away, Mattsson said, "That's that. I'll talk to the sheriff—I think we should have a cop here anyway."

"That's up to you and the sheriff," Lucas said.

"Yeah. Okay. I'm sorry I dragged you over here. What've you been up to? Have you been down here all day?"

Lucas told her about talking to Toby, in Owatonna.

"I don't know the first two guys, but I know Dan Weil," Mattsson said. "Over-the-top gun nut. He bought a creek bed off a bunch of farmers, brought in a bulldozer and cut a strip right along the creek, more than a mile long, piled up fifty feet of dirt at the end of it. Guys go out there with .50-cals, try to hit targets at a measured mile."

"He live out there?"

"No, but he doesn't live far from it," she said. "You want to run over and talk to him?"

Lucas did. "What else we got to do?"

.   .   .

Weil lived in a neat ranch-style house out in the countryside, with apple and plum trees spotted around the two-acre yard, and a big metal-sided garage/workshop off to one side. Weil was a civil engineer, and worked out of a studio attached to the end of his garage. A tall thin man with round, gold-rimmed military-style glasses, he had cold blue eyes and a prominent nose under a sandy crew cut. He wore an olive drab shirt with epaulets, jeans, and cleated boots. He invited them in, and sat on a drawing-board stool while they took a couple of leather visitor's chairs. A line of five heavy gun safes sat at one end of the studio.

"All kinds of stuff," he said, in answer to a question from Lucas. "I got more work than I can handle—driveways, embankments, flowage ditches, surveys for building slabs. Anything you'd use a bulldozer or a Bobcat or a grader for."

Mattsson asked, "How well did you know Horn?"

"Not well." He seemed to think about that for a second, then added, "He was out here often enough. He wasn't one of the big-caliber, long-range guys. He shot small stuff out to five hundred yards or so: .22-250, .223. Biggest I ever saw was a 6mm Remington. Had an old .220 Swift if I remember correctly. Said he used to bark squirrels with it. But he didn't talk much. He hung around, but not out, if you know what I mean. He wasn't a hang-out kinda guy."

"And he was a killer," Lucas said.

"Oh yeah." Weil blinked. "That was the thing about him. He liked killing. He liked death. Most of us guys out here, we're interested in guns, loads, ballistics, technique. We've got guys out here who've never killed a thing in their whole lives. Engineers, a lot of them. Shooting paper. Horn wanted to kill stuff. Came back and told me one time that he killed a thousand prairie rats out in Wyoming. I said, 'Well, that's real good, Mr. Horn.' But you know . . . a thousand? That's somewhat excessive, if you ask me, and I'm a gun nut."

Weil hadn't seen him, or heard of him, since the attack on the woman in Faribault. He wasn't surprised about the attack: "Of all the guys who've come out here, if you'd told me what happened without who it was that did it, I'd have guessed Horn."

They talked awhile longer, and Weil said, "Wherever he is, he won't stay away from guns. If I were you, I'd take his picture around to every gun range in the country. Somebody'll recognize him."

Lucas: "We can do that. Not a bad idea, either."

As THEY WERE LEAVING, Weil asked them what they shot. Mattsson said a Glock 9mm, and Lucas said a .45, and Weil said, "A .45, huh? You any good with it?"

Lucas said he was pretty good, and ten minutes later, they were all out at the range, banging away at steel plates with pistols. When they got done, Weil said to Lucas, "You *are* good, for a cop," and to Mattsson, "You're above average. Most cops don't shoot for shit."

"What does it mean," Lucas asked, "barking a squirrel?"

"You get a squirrel way up in a tree, and you're out there with a .223 or something. You hit a squirrel with that, it'll blow the meat right off the bones. So what you do is, you shoot the tree bark right under its head. The concussion and the fall kills the squirrel. Supposedly."

"That'd take a good shot."

"It'd take an okay shot," Weil said. "Not great."

WHEN THEY LEFT WEIL, Mattsson said, "Well, that was fun. What's next?"

Lucas ran a hand through his hair: he smelled like burnt gunpowder. "You know, I'm running around in circles. All of us BCA guys are running around in circles. What I really need is what I told my boss I was going to do, which is go home and think about it some more. Not talk to anyone, not mow the grass, but sit in a quiet spot and think about it."

"You keep saying that."

"I keep trying to do it, and keep getting interrupted," Lucas said.

"I'll call you first thing, if anything happens tonight."

"Yeah, well . . ."

She leaned back against the door of her truck. "You think it's a fool's errand?"

"Probably," Lucas said. "The thing is, I could be completely wrong. Having a cop there could keep the Scott family from being murdered. So . . . tell your guy to stay awake."

She nodded. "If you think of something, call me."

Lucas went home to think.

14

Late that same afternoon, R-A was standing behind the counter in the hardware store, while another clerk, Dick, was out in the small engine shop demonstrating a STIHL brushcutter before loading it in the back of a customer's truck.

Andy O'Neill, who ran the local carpet store, wandered in, carrying a broken white PVC cap. "Hoped you were still open," he said. "Run over the goldarn vent pipe for the septic with my lawn mower. You got any caps like this?"

"Six-inch," R-A said. "We oughta have a few. You bust the pipe, too?"

"Just down to ground level. I'm gonna cut the broken part off with a hacksaw, stick the cap on. Never wanted it sticking up like that, anyway."

"That oughta work," R-A said. He took the cap and led O'Neill back to the plumbing section, found the replacement cap. "You need a hacksaw?"

"Got one," O'Neill said.

When he was ringing up the sale, R-A caught O'Neill . . . *peering* at him.

"What? I got a hickey on my neck?"

"No, no," O'Neill said. He was a tall man, as heavily muscled as R-A. "I been watching that Black Hole investigation thing. This girl over in Zumbrota says some postal clerk did it. They had a picture of him. You look like his brother, or something. You related?"

"Not unless my mother was doing something I didn't know about," R-A chuckled. "They don't catch that guy, maybe I better grow a beard."

"Does look like you," O'Neill said. He hunted through the candy rack for a moment, found a candy bar. "Give me a Snickers, too. I don't want it on the same receipt. My old lady looks at receipts."

"Know how that goes," R-A said. Though he didn't.

R-A WENT HOME IN A STATE: he wheeled Horn out to the living room and said, "Soon's that sonofabitch thinks about it long enough, he's gonna mention it to someone. Then it'll get around town, and the law's gonna come lookin' for me."

"Not against the law to look like somebody else," Horn said.

"But . . . there's probably other stuff," R-A said. "Maybe some evidence that we don't know about, but they're looking to hang on somebody. Maybe some of that DNA. There was enough of it in Mary Lynn's pussy, when I put her down the well. If they test me on it, I'm done."

"What are you going to do?" Horn asked.

"Well, I know you got nothing against killing people," R-A said.

"Against *you* killing people. I'm not killing *anybody*, not in this condition," Horn said.

"Well, shit, I don't exactly have a problem with it, either," R-A said. "How'm I gonna do it? A gun's so goddamn loud in the night."

"Baseball bat?"

"Jesus Christ, Horn, this isn't some drunk blonde," R-A said. "O'Neill's a big guy. Carrying rolls of carpet around, he's probably twice as strong as me. He'd take a baseball bat and stick it up my ass."

"Just kiddin' you," Horn said. "Think what you got downstairs."

R-A thought, then his face brightened. "Your old Ruger."

"That's right. Not a lot of accuracy if you're shooting more than twenty feet, but if you're shooting at two inches . . ."

"Goddamn: I don't think of you as being a dogcatcher," R-A said.

"Neither do I, and I never did. There was a lot more to it—"

"Okay, okay. I apologize." R-A rubbed his face. "Even so, they'll tear the town apart when they find them."

"Sure, but what's worse—them tearing the town apart looking for a gunman, or coming to you directly and asking for a DNA sample?"

"I dunno, I dunno."

"Got away with a .45 right here in town," Horn said. "O'Neill's out there on the edge, must have a two-acre lot."

"The Ruger. Gotta do it soon," R-A said. "Tonight. We can't have him talking to anybody."

"Maybe he already has," Horn said.

"Nothing we could do about that," R-A said. "We gotta play it like he hasn't said anything."

There was still light coming through the curtains, and would be for another hour or two. Horn said, "You can't go out there until after dark. We've got time to plan it out."

R-A said, "This could be the thing that kills me."

"Maybe," Horn said. "But you had a good run. If you still *really* don't want to be caught, I'd think about running up to Alexandria, find yourself a blonde. Maybe even tonight. They won't believe you'd be in two places in one night."

R-A scratched his neck, under his chin, thinking about that. "That'd be one hell of a night," he said after a few seconds. "I'd have to take O'Neill first, and that'd have to be after dark. Could I get up to Alexandria in time to do any good?"

"I don't know. Figure it out."

R-A: "Mattsson. Maybe they do get me, but I'm gonna get her first. I swear to God."

So THEY PLANNED IT OUT, sitting in the living room. R-A had a few drinks, getting his guts up, and went down to the basement and got Horn's Ruger Mark II .22 auto. It had a very long barrel, and was poorly balanced. He could live with it.

"Go up to the door, shoot him, kick the door shut, shoot the old lady," R-A said, demonstrating the moves to an unnaturally intent Horn. "Gotta remember the part about kicking the door shut. If somebody hears *bang!* they might let it go. If they hear *bang! bang! bang!* they'll be looking out the windows."

"There won't be much of a bang, but there'll be some," Horn said. "It won't sound much like a gun. I never had anybody come out and ask, 'You shoot something?'"

"I'll take it down the basement before I go . . . see what it sounds like."

"Don't go running out the door after you shoot them," Horn suggested. "If somebody *does* hear that first bang, and looks around, and they see somebody running, they'll be looking around for sure."

R-A was sitting on the couch and popped the magazine on the Ruger. He was about to push one of the shells out with his thumb and Horn said, "Don't!"

"Don't what?"

"Those shells are gonna have my prints on them," Horn said. "I imagine you'd want to keep them on there. And not yours."

R-A looked at the magazine. "Yup." The magazine had a long slot down the side, and R-A counted the shells. "Ten of them. I'm gonna have to shoot one, to make sure it's still working, that the spring hasn't gone flat."

"You can do that down the basement. There's another magazine down there, too. It's not loaded. I'd polish off some shells, then load it up, wearing gloves, of course. Just in case you need to re-load."

"Good. That's good," R-A said. "I'll do that." He pointed the gun at Horn's head, but Horn didn't bother to flinch. "Gotta remember: jack one in, safety off, one shot, boom, kick the door shut. Jack one in, safety off, one shot, boom, kick the door shut."

"Here's another thing," Horn said. "Lot of people got those cheap game cameras now. They put them up in trees, set for night hours. You need something to cover your face—a sock or a ski mask, and a hat."

"That's good," R-A said. "That's a good idea."

"And don't forget: you need to type up that note."

"Getting really fuckin' complicated," R-A said.

"Confusing is what it is," Horn said. "When it comes to the cops, confusion is your friend."

BY THE TIME they got it figured out, and R-A had gone down to the basement and fired a round into a hard-foam archery target, and then come back up, and finished typing the note he'd leave by the blonde's body in Alexandria, red sunlight was streaming in through the low west windows in the parlor. It'd be dark in half an hour.

"Got to do it," R-A said.

THE NIGHT was almost always quiet in Holbein. Sometimes the kids would be out in the warm twilight, playing war with apples picked off neighborhood trees, and you'd hear shouting when somebody got ambushed or hit behind the ear with an unripe Haralson; or, if they were a little older, necking in the shadows. Three nights a year, a carnival would be in town, and you could hear it for miles around, and then there was the Fourth of July, which could get loud . . . but otherwise, the nights were slow and quiet, and a banging screen door was as noisy as it got.

The O'Neill house was right on the edge of town. The house faced neighbors on the other side of the street, but behind it, to the east, it was nothing but corn and soybeans all the way to the Mississippi.

After thinking it over, and thinking about the long hike he'd made back from Zumbrota, R-A parked almost a mile away, two big cornfields east of the O'Neill house. He'd come up from the back, and if he had to run for it, he could disappear into one of the cornfields and make it back to his truck in ten minutes or so. There was even a place to park, down through a pasture gate behind a screen of ditch weeds.

At least, that was what he figured out, after driving around for a while. He parked in the pasture and turned his truck lights out, and sat. If the owner of the field came along, he'd have no excuse for being there, so he took along a bottle of bourbon, put it in the backseat. If somebody jumped him, he'd say he'd pulled off where the cops wouldn't find him, because, well, he was driving drunk.

Or, he could just kill the guy.

He'd work that out if it happened.

He looked out the window, tempted to take a drink. Full dark. He unscrewed the cap on the bourbon, took a hard swallow.

THE FIRST PART of the plan went wrong.

From the road, R-A could see reasonably well: the moon was probably three-quarters, and the stars were bright. He walked across the narrow pasture to the cornfield—he could see the lights in the back windows of the O'Neills' house—but as soon as he got in the corn, he couldn't see anything. Worse, the rows ran in the wrong direction, at right angles to the direction he wanted to walk. After crashing through thirty feet of corn, he made a right turn, walked down the row, climbed the fence at the end of it, crossed the ditch to the road, and started jogging west. The gun was in the game pocket of a hunting shirt, and banged against his butt as he ran.

He crossed another narrow gravel road, crossed back over the ditch to the cornfield, and in this one, he found, the rows ran in the right direction. He walked along, arms and hands in front of his face so his face wouldn't get cut by the corn leaves, and after eight or ten minutes, hit the fence behind the O'Neills' house.

The trip from the truck had taken almost twenty minutes, far longer than he expected. He'd stick to the road going back, he decided, at least until he saw lights behind him.

THE SECOND PART of the plan went well, at least from R-A's perspective. The O'Neills didn't bother to draw a lot of curtains in their house, especially on the sides. After pulling the ski mask over his head, R-A crossed the fence line and moved slowly—he was an experienced hunter—across the backyard, watching especially the house to the left side of the O'Neills'. There were lights over there, but he never saw anybody moving inside.

The O'Neill kitchen, he decided, was at the back of the house, because Mrs. O'Neill (Lucy? He thought that was right) was standing framed in a small high window. That'd be the window over the kitchen sink, where she was doing dishes. There were lights in the front of the house, and the peculiar blue glow of a television.

That would be Andy, watching the TV while his wife did dishes. R-A watched and listened; the neighborhood was quiet. More than quiet: it was still. He'd go for the front door, he decided. Take Andy O'Neill first.

He moved down the side of the house. There was a lit window on the second floor, under a dormer. A bedroom?

At the corner of the front porch, he knelt, concealed by a clump of arborvitae. Still time to turn back . . . but he couldn't. Andy was a talker.

Took a breath. Muttered to himself: jack a shell into the chamber, pistol now cocked, flip the safety off. Check the safety again. Wait some more. Check the safety a third time.

He took a last look around, and a deep breath, stood up, walked around the corner of the house and up the porch steps. The front entrance had both an inner door and a screen door. He tried the screen door and found it unlocked. He pulled it just slightly open, then rang the doorbell.

O'NEILL CAME to the door with a querulous look, impatient with the interruption, but not quite annoyed. R-A saw him coming and turned away, as though he were looking out across the lawn, but at the same time, kept his left hand on the handle to the screen door. As soon as he heard the door open behind him, and O'Neill saying . . . "Yes . . ." he turned and pulled open the screen door and swung the pistol up. With the muzzle two inches from O'Neill's forehead he pulled the trigger twice, the gun went *whump whump* and O'Neill went down.

Mrs. O'Neill in the kitchen called, "Andy? Andy, what was that? Who's there?"

R-A hopped across O'Neill's body, kicked the door shut, and ran across the living room carpet to the kitchen door and got there just as Mrs. O'Neill stepped into the doorway. He was leading with the muzzle of the gun and *whump whump* and Mrs. O'Neill went down, but maybe not dead, and he stepped close and fired again, this time with the muzzle one inch from her temple, *whump.*

Five shots, four rounds left.

Then, from upstairs, "Mom? Mom? What was that?"

R-A turned back to the living room. He'd seen the wide steps going up, over the built-in bookcase, and he ran back through the kitchen door and turned toward the staircase, and saw the girl there, maybe ten years old, staring openmouthed at her father's body by the door, then she saw him, and quick as a flash, turned and ran back up the stairs.

R-A was right behind her, slamming up the stairs, around the landing, saw a door closing, locking, kicked it as hard as he could, felt it give, but hold, kicked it again, close to the knob, and it caved, and he kicked it again and was in, but as he went through he heard the window shatter, and inside the door saw the girl at the window about to go out on the porch roof and he fired four times into her back, *whump whump whump whump.*

She was terribly hurt, but not dead yet, and rolled over on her back, and looked up at him, her eyes already going hazy, and she asked, "Why?" He leaned forward and tried to fire again, into her forehead, but nothing happened. He looked at the gun: empty magazine. He ejected the empty mag, slapped in a new one, and fired the last shot and the girl's eyes shuddered and closed.

She was dead, but the window over the porch was shattered, no way to put that back. He turned off the room light and shut the door, and turned off more lights as he ran back down the stairs.

He stepped over to Andy O'Neill to make sure he was gone; and he was. And then over to Mrs. O'Neill. Gone. He turned out all the lights on the first floor, and with the house dark, left by the side entrance. He jogged across the backyard, crossed the fence, catching the crotch of his pants on the top strand of barbed wire. He carefully unhooked it, and ran through the cornfield.

The night was as silent as ever. Still. He ran on to the far fence line, then out of the field, out to the road, and along the road to the pasture where he'd parked.

BACK AT THE HOUSE, Horn was waiting. "Done?"

"There were three of them. I didn't know about the kid, but it wasn't a problem."

"What about the gun?"

"If they come for me tonight, it's only because they knew I did it. The gun wouldn't make much difference . . ."

"Roger, everything makes a difference," Horn said. "The gun would be conclusive. You've got to get rid of it."

"Not yet. Not tonight. Tomorrow, I'll hide it so they'd never find it," R-A said. "I'm not going out tonight without it."

"If they hang you with it, it's not my fault," Horn said.

They'd worked the whole plan through, but R-A was high on adrenaline and said, "I gotta roll. Gotta roll."

"Then roll. But roll slow. You don't want to get stopped by a cop, with that pistol in the car." Horn sniffed. "You been drinking?"

"Not much, a quick jolt."

"Go use some mouthwash or toothpaste or whatever you got. You don't need to get hauled in for drunk driving. You don't need a cop to remember you."

"All right. I've got some gum, just for that thing."

And Horn said, "Give me one minute before you go. What was it like, up there at the O'Neills'? Had to be good . . ."

.   .   .

R-A HEADED NORTH in his truck. All he had to do was find a blonde out in the open in Alexandria. Choke her out, drop the typewritten note on her chest. If it didn't work out, it didn't work out. He had to remember that: if it didn't work out, it didn't work out, and he'd turn around and go home. A ten percent risk, that was okay. Maybe a twenty-five percent risk. Anything more than that, turn right around.

The route took him through the Twin Cities. He hadn't gotten there when he glanced at the dashboard clock and was surprised how late it was. He worked it through his head. He'd pulled into the ditch around 8:45. It hadn't gotten dark enough to move for another ten minutes, and then it had been twenty minutes to the O'Neill house. He'd been in the house for probably five minutes, then another ten minutes back to the car, running all the way. So: 9:30 at the car, then back to the house, talking with Horn, he probably hadn't left the house until 9:40 or so. The bars in Alexandria closed at one o'clock, and it took three hours to get there.

He was too late! He wouldn't get there until closing time, and he didn't even know exactly where the bars were.

He slowed, thought about turning around. Giving it up. But: he'd mailed that first letter from Sauk Centre, and on the way out of town, had stopped at a bar for a couple of drinks. He knew how to get there, he knew where the bars were—there were a bunch of them on one big street, quick to get there from I-94.

Hell, Sauk Centre was as good as Alexandria. He'd have only an hour or so to operate, he'd have to get lucky. But if he got lucky, the cops wouldn't know what hit them. They'd be jumping around like their feet were on fire and their asses were catchin'.

One thing he couldn't do was drive slow. He'd have to drive fast, and then drive slow coming back. He did that, his back tense, waiting for the flashing red lights to pop up from behind a dip in the road. . . .

Never happened.

He got to Sauk Centre an hour before closing; found the first two bars almost empty, a few lone divorced guys looking into their beers. The third bar, the Rusty Gate, had an available blonde, sitting with a nice-looking brunette, but the ages were wrong. He needed *young.* . . .

He found a young one, all by herself, talking to the bartender at a place called College Town. Four cowboy-looking guys were shooting pool at the back of the bar, while another one, with his girlfriend, watched. A half dozen other couples were scattered around in booths.

R-A took a stool at the bar, ignoring the blonde, and the bartender came over and said, "Getcha?"

"Got Bud on tap?"

"Yup."

The bartender went and got it, and when he came back, R-A asked, "You about to close?"

The bartender looked over his shoulder at a clock and said, "You got a half hour."

The bartender went back to talking with the blonde, something about a traffic stop down in Iowa, and the Highway Patrol had taken somebody's car apart looking for dope, and whoever it was never smoked dope or anything else . . . hardly even drank.

R-A couldn't follow it all. He studied the girl in the mirror behind the bar, and God help him, she was perfect. She had large, strong breasts and a small waist, blond ringlets down to her shoulders. She was wearing a white cotton sweater, with the sleeves pushed up to her elbows, and he could see the dark shadow of a black brassiere.

If he'd been ready for another one, for a real one, he'd have put her on his list, and would have watched her for weeks, and then would have closed in . . . and . . .

He got lost in the fantasy, sipping the beer, and the bartender came over and said, "You want another?"

R-A came back and looked at his glass. The beer was almost gone.

The bartender said, "I only asked, because if you want a third one, you'll be right at last call."

"Gimme another," R-A said, swallowing the last of the beer and pushing the glass across the bar.

IT WENT LIKE THAT for fifteen minutes, the cowboys in the back laughing and jostling each other around, and R-A got a third one at last call. The bartender and the blonde were running down, and there was a burst of laughter from the back, and then three of the cowboys walked out toward the front, and two of them draped arms around the blonde, from opposite sides, and one of them asked, "Which one of us you goin' home with, sweet thing?"

The blonde pressed a finger to her perfect lips and her eyes opened wide and she said, "It's so hard to choose . . . but, given the circumstances, maybe I'll just go home with my husband."

The third cowboy said, "Goddamned right. Get your cookies in the oven and your buns in the bed."

She frowned and said, "George, that's so old and stupid. Don't say that stupid shit because—"

"It makes you look stupid," said another one of the cowboys.

"Never made any claims otherwise," the husband said.

They were all on their feet, moving around, and went out the door in a group.

THAT WAS THAT. R-A finished his third Bud, nodded to the bartender, and went out to the street. Sinclair Lewis Avenue. Other bars were closing around him, up and down the street. Not an unaccompanied woman in sight.

"Well, shit," R-A said.

MATTSSON WAS ASLEEP in her apartment, but not at ease: too much going on, too many possibilities to think about. When the phone rang at 1:15, she was not entirely asleep, nor was she entirely surprised. The pressure was such that something *had* to happen.

She kept her phone on her nightstand, picked it up and looked at the screen. There was no name, just a number, from Wisconsin. Thinking, *Wrong number*, she punched the answer bar and said, "Hello?"

"Hello, Catrin . . ."

She sat up: not a voice she recognized, and she had a good ear and a good memory. "Who is this?"

"Well, this is Jack Horn. I understand you've been looking for me."

"Is this a joke?"

"No joke, Catrin. You've got a pencil?"

She fumbled the bedside lamp on and found a pencil and a slip of paper: "Yes."

"Marsha Wells. Picked her up outside the He's Not Here bar on Hennepin Avenue. You don't have her on your identified list yet, but she was in there. In the hole. You want to know what I didn't like about her?"

Mattsson was crawling across the bed to her hardwired phone, while punching up the contact list on her cell. She found Davenport's cell number and began punching it into the hardwired phone as she said, "I'm scared to ask."

Horn laughed. "What I didn't like was, she gave up too easy. I mean, I took her and . . . I took her and beat on her a little, to soften her up, but when I started fuckin' her, she was like a rag. She just gave up. See, what I did was . . ."

THE PHONE WENT OFF on Lucas's bedside table and he groaned, and fumbled for it: didn't recognize the number. He punched "answer," and said, "Yeah?"

MATTSSON HAD THE EARPIECE of the hardwired phone clamped to her ear, hoping Horn wouldn't hear Davenport answer. As soon as she heard Davenport say, "Yeah?" she interrupted Horn's rambling description of his rape of Marsha Wells. She said, maybe too loud, "Yeah, Mr. Horn, this is all pretty awful, but how do I know you're really Mr. Horn? I mean you say you killed what's-her-name, Marsha Wells, is that right?"

She moved the mouthpiece of the wired phone close to the speaker on her cell phone, so Davenport could hear Horn.

"Yeah, that's right. Marsha Wells. Grabbed her, fucked her good, got me a piece of rope and put it around her neck, and was strangling her while I fucked her that last time. You know what happens when you're fuckin' some chick while you're strangling her . . ."

"Yeah, yeah, yeah, but how do I know that you're not down in some bar someplace with Dick Wolfe or Bobbie McCauley and you're not pulling my leg? If you're really Horn, how'd you get this number?"

"You can find anything on the Internet, if you look long enough," Horn said. "What I did was . . ."

Lucas hung up and when Weather asked, "What?" he said, "Holy shit, Catrin Mattsson's talking to Horn." He called the duty officer and said, "This is Davenport. A Goodhue deputy named Catrin Mattsson, lives in Red Wing, I got her number here, she's talking to the Black Hole killer right now, right this minute, she's keeping him on the line, we need to know where he's calling from."

"You know what carrier . . . ?"

"No, no, I don't know a fuckin' thing. Just find it, find where he's calling from, what the number is. . . . Here's her number . . ."

"Get back to you." And the duty officer was gone.

Horn finished with his pornographic description of the final attack on Marsha Wells, then said, "I saw you on TV. I really like your looks, Catrin. Bet you wouldn't give up, would you?"

"I'd tear your fuckin' heart out," Mattsson said. Davenport had hung up, and she was hoping against hope that he was tracing the call. "If you're really Horn."

"I'm really Horn," he insisted.

"If you're really Horn, what were you doing in that ditch when Little Kaylee saw you?"

After a moment of silence, Horn laughed and said, "Little Kaylee. I won't tell you what I was doing, but I had a good reason for being in there. And I'll tell you what, I was never one of those peter-whatever-you-call-'ems, peterists?"

"Pederasts," Mattsson said.

"Yeah, I was never one of those. But Little Kaylee, she could get me in that habit, you know what I mean. That long blond hair and all."

"You touch her, I'll kill you."

Horn laughed again. "Just kiddin' you. I like a little tit on my girls. Listen, I don't think you can trace this call, because I took precautions, but I better go anyway. I just wanted to chat. I'll tell you what, Catrin: I really do like your looks."

HER PHONE BURPED: a message coming in.

Horn asked, "What was that?"

"What was what?" She thumbed the message tab; a note from Davenport that said, "Keep him talking."

"That noise?"

"I don't know. I thought it was you. But don't go, give me one little clue, one hint here: not about you, about this Wells woman. We need to track her, see if we can get dental records. Was she from the Twin Cities? Where would we find that?"

"Come on, I know you got computers . . ."

"You'd be surprised what isn't in the computers . . ."

"Ah, shit, you bitch, you're keeping me on the line. Fuck you."

He was gone.

SHE SAT LOOKING at the phone for a minute, then went back to the hardwired phone and keyed in Davenport's number. When he answered, she blurted, "You get him?"

"He was calling from Sauk Centre," Lucas said. "He was calling on Mary Lynn Carpenter's cell phone—so he was real. I yanked the Sauk Centre chief out of bed, he said he'd put every guy he had on the road, take down every tag that they see. But Horn could have been out on I-94 by the time they started looking—and we'd have no idea which way he was traveling."

"Goddamnit . . ." Mattsson was so cranked that she found herself standing on her bed, without knowing exactly why. She sat down and said, "Now what?"

"We're hoping he doesn't pull the battery on the phone. We're hoping that we can call him on that phone in about two hours . . . and that he doesn't answer. If we can do that, we can get pretty close to where he's calling from. If we can call him a second time, we'll get even closer."

"He's gotta be from down here. He *can't be* from up north," Mattsson said.

R-A HAD BEEN out on I-94 when he called, because like everybody else on the Internet, he knew that the cops could find the cell phone tower that the call had come from. He clicked off, and tossed the phone on the passenger seat.

He'd had a few beers, and now really didn't want to get stopped, so he took it slow going back south, around the Cities. Stopped once at a truck stop to pee and buy a pack of cigarettes.

He was most of the way home when the cell phone rang. That froze him. He didn't answer, but he thought, What if all they had to do was call? And if the phone company could find out where the phone was, to forward the call, couldn't the cops do that, too? Now he was scared.

He looked for a side road—the phone had stopped ringing—but no side roads came up for a long minute, then another minute. The phone didn't ring again, but R-A didn't think he could wait: Were they coming for him right now?

Then a turnoff came up, and he went down a blacktop road for a quarter-mile, did a U-turn, jumped out of the truck, the phone in his hand, and got into the toolbox in back. After carefully wiping the phone down, he laid it on the blacktop in front of his headlights, and beat it to death with a ball-peen hammer.

Nobody came after him.

He made it home in fifteen minutes. Didn't talk to Horn.

Crawled in bed and pulled the covers over his head.

Nobody came . . .

He couldn't sleep, but lay there, his mind racing, tracing what he'd done that night. He hadn't gotten a blonde, but hadn't gotten caught, either.

As he finally drifted toward sleep, he was thinking about the girl on the bar stool, and how perfect she was, and then thought about Mattsson, and how perfect she'd be, and then thought about the feeling of satisfaction that came from beating the phone to death.

Then he was asleep.

Lucas called Mattsson a few minutes before three o'clock. "We rang him. The phone was still operating. He was on Highway 52 just south of Cannon Falls. So, you were right: he's from down south."

"I knew it. I knew it."

"And you were right. But: he was moving. He wasn't where he lives, yet. He could have been headed for either Holbein or Zumbrota. One of those two places, I think."

"What do you want to do?"

"We're going to give him time to get home. I'll be in Zumbrota, because . . . I don't know, because that's where Shaffer was found. We'll have the cops from both Zumbrota and Holbein ready to go. We need you guys from Goodhue to have a couple people ready—"

"I'll take care of that," she said.

"That's why I called you," Lucas said.

"Good. I'm coming to Zumbrota with you," she said. "Where do you want to meet?"

"Five o'clock at the Zumbrota police headquarters," Lucas said. "You know where it is?"

"Of course."

"See you there. And, Catrin . . . bring your above-average guns."

15

Lucas got to the Zumbrota city hall, which housed the police headquarters, a few minutes early. He parked on the side of the building, the sun still trying to find its shine, and a sleepy-looking chief came to the door and held it open for him.

Lucas said, "Thanks," and followed him back to the police wing, which had standard office cubicles for the cops, and an oval conference table. Two more cops were already sitting there. "Coffee?"

"Yeah, that'd be fine," Lucas said. He saw an SUV go by, headed into the parking lot, and he added, "There's Mattsson. I'll get the door."

He walked out to the lobby and saw Mattsson already walking over, her hands in her jacket pockets and shoulders hunched against the predawn cool. "If he's really close by, he could see us getting together, all the lights," she said.

Lucas looked around and said, "Yeah, I suppose. I'm not sure anyplace else would be better."

She looked around and said, "Probably not. But why five o'clock in the morning?"

"To give him time to go to sleep," Lucas said. "If he kept the phone, and didn't pull the batteries, we're hoping it'll ring a few times. What we're *really* hoping is that he turned it off, so that it *won't* ring. It'll still be registered with the system, and we'll be able to nail it down. We'll keep calling until we get a good fix."

"What's the worst case?"

"He pulled the batteries and threw it in a ditch. If he did that, we won't get him now, and when we do catch him, he wouldn't have it, as evidence. That's worst case." Lucas looked at his watch. "They'll start calling him two minutes from now."

Mattsson looked out at the quiet, dark town. "There oughta be a bigger ceremony," she said.

THEY WENT BACK into police headquarters, and the chief had two cups of coffee waiting for them.

They didn't say much, until Mattsson said, "Getting kinda tense, here," and one of the other cops asked, "What exactly are we gonna do if we get a good fix?"

"Depends on how good it is," Lucas said. "If it's really good—the phone's got a GPS function, and if they get some time with it, they should be able to tell us what house it's in. With less time, we'd probably at least be able to tell what block it is in."

"If we know that," the chief said, "I'll be able to tell you, ninety percent, which house we should look at first."

"Got a judge ready to sign a warrant if we get an address," Mattsson said. "He'll sign it and fax it over. He said he'll be sitting by the phone from four forty-five on, and if we get a solid fix, we'll have it in one minute."

THEY WAITED. Finally Lucas said, "Either things have gone really bad, or really good, and they're working it hard."

One of the cops pulled a leather money clip out of his pocket, pulled dollar bills out of it, and said, "I got four bucks says it's gone wrong."

The chief said, "Goddamnit, Mikey, why'd you have to go and say that?"

A minute later, Lucas's cell phone lit up and then rang and he punched the "answer" tab and the "speaker" setting, and the tech on the other end said, "The phone is dead. He must've pulled the batteries or trashed the phone. It's not signed on anywhere."

"Goddamnit. You're sure?"

"Yeah. There's only one answer to this—the phone either registers, or it doesn't. If there's a battery in it, it'll show up. If there's no battery in it, or the battery's dead, it won't. Or, a third choice—it could be buried, or something. Most likely, he either pulled the battery or trashed it."

"All right. Listen, ping it every ten minutes," Lucas said.

"For how long?"

"Forever," Lucas said. "Keep pinging it forever."

MATTSSON GOT UP, walked out to the lobby, in disgust, then turned and walked back. She asked Lucas, "What're you going to do?"

"See if I can get breakfast somewhere," Lucas said. "Probably go back home."

"There's nothing here in Zumbrota, but there's an all-night pan-cake place on the highway up in Holbein," the chief said. "I've eaten there a few times, never actually gotten food poisoning."

"The Teepee," Mattsson said. "That's good enough. Goddamnit, I thought I'd be outside somebody's house right now, getting ready to kick the door."

THE TEEPEE was a red A-frame pancake house with faux Indian signs painted on the roof, and four cars parked outside. One skinny trucker sat on a bar stool drinking coffee, looking them over when they walked in, and two heavyset guys hunched over eggs and sau-sage in a booth. The waitress was talking to the cook through a service slot, and followed them to a corner booth.

"How you doing, hon?" she asked Mattsson. She plopped two plastic water glasses on the table and took a long look at Lucas.

Lucas said, "I'm also a cop, but I'm not a 'hon.'"

"I decide that," the waitress said. "I figured you were another cop, or the two of you was just up from the Motel 6."

"Hey!" Mattsson said. "He could be my dad."

"Doesn't look like your dad," the waitress said. She gave Matts-son a broad wink.

"I'm sitting right here," Lucas said.

"So shoot me," the waitress said. "You all want coffee?"

THEY GOT PANCAKES and lots of butter and syrup, and Lucas got a Diet Coke and Mattsson got coffee, and they talked about the phone call she'd gotten from the killer. Mattsson went out to her truck and got a notebook, and brought it back, opened it as she sat down and said, "I wrote it all down. I got it pretty much word for word."

She recited the entire conversation, and when she finished, Lucas said, "He called you a bitch and hung up."

"Yes."

Lucas thought about it for a minute, then said, "He still had Carpenter's phone—so he keeps trophies. At least, some trophies."

"If we ever figure out who he is, that'll hang him," Mattsson said.

"Unless . . ."

"It's in a ditch," they said simultaneously.

THEY FINISHED the pancakes and got another round of Diet Coke and coffee, and Mattsson asked, "I've been thinking about what you said about working for the BCA. If I put in for it, what are my chances of getting hired? I've got a good clearance record, I could get one of your guys to recommend me."

Lucas studied her for a moment, then said, "That fuckin' Flowers."

She said, "Well, yeah, Virgil. We've talked a few times. He helped me out on a hijacking case. You guys don't get along?"

"We get along fine," Lucas said. "He's one of my guys. If Virgil recommended you, that'd be a step up. I'd chip in. You're smart and you're not afraid to stick your face into it. I gotta tell you, though, things get seriously political up there, and the question is, how well do you deal with office politics?"

"I do sometimes get impatient . . ."

They were still talking about that at six o'clock when Mattsson took a call. "Duty officer," she said, looking at the screen on her phone. She answered, listened a moment, then stood up and said, "What!"

Everybody in the place turned to look at her, and she started toward the door and called to Lucas, "Pay the bill. We gotta go! Like, right now!"

The waitress called, "Twelve forty-eight," and Lucas threw a twenty at the table and hustled out after Mattsson, who was halfway to her truck.

"What?" he shouted.

"We got a triple murder," she called back.

"Where?"

"Right here," she shouted. "A half-mile from here."

"What is it about you? Every time we talk, somebody's dead."

"Fuck you," she said, but in a collegial way this time.

SHE TOOK OFF, lights and siren, with Lucas behind her, off the highway and through the middle of town, cars pulling off the road to let them by. They went through the small business district, and out to the edge of town, where two cop cars sat next to a semi-stately two-story house. A crowd of neighbors was gathering across the street. Mattsson pulled right up to the edge of the yard, Lucas parking across the street, and they both climbed out and hustled toward the chief of police, who was there in jeans and a flannel shirt, and a cop in uniform.

The chief said, "My God, that was fast. Where were you?"

"At the Teepee," Mattsson said. "What happened?"

The chief nodded at the cop. "George was on patrol, and he drove by." He said to the cop, "You tell 'em, George."

THE COP WAVED a hand at the front porch and said, "I was driving by, because, you know, we was waiting on you and that phone call. So the chief called and sez it was all off, the phone was dead, and I was heading back in, and looked up there and I could see the window was busted out, above the porch. Could see the sun off the other windows, but that one window was like this black eye, with the curtain there, flapping out the window. At first I just figured the window was open, then I seen it was, you know, busted out, and there's something out on the roof. I don't know, I just thought, I don't know, that weren't right. So I walks up the front walk and go to ring the doorbell, and I look through the window on the door and seen Andy laying there on the floor in a big pool of blood."

The cop started screaming for help, and for the first time in his life, took the gun out of his holster and pushed open the door, "with my knee, so I didn't mess up any prints. I had to make sure, you know, that the people inside was dead, that they didn't need help. Medical help."

He found Lucy O'Neill at the kitchen door, obviously dead, like her husband. He knew the O'Neills had a daughter, and since it was unlikely that either of them had been killed upstairs and dragged down, he followed his muzzle to the second floor, where he found young Janice O'Neill dead on her bedroom floor. He'd had his phone live the whole time, and he cleared the second floor and then, when the chief arrived, ran down to meet him.

Now he looked back up at the house: "Never in my life seen anything like it," he said. Then he started to cry and the chief patted him on the shoulder, and the cop tried to get himself back, saying, "I never touched anything in there, except the floor, with my shoes. Oh, and I had to turn on a light switch in the little girls' room."

"You did good, George," Lucas said. "That's a real professional job of it."

And to Mattsson, "Let's go look. I'll get the crime-scene crew down right now."

He got on his phone and made the call to the BCA duty officer, told him the situation, then followed Mattsson up to the house, across the porch, and then, carefully, through the front door.

Andy O'Neill was on his back, his sightless eyes still open. Lucas said, "Shot with a .22."

"Uh-huh. Blood spatter." She pointed at the door, at a streak of blood toward the bottom. "Like he hit his head on it going down."

They moved over to Lucy O'Neill—more .22s, and Mattsson said, "Got brass. He was shooting an auto."

Lucas moved back to Andy O'Neill, looked around, spotted a shell, then two more as he stepped back to Lucy O'Neill. He said, "With any luck, some of them will have thumbprints."

THEY WALKED CAREFULLY up the stairs. Before they went up, Lucas said, "Walk right on the edge of the stairs. If he was hurrying, he would have been in the middle, and we might find a tread."

At the top landing, they looked down to their right, saw lights and an open door. Lucas led the way down the hall, stuck his head in the room, and saw the girl curled on the floor just inside the window. She was wearing fashion jeans, a black blouse, and one black leather shoe. She had a black cord around her neck, strung with a pewter symbol of some kind, a winged heart.

"She heard the shots from downstairs," Lucas said. "Maybe . . . looked down the stairs, then ran back up here and tried to go out the window."

They peered out the window and saw, on the porch roof, a school backpack. "Threw the backpack at the window, but the shooter got to her before she managed to get out," Mattsson said. "Where's her other shoe? Did the guy take it?"

"By the bed," Lucas said.

"Got it."

Lucas looked at Mattsson and said, "I think . . . I'd bet a million bucks that this is our guy. No way this town is going to get a triple, right when we're hunting down the Black Hole guy. He came here and killed them for some reason. This isn't simple craziness. He picked on them because they knew something. We need to talk to everybody they knew. Starting right now."

"I'll get the whole goddamn sheriff's department down here," Mattsson said.

"I can get at least a few guys, plus the crime-scene crew," Lucas said. "We need to talk to the neighbors right now. He fired nine or ten shots, sometime during the evening—it looked to me like the woman downstairs was washing dinner dishes."

"Yeah . . ."

"The girl broke the window out, so he was shooting, at least four shots, with an open window. When he shot the man, the door had to be open. That's more shots. Somebody had to have heard the shots."

Mattsson looked at the girl, then up at Lucas. A tear trickled down one cheek and she wiped it away and said, "If I find this guy, and if he does anything other than get down on his knees with his hands up in the air, I'm gonna kill him."

Lucas, with an image of Letty in his mind, said, "See, there's one difference, right there, between us older BCA professionals, and you younger sheriff's deputy amateurs."

She tipped her head away, and her eyes narrowed, waiting for the insult. "What?"

"As an old pro, you'd never, ever, tell *anyone* that," Lucas said. He was smiling, the hard, feral smile that tended to frighten people. "You'd just do it."

She poked him in the chest with her index finger. "You're right. I do have some things to learn. Thank you."

THEY WENT BACK DOWN the stairs and made their calls for help, then got the Holbein cops—there were four of them now—to find the immediate neighbors and send them back to their own homes, where they could be interviewed. Lucas and Mattsson started with the closest house, the Carson family, Randy, Sheela, and their sons Bob and Don.

They hadn't heard a thing.

"Our front door was open, but I didn't hear anything like a shot. Not even a backfire," Randy Carson said. The two boys, sitting on the couch with their mother, nodded: Bob, the younger boy, maybe fourteen, said, "I was upstairs on my bed, reading a comic, and I thought I heard something, but not a shot. I thought maybe Dad or Don were doing something out in the garage."

"What time was that?" Mattsson asked.

The boy pressed a finger against the side of his nose, thinking. "It was dark, but I don't know the exact time." He looked at his brother and said, "You came up. I was still reading the comic, and you were talking to Nina."

"Who's Nina?" Lucas asked.

"His girlfriend," Bob said.

"Sorta my girlfriend," Don said. He dug his cell phone out of his pocket and said, "She called me at nine-oh-three, and I came up to my bedroom to talk to her."

"I heard the noise just a few minutes before that," Bob said.

Mattsson: "So around nine o'clock, give or take."

"I guess so," Bob said. "But it wasn't any shots. We all go hunting, and I know what shots sound like."

WHEN THEY WERE DONE with the Carsons, they went to the next three closest houses. Nobody had heard anything.

"That's not right," Lucas said, as they left the last of the interviews.

"Could have been a silenced pistol," Mattsson suggested.

"Where would he get it?" Lucas asked. "You don't get a silencer down at the hardware store."

She shrugged: "I don't know. I've never dealt with a silencer. Never even seen one, except on television. What else could it be?"

Lucas rubbed an ear, then took out his cell phone and made a call. There was no answer, so he called it again, and this time a man answered. "What?"

"This is Davenport," Lucas said.

"Oh, shit. What happened?"

"We got a triple, down in Holbein. I'm trying to figure something out. The killer shot a man in an open doorway, at least two shots. He shot a girl in an open window, at least four more. The people in the nearest house, maybe"—he looked at the Carsons' house—"maybe a hundred fifty feet away. Their door was open, they didn't hear anything like shots. Quiet night, right around nine o'clock, no traffic nearby."

"You know what caliber?"

"Looks like a .22," Lucas said.

"Is this the Black Hole guy? What's his name? Horn? The dog-catcher? Shooting with an auto, you found some brass on the floor?"

"Yeah, we did find some brass. We think it's Horn. Why do *you* think it's Horn?"

"Because Ruger made a sound-suppressed .22 auto pistol, the Mark II, for pest control officers. It's a Class II weapon, so it has to be registered with the ATF. You might want to check with them."

"Wayne: thank you."

"Also: the Mark III, that's the current model, some versions have a threaded barrel for suppressors or compensators, so that'd be another possibility."

Lucas rang off and Mattsson said, "What?"

"There's a pretty common pistol that was sold with a silencer, to pest control officers."

She looked down at her shoes, then back up, and turned in a full circle, looking at the neighbors and the houses up and down the silent street. "Horn. Where in the hell is he hiding? He can't be hiding in *this* town."

"What could the O'Neills have known, that they wouldn't call in?" Lucas asked. "Could they have been hiding Horn? That seems crazy."

"When Crime Scene gets here, you gotta have them tear the place apart. But I don't believe they were hiding him," Mattsson said. "I don't believe it. I think one of the O'Neills saw the same thing Shaffer did, and he knew it, and he had to shut them up."

16

The next three hours were busy. Jon Duncan showed up with two other BCA agents and the crime-scene crew, again. Bea Sawyer said to Lucas and Mattsson, "We gotta stop meeting like this."

"It's pretty goddamn bad," Lucas said. "There's a dead girl up there, reminds me of Letty."

Sawyer patted him on the arm and said, "Aw, boy. But you'll get the guy, okay? You'll get him."

"Won't get the girl back," Lucas said. "Listen: one thing we need to know right away: Were the O'Neills hiding Horn? If they were, you should be able to figure that out."

"We will."

Duncan said, "We were wondering what he was doing here at nine o'clock, up in Sauk Centre at one, and then down here at three? Just trying to decoy us up north?"

Mattsson nodded. "I gotta believe it was."

. . .

HORN WAS CLOSE BY, but where? Mattsson was almost certainly right, Lucas thought—he couldn't hide in Holbein, or any of the other nearby towns. Everybody they talked to said he hadn't had any real friends, and even if he had one, how could he have hidden for all those years?

Not right.

WHEN THE SCENE at the O'Neill house was running smoothly, Lucas told Mattsson he was going home: "We'll have a bunch of guys down here, we'll keep pinging that phone, in case it comes back online. . . . If you think of anything, let me know. When we get a time of death, get your people and the city cops to knock on every door for six blocks in every direction and ask who they saw driving around."

"What're you going to do?"

"Take a nap, first thing. Then go back to the books. There's gotta be something."

HE PULLED OUT, and he held up a hand to her as he went. Smart, good-looking woman: maybe a little rough around the edges, but he was starting to get a vibration from her. Old enough to be her dad? *I don't think so.* He didn't know anything about her personal life, but there was that vibration . . . and if he hadn't been so happily married, he'd have happily gotten her ankles up around her ears.

He'd just thought that, when a name popped into his head. Flowers. That fuckin' Flowers was a friend of hers. Few tall, well-built single blondes who were friends of Flowers had gotten away with their honor intact.

He punched the phone button to bring up the car's cell connection, then used the hockey puck to select Flowers's name, and called him. Flowers answered on the second ring. "Where are you?" Lucas asked.

"Down in Le Crescent. Not in the boat. Working."

"On your mystery case."

"Lucas, if you want to know about it . . . but I promise you, you're better off not knowing."

"All right. I'm up in Goodhue County, in Holbein," Lucas said.

"Early for you," Flowers said.

"We got a triple."

"Uh-oh! That's gotta be a first for Holbein."

"It's the Black Hole killer. I'm working it with Catrin Mattsson," Lucas said. "Your name has come up, a time or two. Got me curious: You work any night shifts with that girl?"

Flowers didn't say anything for a moment, then, "I'll be goddamned. Calling me up at the crack of dawn to find out—"

"It was not the crack of dawn I was asking about," Lucas said. "Virgil, you are *such* a slut."

"I am not," Flowers said. "Unlike some people I could think of, I'm just a friendly guy."

LUCAS WAS SO SLEEPY when he got home that he said, "Good morning," to the housekeeper and fell into bed. He slept soundly until eleven-thirty, woke up with a tiresome idea at the back of his head, made a couple of phone calls, then a third one to Mattsson.

"This is your dad," he said.

She laughed. "I knew that'd piss you off."

"What're you up to?"

"I'm sitting at my desk bouncing a ball of Thinking Putty off a whiteboard," she said.

"That's the stretchy blue stuff?"

"Mine's called 'amethyst blush,' but yeah. Why?"

"I'm driving over to Eau Claire, to interview this Heather Jorgenson woman, the one who got away from Horn. You want to sit in?"

"Why? I wish I'd been there when Duncan interviewed her, but I never got an invitation," Mattsson said. "On the other hand, after I read the interview, I couldn't think of anything else to ask her."

"I want to go at her from a different direction. I'm bringing an old friend along to help out."

"All right, I'm in," she said.

"You're closer to Eau Claire than I am, but I'm all interstate highway, so . . . I told Jorgenson that I'll be at her house at three o'clock. She's got to be to work at five."

"Plenty of time. Give me her address," Mattsson said.

Lucas gave her the address, then said, "There's a Red Lobster near the intersection of I-94 and 53, not far from Jorgenson. We'll get there about two, have a late lunch. If you've got time, we could have a pre-interview chat, see where we're at."

"See you there. And then."

·   ·   ·

IN LUCAS'S OPINION, August was the best month of the year in Minnesota. Under normal circumstances, he'd have spent at least a couple of weeks at his cabin on Lost Land Lake, in northern Wisconsin.

"September can be almost as good," he told his friend Sister
Mary Joseph, as they crossed the St. Croix River bridge into Hud-
son, Wisconsin. "I can still make it up there, in warm weather, if I
can get this guy in the next couple of days."

When Sister Mary Joseph had been five-year-old Elle Kruger, she
and Lucas, with their mothers, had walked together to the first day
of kindergarten at the local Catholic elementary school.

"Who's going to take Letty to Stanford?" Elle asked.

"Well . . . everybody. She wants to go out there on her own, of
course, preferably in a Greyhound bus. She said she wanted to catch
the scent of America—I think she was reading *On the Road* last
week. We told her she could catch an equally valid scent in the back
of a Delta MD-90. And the closer she sat to the can, the more valid
it would be."

The nun laughed and said, "So you're all going?"

"Yup. Drop her off, check the campus for any suspicious-looking
young men . . ."

"Of which I'm sure there will be many . . ."

"Then go back up to San Francisco for a quick vacation. Try to
get used to the change."

Elle said, "I am going to miss that girl. I hope she comes back to
the Twin Cities. I'd like to see her grow up."

Lucas said, "We're all gonna miss her. Sam cries every night, before he goes to sleep, knowing the day she leaves is one day closer."

They talked about Letty, and her history, for another few miles, then Elle got a transcript of Duncan's interview with Jorgenson and started reviewing it. They stopped once, so Lucas could get a Diet Coke at the Menomonic rest stop, and got to the Red Lobster a minute after two o'clock. Lucas spotted Mattsson's SUV in the parking lot and said, "She's here. She's got a mouth on her and shows some signs of intelligence, so . . . be aware."

"I will take care," Elle said. She looked out at the Red Lobster storefront: "Mmm, mmm, mmm. Seafood on the coast of Eau Claire, Wisconsin."

LUCAS LED THE WAY INSIDE, found Mattsson in a booth. She did a quick double take when she realized that Lucas's friend was a nun. Elle no longer wore the traditional habit, but a tarmac-colored dress and gray stockings, with a little white coif perched atop her head.

Lucas let Elle slide into the booth across from Mattsson and sat beside her, and said, "Elle Kruger, aka Sister Mary Joseph, this is Catrin Mattsson, aka Goodhue County sheriff's investigator. Catrin—Elle."

Mattsson nodded and said, "Uh . . ."

"She's a shrink," Lucas said. "Head of the psychology department at St. Anne's, up in St. Paul. She's helped me out, from time to time, on . . . delicate matters."

"Pleased to meet you," Elle said.

Then Mattsson surprised Lucas with a gently probing series of questions about psychology and police work, drawing Elle out in a way that Lucas hadn't seen before. He was even more surprised by Elle's somewhat skeptical attitude toward her ability to help.

"You help me all the time," Lucas said.

"I've never told you this, but when you ask me to help, my primary function is to make *you* think. To get you off your butt—excuse me—and quit your lazy ways and get to work." She turned to Mattsson and said, "One thing you have to know about Lucas is, he exploits women. Because he's good-looking and charming. He picks out smart women and gets them to do his work for him. That includes his wife and daughter. And me. And you."

"I met his daughter, and even drove around with her for a while," Mattsson said. "She seemed astonishingly intelligent."

"Exactly. Lucas has unconscionably, but not unconsciously, exploited her brains from the time she was a middle-school kid. He even got her to shoot a cop."

"What?"

That took some explaining, and when Lucas was done, Mattsson squinted at him and asked, "Are you exploiting me? Dad?"

Lucas looked around for a waitress and asked, "So . . . we're all for the shrimp platter?"

HEATHER JORGENSON was living in a pale yellow ranch house with green shingles and a two-car garage, a satellite dish on the roof. A six- or seven-year-old cranberry-colored Cadillac sedan sat in the driveway.

Jorgenson met them at the front door, nervously twisting her hands, and invited them in. A sunburned guy with bleached-white teeth named Rex was lying on the couch watching the Golf Channel. He rolled off the couch when they walked in, and said, "Whelp, I got a lesson in twenty minutes, I better get to work."

"Work" was a golf course, where he was a teaching pro. When Rex had gone in the Cadillac, Lucas introduced Mattsson and Elle; Jorgenson settled the other two women on the couch, and Lucas in a La-Z-Boy. "I have to tell you that I'm a little upset by all this," she said. "I never believed that Horn was still out there. I thought he'd crawled off somewhere and died, or was gone to Brazil or something. I mean, I am *so* scared. I got Rex to put his gun under the bed."

"I think he'd have a hard time finding you, that you wouldn't hear about it before he got here," Lucas said.

"Oh, pish," she said. "If he knows anything about computers, he could find me in ten minutes. I mean, I looked in the White Pages, and there I was. No way to get it off there, either."

"I won't tell you he's not dangerous," Lucas said. "I'm sure you've heard about the shootings in Holbein."

"Just awful. And you don't have to tell me about dangerous. I would've been in the Black Hole if I hadn't had my knife that night. Sometimes I wake up, I just start to cry. . . ."

"That's not uncommon, it's a form of post-traumatic stress," Elle said. "Have you talked to your doctor about it?"

"Years ago," Jorgenson said. "He gave me some pills and they helped. I've saved a few, and I'm thinking about going back to them again. Don't have enough for a week, though."

"You'll only need a couple," Lucas said. "Because I'm going to get him soon."

She smiled at him, tentatively, and asked, "Why do I believe that?"

Mattsson said, "Because he's good-looking and charming."

·   ·   ·

THEY CHATTED for a few minutes. Jorgenson was working at the Beerateria in downtown Eau Claire, a bar that specialized in craft beers. The money was okay, she said, and she and Rex got along okay, and had pooled their money to buy the house they were in. They were talking about getting married, and this time, she thought, Rex was serious.

Elle said, "When you talked with Agent Duncan, he asked you about the sequence of events that night. We've all read through that. We'd like to do something a little different, but I have to warn you, it won't make you feel any better."

"Well . . ." She looked from Elle to Davenport to Mattsson. "What?"

"We want to get you very, very relaxed, with your eyes closed, on the couch here, and then we want to take you back through the whole sequence," Elle said. "We want you to try to visualize it, rather than think about it. Like you're dreaming it."

"You mean, like, have a nightmare about it?"

"Not exactly," Elle said. "Because you'll be in control. Once we get you relaxed, we'd like you to stay in the dream as long as you can."

"Okay. If you think it'll help."

ELLE MOVED JORGENSON to the couch, pulled the drapes over the picture window, brought another chair from the kitchen, so she could sit close to Jorgenson's head. She started by asking about Jorgenson's relationship to Rex, got her laughing a bit, then about her parents, who were both still alive, and living in the house where

Jorgenson had grown up. "My oldest friend still lives there . . . beside my parents, she's the only one in town who knows exactly where I am."

Elle took her through her school years, then a couple of years at a community college, where she trained in food service management. When she took the job at Auntie's, she'd thought she might eventually wind up as the manager, or even, in due time, the owner.

"That didn't happen, because of what happened with Horn," she said.

She started talking about the moment she was kidnapped—of her fear of dying, of the panic-stricken thrashing inside the heavy canvas postal bag. Elle slowed her down: "You're going way too fast. Tell me, what was that night like, at Auntie's? A lot of people there that night? Was it hot or cold outside? Could you see the stars when you went out?"

Elle asked a lot of safe questions that elicited brief, easy answers. They could feel Jorgenson slipping into the dream. Her words came more slowly, and her voice dropped a half-octave. Then, "There were about six bags of garbage when I finished, and one of them, with the grease pit stuff, really smelled. I took that out first because I wanted to get it out of the place."

The dumpster was high, and she had to stand on tiptoe to flip the cover back. "Had to keep the cover down because, if we didn't, people would come at night and throw their garbage in it. When I started closing the cover at night, I saved the store fifty dollars a month in garbage bills."

She threw in the first bag, walked back to the diner and got two more bags and threw them in . . . and the canvas bag came down over her head.

She began moving on the couch as she talked about it, her sentences growing choppy, and Elle patted her on the arm and said, "Easy, easy, we're on your couch, right at home. . . ."

The bag was rough and thick and dark and she really didn't understand what had happened. She couldn't see and could hardly breathe inside the bag, and then she was knocked to the ground, and the rope around the edges of the bag was tightened, binding her legs together above the knees. She began screaming and fighting against the bag. Her legs were free below the bag, and she tried to kick the kidnapper. But he picked her up, threw her in the back of his truck, and wrapped her ankles and legs with silver duct tape— she knew it was silver duct tape because some of it was still on her legs when the cops got to her.

Then he'd slammed the truck door, had jumped into the driver's seat, and she'd felt the truck accelerate out of the parking lot, missing the exit curb-cut and bumping over the curb. "That was easy to do, I did it myself," she said.

She knew she was on the backseat of a cab-and-a-half, because the seat on which she was lying was flat and narrow, and she could feel herself jammed between the back of the seat and the back side of the driver's seat. Inside the bag, she'd nearly panicked. But not quite. She'd been fighting the bag and screaming when her hand hit the knife in her uniform pocket.

The knife.

A Leatherman with a long serrated blade. She fumbled it out, opened the blade, cut the rope edge on the bag, "like cutting butter," then pushed her hand down to her ankles and cut through the tape.

She'd stopped struggling as she did that, but as soon as she'd cut her legs loose, she screamed some more, and struggled against the bag, hoping to fool the driver, keep him from looking back at her, as she hitched the bag up and slipped out of it.

When she was out, she'd pushed herself up with her left hand, her bottom hand, and found herself directly behind the driver. She hadn't hesitated. She'd stuck him in the back and neck repeatedly. . . .

"I was so *angry*. I was *insane*. I wanted to kill him." She was reliving it, her arms jerking as, in her mind, she stuck the driver again and again.

The truck had rolled, she'd gotten out, she'd run to a house not far up the road . . . the cops had come . . . the truck had belonged to Horn.

Horn was never seen again.

WHEN SHE FINISHED, she exhaled, and some tension, which had been building up in her body, visibly eased. Elle looked at Lucas, and he said, quietly, slowly, "Heather, I have a couple more questions. Just a couple more. You said he threw you on the ground and tied the bag around your legs, then threw you in the truck, taped your ankles and lower legs, and then slammed the door and the truck took off. . . . The way you were talking, that sounds like it was really quick. I mean, *really* quick."

"It was," she said. "I mean, he picked me up and threw me in and slammed the door."

"You said you came up directly behind the driver. So your feet were on the passenger side?"

"Mm-hmm. I came up right behind him. My feet were on the passenger side. I didn't hardly have any room to move."

"When he picked you up and threw you in the truck, did he pick you up around the waist?"

"Uh . . . I uh . . . I was trying to kick, he was holding my feet. He picked me up by my feet . . ."

"And he threw you into the truck . . ."

"Let me see, I . . . yes, in the truck."

"When you took the garbage out to the dumpster, did you see the truck? You didn't mention that."

"No . . . I never saw it."

"How far did he carry you before he threw you in the truck?"

"Oh, not far. He picked me up by, he . . ." She sat up, her eyes flying open, and said, "Oh, Jesus Mary and Joseph. There were two of them."

Lucas: "I thought there might be."

MATTSSON STARED AT HIM, and Elle saw it, and spread her hands in a gesture that meant, "Like I told you . . ."

LUCAS PUSHED A LITTLE FURTHER: "When you stabbed this man, you told Jon Duncan that you stabbed him several times. When you stabbed him, did you really stick him? Or did you slash him, you know, like cutting a sandwich?"

"Oh, no, I stuck him. In and out," she said. She was sitting up now, with her feet on the floor, eyes wide, and she mimed the stabbing, hard, overhand strokes, into Horn's neck, back, and arm. "There was lots of blood . . . the knife got all slippery . . . I remember that, the blood on the knife. I stuck him and stuck him and stuck him . . ."

"Did you see any other trucks? After you got out?"

"No. After the truck rolled over, I got out and I ran into the corn-field, and I thought I heard him coming after me, so I freaked out and ran away and fell down a couple times, and then I got to some woods and I hid in there, but all I wanted to do was get away from there. I saw some lights, I was trying to get there, but I didn't see a truck. . . . I went down in this dry crick and crawled and crawled a long way, my legs were all cut, and then I was in another field, and then I stood up and ran. I had to cross the road to get to the Mar-shalls' house—the Marshalls were the lights up the road. I saw the taillights in the ditch where the truck was . . ."

"You think there could have been another truck? Another vehicle?"

"If it had been right behind Horn's . . . maybe. I was in that field for five or ten minutes, I guess. . . . Heck, I might have been in there for fifteen minutes, I don't really know. If the other truck had been right behind Horn's, I wouldn't have seen it. Especially when I was down in that crick."

LUCAS HAD no more questions; neither did Mattsson. Elle shooed them out, said, "Go sit in the cars. I want to sit here and talk with Heather for a while."

OUTSIDE, MATTSSON SAID, "Whoa. That was *something*. That was like a movie. The hair was standing up on my neck when she was talking about stabbing him, and then realized there'd been a second guy. . . ."

"I believe her," Lucas said. "I think she stabbed him in the back of the neck, in and out, maybe five or six times and maybe more. I'm pretty sure they would have been deep, penetrating wounds— when you think of the way she was sitting in the truck, it would have been easy to stab him, and a lot harder to slice him. Easy to go up and down, a lot harder to pull back and forth."

"How did you get to the idea that there were two people?"

"First, because we can't find Horn anywhere, and nobody ever saw him after he attacked Heather. That's fairly improbable. From her description of the attack, in Duncan's interview, which sounded real to me, I'd say he either had to get to a hospital, or die. Three-inch wounds down the neck and spine? I'm sorry, but that's big trouble. He didn't get to a hospital. We know that for sure."

"So . . . he's dead?"

"That's what I think. If he didn't die immediately, the second guy probably killed him and ditched his body somewhere. I think the second guy still lives in Holbein, and he's the guy that Shaffer ran into."

Mattsson smiled as she realized what Lucas was thinking. "That's why Horn's name was written in Shaffer's book," Mattsson said. "The second guy had the notebook, and wrote it in there, so we'd all be looking for Horn. We'd be looking for a dead guy."

"That's what I think," Lucas said.

"You said, 'First, because we can't find Horn.' Was there something else?"

"You ever try to get a grip on a big strong angry woman?"

"Not since I was on patrol. I let the guys do that now. But I see what you mean. It's sorta not a one-man job."

"Heather's driver's license, when she was kidnapped, said she weighed one thirty-five," Lucas said. "In my experience, the weight on a woman's driver's license is what she'd like it to be. In reality, you could add about twenty pounds to that."

"That's a little sexist," she said.

"Lemme see your license."

"No way."

"See?"

"I'm not twenty pounds heavier than my license says," Mattsson said. "But I'll give you the argument."

"The pictures of Horn show a tall, thin guy. His driver's license says he was six feet tall, and one seventy. I'm saying that a lone hundred-and-seventy-pound man would have a hard time throwing a struggling hundred-and-fifty-pound woman into a truck, without help."

"And the truck," Mattsson said. "She didn't see the truck in the parking lot."

"That's right. He sure as hell didn't carry a struggling hundred-and-fifty-pound woman around to the front of the diner and throw her in the truck, even if her sense of time was off. She said it was quick, and I think it was, because I think the other guy drove the truck back there to get her."

"I buy it all. Horn's dead, we're looking for a partner," Mattsson said.

"Yes, we are."

"Jesus: tall, good-looking, charming, and smart. It must be a burden."

"I try to carry it gracefully," Lucas said.

· · ·

ELLE TALKED TO HEATHER for another fifteen minutes, and when she came out, Lucas asked, "What do you think?"

"She'll be all right," Elle said. "I told her to get down in a crowd of people tonight, and maybe have a few beers in the back room. Laugh—make herself laugh."

Mattsson: "That's what I would do."

"No guarantees," Elle said. "She could jump off a bridge tomorrow morning. I have a friend here at Luther Hospital, in the psych department. I'll ask her to check on Heather tomorrow, see if she wants to talk some more."

Lucas nodded, and then said, "We had to talk to her."

"I agree. The truth had to come out. Two of them," Elle said. "Interesting. If everything breaks just right, I could get a paper out of this."

LUCAS LAUGHED, and Mattsson smiled, and then Lucas said, "Give me one more minute. I need to talk to Jorgenson again. Just a minute."

He went back and knocked on the door, and when Jorgenson answered, he said, "I thought I ought to tell you—I'm not positive about this, but I'm almost sure that Horn is dead. I don't think you have to worry about him. Officer Mattsson and I have been talking about it, and we think that maybe the other man, the real Black Hole killer, the current one, probably killed him after you wounded him."

"You think? I want to believe that."

"That's what we think. You still be careful, but . . . you're okay."

17

Lucas and Elle didn't get back to the Twin Cities until after seven o'clock. Mattsson said she was going to look at the path of Jorgenson's flight through the cornfield, to see if she could estimate how long it took between the truck wreck and the arrival of the cops. She'd see him in the morning.

Lucas told Weather what they'd learned: "If Horn's dead, you guys have wasted a lot of time," she said.

"It was something we needed to know," Lucas said. "Something critical."

MATTSSON SHOWED UP the next morning for the daily case conference, came straight into Lucas's office: "Did you tell them that Horn's dead?"

"Not yet. I'm just about to, at the meeting," he said. "It's not like we're competing against them."

"How about if I told them?"

Lucas looked at her for a moment, then pointed at his visitor's chair and she sat down. "You remember what I said about how it gets kinda political around here? Jon Duncan is eventually going to be an important guy. He's got that command presence, and, though he really seems to be a good guy, he's never been around an important ass that he didn't kiss."

"I see that in him," Mattsson said.

Lucas said, "The problem is, we went over and interviewed Jorgenson after he did, and we got something critical that he didn't. Might not make him look so good. I don't have to worry about that, but you'd like to find a spot up here."

"I understand that," Mattsson said. "But let me break the news— I want to try out those political chops."

Lucas leaned back in his chair and said, "You got about one minute to get it together."

She said, "I've been thinking about it all night."

Lucas looked at his watch: "Let's go."

DUNCAN CALLED THE MEETING to order, summarized in thirty seconds the investigations of his crew in the Sauk Centre area—not much there.

"The phone trace began in Sauk Centre, wound up way south of Highway 52, looked to be heading back to Zumbrota or Holbein. Now, from what the crime-scene crew says, it appears that Horn killed the O'Neills earlier in the evening, drove to Sauk Centre to make the phone call, and then drove back. We now think that he actually lives south, and all that stuff about Sauk Centre and Alexandria was an attempt to pull us up north."

"We don't even know for sure that Horn killed the O'Neills," one of the agents said. "I admit it'd be a weird coincidence . . ."

Duncan waved him down: "We know now. It was Horn. The crew was working all day and most of the night on the O'Neill scene, you'll all have summaries in your paperwork. As you all know, we picked up a lot of .22 brass from the floor of the O'Neill house. About fifteen minutes ago, Don Abernathy confirmed that we had several partial fingerprints, mostly thumbprints, on the brass, and they match the prints that Horn had with the feds. He was finger-printed in Holbein when he was hired on at the police department. So. Where is he?"

There was a flurry of conversation about that and Mattsson looked at Lucas, eyebrows up. Lucas held up a finger and asked, "Is Don still upstairs?"

Duncan said, "I'm sure he is."

"Let's give him a ring," Lucas said. "I've got a question about the prints."

"Which is?"

"I want to know how old they are."

Duncan stuck a finger in an ear and rattled it around for a sec-ond, then said, "Sure," and reached for the speakerphone and punched in a number. Abernathy was on the line a minute later.

"Don, we have a question for you," Duncan said. "Do you have any idea how old those prints were?"

Abernathy cleared his throat and said, "They are somewhat old—can't really tell how old, but they're not real new. What we're seeing is not the oil or perspiration from the friction ridges, like you see on fresh prints. We're seeing some faint corrosion in the brass, caused by finger oil or perspiration, that follow the pattern of the friction ridges. There's no doubt that they belong to Horn, if that's what you're worried about."

Lucas asked, "Could they be ten years old?"

Abernathy said, "Yeah, once they're etched onto the shells like that, they're pretty permanent. They could be fifty years old."

DUNCAN ASKED LUCAS, "That everything?" and Lucas nodded and Duncan said, "Hey, Don, thanks," and then rang off. He looked at Lucas and asked, "All right. What's up?"

Lucas pointed a finger at Mattsson.

"LUCAS AND I were reading your interview with Heather Jorgenson," Mattsson said, speaking directly to Duncan. "We got to talking about it when we were out there yesterday morning on that phone-tracing business, and then the O'Neill murders. We thought there was a lot of good stuff in there, but we wondered if we could drill deeper if we had Jorgenson talk to a psychiatrist or psychologist.

"Lucas has a good friend who is the head of the Department of Psychology at St. Anne's," she continued. "We went over to Jorgenson's late yesterday afternoon, with the psychologist, Elle Kruger. Kruger put Jorgenson into, mmm, what I guess you'd call a state of regression. She didn't exactly hypnotize her, but it was over in that direction.

"After interviewing her in this state, in which she more or less relived the attack at the diner, and then her attack on Horn, a couple of things became evident."

Duncan was twiddling a yellow pencil and he stopped and

crossed his legs and said, "I gotta tell you, the suspense is killing me. Just tell us."

Mattsson smiled at him and said, "First off, she realized, and we agree, that there wasn't one attacker, but two."

Somebody said, "Whoa."

Duncan was chewing on his lower lip. "I could buy that. Tell us why. Give us the scenario."

Mattsson outlined it: a woman who they believed might have weighed as much as a hundred fifty pounds, or more, being bodily lifted and thrown in the back of the truck by a man who probably wasn't twenty pounds heavier. The mysterious appearance of the truck within seconds of the attack. The even more mysterious disappearance of Horn.

"There were theories that he ran off somewhere and died. We think he was picked up, by an accomplice in a trailing car or truck. Kruger took Jorgenson on a minute-by-minute reconstruction of her flight after the truck went in the ditch. She wouldn't necessarily have been aware of a second vehicle. Quite a bit of her run was down in a dry creek bed. She couldn't have seen another truck from there. I went over there last night and walked up the same creek bed—she couldn't have seen anything until she recrossed the road to the house where she called the police from."

Duncan: "You said, 'First off.' Is there anything else?"

Mattsson nodded. "Kruger got Jorgenson to relive the stabbing. She had a razor-sharp, serrated blade with a nasty point, three inches long. I got the name and model from her—it was the first model of a Leatherman Super Tool—looked it up, and it's a serious weapon. In the reenactment, she seemed to think she stuck him at least five times in the neck and spine."

Duncan twitched the yellow pencil at her. "The reason that Lucas asked about the fingerprints, and how old they are, is because you think . . ."

"Horn is dead," Mattsson said. "We think he's been dead for years. We think the real Black Hole killer has been dragging him out in front of us because he wants us looking for Horn. Horn's probably been in a hole out in the woods ever since he attacked Jorgenson."

A long silence, and then everybody started talking at once. Lucas jumped in. "Little Kaylee said she saw this postal clerk, Sprick, in the ditch near where Shaffer's body was found. We have another woman who's identified Sprick as having been in her shop, the one Mary Lynn Carpenter ran, several times a year. He doesn't look anything at all like Horn. And you know why Kaylee saw him in the ditch? I suspect it was because he was walking back to Holbein. He drove Shaffer down to Zumbrota to throw us off. It's a good hike back, but half of us in here are runners, and we run distances that approach that. It's an easy walk, really, if you've got a couple hours. He had all night. Everything here points to Holbein: the last cemetery that we know for sure that Shaffer was in . . . the O'Neill murders."

MORE SILENCE, then Duncan asked, "Show of hands. How many people think Horn is probably dead?"

All the hands went up, including Duncan's.

"Okay," he said, "we gotta turn this train around." To Mattsson, with one last poke of the pencil: "Nice piece of work."

.   .   .

LUCAS WENT back to his office, trailed by Mattsson. Lucas said, "You done good. You didn't embarrass him, left him in charge."

Mattsson: "Now what?"

"Now there's going to be some more grinding. We have a real shot at him now. We're not chasing a ghost," Lucas said. "We're going to throw a net over Holbein, the whole town, and sieve it out."

"Goddamnit: I'd like a gunfight," Mattsson said.

"Innocent people get killed in gunfights," Lucas said.

"Okay. I want a gunfight where no innocent people get killed. Only the Black Hole guy."

"Careful of what you wish for," Lucas said. "In the meantime . . . I gotta catch up with my guys."

MATTSSON LEFT and Lucas went looking for his secretary, and found Sands, the director, instead. "I found you," Sands said. "What's that fuckin' Flowers doing?"

"Working a semi-low-priority case down south."

"Excellent. He's right on the spot," Sands said. "We got a call from the Winona County sheriff's office that some drunk reporter from a shopper newspaper down there was found dead in a ditch."

"Dead from drinking?" Lucas asked.

"From what I'm told, he might've been, except for the bullet holes in his back."

"All right. Who's handling the crime scene?"

"The sheriff's office has got a competent guy, I'm told. He's on top of it. There's not much of a crime scene—the guy was shot and thrown in the ditch, off a blacktop road, not found for at least a couple days. But they want us to take a look, Virgil particularly," Sands said.

"I'll talk to Virgil."

"Interesting, that thing about Horn being dead," Sands said, as he drifted away. "Who woulda thought?"

LUCAS CALLED VIRGIL, who said, without saying hello, "I'm already on the way over."

"The newspaper guy?"

"Yeah. Not much of a newspaper, and not much of a guy, from what I'm told, but he's definitely been murdered."

"Stay in touch," Lucas said.

HE CHECKED with Jenkins and Shrake. Jenkins said they'd be done in two more days, that they'd be back with Bryan and all the paper-work they'd found in the trunk of his car, since Florida didn't want him for anything. And that they were tired of Florida. "You know they allow alligators on the golf courses down here?"

"I don't play golf," Lucas said. "But I'm guessing that's what they call a water hazard."

DEL WAS out of touch.

.   .   .

A LITTLE AFTER NOON, Lucas went home, taking the updated murder books with him. Weather wasn't yet home, because she had an afternoon patch job on a guy with skin cancer. Lucas thought an intensive search of Holbein, and perhaps Zumbrota, was likely to turn something up, so he finished reading the last of the murder books, and when he was done, dumped the books on the floor and took a nap.

AFTER THE NAP, he went for a run, and Weather called as he was going out the door and said she'd be a little later still. After a hard four miles, Lucas stood in the shower for a few minutes, then dressed again and found Letty downstairs with fifty pounds of gear she'd need for Stanford: "What I really need is a new laptop. It's gonna have to be a heavy-duty one. I don't want a low-rent Dell."

His phone vibrated, and Lucas looked at the screen. He said, "Duncan. Maybe something happened," and clicked "answer."

"What are you up to?" Duncan asked.

"Just finished scrounging through the murder books again. Why?"

"We've taken over the Holbein City Hall lobby down here, and we've got people walking all over town, spreading the word that the killer may be here. Well, a woman came in a few minutes ago, name is Barbara Neumann, to tell us that Horn was *not* friendless, like we've been told. There's a Mayo clinic here, and Horn apparently got himself poisoned with some kind of weed killer—nothing serious, eczema, a rash, painful, I guess, but not much more. Anyway, he had to come back a dozen times, for treatment and tests, make sure he didn't have any liver problems and so on. The woman said that a social worker named Rachel Cline seemed to have gotten pretty friendly with him. I don't know what that means, and Neumann doesn't either, whether the friendliness was personal or professional. But: to make a long story short, Cline is in the Twin Cities now, working at Fairview Southdale."

"So we're *not* assuming that Horn is dead?"

"I'm assuming that," Duncan said. "What I'm hoping is, Cline knew him well enough to know who another friend of his might be. That fuckin' Horn is the most impenetrable personality I've ever run into. Didn't do anything but pick up live dogs and dead skunks, shoot guns, and drink. Anyway, I'm sorta looking for somebody to run over to Southdale. Cline is there now, and she knows we want to talk to her."

"I can leave in one minute," Lucas said. "Where is she, exactly?"

CLINE WAS a tall honey blonde who wore heavy black-rimmed spectacles that made her look like she wrote book reviews for the *Wall Street Journal*. She gave Lucas a firm shake and said, "I can assure you, I was not a friend of Horn's. Any kind of a friend."

They were sitting in an otherwise empty lounge area outside the office of the Case Management Team.

"But you were friendly with him—professionally, at least."

"Yeah, but I knew he was a creepoid," she said, hugging herself. "He tried to be friendly with me, but the only things he could talk about were shooting . . . things."

"Why was he talking to you at all?"

"He couldn't pay his clinic bill. I mean, he had to be treated, but he had no money. He had this cheap-ass insurance from the city. You had a choice—you either took a high maximum payment with a high deductible, or vice versa, low max, low deduct. He took the high max, high deductible, and he couldn't make the deductible. We worked out a payment plan with him."

"So . . . you didn't know who he hung with. If he hung with anybody."

"I saw him with a guy once, when he was being treated, and I think it was a friend. I don't know who it was." She leaned toward Lucas, intent on the memory. "What I remember was, there is a place in Holbein called Arlo's Finer Meats, and Horn and this other guy were carrying a dead deer—I think it was a deer—into the back. They had a deer-processing thing there. The reason I remember, in particular, is that my ex-husband was a deer hunter, and I've seen a lot of dead bucks. This deer had *huge* horns. Horns like I'd never seen. That's why I'm not even a hundred percent sure it was a deer—it was just so big. Like an elk. But not that big, maybe."

"You remember what year this was?"

"Not the year, but I can tell you it was probably a year before he attacked that woman."

They talked for another ten minutes, but she had nothing else. Lucas thanked her, went to his car, and called Duncan.

"Big deer," Duncan said. "Huge deer. I'm heading over to Arlo's. I wonder if they might have shot it at a game farm? That's where you get the biggest bucks."

"It's a possibility," Lucas said.

"Lucas: thank you."

. . .

LUCAS WENT HOME and found Letty waiting to talk to him. "I've been reading the murder books again," she said. "I've got a question about the ropes. There were fourteen ropes found down in the Black Hole. Seven of them were quarter-inch nylon, three were quarter-inch polypropylene, two were three-eighths-inch nylon, and two were three-eighths-inch polypro. All of them were within a couple of inches of thirty inches long, and they all had knots tied at both ends."

"So his hands wouldn't slip when he was strangling the women with them," Lucas said.

"But here's the thing—even though they were extremely similar, they didn't all come from the same length of rope. It wasn't one rope he was cutting to get seven lengths of nylon. The lab says there are subtle differences in chemical composition and even in weave, by different manufacturers. So, the killer got them at some place with a lot of rope."

"Or a lot of different places with a lot of different ropes," Lucas said. "They've checked the hardware stores everywhere, got no good information—even checked the marinas, because nylon's used by boaters."

"There's gotta be something weird about going someplace and buying a two-and-a-half-foot rope," Letty said. "What could you use it for, besides strangling people?"

"Lawn mower starter cords, boat tie-downs, I dunno." Lucas thought about it for a few seconds, then said, "Think it over. There might be something in there."

. . .

WEATHER CAME IN AND SAID, "You guys are on television again. That Mattsson is a *very* attractive young woman."

Lucas tried to think of a reply, but nothing came to mind. So he said, "What are we on television about?"

"About Horn being dead. About looking for another guy. At least, that's what the promo said."

"*What?* Jon wasn't going to release that yet."

Letty, who'd worked at Channel Three for several years, as a student intern, said, "If you've got agents running all over Holbein and Zumbrota, how long did you think it'd stay confidential?"

Lucas settled back in his chair. "All right. Not long, I guess."

"Well, get up. Let's go watch," Letty said.

THEY ALL WENT TRAIPSING into the family room, where Sam was playing with Legos in front of the TV, and Gabrielle was watching him work. They sat through an advertisement for Hyundai automobiles that were being blown out at record low prices while the boss was on vacation in Canada.

Then the anchorman came up and said, "Breaking right now! An exclusive from Channel Three's crime team! We're switching you to Holbein, where . . ."

They switched to an excited reporter in Holbein who said, "Greg, we've confirmed from a number of sources that the agents of the Bureau of Criminal Apprehension are literally swarming through the towns of Holbein and Zumbrota, looking for a mystery 'second man' in the Black Hole case. And get this, Greg! The BCA now be-lieves that Jack Horn is dead!"

There followed shots of agents and cops coming and going from the Holbein police headquarters, and a shot of Duncan, in plain clothes, consulting with Mattsson, in her deputy's uniform. "Those two are getting pretty friendly," Lucas said, genuinely amused. "A few days ago, they were screaming at each other."

The reporter tried to interview Mattsson, but she brushed him off: "You need to talk to Jon Duncan. *Everything* goes through him."

"But are you closing in? Do you have somebody in your sights?"

Mattsson smiled and shook her head, but the smile said, "Yes."

Duncan did say a few words, and Letty said, "He has nice hair and a good smile."

"Good hair is important," Lucas said.

"That's all you got?" Letty asked. "They're closing in, and all you got is, 'Good hair is important'?"

"This killer is not a dumb guy," Lucas said. "I'm not sure they're as close as they think they are."

Lucas was drifting away from the TV when the anchor said, in the same excited voice, "The C-Team also has an exclusive inter-view with Little Kaylee Scott, who may have seen the Black Hole killer again, and this time he was stalking her in her own neigh-borhood."

"Ah, shit."

"That could be a big deal," Letty said.

"It's not," Lucas said. He took one minute to explain.

Weather said, "TV. It's like if you're not on it, you don't exist. The single most pernicious idea in our culture."

18

R-A and Horn were watching the news at the same time as Lucas. R-A was down four half-glasses of bourbon, and feeling a little wobbly.

"Those fuckers are all over town," he said. "They're not exactly going door-to-door, but it's pretty close. They'll be knocking here anytime."

"Well, don't let them in," Horn said. "They get a look at me, and it really *is* all over."

"Can't take a chance of that, no way," R-A said. He stepped toward Horn, and then Mattsson was on the TV screen, and R-A said, "Ohhhhh . . . Jesus."

"Run back to the bathroom, stroke boy," Horn said. "Run-run-run-run."

"Shut up."

"You still think you're gonna get her? Looks like she's hanging out with the state cops now."

"I'll get her," R-A said. "Too bad you won't be here to see it."

"C'mon, R-A, are you—"

He stopped talking because R-A stepped behind him and snapped his head off.

NOBODY CAME to the door the first night of the big Holbein-Zumbrota hunt. R-A was keeping his pickup in the garage for the time being, and was getting around in his ten-year-old Suburban. After pulling on some plastic kitchen gloves, he loaded Horn's mummified corpse into the back of the Suburban, on a plastic sheet, tossed the head on top of the pile, and tied up the bundle. Horn was still wearing the clothes he'd been killed in, though you couldn't see much blood after fifteen years of rot.

Horn's wheelchair, which had once belonged to R-A's father, he carefully washed, out behind the garage, with the Scrubbing Bubbles. When it was clean and dry, he folded and put it in the garage's storage loft.

At nine-thirty, he drove out of town, heading east. He thought about dropping the bundle on top of the Black Hole, which would be funny, but too risky. After driving around for a while, down narrow and narrower country roads, watching for headlights and nearby farm lights, he said screw it, spotted some tall weeds in a ditch, and threw the bundle into the ditch and the head after it.

He didn't particularly try to hide it. He was familiar with the countryside, and the way isolated neighbors watched out for each other. The thing that would create the most suspicion was a car parked on a road for a while, without good reason. He really didn't need somebody wondering whose car that was, and what was going on.

And he didn't really care if Horn was found: what he really needed to do was get him out of the house.

With Horn in the ditch, and no lights in sight, R-A turned around and headed back into town. Instead of going home, he drove a loop through it, a block over from the police station. There were all kinds of lights on, and a half dozen cars in the parking lot. Cops were still at it.

He stopped at the K-Bar, run by a former marine who'd never gotten over it, had a couple of margaritas, and listened to the other guys at the bar talk: all of it was about the cops in town, and speculation about who they were after, and that the same guy had killed the O'Neill family.

"Tell you what," said one of the local blowhards, "if the town gets ahold of the guy before the cops do, I wouldn't be surprised we had our first lynching. If they catch the sonofabitch, and if they don't kill him on the spot, and if he gets convicted and doesn't pull some technical shit on the court, then he'll get life. He'll be living better than a lot of the street people you see up in the Cities. Way better. Good medical care—"

"Wouldn't want to spend all my days locked up," said another guy.

"Either would I, but that'd be better than going to the chair," said the blowhard. "But he's gonna wind up in one of our country-club prisons, when what he should get is about four feet of rope up in a tree."

A couple guys nodded, but a couple more said, "Don't know about that," so it wasn't entirely unanimous.

R-A finished his second drink and left. Nobody said good-bye, because R-A was not especially well liked.

Back home, he found Horn sitting in the living room, in the wheelchair. He no longer had the duct tape around his neck, which had held his head upright for the past decade and a half. R-A was not especially surprised.

"You didn't think you'd get rid of me that easy, did you?" Horn asked.

"No, I really didn't," R-A said.

"So what are we doing?"

R-A said, "Mattsson."

19

All during dinner, with Letty chattering away, more and more excited about going out to California, and Sam fretting about it and Gabrielle throwing mashed squash at him, and all during that, and the subsequent cleanup, Weather would catch Lucas's eyes with a little smile, and Lucas knew precisely what that meant, and it was fine with him.

They'd go to bed a little early, he'd be a little tired, and instead of staying up to read, he'd just tell everybody that he (yawn) really needed some sleep.

As he passed Weather in the kitchen, he muttered, "Brace yourself, Bridget."

"I got all the bracing you can handle, big guy."

They both laughed because it was so stupid.

AT NINE O'CLOCK, still bouncing off each other a bit, with Letty in the second hour of a phone call with her best friend, who was also going off to school, Lucas and Weather both drifted away to their computers to answer any late e-mails before they actually got it on. Lucas had nothing interesting, dropped the lid on his laptop, and climbed the stairs to stick his head into Weather's office, when his phone rang.

He dug it out of his pocket and looked at the screen as he stopped in Weather's doorway. "Duty officer," he told her.

"Oh, God. Maybe they caught him," she said.

"If they did, they won't need me," Lucas said. He answered: "Davenport."

"Lucas, this is Bob Rogers. Man, the ATF is telling us that Del and one of their officers was shot down in Texas."

"What!" He groped for a chair and sat down, bent over the phone.

Weather: "What? What happened?"

Lucas turned away, put a finger in his off-ear: "How bad?"

"They can't tell us. They're both being taken to a hospital in El Paso. The ATF guy I talked to said that there was a big shoot-out, some old people with machine guns. There's some kind of firefight going on right now. Or was. This all went down an hour ago."

"What about Cheryl? Has anybody notified her?" Lucas asked.

"Oh my God," Weather said.

"We're on the way," Rogers said. "That's the first thing we got going. We think somebody ought to get down there, and he's your guy, and you're old friends, we thought . . ."

"I'm going," Lucas said. "Give me ten minutes to get back to you. I'm going."

He hung up, white-faced, and stared at Weather, who said, "Who? It's not Del?"

"Yeah. He's been shot. He's in an ambulance going to El Paso, we don't know the condition," Lucas said. "I gotta go. I gotta find out how to get down there, probably aren't any flights at night—"

"Lucas, you're rich," Weather said. "Rent a jet."

Lucas looked at her and then down at his phone, thumbed through his contact list, and pushed a number that, under normal circumstances, he only called a couple of times a year.

The governor answered: "You got the Black Hole guy."

"No. Do you still have that jet?" Lucas asked.

"Yeah?"

"I need it to go to El Paso. Right now. I'll write you a check for whatever it is."

"What happened, Lucas?"

"Del Capslock—you met him a couple times," Lucas said. "You said he looked like he fell out of a boxcar."

"I remember."

"He was on an ATF job down by El Paso, involving some gun-runners from here in St. Paul. He's been shot, we don't know his condition. He's my guy . . . my friend."

"All right. My plane isn't actually here. It's part of a co-op flight program. But some plane will be here," the governor said. "You get started to Holman Field, I'll call the FBO, and I'll call you back and tell you where to go. You can write the check later."

"I'm gonna call his wife, Del's wife, see if she wants to ride along. She will," Lucas said.

"That's fine. My plane seats sixteen, you'll get something simi-lar. Go."

"Thanks, man."

.   .   .

LUCAS HUNG UP AND SAID, "We're set. I'm going."

Weather took his arm and said, "I can't go, the kids . . . But you should take Letty. Letty to take care of Cheryl . . . no matter what's happened."

Lucas thought for a second, then went to the door and shouted, "Letty!"

She was downstairs and shouted back, "What? I'm on the phone."

Lucas: "Del's been shot. We're going to El Paso. Pack some clothes. You got five minutes."

After one second of silence, Letty yelled, "How hot's it gonna be?"

THEY WERE OUT THE DOOR in seven minutes, Letty driving Lucas's SUV, Lucas on the phone in the passenger seat.

Cheryl said, "Of course I'm going. That goddamned fool, I told him this was going to happen, running around like a kid playing guns after, after, after . . ." And she began to sob.

Lucas said, "You're gonna need some hot-weather stuff, some blouses and shorts and jeans. Just throw them in a bag. We'll be there in four or five minutes. We'll buy more clothes in El Paso, if we need them."

"I'm doing that now. . . ." She began sobbing again.

Lucas said, "We're coming, hang on, we're coming . . ." He hung up and said to Letty, "Slow down, you're gonna kill us," and, "You got the AmEx card I gave you?"

"Are you kidding me? It's practically glued to my body."

"Good. You gotta take care of Cheryl. Anything she needs, put it on the card. Anything."

CHERYL WAS a middle-aged nurse who looked as though a hurricane had been blowing through her hair, and whose eyes were red and swollen from crying. She threw a carry-on-sized suitcase in the back of the truck and asked, "Have you heard anything more?"

"Nothing, what about you?"

"He was alive when they got him to the hospital, but the ATF guy is dead," Cheryl said. "Del's shot bad, Lucas, he's shot bad . . ."

"One goddamned place in the world that they'll know about gunshot wounds, it's gonna be El Paso," Lucas said. "If they got him there alive, he'll make it."

"Oh, God . . ."

THE GOVERNOR CALLED and gave them directions to the fixed-based operator. "There's a guy named Jeff there, he's putting together a flight plan. There were two pilots on stand-by, both from Washington County, they're on the way, and supposedly, they're both sober."

THEY GOT TO THE FBO, found the plane in a pool of bright light outside a white-painted hangar. Jeff was inside a small office, and he said, "Hello," without a smile, and added, "The governor says you've got a serious situation."

"We do," Lucas said. "How soon can we get going?"

"The plane's prepped and ready to go. When . . ." A door banged open at the end of a hallway, and two men came through, pulling nylon bags. ". . . the pilots get here, and here they are. They're the best we got."

THE PLANE WAS BIG, white and shiny with comfortable seats and a bathroom twice as large as those on commercial airliners. Twenty minutes after the pilots arrived, the jet powered off the runway and they were gone in the dark.

A moment after they took off, Lucas's cell phone rang. The governor again:

"Are you in the air?"

"Just left."

"Del's at the University Medical Center of El Paso. It's a Level 1 trauma center, so that's where you'd want him. They're operating on him now. Our information is that he was hit three times, two of the wounds, you know, serious but not life-threatening, but the third one, the third one was bad. That's all I could get. There'll be a limo waiting for you at the FBO in El Paso."

"Governor, I can't tell you—"

"Yeah, don't. You guys are about half of my entertainment. I'd hate to lose one of you."

THE COPILOT came back as Lucas was ending the call, to fill him in on the flight plan, and said, "You can use your cell phone, but I gotta tell you, we're not going to cross any big metro areas going down there. You might get good links when we're crossing the freeways, but reception is going to be spotty. If you need to make any calls, you better make them now."

THE FLIGHT took a little less than four hours, Letty and Cheryl sitting across a narrow aisle from each other, talking quietly. Cheryl broke down twice, sobbing, and she told Letty that as a nurse, she'd seen a lot of gunshot wounds, and that none of them were good. "They just tear you up. They tear your insides to pieces. Oh, God, I hope his spine . . . I hope . . ."

Lucas looked out the window at nothing. The shooters, as far as he could tell, were the same old folks that he and Del had joked about since the investigation had begun. Old, doddering, seventy-plus senior citizens. They'd been laughing about the possibility that they were involved in wife-swapping orgies, about getting their false teeth mixed up in their various glasses in that four-way twist-up, laughing.

Laughing, because the suspects were old and wrinkled. They'd overlooked the relevant facts. They were old, but they weren't feeble. They were gunrunners and coke dealers, working with some of the most vicious people in North America. There was more to them than age, and he and Del hadn't paid proper attention to that.

At some point, one of the pilots said, "We're about a third of the way down there, folks. Glen and I grabbed a bunch of sandwiches at a Jimmy John's, and there's some water and Pepsi."

·   ·   ·

THEY ALL ATE SUBS and drank Pepsi, and then Lucas got another call, this one from an ATF agent named Miguel Colson.

"We've been talking with your governor, and he asked us to call you directly, to fill you in with what we know."

"Appreciate it," Lucas said.

"We were all over these old guys. We watched them unload two bundles of rifles the day before yesterday, and we were covering those. We've got those nailed down. We'd also heard that all the rest were going out in one batch, with the payment in cocaine, so we decided that instead of an early bust, we'd go for the big one. Del agreed."

"He would," Lucas said.

"Yeah. The meet was out north of El Paso, up in New Mexico. We had precise information on the location, from our bugs, and got out there early. We were all set up, six guys on the ground, eight more trailing in vehicles. Del and Carl were on the ground, on foot, down an arroyo that ran through the meeting site—this was really out in the sticks. Anyway, the buyers showed up, these were a couple of unknowns, but the sellers knew them pretty well, it was all first-name stuff.

"The buyers were driving a Land Rover, so they were prosperous. Anglos. They pulled in, we were monitoring, and there was some talk, and the buyers were looking at the guns, and the sellers were checking the cocaine, and then they were all, 'See you next time.' We pulled the trigger, we were all over them, SWAT gear, helmets, lights, everything, and the old motherfuckers in the RV ran for it. I couldn't fuckin' believe it. They left the buyers standing there with their dicks in their hands, and took off down this arroyo,

and Del and Carl showed themselves and these guys opened up
with M-16s, full auto, mostly missing everything because the RV
was falling apart, smashing down that riverbed, but they hit Del and
Carl, Del and Carl were right there—"

Lucas cut him off: "How bad's Del?"

"He's pretty bad, man. Took one in the guts. He was hit in the
arm and leg, not so bad. Carl's dead. Carl's gone." Colson sounded
frantic with grief and anger. "We had them both down at Thoma-
son in like fifteen minutes, didn't wait for the ambulance to get
there, threw them in a truck and took off."

"We heard an ambulance," Lucas said.

"Yeah. We met up eight or ten miles south down the road, trans-
ferred them. . . . I think Del would have died if we'd waited. Carl
did, Carl's gone, man."

"What happened to the shooters?" Lucas asked.

"They're dead. All of them. We think we hit two of them right
after they opened up, just hosing down the RV, but they got a ways
down that arroyo, don't know where they were trying to get to, but
they went over this ledge-like thing and got hung up, and then kept
grinding away until the tires caught fire. Then we think one of the
old guys went through the RV and shot two of the old people, who
were wounded, then shot his wife, and then ate his gun."

"Jesus Christ."

"No, he wasn't there," Colson said.

"So what do you think? We're in the air, with Del's wife."

After a moment, Colson said, "The docs here are supposed to be
really good. I don't know. Fifty-fifty? I don't know."

"We're coming," Lucas said.

After a long silence, Colson said, "They were old people."

·   ·   ·

THEY FLEW INTO El Paso International, and the limo was waiting, just as the governor said it would be. The pilots would check in to a local motel, and said they'd be available as long as they were needed, and as long as Lucas would pay them. He said, "No problem," and got in the car.

"Please, please don't let him be dead," Cheryl said, as they rolled across town. "Don't let him be crippled."

Lucas had been in far too many emergency rooms in his life, and a couple of times, the emergency was him. He'd gotten to dislike the odor of the places, like the back rooms of a butcher shop, with an overlay of alcohol.

Two big guys were standing inside the door and Lucas read them as federal. When Lucas, Letty, and Cheryl came in, they turned suddenly, like they might need their guns, and Lucas said, "Minnesota—Del's wife, I'm Davenport, with the BCA."

One of the guys was Colson. He was as tall as Lucas and thicker, with brown hair worn longer than most cops', and a tight bristly mustache; he looked like a Texas rancher on a TV show. He shook Lucas's hand and introduced the other man, John Sanchez, also ATF.

With the introductions done, Colson stepped up to Cheryl and put his arm around her shoulders and said, "Del's gonna make it. You gotta believe that."

"Where is he?" She'd been alternately calm and frantic during the plane ride, and in the car, but now, in the familiar zone of a hospital, she pulled it together.

"He's still in the OR, but one of the docs came out a while ago and said they're closing him up."

"Let's go. . . . Where's the surgical waiting area?"

"This way . . ."

THEY WAITED for nearly an hour, sitting around looking at old magazines, with Colson and Sanchez filling Lucas in on the firefight. They'd both been there, in vehicles.

"I'll tell you," Sanchez said, at the end, "what Carl and Del did looks stupid, not that I wouldn't have done the same thing. There was no reason to shoot anyone. There was no way to get away, no point in running. They more or less showed themselves to flag these old people down, you know, let them know that running wasn't an option. Carl was hit in the head, and was gone. Del got sprayed from the other side of the RV, down lower. He was lucky because he was wearing a vest with heavy plates, we insisted on that. The plates stopped three rounds that would have killed him for sure, but his arms and legs weren't protected, and when he tried to stop them he had his hand over his head and that apparently pulled the vest up. The slug that did the most damage clipped the bottom edge of the vest, punched through the nylon and into his lower stomach."

Colson looked at his watch: "Carl's wife, Jennie, is coming up from San Antonio by car. There were no commercial planes and it looked like a private deal would take a long time to set up, so we called the state guys and she's on her way with a bunch of state troopers doing a relay. It's usually a seven-hour ride, but the troopers say they'll have her here in five. It's been five now."

"Mmm, where is he? Carl?" Lucas asked.

"He's here. They've got a temporary morgue in the hospital," Colson said. "The medical examiner's right around the corner."

"I'd just as soon not be here when Jennie shows up," Sanchez said. "But I got no choice."

LUCAS PROMPTED THEM for the rest of the firefight:

After the people in the RV opened up with the full-auto weaponry, the ATF guys opened up on the RV, and the four people inside were all eventually killed, one way or another, but Del and Carl Lanning were already down.

Colson and Sanchez kept going back and forth about what had happened and how it had happened and why, and Lucas finally said, "You didn't do anything wrong: this shit just happens. Just like a couple patrol cops get a call about a possible store robbery, and they roll on it, and it turns out to be three ex-army guys with M-16s, when they were expecting a gangbanger with a piece-of-shit .22."

They both said, "Yeah, yeah," and went right back to who, what, why, and how.

Lucas knew exactly why they did that, because he'd done the same thing.

AT FOUR-THIRTY, Sanchez got a call, listened for a second, then said to Colson, "Jennie's here." They left. Cheryl said, "This is so awful. I feel like I oughta go down and say something, but I can't, because my man's still alive, and she'd be thinking, Why's her man still alive, and mine's dead? I don't think I could handle that very well."

Letty patted her on the arm: "Maybe later. Maybe we'll see her after we talk to Del."

AT FIVE O'CLOCK in the morning, a tall, solemn surgeon came out of the OR and walked down toward them, still in his operating gown, with a small splash of blood at just about the belly button, and said, "I could use a cigarette."

Everybody was standing, and he looked at them and said, "He's closed up, he's breathing, he's got no more leaks that we can see, and he's got blood. There are numerous possibilities on the down-side: stroke and blood clots, but the slug didn't hit much bone, so we're better off there, not a lot of fat punched into the bloodstream. He lost a chunk of his liver, but he's got most of it left."

"He's going to make it," Lucas said.

The doc said, "I can't make that promise, but he's seventy-thirty. Two-to-one he makes it. He's in good shape, and that helps. They got him here in a hurry, and that not only saved his life up front, but makes the recovery that much more likely."

Cheryl, whose hands were clenched in front of her, began sobbing, and Colson said, "This is his wife."

The surgeon tipped his head and then said, "I'm sorry. I would have been more diplomatic if I'd known. I was told his wife was in Minnesota."

She said, "That's fine. I'm a surgical nurse, I listen to docs all day. But I just, I just, I just . . ."

Lucas gave her a squeeze. "Don't worry, they got it covered. They got it covered."

. . .

LUCAS WILLED HIMSELF to believe. An hour after they talked to the doctor, they briefly saw Del as he was wheeled unconscious to the Critical Care Unit. He would not be awake until mid-morning, they were told; they should get some sleep.

Lucas got them rooms at a Hyatt near the airport. The limo had gone, so they took a cab over. Cheryl nearly fell asleep in the cab: some of the stress backing off. They checked in, Lucas said good night to the two women, and they all crashed.

20

"Finding really big spuds is getting harder and harder," Horn said. "That's a good one, though."

"You know what you can find?" R-A asked, as he carved the baking potato on the kitchen counter. "You got those big red sweet potatoes. The only thing is, they're harder than regular potatoes. Be like hitting somebody with bare knuckles."

"Could try it sometime, if the cops don't get you first," Horn said. Horn was looking a lot better, like he'd looked eleven or twelve years earlier, when he was alive. R-A was beginning to regret not getting rid of the body years before.

R-A finished carving, dried the potato with a paper towel, looked at it, said, "Close enough, I think." He picked up a thin plastic glove, the kind food handlers wear, pulled it on, and slipped his four fingers into the holes through the potato, with his thumb wrapped around the bottom.

The fit was too tight, and he pulled the potato off his hand, did a little more whittling between the fourth and fifth finger holes, and tried again. This time, the fit was right: like a pair of brass knuckles, but made out of a big Idaho baking potato.

"This should put her down," he said.

WHEN GOING AFTER WOMEN in the past, they'd tried several methods. The postal bag had worked well the first four times, but the fifth, with Heather Jorgenson, had been a disaster. They decided that in the future, the woman's hands, feet, and mouth had to be securely taped. To do that, they had to be taken down in a hurry.

Their first thought had been chloroform or ether. Chloroform had been almost impossible to get without leaving a trail. Ether was tough to get, too, according to all the available sources at the time. Then they found out about John Deere diesel starting fluid, which is almost pure ether, and which they carried in the store. They'd turn the can upside down, punch a hole in the bottom with a nail to release the spray propellant, and then pour the ether into a bottle. And there you were.

One problem: induction was really slow. You could grab a woman, pull a bag over her head, with a rag inside, soaking wet with ether, and it might not knock her out for good for five minutes. She'd be screaming her head off all that time. Then, when she woke up, she'd be puking all over everything. Worse, you stank of ether. If you were pulled over by a cop, you'd be doing the stupid human tricks in one minute—and if the cop looked in the car, you'd either have to kill him, or hang.

So ether and chloroform were out.

Then R-A read somewhere about sapping people with potatoes.

Usually, it'd be a potato in a sock, but after practicing with it for a bit, the method turned out to be unreliable. Better to fit the potato on your hand, punch them right in the mouth. They'd go down for the count, and by the time they were reoriented, they'd be trussed up like a Christmas turkey.

Quick, efficient, effective—and the potato would go out the truck window, to be run over by the regular traffic.

THE HARDEST PART of his investigation had been finding out where Mattsson actually lived. R-A could find a name, but not an address, on the Internet. She wasn't listed in the county property tax records, which meant she was renting somewhere. He mentioned to a clerk at the store that he was looking for an old friend that he'd lost touch with, and the clerk suggested the court records for lawsuits and such.

That sounded smart, so R-A ran into Red Wing and found her in the court records: a divorce. The papers were being served to a downtown address, and when he went to look at it, found a storefront, with a locked door and a staircase off to one side. The mailbox said C. Mattsson. He took a look at the lock; he knew locks, because he sold them.

The lock was old, and not very good. Even better, the door had a glass panel, and if he could cut through the glass, he could slip his hand inside and unlock the door.

On the way back home, he stopped at Walmart and bought a pay-as-you-go cell phone, for cash. A burner, the dopers called them.

What else? He'd be climbing that stairs in the dark, and if he was wearing his usual boots, she might hear him coming. He had a cozy pair of moccasins for wearing around the house in winter. They oughta work.

"YOU BETTER MOVE FAST," Horn said, as sun spun down in a clear blue sky, and the night began coming up. They were sitting in the living room, looking out over the lawn. "You don't have many days left, before they come in here."

"I can get away with it," R-A said.

Horn made a farting noise. "You got no chance. Fuck her while you can. Take a gun with you."

"If I have to use a gun, I'm probably cooked anyway," R-A said.

"The gun's for you," Horn said. "Gives you a choice."

R-A rattled the ice cubes in his glass, and thought about it.

THERE WAS A BAR in Red Wing called The Blue Ox, two blocks from Mattsson's place, and that was where R-A set up. He got there at ten-thirty, nervous as a hen in a weasel house, and drank beer. Not too much beer, but some, maybe a six-pack spread over two and a half hours.

Every half hour or so, he'd tell the bartender to watch his stool, he had to pee. He'd stop at the men's room, then go out the back door, walk down a block, and check the lights in Mattsson's apartment.

An SUV was parked out front, and he assumed it was hers—there weren't any garages around, and no other cars parked within a couple hundred feet. If she came out the door and he punched her, and then there was a guy behind her, an unknown lover . . . maybe another cop with a gun . . .

He *would* have a reason to carry a pistol. He'd brought it with him, because this whole night would be different. The other women he'd taken were usually drunk, often out of shape, unsuspecting, easy to take down. Mattsson could be a whole 'nother thing.

THE LIGHTS WERE still on at midnight, but fifteen minutes later, were off. He wanted her a little groggy, so he gave her another fifteen minutes to get settled in bed, had one last beer, paid, and walked out of the bar.

He took his time walking down to the apartment. He'd done this nearly two dozen times, but was still jumpy, waiting for a cop car to turn the corner. He got to the Suburban, pulled on a jacket, checked the pockets: tape, plastic gloves, glass cutter and cutter guide, potato. The cutter guide was simply a piece of cardboard with a fist-sized circle cut out of it.

The tape had been pre-pulled, the end of it folded over, so he wouldn't have to scratch around for the end. He took a breath, started the truck, drove around the block, and parked behind Mattsson's SUV. Sat for a moment, sticking two pieces of tape across the top and bottom of the glass cutting guide, checked the block again, then got out, eased the truck door shut, and walked over to her door.

He stuck the guide to the door's window, adjacent to the handle inside, and then ran the glass cutter around the inside of the cut-out circle of the guide. The cut was gritty, but quiet: he could feel the cut with his fingers, but he couldn't hear it.

When he'd run around the initial groove a half dozen times, he went back to the truck and dropped the cutter guide and the cutter into the backseat. Another check, and he pulled on heavy plastic gloves, then stepped back to the door with the roll of tape. He stuck a strip of the tape inside the scored circle, and stuck the other end to the back of the glove on his right hand. With his left thumb, he put pressure on the glass circle, pushed, pushed, heard it crack, and then it popped. The tape kept it from falling inside and shattering. He fished it back outside, walked over to his truck, got in, and drove away.

A block down the street, he pulled over again, dumped all the tools except the thin gloves, the tape roll, a flashlight, the burner, and the potato into the back, and watched the windows in Mattsson's apartment. No lights. He waited, slumped in the front seat, and then a cop car did turn the corner, and rolled slowly down the block, past him, past Mattsson's, without slowing, to a stoplight. The car turned right on red, and rolled away. . . .

R-A let out a breath.

Waited another ten minutes, then drove around the block again, looking for cops, and rolled to a quiet stop behind Mattsson's SUV. Checked the block. Pulled on the moccasins and gloves. Got out, walked over to the door, stuck his hand inside, turned the knob. The door popped open. He listened, but expected no alarm, and didn't get one.

The moccasins were good, and he climbed the stairs about as quietly as humanly possible, though he still created the occasional creak. He heard nothing from Mattsson's apartment. Got to the top, and found four doors. He would have had no idea which one was hers, except that three of them had no number, and the fourth showed the numeral 1.

Another deep breath, a long listen, and he took the cell phone and potato from his jacket, slipped the potato on his right hand, and made the call.

MATTSSON'S EYES clicked open. Her cell phone was a foot from her head, on the end table, waiting for the killer's next call.

She picked it up and looked at the screen, which had nothing but an unfamiliar number. She picked up the hardwired phone and punched in Davenport's cell phone number, and at the same time, she said, "Mattsson," into her cell.

She recognized his voice with the first syllable. "How you doing, Cat?"

"Nobody calls me that," she said. Davenport wasn't answering. "I am coming for you."

"Well, I know that," the killer said. "There'll be a big gunfight somewheres, and I'll have my .30-06 B-A-R and take a couple of you-all down, and then you'll kill me, and guess what, we won't be even. I'll be about twenty ahead. You know what I'm saying?"

"That's crazy," Mattsson said, then almost bit her tongue. Wrong word. "You need treatment. You need help. You really do . . ." God-damn Davenport wasn't answering. "You need to come in, because you don't have to die."

The killer laughed, a chuffing laugh, and said, "You ain't gonna let me give up. Be honest, Cat. Ain't gonna happen, not after I smoked that state cop. Anyway, I'm sure you're tracking this by now, so I gotta go away. I just wanted to call you and tell you I left another little present for you up at the Black Hole. I know I'm gonna die, so, you know, a man's gotta have some fun. . . ."

He laughed a last time, and signed off.

Mattsson said, "Shit!" and jumped out of bed, called the Goodhue duty officer and was shouting at him, getting whoever was out
there over to the Black Hole, more than one guy, everybody available, stop anyone on nearby roads.

She finished with the instructions, dressed, pulled her shoes on,
grabbed her car keys, purse, gun, and headed for the door, leaving
the lights on behind her.

No time, no time, she thought. *He'll be long gone.*

She fumbled the chain off the door, yanked it open.

And there he was: she knew it the instant she sensed him.

R-A HIT HER, hard as he could, right on the point of the chin. The
potato split and went flying and Mattsson went straight to the floor,
and R-A was on top of her, like a tiger on a goat, slugged her again,
rolled her, threw a twist of tape around her mouth, turned, taped
her legs, turned again, wrenched her arms behind her. She was
starting to struggle, just feebly, and made a loud moaning sound,
and he taped her hands, and then wrapped more tape, sloppy but
tight, across her lower face and mouth, threw more tape around her
lower face, ankles, more around her arms, and more around her
head. Then he dragged her fully inside, and pushed the door shut.

Her cell phone rang, but he kicked it away: didn't want it anywhere near her.

He worked quickly, more wraps around her ankles, her arms
and hands. She moaned again and started to struggle, but there
wasn't anything in it. He checked her pockets for weapons, found
her pistol, but no knife. He left the pistol on the floor, wiped and

tossed the burner—he didn't need it anymore, and was afraid that if he carried it even a block, it would give the cops something they could use, like a location and time.

R-A looked around for anything he might have inadvertently dropped, that could give him away. Nothing. He was breathing hard, he realized, his heart going like a trip-hammer. He took a few seconds, tried to calm down, then picked her up, over his shoulder, carried her out into the hall, kicked the door shut again, and went down the stairs.

The streets were empty. He left her lying inside the door, walked quickly out to the Suburban, opened the back, then walked back, picked her up, and threw her inside. He climbed in after her, and took a quick couple of turns of tape across her eyes, to blind her.

A moment later, he was headed south out of the city. The available Goodhue cops should be heading west, toward the Black Hole.

He could loop around, and avoid them all.

With any luck . . .

His luck held.

He took her south to the town of Frontenac, then turned west and south on County 2. On the way, Mattsson apparently recovered from the punch, as he'd hoped she would, and began kicking at the inside of the truck, her boots pounding at the panels below the windows. After one particularly loud flurry, he started to laugh, and shouted back at her, "If you keep kickin', you'll wear yourself out. Then how're you gonna fight me?"

That stopped her.

· · ·

THE BLOW to the head hurt Mattsson: she'd toppled backwards, and the back of her head cracked against the wooden floor, a second blow nearly as severe as the blow to her chin. Then the killer was on her, and he hit her again. She lost consciousness for a time, but she had no way to know how long. When she began to come back, her ankles and arms were already taped.

She was naturally a bit claustrophobic, and being bound, gagged, and blinded triggered all the phobia she had. She began to struggle against the tape, and then, because she could bend her legs, to mindlessly kick the panels on the inside of the truck.

The killer shouted something at her. She didn't know what he said, but it stopped her kicking, because it interrupted the panic that had gripped her. When she'd controlled her breathing, she systematically tested the bonds on her legs, hands, and arms; and finding a cut in the carpeting of the truck she was in, she tried to scrape the tape off her eyes. If she could only see, she might make some progress. So she scraped, and turned, and scraped, and ripped up her forehead and both of her ears, and got nowhere.

She could get some leverage on the tape around her ankles, and tried to kick off her boots, but failed. Her arms were taped close to her body, and her hands were bound so tightly that she couldn't feel her fingers.

The truck rolled on for a long time. Occasionally, she heard another car pass, but even that ended. The driver turned onto a gravel road, and that continued for several minutes, and then they were back on blacktop. He was picking his way across the countryside.

A new tactic: she straightened out the best she could, then rolled back and forth across the inside of the truck, trying to find something—anything—in the truck that she could use somehow.

She found nothing, and she began to panic again.

This could be it, she thought. She wouldn't give up, but if he simply decided to strangle her, she was done. He was a madman, so she doubted that there would be any way to placate him. She had to work him, somehow. If she got the tape off her eyes, if she got it off her mouth, she had to talk to him, work him. She had quick hands, if she could get her hands free and get close enough to him, if she could blind him, scratch his eyes . . .

The ride seemed to go on forever.

Then it ended.

R-A USED THE REMOTE to open the garage door, drove in, killed the engine, closed the garage door, and as it was rolling down, turned and called, "Honey, we're home."

Mattsson did nothing; no more kicking.

R-A said, "Okay, be that way." He climbed out of the truck, went around to the back, opened the cargo doors, grabbed the tape between her ankles, dragged her halfway out of the truck, then tossed her up on his shoulder again. She struggled against him, but she was so bound up that it was hopeless, and so she stopped.

R-A carried her through the door into the house, where Horn waited in his wheelchair. "You got her."

"Yes, I did," R-A said. "Slick as a whistle."

"Taking her straight down the basement?"

"Yup."

Mattsson heard it all, but didn't understand—it was the killer's voice on both sides of the conversation.

R-A walked through the house to the basement door, with Mattsson still over his shoulder, dropped down the steps, banging her feet against the wall a couple of times, then around the corner and into the bomb shelter. He put her down on the concrete floor and said, "Don't go anywhere, I'll be right back."

He was back in a minute, with another roll of tape and a box cutter with a razor blade. He said, "If you fight me, you're gonna wind up getting cut, and it won't do you no good. I'm working with a razor here."

Sitting on her legs, to pin them, he taped her legs around her calves, then cut the tape off her ankles, peeled it away, then cut the laces on her boots and pulled them off with her socks. Then he re-taped her ankles with several wraps of tape.

Her arms were pinned by more wraps, and he left them, but peeled the tape off her wrists, then re-taped them, behind her back. Then he cut the tape that wrapped her eyes, and she looked up at him for the first time; her eyes as hard as marbles, and angry.

"Mmm, you *are* upset," R-A said to her, in a teasing tone. "I'm going to leave that tape on your mouth, 'cause I don't want to hear you pissing and moaning."

SHE MADE SOME NOISES, but they were unintelligible, and he ignored them. He rolled her onto her stomach, sat on her back, straddling her, and began to cut her clothes away. That freed her arms, but as soon as her clothing was gone, he got the tape out again and, lifting her by her throat, again bound her arms to her sides. She began to flop around, so he waited until she was on her back, said, "Them's some nice titties," and backhanded her face, hard, and she stopped fighting.

He rolled her back over and cut her pants and underpants off. That done, he dragged her to a corner of the room and propped her up, and stepped away, and began taking his own clothing off.

He had to take off his boots to take off his jeans, but then he put the boots back on. When he was naked, R-A didn't look like much: a wrinkled forty-something alcoholic with way too much wobbly fat around his waist, dead-fish pale below the neck and above the elbows, red nose. He had heavily muscled arms, and hard shoulders. He said, "I guess you know what's coming next. I'm gonna fuck you."

He dragged her to the weight bench, bent her over it, facedown, sat on her back, and took a half dozen wraps of tape around her neck and the bench. Then he cut her legs free and wedged himself between them.

And raped her.

After a while, he raped her a second time.

After another long time, he cut her neck free and said, "Okay, Cat, here comes your big chance. Here it comes, and you better grab it, because if you don't, it's gonna be nothing but fuckin' you, until it's time to get the rope."

MATTSSON HAD NO IDEA what he was talking about. The rape, bad as it was, didn't affect her much: it hurt, but she knew she could get over it. She did everything she could to avoid giving him any pleasure at all: she simply took it, without any reaction. Maybe later she'd need a shrink, maybe she'd need medical care: but that was later. What she needed now was to get loose.

Of course, if she did get loose, she'd kill him.

And he said to her, "Here comes your big chance . . ." and cut her neck free.

She turned her head: What could that mean?

R-A ROLLED HER off the bench, leaving her legs free. He dragged the bench out of the room, came back, picked up the box cutter and the tape, which he'd left against a wall, and tossed them out through the door, toward the bench. He picked up his clothes, and the scraps of Mattsson's clothes, and tossed them out on the bench. And finally, he held up a key and said, "This is what you're fighting for."

MATTSSON WAS still lying on the floor, watched as he went to the door, pulled it closed, stuck the key in the lock, and turned it. They were locked in.

The room was probably fifteen feet long, and eight feet wide, nothing but gray-painted concrete block, some bare-bulb lights set in ceramic fixtures between the two-by-eight joists, and the door.

R-A came back to her, grabbed her ankles: she tried to kick him, and then tried to kick his hands off her, but he had a grip like iron, and twisted her ankles, rolling her over on her stomach again. He sat on her legs and said, "Hold still, there. I'm taking the tape off your wrists."

She stopped fighting, and he peeled the tape away, then jumped
back, away from her. She lay still for a moment, then glanced back
at him, calculating the distance, and suddenly lurched away from
him, to her feet, and turned to face him.

They were both naked in the cold room. Mattsson was on the
balls of her feet, rubbing her hands, trying to get feeling back into
her fingers, while R-A leaned against the far wall, waiting.

When her hands were coming back, she pulled the tape off her
mouth and croaked, "Why?"

"I do like the pussy," R-A said, "and I do like the killing, I got to
tell you. I like the sound it makes, when you're choking somebody
out. But that's not for a while, yet. It might not be at all, if you can
take me."

"Where are we?" Mattsson asked.

"Down my basement."

Her tongue flicked out: it felt dry as dust. "I mean, what town?"

"Holbein."

She looked around and asked, "I'm supposed to fight you?"

"That's the only way you're gonna get out of here."

Mattsson pushed away from the wall behind her, and R-A did
the same thing.

MATTSSON HAD BEEN judging him. He was out of shape, she
thought: a lot of muscle, but a lot of fat, too. If she could get
close enough, with either hand, she'd go for his eyes. Getting close
enough would be a problem; when she moved away from the wall,
he did, too, and then he fell into a boxing stance.

Mattsson took a step and he watched, then moved in on her and said, "Come on, come on, what are you gonna do? You're a cop, you must've had—"

She waited until he was halfway through whatever he was going to say, and launched a roundhouse kick at his head. Nearly got him, but he pulled back in an eyelash of time and her foot just kissed his nose, just flicked it.

R-A blinked and stepped inside as her leg recoiled and hit her on the side of the face with a roundhouse right hand, like being hit with a brick, and she went down. Dazed, she tried to scramble back up, and he kicked her in the hip with a heavy boot and she went down again and he was on her, straddling her, beating her, and she was blacking out and nearly gone when he said, "A kick's too slow, Cat. Something to remember for next time. But now, you got me all hot and bothered. Time for a little more fuckin'."

He raped her again.

She was like a rag, after the beating, no way to resist.

She was on the concrete floor, blood seeping from her nose and mouth, when she heard the door open. He threw a cloth at her—an army blanket, as it turned out—and said, "See you later. You better get some rest, because you're gonna need it."

Then he was gone, and the room was thrown into a deep, abiding darkness.

21

Lucas woke up at nine o'clock, with a little more than three hours of sleep, when Letty called. "Cheryl's up, we're going pretty soon."

"Fifteen minutes, wait for me," Lucas said. "Did Cheryl hear anything more?"

"Not a thing—which I think is good," Letty said.

DEL WOKE UP at ten o'clock, the three of them sitting around the foot of his bed. When he stirred and opened his eyes, Cheryl was bent over him, and she said, "You fuckin' moron."

He groaned, "Hey, sweet."

"Don't call *me* sweet. . . ."

Lucas half-pushed her out of Del's line of sight, and bent over him. "You fuckin' moron."

"Hey . . . I don't hurt much."

"You *are* hurt," Lucas said. "Believe me. And you *will* hurt. What the fuck . . ."

Cheryl pushed Lucas out of the way and cried, "Baby . . ."

Lucas said, "I'm not calling you baby, I can tell you that . . ."

Letty moved in: "How're you doing, Del?"

"I don't know, how am I?" He seemed slightly confused by all the bodies, his eyes unsteady.

Cheryl said, "You're fine. You'll be in bed for a few days, and we'll get you home. No spinal involvement . . . I mean, you're gonna hurt, but then you've been shot, so, what do you expect? How many times have I told you—"

"I'm really gonna be all right?"

Lucas moved Cheryl aside again and said, "They say there's no problem about transplanting a new dick. The thing is, they've only got a batch of 'smalls' right now."

Cheryl and Letty, simultaneously, "Lucas!/Dad!"

Del coughed and said, "Jesus Christ, don't make me laugh."

And his eyes closed.

DEL KEPT WAKING UP and falling asleep. He was asleep and Lucas and Letty were in the hallway, talking quietly about finding some breakfast, when Lucas's cell phone rang. Jon Duncan calling. He almost ignored it: BCA agents and Minneapolis cops had been calling all morning, along with Rose Marie and the governor.

But he took it: "Davenport."

"How's Del?"

"He's gonna make it, but he's hurt bad."

"That's what everybody tells me," Duncan said. "God, I hope

that's right. I hope that's good. But . . . I didn't call about Del. Lucas . . ."

"What?"

"Catrin Mattsson. Nobody can find her. She isn't at home—she left in the middle of the night, in a hurry. Her gun and cell phone were on the floor inside her door."

"Oh, Jesus. Jesus. He's got her."

"We don't know that, but we're afraid that's what it is," Duncan said. "I don't have all the details yet. I'm at home, just heading out there—"

"*I know that,*" Lucas was almost shouting. "He's got her, Jon. Holy Jesus, I got to get back there."

He rang off, and Letty asked, "What?"

"Black Hole guy," Lucas said. "He's got Catrin."

Lucas's instinct was to grab a cab to the airport and fly back to Minnesota *right now.* He couldn't do that: there were people to call, arrangements to make. He got the pilots headed back to the airport, then talked at a hundred miles an hour at Letty.

"You've got to take care of Cheryl," he said. "Everybody's happy about Del, but I can tell you, he's not out of the woods. I don't know what's going to happen, so I'm going to have to lean on you. Put everything on the AmEx card. This won't take more than a couple of days."

"How do you know that?"

"Because that's how long I've got to get her back. We believe he abuses the women for a while before he kills them."

"You mean, rapes them." Looking at him with the stillness she'd shown a few other times, since Lucas had first met her; like just before she'd shot a cop.

"That, and whatever else turns his crank," Lucas said. "But it gives me some time, some little bit of time."

"The other guys . . ."

". . . won't get him back," Lucas said. "It's on me."

LUCAS WENT BACK to Del, leaned over him and said, "I want to stay, Del, but I gotta go. That Black Hole killer's got Catrin Mattsson, the woman cop we saw at the hole. God only knows what he's doing to her."

"Take off," Del said. "Get him. See you when I get back."

Lucas was back at the airport in a half hour, and gone in forty-five minutes. He asked the pilots to tell him when they got close to a metro area, or crossed an interstate highway, so he could use his cell phone. They passed west of the Amarillo area, over I-40, and he called Virgil Flowers.

"How jammed up are you?" he asked.

"Pretty jammed," Flowers said. "This killing has gone all weird. What's up?"

"The Black Hole killer's got Catrin Mattsson."

"What!"

"Yeah. I'm shredding the murder books, but I've already been through them twice, looking for anything. . . . I don't know why I'm calling you, except that you know Catrin."

"Listen, Lucas, she and I never had any kind of close relationship," Flowers said. "I mean, if I could help you out in any way, I'd drop everything and haul ass up there. But I don't know what I could do. This thing down here . . . I don't want it to get away from me."

"All right. Goddamnit, Virgil, I got nothing, I'm desperate. I'm calling you so you can tell me what to do."

"I don't know, man. All I know about the case is what I've seen on TV, that little girl and the mailman guy."

"All right. Stay with your case, but if you think of anything . . ."

"What are you going to do?" Flowers asked.

"Duncan's group is tearing Holbein and Zumbrota apart. I think maybe my best shot is to go over to Durand, Wisconsin, and find someone who knows somebody from Holbein or Zumbrota. I don't know how to do that, but that's what I'm going to do, if I have to go around and knock on store windows."

"Let me think about it," Flowers said. "I'll get back to you."

"I'm counting on you," Lucas said.

Flowers said, "I'll tell you one thing. Catrin's got this tough-girl act, but under the act, she really *is* tough. Smart. I think she could string this guy out for a while. Don't stop pushing it."

Lucas made another call, from west of Omaha, over I-80, to Duncan.

"Jon, what's going on? What can I do?"

"Anything you can think of. We've got everybody working it, we know what happened, how he got her, but where she is now . . . we got no idea."

"Then give me what you've got."

Duncan said that when the sheriff's officers got to the Black Hole, they'd found nothing—and Mattsson hadn't shown up. They'd tried to contact her and failed, and so they'd gone to her apartment, and found that somebody had broken in through the street door.

"He knew what he was doing—used a glass cutter to cut through the door panel."

Worried now, the cops had gone into her apartment, where they found her Glock, her cell phone, and a burner—a pay-as-you-go phone, that had been thoroughly wiped. The phone had been used to call Mattsson, a minute before Mattsson had called the Goodhue County duty officer. The phone had been purchased from a Walmart, but they didn't know which one, and were working with Walmart's inventory people to see if they could track it down.

"What he did was, he called her at 1:07. She was in bed. They talked for only a minute, and he apparently told her that he'd left another body at the Black Hole site.

"Less than a minute after the call ended, Mattsson called the duty officer at the Goodhue County sheriff's office and told them to get everything started toward the Black Hole, and why. They did that.

"But he called from Red Wing, not up by the Hole," Duncan said. "In fact, we think he called from right outside Mattsson's apartment door. She wears pajamas: they were on the floor next to her bed. We think she got dressed in a big hurry, picked up her weapon and ran out the door, and he punched her out right there. There are chunks of potato in the hallway and on the floor inside the door. We think he used the potato like brass knuckles, see . . ."

"I know about that," Lucas said. "You got any video of the street?"

"Not a thing," Duncan said. "We've gone up and down the streets around there, looking for a camera that might have caught him, but we've come up empty so far. We're still looking."

"And nothing yet in Holbein."

"No. People here are getting a little surly: the newspaper editor thinks they're getting unfairly blamed for harboring this guy."

"Ah, bullshit."

"Yes. But that's what he said."

LUCAS RANG OFF, then called Weather before they dropped the cell signal, told her he was on the way back, and about Del and Matts-son. He made a final call to Duncan as they crossed I-90 in southern Minnesota; nothing had changed.

"I'm going to Durand," he said. "I think that's where we've got the best shot, short of you guys turning somebody up in Holbein."

"Stay in touch."

FIFTEEN MINUTES before landing, Lucas went to the plane's over-sized bathroom, gave himself a cold sponge bath, changed into jeans and a vintage RL flannel shirt, and jammed the morning's clothes back into his overnight bag. They landed in St. Paul in the early afternoon. Lucas's truck was waiting in the parking lot. He thought about starting straight for Wisconsin, but decided he needed to stop home first, a half-hour detour.

No time, he kept thinking. *No time.*

He parked in the driveway, went into the garage through a side door and opened the cache he kept under a step that led up to the housekeeper's apartment over the garage. He'd built the cache himself, and carefully, so that it was essentially invisible. Inside were several cold guns, a silencer, a lock rake, and a few other items that he didn't really want anyone else to know about.

Among them was a bottle of little gray pills, known in the truck driving trade as little white pills: the best speed he'd ever encountered. He'd gotten them from a line foreman at the Ford plant, when there still was a Ford plant.

He shook four of the pills into his hand, popped one and put the other three in the breast pocket of his sport coat. Weather walked into the garage from the kitchen as he was closing the latch on the cache, and said, "I heard you come in. Anything new?"

"No. I'm on my way to Wisconsin," Lucas said.

"Space those pills out. The third one can fool you—you'll feel sharp, but your reflexes start to fall apart. Don't kill yourself."

"I won't."

"Don't let anybody else kill you, either."

He kissed her and gave her a squeeze and said, "I'll keep the phone plugged in. Call me anytime."

DURAND WAS an hour out of St. Paul, even at the speeds Lucas was driving. The amphetamine had kicked in: he was clearheaded and focused. He was crossing the St. Croix River when he got a call. Virgil Flowers.

"You still planning to go to Durand?" Flowers asked.

"Yeah. I'm on the way."

"I'm looking at my Pad," Flowers said. "The population is about two thousand people. Quite a few of those will be kids."

"Yeah?"

"So there probably aren't more than fifteen hundred adults. Get the Durand cops to call everybody they know. All their friends and relatives and everybody else. Ask who knows somebody from Holbein or Zumbrota. Then ask all those people to call everybody *they* know, and so on. It's like a tornado-warning phone chain. You'll get a lot of duplication, but you'll touch everybody in town—at least, everybody with a phone—inside fifteen or twenty minutes, figuring each call at a minute or so each."

"Virgil: we need to do that. Right now. You do it, you can explain it better. Call the cops and tell them that. There's a sheriff's office in town, along with the cops. . . . Call them both and get it going."

"How far out of town are you?" Flowers asked.

"Maybe forty-five minutes."

"Could have something by the time you get there," Flowers said.

LUCAS WAS HEADING down the hill toward the Chippewa River bridge when he took a call from an unknown Wisconsin number. He answered, and was talking to a Durand cop. "We responded to that call from your agent Flowers, and we've got a couple of things for you. You need to talk to Shelly Linebarger at Andrew's Rentals and also to a Melissa Saferstein at the Book Nook."

Lucas got the locations, and after crossing the bridge, turned north for two blocks and spotted the rental company in a standard concrete-block-and-tin-roof building on the east side of the highway. He hopped out and went inside, where three clerks, two men and a woman, were standing in a cluster behind the service counter, and turned to look at him.

He said, "I'm Lucas Davenport and—"

"We've been waiting for you," the woman said. "I'm Shelly. We've got a customer from over in that area. He's rented towable cement mixers from us a few times."

The renter's name was Bob Bonet. They had a Visa card number for him.

"He's rented here a half dozen times. I asked him once why he comes all the way over here, and he said he could save quite a bit of money over rentals in the St. Paul area, where's the next closest place he could get these one-and-three-quarter-yard mixers. I don't know exactly where he lives, but it's in the countryside by Holbein."

"You ever see his truck?"

"Yeah," one of the men said. "Every time he comes over. It's a red Chevy dually, maybe four or five years old."

Lucas said, "Huh." And, "Big guy? Tall as me?"

"Almost as tall—and a lot wider."

Lucas got the Visa number, said, "Thank you," went back to his truck and phoned the number to Duncan, who was in Zumbrota. "We got to check it, but I got a down feeling about it—he's a big guy. Our guy isn't that big, I don't think."

"Gotta look," Duncan said. "We'll roll on it as soon as I can track the Visa number, and get an address."

"Stay by your phone, I may have another one coming," Lucas said.

THE BOOK NOOK was a narrow book-and-magazine store on Main Street, with about as many knickknacks as books; crystals hung in the windows over a sleeping red-and-white tomcat.

Lucas went inside and found Melissa Saferstein, whose candidate was the man who stocked her books from local and small presses—hunting and fishing books that focused on the North Woods, a variety of nature and photographic works of red barns and coyotes stalking field mice; like that.

"Davis Tory. Davis, not David. Not Davy, for sure, he told me that straight-out. There's something a little off-center about him. He's a little too tense," she said. Saferstein was a blonde, pushing hard at middle age, if not yet quite there.

"You ever feel uneasy about him?" Lucas asked. "Like he might come on to you?"

"Oh . . . no, I couldn't really say that. He just seems really tense to me. I always thought it was because he works so hard. Doesn't take time to schmooze, he just comes flying in the door, runs back and forth with his book boxes, and boom, he's gone. And his language is atrocious. It's motherfucker this, and goddamn that, and a few other words that I won't repeat."

"Big guy?"

"No, a fairly small guy," Saferstein said. "Muscular, I guess from carrying all those book boxes around all the time. But, not too big, bald. One thing: he always takes a minute to say hello to the cats. He likes cats, and they like him."

A black cat was at that moment walking across the counter to Lucas: he held out a knuckle for the cat to sniff, and then gave it a scratch behind the ears.

"Like that," Saferstein said.

She had both an address and a phone number for Tory. Lucas wrote them down, and called Duncan again. "This guy's got the right build. He's from Cannon Falls, which is close, but not exactly the big cigar. We've got to look at him, but I've got my doubts."

"Anything's better than sitting around on our hands," Duncan said. "You got a third guy?"

"Not yet," Lucas said. "I'll go up and talk to the cops, and see what they think."

.   .   .

HE DROVE THROUGH TOWN, then up the hill to the government center. There was nobody in the police department office, and only one officer in the sheriff's office—the guy who was running the communications.

"They're all out on the street, trying to make sure we didn't miss anyone. Going out in the nearby countryside, too," the deputy said. "If we didn't get everybody in town, I don't know who we could have missed. Some people are complaining that they've been called eight or ten times. We've got about thirty names for you, people from Minnesota, but we've been plotting them on Google, and most of them are from up around the Cities. Outside your zone, anyway. The two you got were the only close ones."

"So you're slowing down?" Lucas asked.

"Afraid so—nobody else to talk to. Sorry it wasn't more help."

"WE DON'T KNOW it wasn't, yet," Lucas said. "If you get anything else that looks good, call me." He left his number, and walked out to the truck, looked at his watch. Six or seven more hours of day-light, not much more than that. He sat for two minutes, thinking about it, could feel the panic rising in his throat. He was nowhere: nowhere. And he had the sense he'd just wasted half a day. How much time did Catrin Mattsson have? Where was she? What had the killer done to her?

Wherever she was, whatever had been done to her, hadn't been done in Durand. He got in his truck, and pointed it at the Missis-sippi River.

22

attsson was beginning to lose contact. She kept trying to wrench her brain back to the reality of her situation, trying to concentrate on what she might do, but then she'd blank out. She had no idea how long she'd been in the room. Sometimes, she thought she'd been in it for a couple of hours. Other times, a couple of days. Other times, more frequently, she thought she was dreaming, and that she'd wake up safe in her bed, covered with sweat from the nightmare.

One of the things she'd done as an investigator was to handle the rape cases, because a lot of victims simply weren't ready to talk to men after an attack. She'd always bought the argument that rape wasn't about sex, it was about power. Her faith in that view had been shaken. The killer was about violence, domination, power, whatever you might call it. But he was also all about sex.

Another item of faith that she was dropping behind: when she was dealing with rape as a cop, and as a woman, she'd always thought that rape was about the worst that could happen to you. Maybe it was, in the normal range of attacks on women . . . but for her, the rapes were a minor part of her immediate problem.

They hurt her, but wouldn't kill her.

But this man was killing her, literally killing her, inch by inch. He was beating her to death. When she went down for good, she sensed, there'd be one last rape or two, and then he'd strangle her, and by then, she'd be in no shape to resist.

HE'D SO FAR beaten her twice, and raped her five times. He'd make her get to her feet, and then it'd start: he'd take up a boxing pose, and start hitting her, and he'd scream at her, "C'mon, Cat, let's see it, punch back, goddamnit, let's see a little fight, this is no fun," spraying her with saliva as he screamed.

He was bigger than she was—not taller, but probably fifty pounds heavier, with arms like a gorilla, long and muscular. And he was fast. She'd try to block the punches, but he'd hit her as fast and as easily as if he were hitting a speed bag. Just bang-bang-bang and she'd go down and he'd have her by the hair, throwing her around the room, smashing her against the door, letting her get back to her feet and then going again, and when she could no longer resist, he'd rape her.

WHEN HE WAS DONE, he'd drag the weight bench out of the room and lock her in. After the first beating, she managed to crawl to the door. The lock was a heavy steel box; she could feel the keyhole, but no light came through it. The door fit tight, which was disappointing. She'd once seen a movie where a man locked inside a room had slid a newspaper under the door, then used a pin to push the key out of the lock on the other side. It'd fallen on the paper, and he'd pulled the key under the door. . . .

That wouldn't happen here. She didn't have a newspaper, and she didn't have a pin. In fact, she had nothing at all, except a green army-style blanket wrapped around her shoulders.

She was in a barren rectangular room with concrete walls. When he was in the room with her, she'd seen joists overhead, with a half dozen lights set behind hard glass panels, between the joists. There was nothing obvious, like a protruding nail she could use, not even a sliver. There was a steel bar, which would have made a weapon, but it was held in place by two heavy steel sockets. After the man finished raping her the last time, he'd done a half dozen pull-ups as she lay on the floor, looking up at him with one eye—the other had been bruised closed—and couldn't believe it.

After the first attack, she'd lain in a corner of the room. She was naked: he'd taken her clothes with him. When she'd recovered a bit, she'd crawled around the room in the dark, patting the doors and walls, but there was not a scrap of anything useful in the room. She went back to her corner, and her blanket, and waited. How long, she didn't know.

Then he came back, and did it all again.

She got to her feet, and got her hands up, and he laughed and said, "Atta girl, let's box." She'd staggered around the room, her good eye going to the door—could she run for it? Probably not, but if she got out in the basement, she might get lucky. If there was a workbench with a hammer or a hatchet or a wrench . . .

Distracted by the thought, she never really saw the punch that broke her teeth and knocked her down. She didn't want to get back up, but she did, but she'd lost all discipline and went for him, wind-milling, shrieking, and she got him, slashing one cheek with her fingernails; and he shouted at her, and then hit her again and again, knocked her against the wall and broke her nose with a wind punch, and she sagged to the floor again, and he dragged her by her hair, smashing her into the wall, then let her lie, moaning, as he dragged the weight bench back into the room.

SHE BEGAN to understand that she was going to die. She didn't wel-come the idea, but it wasn't completely repellent, either. Sometime during the last beating, he'd broken one of her ribs, as well as her teeth and nose, and when she moved, or coughed, the pain from her cracked rib lanced through her entire body cavity.

EVEN WITH THE BLANKET, she was freezing. Outside, the day must be hot. Down here, in the basement, naked, covered with concrete grime, it was cold. She wrapped the blanket around herself and tried to think, but she couldn't think. She began to drift, dragged herself back, then drifted again.

This time, he was gone for a good long time. How long, she didn't know, but it seemed long. . . .

R-A DIDN'T SLEEP all that well; he was too excited.

The first attack hadn't really been much—he'd expected more resistance than he'd gotten. Probably, he thought, because she hadn't been ready for what was about to happen to her. The second attack had been more entertaining. She'd really come after him, for a moment or two, and had managed to give him a pretty good scratch down his cheek. That would take some explaining.

"Goddamned stupid thing to do," Horn told him. "They're out looking for a kidnapped female cop, and here you are, a single guy, the kind of guy they're looking for, and you've got a big scratch right down your face. What are you going to tell Roy and the other guys? I cut myself shaving?"

"That had crossed my mind," R-A said.

"Oh, for Christ's sakes. You gotta think of something. Go look at yourself in the mirror."

He went and looked at himself in the mirror, and Horn was right. She'd cut him from the upper corner of his right ear all the way to the corner of his mouth. The cut looked like nothing more than a fingernail scratch from an angry woman.

He checked the time: six-fifteen in the morning. He had an idea, but he had to hurry. He shaved and showered, got dressed, and with Horn shouting after him, "I don't think this'll work," he half-jogged up to the store, went in, locked the door behind himself, turned on the lights, and hurried to the back. The first clerk would be arriving in ten minutes or so.

On the back wall of the store, a heavy-duty Peg-Board held racks of gardening tools against the wall. He noticed a couple weeks before that the rack was shaky—nothing dangerous, but shaky, as if one of the screws that held it to the wall had pulled out.

He got a step stool, found the loose screw, pulled it out; Horn, coming up behind him, said, "Now we got two loose screws."

"Fuck off," R-A said.

The next screw was tight. He got a big Phillips screwdriver and took it out, and then shoved it back in the wall with his fingers, enlarging the hole. The third screw was also somewhat loose, like the first one, and he pulled it out and dropped it on the floor: now the whole rack of tools wanted to tip.

In the auto section, he found a vanity mirror that clipped to a car's visor, pulled the wrapping off it, and looked at the scratch again. Already swollen a little, and starting to heal. He'd need to draw some blood. He got a nail from the hardware aisle, and the mirror, and took it back to the rack.

Sat on the step stool and waited.

The clerk named Roy showed up at four minutes to seven o'clock, right on time. R-A heard the key rattling in the lock, and then Roy calling, "Anybody home?"

"Yeah, it's me," R-A called back. "You want to get the front shades?"

"Got 'em," Roy called.

R-A looked in the mirror, tilting his head just so, and dragged the nail down the length of the scratch. Blood began seeping out.

Good enough. He threw the nail back behind the tool rack, put the mirror on a shelf, and then pulled the tool rack over on himself.

THE CLATTER sounded like the end of the world. All the hand tools came off, and a dozen rakes and a limb saw, smashing down through the adjacent bolt rack. The tool rack was made of three-quarter-inch plywood, eight feet long, four feet high, and it hit him hard— he didn't have to fake the fall beneath it.

Then Roy was shouting, "What happened? What happened? R-A, are you okay?"

"Get the fuckin' board off me," R-A groaned. "Ah, Jesus. That hurt."

Roy was two feet away from him, looking down. "You're bleeding. Let me get this . . ."

Roy helped him up, and R-A put his hand to his face, then took it away and looked at the blood. There wasn't much, but there was enough. "How bad is it?" he asked.

"Not too bad," Roy said. "You gotta put something on it. We got some triple antibiotic ointment in the first-aid kit. You'll need a couple Band-Aids." Roy looked around at the wreckage. "Jeez, how'n the heck did this happen?"

"Screws must've pulled out of the drywall," R-A said. "That hurt. Wasn't the tools, so much, but that board is heavier'n hell, and I had to go and pull on that rake. Got hung up on the hook, and the whole shebang come down on me. You guys gotta put it back up, but screw it in there good. If this had fell on a customer, we'd be going to court. Goddamn, that hurt . . ."

"Maybe you ought to take a break," Roy suggested.

"Yeah. Think I'll go stand in the shower for a while. . . . Goddamn, that hurt. That really hurt."

He put a limp on, going out the door. Called back, "Hey, Roy? Why don't you call Gene, see if he can come in early to help out? You need me, I'll be down at the house."

"Yeah, yeah. Take it easy."

HORN THOUGHT it was hilarious, but he was also impressed: "You could do Shakespeare. Or maybe one of those Mexican soap operas, anyway. 'Course, Roy isn't the sharpest knife in the dishwasher. You might want to keep that scratch out of sight. At least, until, you know, you get rid of her."

"She's breaking down already," R-A said. "She won't fight anymore. I'll fuck her a couple more times, then get rid of her tonight. Gotta go up to the store and get a rope."

"Why don't you just shoot her?"

"What's the fun in that?"

"You shot the O'Neills . . ."

"That was business, not pleasure," R-A said. "Nope, I need a rope."

"After you get rid of her, if I were you, I'd take every bit of junk you got in the garage and throw it in that bomb shelter, so maybe they won't do that science shit on the floor. There's gotta be blood soaked into the floor and walls," Horn said. "Because I'm telling you, they're gonna get to you, and sooner instead of later. There probably aren't three hundred single guys in town, and they'll be looking at all of them. You might get through today, and maybe tomorrow, but she better be gone by then."

ALL MATTSSON HAD were her fingernails and the blanket. For a long time, she used the blanket to wrap around herself, as her mind drifted away from her. When it came back, she tried to think of something that she could do with the blanket; could she shred it, make a rope out of it, use it somehow?

That was all bullshit, she thought. That was like some old TV show, where the guy invents an anti-tank weapon with a hairpin and a jar of Vaseline.

But she had her fingernails. If she could just get at an eye . . . if she could get at an eye, and then, after he was blinded or partly blinded, she could try to stay to that side of him, and maybe get the other . . . But she couldn't get close enough.

She thought about it.

Fingernails and a blanket.

R-A WATCHED TELEVISION all morning, clicking around to local news channels. Everybody was looking for him, he thought, with some satisfaction. They were going crazy out there. Most of the search was in Zumbrota and Holbein, but a crime-scene crew was shown working in Red Wing, at Mattsson's apartment.

A little after noon, having eaten a lunch of tomato soup and grilled cheese sandwiches, R-A got his keys and went down to the basement. Outside the door, he stripped down—getting undressed during a violent rape was a lot of trouble, if there were any resistance at all, and he liked at least a little resistance.

When he was ready, he shouted, "Coming again, Cat." He put the key in the lock and braced his feet, in case she tried to kick it open. She didn't. He opened it just an inch and looked through the crack between the door and the jamb.

Mattsson was on her feet on the far side of the room.

"What the fuck is that all about?" R-A asked. He stepped inside, pulled the door shut, locked it. He dropped the keys on the floor and sidled toward her. "Your suit of armor?"

Mattsson had ripped the blanket into strips and wrapped the strips in multiple layers around her head—around her forehead, across her nose, across her chin. Then she'd folded the rest of the blanket into a thick pad, and with three more strips, tied the pad down the front of her body.

Her arms hung free.

"You think that's gonna protect you?" R-A asked as he moved in on her.

She said nothing, but moved back into a corner, and crouched.

"Come on, get up," R-A said. In a crouch like that, she'd be harder to hit. Back in a corner, he couldn't maneuver around her. "Get up and fight like a cop."

"Fuck you, fat man," she said. "I'm gonna pull that pathetic little dick right off your fat gut."

Get him mad, she thought. She flicked her fingernails against the palms of her hands. She'd found one good use for the concrete walls—she'd used them to hone her nails, which were now as sharp as a cat's claws.

"Get up here, you . . ." and his hand arced at the top of her head and he grabbed her hair . . . as she thought he might. When he pulled, instead of resisting, she launched herself straight up toward his face and slashed at his eyes with both hands.

And missed.

Slashed his face, but missed his eyes. He screamed and staggered backwards, but didn't fall. She went back to the corner and her crouch. He was so angry that he hurtled at her, and just before he would have crashed into her, she launched herself again, and they collided, his weight knocking her backwards, but her claws were slicing at his face again.

He hit her in the face, but the pads took the blow, knocking her back but not down, and she tried for his eyes again. He hit her twice in the body, twisting his face away from her, but again, the heavy padding gave her some protection.

Again he came straight at her, but this time, his arms full-length in front of him. Her nails sliced up his forearms, but he got a hand at her throat and smashed her head against the wall, and she sliced at his hands, but he held on, and smashed her again, and this time she blacked out for a second, and then he was beating her down and unconscious.

When she came to, her eyelids fluttering, her head and body had been stripped of the padding. She didn't know exactly where she was, or what had happened to her, but then a dark object . . . a head? . . . blocked out some of the light, and R-A said, "Here he comes again."

He raped her only once, then dragged the weight bench out of the room and said, "You cut me up good that time, Cat. You better think of something else, though. Your armor's gone, and when I come back, I'm bringing my rope."

She said, "Fuck you," and passed out on the floor.

23

Lucas was coming up to the Red Wing bridge on the Mississippi when his phone rang. Letty calling from El Paso.

"What's up?"

"They've taken Del back into the operating room," she said.

"Ah, no. Why? How bad?"

"They say he's sprung a leak—that's Cheryl's language, not the doctor's. The doctor told me that it wasn't unusual. The shot that did all the damage just nicked the point of his pelvis and sprayed some bone fragments back into his intestinal cavity. He started running a fever and they think they have some contamination to clean up. The doc said they should be able to handle it, but it's not good."

"Ah, man. Ah, man, I oughta be there," Lucas said.

"Not until you get Catrin back," Letty said. "When will that be?"

"Tonight. I'll get her back tonight."

"I'll call you when they take Del out of the operating room,"

Letty said. "Cheryl's trying not to freak out. You call me when you get Catrin."

"Deal," Lucas said. "You turned out to be a pretty good kid, you know? Even if you do date soccer players."

He called Duncan, and asked where they were.

"We took about ten guys to interview Bonet. He pronounces his name bone-ay. Anyhow, he's not the guy. We know that because he was at a party here until sometime after twelve last night, with his wife. He couldn't have gotten to Red Wing even if he fit the rest of the profile: he's big, he's too young, and he's got a wife who's been with him since high school, and they've got four young kids."

"All right. How about the other guy?"

"We're saddling up right now," Duncan said. "From the facts and figures, he looks better."

"I'll see you there," Lucas said. "I'm crossing the Mississippi."

He turned on his flashers and ran through Red Wing in a hurry, the navigation system taking him up Highway 61, the one that Bob Dylan revisited, and then west toward the town of Cannon Falls.

Davis Tory's house was in the countryside two miles east of the town. Duncan called and said, "We're coming up to Tory's place now."

"I'll be there in one minute if my nav system is right," Lucas said.

"See you there."

. . .

THE HOUSE was a quarter-mile or so down a lane off County 19. Lucas took the turn, accelerated up a long, low hill, and when he came to the crest, saw two SUVs and two sheriff's cars climbing up a blacktop driveway toward a modern house that sat a hundred yards or so back from the road.

Lucas felt a touch of hope: the place was surrounded by a huge green lawn, carefully trimmed. There was a flagpole out front, with an American flag at the top. The house was barn-red, and behind it, off to the side, was a large metal building, the same color as the house.

The place looked obsessively neat, and Lucas was looking for somebody obsessive. The first cops out were wearing vests and helmets, and went to both the front and side doors. Lucas turned up the driveway in time to see somebody at the door of the house—a woman with pixie-cut dark hair in a blue dress. She said something to the cops, and pointed around to the side of the house, and then came out with them.

Lucas pulled up behind the last SUV and got out: Buford, the BCA agent, was there, an M-16 on the car seat next to his leg.

To Lucas: "He's in the barn. That's his wife."

The helmeted cops were leading the woman toward the metal building. She pulled open a door and shouted something inside. A moment later, a man came out, short, muscular, and balding, in a white T-shirt and blue jeans, just as Saferstein had described him.

Buford said, "Shit: it ain't him."

Lucas: "Yeah?"

"The guy would have run, or put up a fight," Buford said. "He and his old lady just look scared."

"Yeah."

LUCAS TURNED AWAY for a moment, looking out across the countryside. Another beautiful day, the corn gone dark green, the soybeans a lighter green, rolling away for miles and miles. And down the road, a white van with a big "3" on the side.

He turned back and walked along behind Buford to the cluster of cops around Tory.

Tory was saying, ". . . can look at the computer. I was on there until after midnight, writing invoices. They should be date-stamped on the program. I'll tell you what, I know you're supposed to have a search warrant and all, but this is no joke: I'm giving you permission to go in the house and the barn and anywhere else you want to go, and look at anything you want."

"You don't have to do that," Duncan said. "But if it's okay . . ."

"I wouldn't do that, if it wasn't for this crazy man running around the countryside," Tory said. "You'd be up to your knees in lawyers, but this guy, somebody's got to get your cop back, this what's-her-name."

"Catrin Mattsson," Duncan said.

Lucas asked, "How'd you know about Catrin?"

Tory, showing a streak of sweat on his scalp, wiped it back with the heel of his hand and said, "It's all over TV. They're not doing anything else."

Lucas said, "Speaking of which . . ."

They all turned and looked down to the road, where the van had pulled off to the side. As they watched, a cameraman came running around the nose of the van, a camera on his shoulder.

Tory asked, "Should I smile for the camera?"

LUCAS LEFT.

He drove to Holbein. On the way, Duncan called and said, "You took off?"

"I'm going to Holbein. I don't know . . . I think the answer is in Holbein or Zumbrota. I don't know what I'm going to do."

"Whatever it is, you're gonna be on your own," Duncan said. "The Red Wing cops found a video camera at a liquor store on Plum Street, which turns into Highway 58, which is the fastest way down to Holbein and Zumbrota. They say they can *almost* read the plates on every car and truck that went by last night. We've got a guy on the way down there, he's going to get some screen-shots off the video and pull the plates, starting with any dark-colored pickups, and then everything else. I'm going over there with Buford, we got a lot of tape to look at . . . I think it might be our best shot."

"What about the other guys?"

"Some of them I've got to send home. They haven't had any sleep for two days now, and they're out of gas. I'm also gonna drop a couple guys off at the Black Hole . . . you know, if the guy's nuts . . ."

"I hear you, Jon. Jesus, if he's already killed her . . ."

"Keep the faith, bro."

·   ·   ·

TEN MINUTES TO FIVE. Lucas went to the bank, found it about to close. He identified himself and told the receptionist, "I need to talk to your president, or your manager. The boss."

A couple of years earlier, Virgil Flowers had been stuck with a similar problem, and he'd partly solved it by the simple expedient of asking the smartest people in a small town who they *thought* the killer might be. He got back a long list, but, sure enough, the killer had been on the list. But Flowers had had more time. Lucas looked at his watch: he had no time, no time.

Flowers's technique had created a scandal in law enforcement circles, where many argued that the technique had been severely unprofessional, and nobody had tried it again, as far as Lucas knew.

Not that Flowers particularly cared about the question of professionalism. Lucas had once been with him when Flowers had tried to stop a killing by shooting the prospective killer in the chest. He'd hit her in the foot.

Lucas had nothing else: his brain felt like it was stuffed with fudge: nothing was moving. So he sat on a black leather couch while the receptionist . . .

"Yes? Officer? Can I help you?"

The branch manager was named Sandy Rodriguez. She took him back to her office and said, "I really want this guy caught."

"We'll get him," Lucas said. "The question we're dealing with now is, will we get him before he kills Catrin Mattsson?"

"My family said a prayer for her at lunchtime," Rodriguez said, as she sat behind her desk. "How can I help?"

Lucas said, "I'll tell you the absolute truth, and trust that you won't go talking to the television people. We've got a huge pile of information that we can use when we get a name. We got two possible names today, and we were able to eliminate them almost immediately."

"That book man, up by Cannon Falls . . ."

"That's been on television already?"

"About fifteen minutes ago."

"Aw, jeez. We're trying not to hurt people . . . anyway, I came here because bankers are smart and knowledgeable about their communities . . . and I want to ask . . . if you were to come up with a list of people who you thought might be able to do something like that . . . from here in Holbein . . . who'd be on your list?"

She looked at him steadily for a few seconds, then shook her head once and said, "Nobody."

"Nobody?"

"Nobody. I can say that, because, I've been thinking about it. So has everybody in town. I talked to three or four . . . or five, or maybe six . . . different people today about it, almost everybody who was in my office today talked about it. We don't know. Nobody knows. We can't come up with a name. We all know people who are troubled, but we wouldn't even suspect that they could do anything like this . . . and for so long. That's the thing. There's a boy in my oldest son's class, he's very troubled . . . but he's fourteen."

"Not him," Lucas said.

"I'm sorry," she said.

Lucas said, "Okay. Then give me five names of people who might know, smart people who know the community. . . ."

.   .   .

LUCAS GOT FIVE NAMES from her, and he hurried along Holbein's
Main Street like a gust of wind, cornering the people on Rodriguez's
list, asking the question, getting shakes of the head . . . and a few
more names. When he ran the names through the BCA databases, he
always found disqualifying problems: too young, too tall, and in one
case, too much in the Hennepin County Jail for the last four months.

LETTY CALLED, as he was walking past a tiny park, with three loose
dogs playing with each other as their owners chatted. "Del's out of
the OR, but he's still asleep," Letty said. "The docs said they got two
tiny holes, and they think they got them all this time. They say he's
strong, and unless something weird pops up, he's going to make it."

"They said that?"

"They did. Cheryl was all over them, and that's what they said,
and she believes them. He's going to be asleep for a few hours.
We're going back to the hotel and try to sleep ourselves."

"All right. That's good, that's good. Jesus, that takes a load off,"
Lucas said.

"What about Catrin?"

"I'll find her. I'm going to find her."

AT SEVEN-THIRTY, he was sitting in the supermarket parking lot,
watching shoppers come and go. The killer had had Mattsson for
eighteen hours. If she wasn't dead yet, she'd be dead soon. Looking

out at quiet streets, at the lights coming on in the windows, at the ash trees marching up the hills . . . What could he do?

He worried it, worked it . . . called the duty officer: "Could you get the DMV to try to run all dark pickup trucks against owners in Holbein and Zumbrota?"

"They're trying to write a program right now that'll do that, but they're not getting it done very quick," the duty officer said. "The whole data thing is complicated, and has all kinds of protections, and all the programming is outdated . . . it's all fucked up."

"Who got them to do that?"

"Jon did—couple days ago. They're still thrashing around."

Lucas rang off, took one of the gray pills from his shirt pocket, swallowed it with a sip of warm Diet Coke. Looked down at the supermarket. The killer could be down there right now. They'd all know him, they'd be chatting with him, but they wouldn't know. . . .

A LIGHT WENT ON.

Of course they'd know him. They didn't know he was the killer, but they'd probably see him every day.

Sonofabitch. He took his phone out, his soul touched by despair, because he knew what he'd find: he'd deleted the photos of Sprick sent to him by Mattsson when he was talking to the candy-shop woman. He'd deleted them for no good reason, except that he always cleaned up his phone; simply a habit.

Sprick. He fired the truck up, hit the flashers, and took off. Sprick was eight miles away, more or less. Six minutes. He didn't know how much time he had left, but with the orange sun sliding down in the western sky, he felt there wasn't much, not much at all.

The killer would get rid of Mattsson's body after dark, he thought, when he'd feel safest, when he could drive around, find a safe spot out in the countryside. He had no time.

Lucas was traveling a bit over a hundred miles an hour when he left town, and never slowed down, except once, to sixty, when he overtook a John Deere tractor using two-thirds of the road, four miles out of Zumbrota.

He was chanting out loud: "Be there, be there."

He had to slow down going through Zumbrota, but got to Sprick's house a little more than eight minutes after he left Holbein. Lights in the window. He parked, the flashers still blinking out into the evening, ran up the sidewalk. Sprick's curtains were pulled, but Lucas saw movement at one of the windows, and banged on the door with his fists.

Sprick opened the door and peeked out. "What now?"

"I gotta take your picture. I got no time, but I need to take your picture," Lucas said.

Sprick was wearing a gray army-style T-shirt, which was fine. Lucas put him against an eggshell-white wall, gave Sprick a ten-second explanation of what he was doing, and used his cell phone to snap a half dozen close-ups.

"Thank you," he said, after checking them. He ran back toward the car, and Sprick called, "Good luck. Get him!"

TEN MINUTES MORE, and Lucas rolled down the hill to the Holbein supermarket again. He hustled across the parking lot and into the store. A cashier was waiting on a woman in the single open check-out lane, and Lucas hurried over and asked, "Where's the manager?"

"What?" She looked at him, sweating, rushed, his hair messed up, like she expected him to produce a gun and a mask.

"The manager! The manager!" he said. "I'm a cop, I need the manager! Right now! Right now!"

The cashier picked up a phone and said, "Manager to checkout. We need a price check on Vlasic Kosher Dills."

Lucas said, "What?"

The cashier said, "You said you needed him right now. That'll get him right now." She turned and looked toward the distant bakery counter, where a heavyset short man in a pink shirt had turned the corner and was half-running toward them. "Here he comes."

"The pickle thing was a code?" Lucas asked, taking a corner of a half-second to be amused.

"Just like in a hospital," she said. "It means 'emergency.'"

"That's neat," said the woman checking out.

THE MANAGER hustled up and asked, "What's the problem?"

Lucas had his ID out: "I need you to get all your people, all the ones who interact with your customers. I need them . . . over there." He pointed toward the beer lane. "Right now. You gotta get them in a hurry. Please."

"What's—"

"Just get them," Lucas said.

THE MANAGER got them, and got a shelf-stocker to stand in the checkout lane to apologize to any shoppers for a short delay. With a half dozen store employees gathered around, Lucas said, "This is really important. I'm going to show you a photograph. Just for one second. I don't want you to look for differences, or why it couldn't be who you think it is: I just want a name of who it might be. Who you think it is with a quick look."

He looked around at the group: "Everybody understand?"

They all nodded.

LUCAS TURNED ON the cell phone and picked a photo, the one in which Sprick looked most stolid, most unremarkable.

He turned the phone around in his hand, then said, "Here it comes." He swung it in a slow arc, in front of their faces, giving each person perhaps a second to look at it.

Nobody said anything for two or three seconds, then the manager said, "Uh, yeah, that's R-A. That's Roger Axel."

"Who's he?" Lucas asked.

THE REST OF THEM were nodding, and the cashier said, "I see him every day. He runs the hardware store."

She pointed out the window, and up the hill. Lucas could see the hardware store sign. He'd been sitting in the parking lot, looking at it. Just as Shaffer would have been, if he'd been in his truck, eating a donut. Then maybe he had an idea, about where you'd make keys, and maybe he dribbled a little jelly into his notebook. . . .

The manager said, "You don't think he's . . ." but he was talking at Lucas's back.

24

Roy, the clerk, called R-A just to see how he was doing.

"I was doing just fine until you called. Woke me up out of a sound sleep," R-A lied.

"Sorry, R-A. When you didn't come back up here after lunch, we thought it might be more serious than it looked."

"Naw, I'm okay. Tired. Been sleeping most of the day. Probably won't sleep tonight because of it. I've been thinking of running up north, go fishing for a few days. If I can't get to sleep tonight, I might just jump in the truck and head out. If I don't show up to-morrow, you boys do the usual. Call me anytime."

"We can do that," Roy said. "Take as much time as you want."

R-A HUNG UP and went to look at himself in the mirror again. The bitch had really cut him up. He had five fiery red scratches down his face; nothing that he would have gotten when the tool rack fell on him. They looked exactly like what they were. He had to get rid of Mattsson, and he had to do it that night. Then he had to get his fishing gear together, and get out of town.

Not that it was a total loss, he thought. He'd relive that fight for as long as he lived, and the aftermath. Best sex of his life.

He opened the cabinet, got out the tube of antibiotic ointment, and smeared it down the scratches. He'd planned to go up to the store as soon as the late guy closed it, and get his rope. He couldn't do that, now, because sure as God made little green apples, he'd run into somebody on the street. He needed to wait until after dark.

Then he'd go down, fuck her one last time, and finish it with the rope. The thought of the rope got him excited.

"Coming to an end now," Horn said, from behind him. R-A could see him in the mirror. "Gonna be seeing you in hell, right soon."

"I'm getting out of here," R-A said.

"Too late for that," Horn said. "Your goddamned dick has done you in. Not that it probably made any difference in the long run. They would have gotten you anyway."

"I still got some rope," R-A said. "I'm good."

Horn started to laugh. R-A turned to him, but Horn had gone; wasn't there anymore. R-A could still hear him laughing, though, somewhere in the house.

LUCAS JOGGED OUT of the supermarket, across the parking lot to his truck, looking up at the hardware store. The windows were dark, with a couple of small neon advertising signs flickering into the growing darkness.

Shaffer had been sitting right here, and he'd thought about the keys. Who makes keys? A hardware store. He walks up to the store, and there he meets the killer, and asks the wrong question.

But the killer couldn't have just shot him in the store. Could he? Or would he have lured Shaffer off to somewhere else? Not something he could know, Lucas thought.

Other thoughts began to impinge. Axel: he'd heard the name before, but where? Somewhere in the murder books? That didn't seem right, but he'd heard the name.

And he thought, *Ropes*. The fuckin' ropes. They were burn-cut on both ends. You had to have a dedicated burn-cutter to do that, and where'd you find those? At a hardware store. Would you go to a hardware store once or twice a year, year after year, and buy a four-foot rope? Probably not. That's something people would remember. But if you could cut the rope yourself, because you owned the place . . .

Shaffer's crew had gone around to hardware stores asking about ropes, but hadn't gotten anywhere—they'd never realized that it wasn't the ropes that were important, but the *cuts*. You could get rope anywhere, but burn cuts, at both ends, only at a hardware store.

And the cut-glass door at Mattsson's apartment: Where would you get glass cut? Who'd know how to do that, neatly and efficiently? A guy who worked at a hardware store.

Axel's name popped back into his head. Yes. He had it: he'd heard it from Toby, the snakeskin dealer. Axel was a big-game hunter and possibly a friend of Horn's. And the woman who'd seen Horn and a friend unloading a huge deer at a butcher shop—Axel, the head-hunter.

All coming together, in the space of fifteen seconds as he hurried across the parking lot, got into the truck, and started it. As he pulled out of the parking lot, he looked in the rearview mirror and saw a line of store employees at the window, watching him go.

He went straight up to the hardware store and parked in front of it, and walked over to the front door. The store was nearly dark, lit by a variety of LED lights on the office equipment and alarms, and a lone fluorescent light in the back. He saw a movement, banged on the door with his fist. A moment later, a man in an apron emerged from the dark and waved him off. Lucas banged hard, again, held up his ID.

The man, tall, thin, and bald, squinted through the glass at him, then unlocked the door, opened it, and said, "We're closed."

"I'm a police officer," Lucas said. "I need to talk to Roger Axel."

"He's not here. He hurt himself this morning when a tool rack fell on him. He had to go home."

"Where's that?"

The clerk pointed down the street. "About two blocks down there, in that big old gray house halfway down the second block."

"Could you give me the address?"

"Hang on a second."

The clerk stepped back into the building and Lucas followed through the door. The clerk said, nervously, "I'm not sure . . ."

Lucas: "I need the address. And while I don't think you've done anything wrong, at this point, I need to warn you, if you call Axel, or warn him that I'm coming, I will arrest you and I will put you in prison for the rest of your natural life. Do you understand what I'm saying?"

The clerk peered at him, and his Adam's apple bobbed a couple of times, and then he said, "You think he's the Black Hole guy."

"I do," Lucas said. "How'd you pick that up?"

"If he's not, don't tell him what I'm gonna say. 'Cause I need this job."

"If he's not, I won't tell him anything," Lucas said. "So how'd you pick it up?"

"Because I think it's possible," the clerk said. "I've known him for six years, and by God, I think it's possible."

"Get the address," Lucas said.

THE CLERK found the address in Axel's personal checkbook, which was lying on his desk. Lucas noted it, and asked, "What about this accident he had this morning?"

The clerk said, "It was strange. He pulled a tool rack down on himself. It sort of made sense at the time, but, if you really think about it, you don't quite see how it happened. One thing was, he got this great big long scratch on his face, like from a nail. If you didn't know it was from a nail, you'd think it was from a fingernail. Like a woman's fingernail."

"I want you to lock up, right now, and go home, and wait," Lucas told the clerk. "Don't answer the door, if it's not a cop."

"Yes, sir," the clerk said, pulling off the apron. "I'll wait until I hear from you."

LUCAS CALLED DUNCAN as he walked out to the car: "Where are you at?"

"Red Wing. Looking at tapes."

"I've got him," Lucas said. "He runs the hardware store in Holbein. His name is Roger Axel. I'm a block from his house and I can't wait. I'm gonna kick the door and go in. Get everybody here, quick as you can."

"Holy shit, Lucas, you gotta wait. You gotta wait—"

"I can't wait. I can't. It's getting dark, and if he's gonna kill Mattsson tonight, he'll do it when it gets dark. Call a judge and get a warrant going."

"Based on what?"

"Based on . . . testimony from the supermarket management which leads us to believe that Axel is the bad guy. Shit, I don't know, Jon, I just know he's the guy. And I can't wait."

Lucas rang off and locked his car as he passed it, and started walking down the block toward Axel's house. Halfway there, he broke into a jog. Would Axel have had the gall to keep Mattsson in his own house, virtually in downtown Holbein? Maybe, but maybe not. Lucas couldn't take the chance of killing him, because if he'd put Mattsson somewhere else, they needed to know where.

He ran.

The streets were empty, but one elderly man in a hat, sitting on his front porch, reading a newspaper by the porch light, turned to watch him go by, a man in jeans and a long-sleeved plaid shirt, out jogging on a hot night. Not something you see every day.

LUCAS GOT TO AXEL'S HOUSE, slowed down, caught his breath, and walked up on the porch. Checked the house number to make sure he had it right. Thought about it for a second, then rang the doorbell. Nobody answered, but Lucas felt the man in the house; felt footfalls. Somebody had moved from one room to another, in a hurry.

Well, hell: he didn't really *need* the job.

He took a step back, and kicked the door. The door was not quite an antique, but it was old, and much used, and blew inward. Lucas went in after it, pulling his .45 as he did, and saw movement to his right and saw Axel there, reaching into a bookcase. Lucas pointed the .45 at Axel's head and shouted, "Stop there."

Axel stopped, his hand still in the bookcase. The facial resemblance to Sprick, the postman, was remarkable. Lucas said, "If you pull a gun out of there, I'm going to shoot you in the head. Pull your hand out."

"Who the fuck are you, and what the fuck do you want?" Axel demanded. He pulled his hand out of the bookcase, empty.

"You know who I am," Lucas said. "I'm a cop, and you've got Catrin Mattsson. Where is she?"

"You're nuts," Axel said.

He turned, and with the change of light, Lucas could see the pattern of fingernail scratches on his face; all doubt disappeared.

"If you don't tell me where she is, I'm gonna shoot you in the gut," Lucas said. "I swear to God. I'm gonna see if I can poke a round through your spine, so even if you come out of it alive, you'll be a cripple for the rest of your life. You got three seconds."

"Got you now," Horn said, from behind Lucas.

Axel said, "No way he's got me. He's only one man."

He said it so naturally that Lucas flinched: snapped a look backwards. Nobody there. "Two seconds," he said.

"Fuck you. Shoot me," Axel said, squaring up with Lucas.

"He's gonna do it," Horn said.

"No, he won't," Axel said. He took a step forward and Lucas did the same, closing up to four feet, the gun still high, and then Axel

juked left. Lucas had been in two hundred fights in his life. He en-
joyed fighting. He was good at it. He'd seen the juke coming, and
swatted the other man with the .45.

Axel went down when Lucas hit him, and Lucas took a quick
look around: there was nobody else in the house. He holstered the
pistol, and when Axel tried to push himself to his knees, Lucas
kicked him in the shoulder, hard as he could. Axel half-grunted,
half-screamed, went down and then rolled, fast, and then rose up
fully on his feet and charged.

Lucas waited until he came in, slipped a wild punch, then hit
Axel hard, on the forehead. The blow straightened him up, dazed
him. He stumbled back, hit a wall, straightened up and lifted his
fists, but only neck high. Lucas hit him in the eye and then hit him
again, and again, and again, all the frustration coming out now, and
Axel went down again, on his stomach.

LUCAS KICKED HIM HARD in the other shoulder, and Axel squealed,
and Lucas stepped to the door and pushed it shut. It was broken,
and didn't close all the way, but it was good enough.

Axel was still facedown, trying to push up, but his shoulders
were ruined, and he was having trouble. Lucas kicked him in the
hip, knocking him flat, then straddled him, grabbed his wrists, and
lifted him off the floor, rotating his arms back and up, stressing
them in Axel's shoulder sockets, and Axel began to scream and
Lucas shouted, "Where is she?"

"I don't have—"

Lucas lifted his arms higher, felt one begin to dislocate, and Axel
screamed, "Down the basement. She's down the basement."

Lucas lifted higher, and felt the second arm begin to dislocate: "She still alive?"

"Yes. Yes. She is," he screamed. "She's alive."

Lucas reached under Axel's neck, lifted him up by his shirt collar, then swatted him with the back of his hand, knocking him to the floor again, then said, "Crawl to the basement door. Crawl there, or I swear to God, I will kick you to death right here."

To prove it, he kicked Axel in the ribs.

Axel tried to crawl, sobbing with pain as he did it. His arms were unable to support his body weight and he wound up shuffling forward on his knees into the kitchen, to a gray door set in the kitchen wall.

"Here," he said.

Lucas kicked him between the shoulder blades, and he smashed forward and down, his face bouncing off the tile floor.

IN THE BOMB SHELTER, Mattsson had managed to crawl back to her corner. She felt she was dying. She was freezing, hadn't had water for nearly twenty hours, had several broken bones. The next time he came, she thought, would be the end, and there was no way she'd be able to stop it.

She had at least the satisfaction of knowing that she'd hurt him. The scratches might provide somebody with evidence that would hang him, and might show somebody that she'd at least fought back. They'd think well of her, the other cops would.

Huddled there, she'd occasionally hear footfalls as Axel crossed one of the rooms on the first floor of the house, above her. Eventually, she would hear him coming down the steps, and when that happened . . .

Then, after a lot of time, she heard running footfalls, and then a louder noise, still muffled, and then a heavy thump. A thump like a body hitting a floor, a sound she'd heard several times in her career, usually when she and another cop were breaking up a bar fight.

She pushed herself up.

LUCAS SNAPPED ON the basement light and pushed Axel down the stairs ahead of him. Pushed harder than he intended, but he was insanely angry, and Axel collapsed and tumbled down them, bouncing off the walls, but at the bottom, managed to come to his knees. His face was a red mask of blood, flowing from cuts in his forehead, and from a broken nose.

He looked around, grabbed a wooden dowel rod off a shelf and used it as a cane to push himself to his feet.

"You swing that thing at me, I'm gonna turn you into a fuckin' Popsicle," Lucas said.

Axel staggered backwards, and with Lucas coming down fast, managed to reach back, snatch a Ball jar off a shelf and throw it at Lucas's head. Lucas dodged and stepped forward and Axel jerked the dowel rod straight up, and more out of dumb luck than anything, rammed it into the bottom of Lucas's nose, a stunning blow that instantly clouded Lucas's eyes with tears.

Lucas had been stunned before. He swung a fist where he'd last seen Axel's head. His head was still there and Axel fell back into a rack of ancient canned vegetables, and sank to the floor.

Several of the jars fell off the shelf and shattered around him, and Lucas bent and grabbed Axel by the shirt again, yanked him out of the mess, and threw him spinning against a concrete wall, where he hit face-first. Axel went down again, and Lucas grabbed an arm and wrenched it back and up and shouted, "Where?"

"Around the corner, around the corner, Jesus, I'm hurt, I'm hurt, around the corner," Axel sobbed. "Don't hurt me no more."

Lucas dragged him around the corner and found himself looking at a gray steel door with a key sticking out of the lock. A light switch was next to it. He turned the key and pulled the door open. The room behind the door was dark: he flipped the switch.

MATTSSON HAD HEARD the fight—sounded like a fight—and a thrill went through her, lifting her to her feet. She pressed back against the wall, waiting, heard the key rattling in the lock.

The door opened, the light snapped on, and Davenport was there, blood running like a creek out of his nose, across his mouth and chin. Axel was lying facedown by his feet.

She asked, "Where the fuck have you been?"

Lucas said, "Catrin. I just, uh . . . just . . ."

HE BACKED UP a few steps, one hand going to his nose, the blood running over his fingers. He nearly stumbled over Axel, who was pushing up with one arm, rolling over onto his back.

Axel looked up at Mattsson and said, "You got me, Cat."

Mattsson looked at him for a moment, then asked, "How bad are you hurt? Who else is up there?"

Lucas said, "I'm not bad, he just . . ."

He was looking at her, and unconsciously shook his head, and she asked, "How bad am I?"

Lucas didn't answer directly. He said, "Gotta get an ambulance . . ." He fumbled in his pocket for his cell phone. She put an arm out, held on to his shirtsleeve, stepped around him, pulling him around a bit, almost as though they were square-dancing, and said, "Just excuse me, I'm just . . ."

There was a crowbar on a workbench, a three-foot-long piece of cold steel. Lucas was turning after her, but she just kept going around behind him, sweeping up the crowbar as she did and she came around to Axel, half-sitting, looking up at her, his eyes widening at the last minute as the crowbar came around and

WHACK!

She hit him, once, at the hairline just above his eyes. The bar shattered his skull, blowing bits of brain matter out to the sides.

Lucas recoiled: "Jesus."

Mattsson looked up at him, held onto his shirt.

Lucas said, "Okay. Now we need a story."

Mattsson fell down, landed on Axel's body and rolled away from him, and Lucas tried to pick her up but she said, "Leave me, make the call."

Mattsson looked up at him, and he crouched next to her and said, "After a fight, I dragged him down here. I let you out, and I was focused on you, when you came out, I was holding you up, and he suddenly stood up and picked up that bar, and you saw it and wrenched it free and swung it."

"That should do," she said, and fainted.

25

Lucas looked around, spotted a mover's pad on one of the well-ordered shelves, unfolded it, spread it on the floor, picked Mattsson up, placed her on the pad, and wrapped it around her.

She started to come around while he was doing that, and said, "I hurt bad. He hurt me bad."

HE SAT on the floor next to her, looked at his phone, pushed the button for Duncan.

Duncan came up instantly and shouted, "What? What?"

Lucas said, "I got her. I got Catrin. She's hurt bad. This guy, this hardware store guy, is dead. Gonna need some medics in a hurry, for Catrin."

"Jesus! Lucas! You got him, oh, Jesus." He was shouting again. "We're coming, we got an ambulance on the way . . . but where are you exactly?"

"I know that," Lucas said. He found the paper with the address on it and read the address to Duncan.

"Ambulance will be there in four or five minutes, cops will be there in two minutes. We're coming fast as we can." Duncan had calmed down just a bit. "What happened . . . did he . . . hurt her?"

He meant raped. Lucas said, "Yeah, I guess. She's pretty out of it. She's hurt. He beat the hell out of her, along with everything else." And he said, "Ah, jeez, I'm getting blood all over everything."

"We're coming. . . . How did this guy get killed? You shoot him?"

"No. I had him on the floor, down in his basement workshop. I turned my back to help Catrin, he came up, she saw him coming, grabbed a crowbar off a workbench and smacked him with it. Right in the middle of the head."

"Aw, boy . . . we're coming, man."

LUCAS CLICKED OFF and looked down at Mattsson; wrapped in the mover's pad, she began shaking uncontrollably as she looked up at him. But her eyes were focused and she said, "Picked up the crowbar . . ."

"That's right."

"I should be unconscious when the ambulance guys get here . . . then I can tell that story when I come back."

Lucas half-laughed: "Yeah, not a good idea to mix it up. You don't have to be too clear, because, you know . . ." He touched his palm to his face, and came away with a blood-smeared palm. ". . . it was all crazy and confusing and we were hurt."

· · ·

"Davenport! Davenport!" A male voice from the first floor.

Lucas shouted, "Down here," and stepped over to the stairs.

Two cops came down, the chief and another guy, the chief with his gun in his hand, both looking frightened. The chief looked at Lucas and said, "God, you okay?" and then, without waiting for an answer, he knelt beside Mattsson and asked, "Is she . . . ?"

"She's breathing, and her eyes were open a minute ago," Lucas said. "But we've got to get her going."

The second cop was looking at Axel: "Don't need an ambulance over here. R-A is . . . well, he's dead."

The chief glanced at Axel, put his gun away and said, "Piece of shit: I should have thought of him." He stood, took a phone out of his pocket, got on it and shouted, "Where the hell are they? Well, tell them to drive faster, we need them here right fuckin' now. What? All right."

He hung up and said, "They're outside. I'll go get them." He looked at the stairs and said, "Don't believe they'll get a gurney up that. Too narrow."

The paramedics took the cushions off a gurney, nestled Mattsson in them, then carried her up the stairs in the lengthwise curl of the mattress. One of them said to Lucas, "Her heart's strong, her blood pressure's a little low . . . she's in shock."

At the top of the stairs, they strapped her into the gurney and ran her outside to the ambulance. "You coming?" one of the paramedics asked Lucas.

"No. But if you've got some gauze pads in there, I could use them."

"WE GOT MEDIA," said the cop who'd come down with the chief. A TV van had stopped down the street, and a photographer hit the ground running, the camera on Mattsson as they loaded her into the ambulance, then panning to Lucas.

The paramedic handed Lucas a bundle of gauze pads. Lucas took them, and saw Duncan's truck swing wide around a corner, flashers burning out into the evening, and Lucas told the ambulance driver, "Hold on, one second."

Duncan piled up close behind the ambulance and jumped out, breathless, and said, "She in there?"

"Yeah. Take a quick look, and we'll send her off."

Duncan climbed into the ambulance and looked at Mattsson and said, "Ah, man. Ah, man, she's hurt. That fuckin' animal, I wanna cry."

Mattsson's eyes fluttered, and she looked up and focused on Duncan. She smiled, showing a line of blood-crusted, broken teeth, and said in a voice that sounded like a rusty gate, "Jon. I know it's my turn, but you're gonna have to handle the media."

"Ah, Jesus, Catrin . . ." He took her hand.

WHEN MATTSSON WAS GONE—the paramedics thought her vitals were strong enough that they should skip the local clinic and take her straight to the Mayo at Rochester—Lucas went inside and washed his face, pinched his nose off with the gauze pads, and walked Duncan through the fight with Axel.

Duncan recorded it, and then sealed the scene until the state crime-scene crew could get there, and the medical examiner's investigators.

"You need to get to the clinic, big guy," Duncan said, when they were done. "Your nose is gonna be the size of a yam by morning."

"Worth it. I got her back," Lucas said.

Duncan slapped him on the back and laughed aloud and said, "Yes, you did. You got her back alive."

Duncan wouldn't allow Lucas to drive himself to the Zumbrota clinic, but assigned a BCA guy to drive, and, after the docs were done with him, to take him home. At the clinic, the docs found nothing broken except a couple of blood vessels. They pushed a bunch of ointment up his nose, along with some cotton wads that looked like pencil stumps. That stopped the bleeding.

"But your nose is gonna look like . . ."

"A yam. I've already heard," Lucas said.

"I wasn't going to say yam," the doc said. "But yam is better than what I was going to say."

THE OTHER AGENT, whose name was Jim, and who was going on his thirty-sixth hour without sleep, drove him home. As they left Zumbrota, Lucas called Letty.

"How is Del doing?"

"Good. And I can tell by your voice, you got her. How bad is she?"

"She's down at the Mayo. She was pretty beat up, raped, teeth broken, probably some broken bones."

"Better than dead," Letty said. "Who was the killer?"

"Guy who ran the hardware store . . ."

He told her the whole story, sliding around the details in the death of Axel, and she filled him in on Del. "He's stable. He'll be back in Minnesota in a couple weeks. Cheryl is going to stay here to take care of him, but I'm going to head back as soon as I can get a ticket."

"I'll pick you up at the airport," Lucas said. "Look for a guy with a yam on his face."

He called Rose Marie Roux. "We got him. And we got Mattsson. He's dead, and she's alive."

"Perfect," Roux said. "I'll call the governor. He wanted to hear. He's going to make a statement."

LUCAS TOOK the next day off, but picked up Letty at the airport that night. The day after that, Shaffer was buried; the funeral had been delayed by the various processes and evidentiary needs of the medical examiner. Lucas and Weather drove up to the Iron Range town of Eveleth for the funeral, with two dozen BCA agents and their wives and husbands, and about a thousand other cops from around the state. At the funeral, June Shaffer gave him a wordless hug, and went on to sit by the coffin with her children.

LUCAS'S NOSE looked like a yam for three or four days, but was nearly back to normal when the family delivered Letty to Stanford. Everybody but Lucas cried when they said good-bye. Lucas didn't cry because he just didn't, but he couldn't speak for a while, and he called her eight or nine times over the next two days.

. . .

Mattsson.

Mattsson was damaged, but out of the hospital in a week. Dental repairs would take a while, her ribs would knit in six weeks, a broken wristbone a while longer. Weather fixed her nose.

She began visiting with Elle Kruger—Sister Mary Joseph—once or twice a week. Her problem involved neither the rapes nor the beatings, as much as the fact that she'd spent too many dark hours looking into the blank hollow eyes of death. She remained on the roster with the Goodhue County sheriff's department for reasons having to do with health insurance, but had been told that a job was waiting at the BCA if she wanted it. She told everybody that she'd want it . . . in a while. Once a week or so, she'd come over and sit on Lucas's back porch and drink a beer, not with Lucas, but with Weather. Talking about life.

Twenty-one skulls were found in the Black Hole. Four were confirmed as taken after death in cemetery thefts. The other seventeen were murders. Nine were matched to missing women during the main investigation, five more afterward. Three were never identified. The BCA sent out 470 DNA kits to families worried that one of the bodies belonged to a relative who'd disappeared.

Most of the skulls, after being released, were cremated by each individual victim's family. The undifferentiated "material"—human remains taken from the Black Hole—was also cremated, after a ruling by the state attorney general about proper disposition.

. . .

Two weeks after the sensational windup of the case, Janet Frost, the *Star-Tribune* feature writer, wrote a semi-investigative feature noting apparent discrepancies in Lucas's and Mattsson's stories of what had happened in R-A's basement. She also pointed out that Lucas had entered R-A's house without a search warrant.

Mattsson rebutted the story on public television's *Almanac* show. She was ferociously angry, and brutally candid about what had happened in Axel's basement. Her story of the multiple rapes and beatings, along with the still-obvious bruising on her face and body, the splints on her arm, the broken nose and teeth, the file shots of Lucas's blood-covered face, and video documentation of the murdered women's skulls coming out of the Black Hole, were so appalling that the *Star-Tribune* was overwhelmed with complaints, subscription cancellations, and a few death threats. The paper stood by the story, but shoveled dirt on it as quickly as the editors could do it; there were no follow-ups.

Frost had also done a long, sentimental first-person follow-up story on Emmanuel Kent and his pledge to starve to death if Lucas, Jenkins, and the Woodbury cops were not brought to justice.

Ruffe Ignace was so pissed off at Frost that he followed Kent after he left his City Hall protest site one night and watched him send another homeless man into a Burger King, to bring back a BK Triple Stacker, a large fries, and a vanilla shake. The next night he was back with a photographer to document it.

The story crushed Kent's protest. Two days later, he picked up his rug and left City Hall, and resumed his can-collecting and his dog- and cat-feeding routine.

FOR REASONS he couldn't explain, Ignace's story about Emmanuel Kent made Lucas feel worse about Kent's situation than he already had. Pure liberal guilt, Weather claimed—a mentally ill man they knew about who went hungry sometimes, and had no shelter, and still spent money on stray dogs and cats; and here they were, by contrast, rich and comfortable and planning a trip to Paris, where the hotel they'd stay at would cost five hundred euros a night. But that was the way of the world, she said, and they gave away a lot of money to organizations that did good work. . . .

Which didn't make Lucas feel a lot better. He was chatting with Jenkins about it, within earshot of a young woman named Sandy, who worked part-time for the BCA as a research assistant. Sandy was a latter-day flower child who took Lucas aside and explained that he and Kent were attached by a karmic thread, and it was stress on this thread that was causing Lucas's uneasiness.

She concluded by saying, "I know you think this is crazy, Lucas, but ask Virgil about what I just told you. He'll tell you, I'm right."

Virgil Flowers. The murder case he was working on had spiraled out of control, as his cases tended to do; but he took ten seconds to tell Lucas, "Sandy's never wrong about this kind of thing. She has a strong insight into the karmic realities, so I would consider very carefully what she said."

"I'm a Catholic, for Christ's sakes," Lucas said.

"Karma doesn't care, Lucas. Karma just is," Flowers said.

A few days after that, Lucas used his connections in the Minneapolis police department to find out where Emmanuel Kent might be, which turned out to be lying under a tree in the circle of grass outside the Hennepin County Government Center. Several other homeless men hung out there. Lucas dropped by, and recognized Kent from newspaper photos.

Kent was a tall man, radically thin by first-world standards. He had the dry, burned face of a man who'd spent too many years outside. He'd shaved recently, not more than three or four days earlier, but hadn't had a haircut in months. A backpack with a bedroll sat on the grass next to him, a pair of shoes sat next to his head. A plastic garbage bag was by his feet, with a couple of Coke cans spilling out of the open mouth of the bag.

He was talking with himself, while paging through a copy of *Forbes*. Lucas walked up, hands in his pockets, still uncertain about what he was going to do. But since he was a cop, he wasn't shy about stopping to stare at Kent, who gradually became aware of the attention.

Kent took him in, said, "You got a five?" Gave him another second's worth of appraisal, and amended, "Or maybe a ten?"

Lucas said, "I'm Lucas Davenport."

Kent took a second to sort through his mental stock of known names, and then said, "Aw, fuck you, man."

They looked at each other for ten seconds or so, without speaking. Lucas, who was wearing a summer-weight black-and-blue-checked wool suit by H. Huntsman, with a dusty red Brioni necktie, and who thought he might possibly have overdressed for the occasion, finally said, "I've been told that we're tied together by a karmic thread."

"That sounds like crazy hippie New Age bullshit, man," Kent said. He got slowly to his bare feet.

"That's something we agree on," Lucas said. "But I kinda started worrying about you. For one thing, why don't you go somewhere else? Like Santa Monica, or Pasadena, or Tucson, or something? Where it's warm all year?"

Kent looked around, up at all the glass and steel towers and said, "Well, this is my home, man."

"Gotta freeze your ass off in winter," Lucas said.

"No, I'm mostly okay," Kent said. "Got places I can go on the really cold nights. They don't make you pray to stay anymore."

"Huh," Lucas said. Then, "Your brother helped you out with a few bucks, huh?"

"Yeah. But that's not the reason that you pissed me off. It's because you never gave him a chance."

"I don't want to argue with you about that, Manny," Lucas said. "Your brother went around with a gun and scared the shit out of a lot of innocent clerks, and when we tried to stop him, he tried to kill some cops."

"That's just your opinion, man."

"No, that's the facts, Manny," Lucas said. "But like I said, I don't want to argue. I thought we might figure out something we could do about your situation."

Kent peered at him again, then said, "What, you want to give me twenty so I'll go away?"

"I know there's no good fix," Lucas said. "If it were up to me, there'd be a window in the government center where you could go for your weed, or whatever else you needed to help you get through the day. But that's not happening. Not yet, anyway. So I'm asking you, what can I do?"

Kent pondered that for a moment, then asked, "You're serious?"

"I am. I thought, I don't know—how'd your brother get the money to you? You're not always so easy to find."

"Got a box at Downtown Copy, Number 171," Kent said. "He sent the money there."

"How about if I send you a Starbucks gift card, or a McDonald's gift card, every once in a while?"

"You trying to cheapskate me, Davenport? Buying me off with a latte?"

"I'm trying to figure out how I can help, so my karmic thread doesn't get twanged," Lucas said.

More thought, then "Money is the most fungible commodity, man. It's not that I'm greedy, but money gets you everything else."

"Yeah, but if I send you money once a month, you'll spend it all on weed, and you'll still go hungry, and I'll still get twanged," Lucas said.

Kent scratched one of his scraggly sideburns, then said, "What if you wrapped like a fifty around a loaded McDonald's card, and sent that to me?"

"I can do that," Lucas said.

"Still won't make up for my brother," Kent said.

Lucas said, "Manny, I'm not worried about your brother. Your brother was an asshole. I'm worried about you."

"Well, fuck you then," Kent said. But he sat down next to his backpack and dug out a blank business card and a pencil, and laboriously wrote his name and address on it, and handed it to Lucas.

"I'll send you something when I think about it," Lucas said.

"How about something now?" Kent asked. "I got mouths to feed."

AFTER THEIR SUCCESSFUL carnal adventure at the farm, which led to the discovery of the Black Hole, Layton and Ginger continued to get it on that summer, but not at abandoned farmsteads. A friend worked in a motel and would give them a room for an under-the-counter twenty dollars, which the counterman split with the maid, 75-25. Layton also got the shirt off Ginger's best friend, Lauren, but that was as far as he'd gotten on that project, before they all went off to different colleges. They would continue to write letters to each other until October, and then Ginger didn't make it home at Thanksgiving, and Layton didn't make it home at Christmas . . . and, you know how that all works, and it's okay. Life moves on.

HORN'S BODY wasn't found until the following spring. His skull grinned up at the bleak Minnesota sky all that winter, as the snowstorms came and went, the snowflakes drifting into his empty eye sockets.

When the body and skull were found, by a man cutting ditch weeds, the cops weren't certain what they had, although a few suspected. A DNA check confirmed those suspicions.

The discovery was a three-day wonder that eventually Twittered away into digital irrelevance, lost amid the noise of the computer age and a universal media that could always find a worse crime.

Then nothing was left, except memories clutched to the hearts of the parents of the young women lost to the Black Hole; and the nightmares of Catrin Mattsson, which she feared would live forever.